Briege,

Hope you have a Lovely

Christmas and enjoy the book!

Love

Michelle Quigley xx

Hush Hush

Michelle Quigley

Copyright © 2014 Michelle Quigley

All rights reserved. This book or any portion thereof
may not be reproduced or used in any manner whatsoever
without the express written permission of the publisher.

All characters in this publication are fictitious and any
resemblance to real persons, living or dead, is purely
coincidental.

Edited by John Hudspith.

Front cover designed by Jane Smith.

Research obtained from www.movilleinishowen.com and
www.wikipedia.org

Printed in the UK

First Printing, 2014

ISBN 978-0-9929983-0-1

To my family with love, especially Sarah for her wonderful stories over the years.

Chapter 1

His piercing eyes stab my soul.

'Molly, did you hear me?'

Doctor Devlin leans over the desk, so close his warm breath caresses my cheek. I had heard him alright. His words had penetrated, like a corkscrew twisting through me. I feel myself glued to the couch, his words ring through my ears and form a tornado in my brain. I had known something was wrong but had never prepared myself for this.

My mind races over the event that had taken place almost four months ago, and every last detail flashes back into my memory, like a projector playing a scene from a horror movie, a scene that I don't want to catch sight of, a scene that I don't want to recall. That night and the awful memories had been sent to a dark corner of my mind, and once there, they had been locked away forever. I'd promised myself those thoughts would never escape; they could stay there, to gather cobwebs and rot. I had hidden it from everyone, including myself!

It was approaching the end of 1938. My friend Emily had heard there was a New Year's Eve dance on in the village of Muff, Donegal, just over the border from Derry, and only a few miles from my home.

'Get yourself dressed up this weekend, love. We're going to a dance,' Emily announced one morning at work, peering over her machine, her emerald eyes wide with excitement. 'It'll be a great night. I heard there's a fantastic band playing.'

'I'll have to think about it,' I replied absently. This was a silly remark to make, Emily will be dragging me along, whether I want to go or not, and usually it's those particular nights that are the most enjoyable.

'What? There's no thinking about it – you're going. You have to, Molly!' If her eyes widened any more they would have popped out of her head.

'Okay, okay then, I'll go before you have a canary,' I said, reluctantly retracting my almost refusal. 'I'm absolutely busted. I owe out so much,' I sighed, pondering over the few outfits that I had bought on buy now, pay later terms.

Emily grinned. 'You're too cautious, Molly O'Connor. Who cares about money? Sure, you'll not need that much anyway. Remember, you only live once, girl!' She waggled her finger in the air before bouncing off her chair.

'Aye, aye so you keep telling me. How the heck do you ever get any work done?' I smiled with amusement, watching her mingle with the other factory girls, working her charm. It wasn't long before almost all of our friends had promised to attend the night out.

'Oh, we'll have such good fun!' Emily rubbed her hands. 'It's been ages since we've been out together.'

'What did you just say?'

'It's been ages since we've been out together.'

2

'Don't exaggerate! We were at a dance two weeks ago. You are forever organising little nights out.' I laughed. She had clearly forgotten.

Mr Doherty, who had been standing a few yards away, peered at her suspiciously, with a look on his face that only a boss gives when he catches his staff skiving. He didn't have to say anything; the expression said it all.

'Oh, aye you're right,' Emily grinned before returning back to her work station. She sat down, tossed her shoulder-length blonde hair and smiled at him sweetly, with a look of butter wouldn't melt.

Emily smirked like a Cheshire cat as we linked arms and entered the dancehall. Her green eyes twinkled with pleasure. A feeling of excitement tingled through me, the pleasant music penetrating my soul, bringing an instant uplifting experience. I was glad to have come out after all. The inspiring beat of the music was enough to cast all thought of money problems from my mind. She was right, to heck with it, we do only live once.

A row of tables ran along both sides of the room, leaving a huge space in the centre for dancing. I glanced around and caught sight of a group of our friends sitting at a table to the left. I was impressed; most of the girls from the factory had kept to their word.

No sooner had we joined them, when two grubby-looking boys made their way across the dance floor towards us.

'Oh no, Molly, they're coming over. Let's pretend we

don't see them or let's make an excuse to go to the toilet. Come on let's ...'

'Hi girls, fancy a wee dance?' they asked at once.

We both hesitated but before we knew it, the boys had taken our hands and we were pulled to our feet. The song began, and soon my body was being whizzed about the dance floor to a fast upbeat tune, my dance partner stepping on my toes more times than enough. I would've forgiven him for treading on my feet once or twice, but he plunged his heavy boots down on my delicate toes so many times that I lost count!

Thoughts of getting rid of him as swiftly as possible soon developed, but to my dismay, after the song ended, he held me close in a vice-like grip. I had no choice but to continue. Emily managed to escape from her partner after the first dance; I, on the other hand, was not so fortunate.

'How about another wee twirl, love?' he questioned in a strong country accent.

Before I could refuse, the beat of the music echoed through the hall, and again I was whisked about in frenzy, with possibly the worst dancer I've ever met. Soon I was regretting not sitting in with my mother after all!

From the corner of my eye, I caught a glimpse of Emily, buckled over in laughter, obviously finding my plight hilarious.

Again the music ended and this stranger continued to hold me tightly.

'What's your name, love? I forgot to ask you. I'm

Daniel. Everyone calls me Dan or Danny. You can call me either. I'm from the village, but I just recently moved to Derry. Where are you from yourself?'

I wasn't sure if I should reply but also knew it would be rude not to.

'Ah, Mo... Molly, my name is Molly,' I answered reluctantly, through gritted teeth. 'I'm from Ballyarnett, just on the outskirts of Derry.'

'Ballyarnett! That's a fine place, Molly. And what brings you down here to Muff? Are you looking to meet a fine Donegal man like myself?' He flashed me a grin and it's only then I notice his stained teeth, yellow like old piano keys.

'You wish,' I whispered under my breath.

'By the way, Molly, is your father a thief?'

'What?' I reply, taken aback.

'Your father, is he a thief? I believe he has stolen the stars from the sky and placed them in your beautiful eyes.' A silly grin appeared on his flushed face.

I cringed. I wanted to yell at him that my father was dead! But I managed to control myself. It was clear he meant no harm. He was obviously just trying to charm me.

My mind began doing cartwheels with thoughts of how to get rid of this creature. I had danced with many men from Muff and they were great – in fact I'd had my eye on a chap from the village for a long time – but this boy had no chance with courting me; not in a snobby way, he was just too much of

5

a pest for my liking.

The music went on and he continued to throw me clumsily about the dance floor, like a rag doll.

'Listen, Daniel, it was great meeting you, but I really need to sit down now, my feet are hurting.'

'Ah, no bother at all, sit down there and rest, maybe I'll see you in a wee while. Maybe I could leave you home?' With a wink and a flash of those teeth, I crumble at the very thought of it. Not in a million years!

'I'm, ah, I'm not sure,' I reply as my mind searches for an excuse to get out of this one. 'Daniel, I'm only sixteen … perhaps I'm too young for you.' I smile sweetly, hoping my words haven't offended him.

'Sweet sixteen and never kissed!' he chuckled. 'Never worry, you're not too young, in fact you're only two years younger than myself.'

'What?' I gasped.

'I'll catch up with you later, Molly.'

'No, Daniel, I'm …'

'I'll see you later,' he interrupted, clearly not listening.

Hopping my way back to our table I found Emily sniggering with amusement.

'I hope you're enjoying yourself!' I muttered whilst removing my shoes. At once the cool wooden floorboards soothed my feet.

'Oh, Molly, I've never seen anything as funny in my

life. We've been watching the two of you the entire time. If only you could've seen the frustration on that pretty face of yours.' Emily laughed. 'I think everyone was so busy watching the pair of you, they were bumping into one another throughout the music.'

'Oh, I'm glad I've been of some use tonight,' I replied with a slight sarcastic tone. 'I wish I hadn't worn these shoes!'

'Ah well, just think of the good you've done for – what's-his-name? Sure you made his night!' Emily flashed another of her cheeky grins.

'I can't believe I've spent almost the entire night dancing with that clown!'

The music came to a halt, the leader of the band took the microphone and announced to the hushed audience, 'Well, ladies and gentlemen I hope you've all enjoyed yourselves tonight. I see we've had some great entertainers in the hall this evening!' He threw a teasing look over in my direction. I quickly replaced my shoes and scanned the hall for anybody other than Daniel. 'You know what's coming next. It's ladies' choice for the final bop of the evening!' he announced with an excited roar. 'I hope you had a great time. Goodnight folks; now, let's end the night with a fast number!'

My eyes fell on Peter Flannigan, but behind him Daniel was trying to get my attention. Peter, I think, is about three or four years older than me. He's a strange character, very rarely speaks to anyone – only to those he's comfortable with. Occasionally he would chat to my brother Donal and I when we fetched eggs from his mother but it was usually only small talk.

I guess it's inevitable that he's odd, given the life he's used to. As a child Mrs Flannigan wouldn't allow him to leave their land. They lived miles from other children, and as a youngster he lacked company from boys and girls of his own age, imprisoned in a world of loneliness, whilst other kids roamed as free as birds around the countryside, getting up to all sorts of mischief and having fun. He seldom attended school; instead he stayed at home to keep his mother company and to help her look after their animals. I felt sorry for Peter; it was clear why he was such a lonely person. He was now an adult, but still imprisoned in the farmhouse with his mother. I shuddered at the thought of having a lifestyle like his. Peter often had a blank expression fixed on his face, his eyes filled with sadness. It was easy to tell there was something missing in him.

I dashed off my seat.

'Hi, Peter, do you fancy a wee dance?'

He looked taken aback. He appeared as shocked as I was that I'd asked him. He wouldn't have been my first choice, but considering the current situation, he would have to do. I'd rather risk a dance with the oddball Peter, than the overpoweringly clumsy Daniel.

'Aye, sure,' he replied at once, in a low, shy voice.

It suddenly dawned on me this was the first time I'd seen him here; in fact it was the first time I'd ever seen Peter away from the farm.

'Did your ma let you out then?'

His expression was like stone, and my smile faded. It was clear from his icy look that he didn't welcome my joke.

Mrs Flannigan probably disapproved of him being down here tonight, much preferring he stayed at home keeping her company.

He led me to the floor and we moved along to the tune in an awkward silence.

The music finally came to a halt. I bid Peter goodbye and returned to my friends, feeling a sense of ease that I'd finally got rid of Daniel.

'Hopefully he got the message he wasn't walking me home tonight when he saw me with Peter. What do you think, Emily?'

'Oh, what do I think? Molly, I think you would make a great pair!'

It was obvious Emily was doing her best not to laugh again.

'Very funny! No, seriously, I think it must've worked.'

My eyes glanced around the hall; thankfully Daniel and Peter weren't in sight.

We scuffled to gather our bags and jackets before making our way outside. We buttoned our coats before stepping out into the slightly chilly air. Emily was still carrying on and telling her silly jokes to anyone that would listen. We always walked home after the dances as it was only a few miles

9

up the road, and, with the fun being so good, we were home before we knew it. However, tonight I was in no form for walking; my feet ached so badly, served me right for not getting rid of Daniel sooner and also for sneaking a loan of my sister Sadie's new high heels that were much too high for dancing in. I chuckled at the thought of her giving off if she caught me wearing them. In fact, the only thing I was wearing that belonged to me was my underwear; even the very bracelet wrapped around my arm was borrowed from my mother.

I ran my hand over my wrist, to find nothing but bare skin.

'I've lost my bracelet!'

The catch on it was loose and occasionally it unlatched itself and fell off.

'I need to find it. My mother will be distraught if it's lost,' I grumbled to myself, the others too caught up in their laughter to listen to my moans. I yelled after them. 'Hey girls, I'll catch up with you soon.'

For the next few minutes I searched frantically for the missing bracelet. My eyes combed the pavement, panic starting to set in. It had huge sentimental value. It had belonged to my mother's grandmother and had been in the family for such a long time. It had beautiful crystals set in a silver Celtic design. I'd adored the magnificent piece of jewellery as a child, often borrowing it and imagining I was a rich princess as I turned my arm to watch the crystals sparkle. I pretended that they were the finest of diamonds.

My eyes were attracted to a prism of light, glinting under the December moonlight. I bent down to pick it up when suddenly a strong hand weighed down on my shoulder.

'Here, let me get that for you, Molly.' He picked up the bracelet and placed it back around my wrist.

'Thanks. I'll have to leave this at home from now on. I couldn't tell you how many times I've misplaced it, perhaps I might not be so lucky next time. It's my mother's, and she would be disappointed if it was lost forever.'

'Aye it's best you do. I'll walk you home, looks like your friends have left you.'

He was right, they were gone.

'Okay, thanks,' I smiled, accepting his kind offer as we began our journey up through the back roads that connected Muff and Derry; it's more of a dirt track lined with huge oak trees than a road. We chatted about the dance and how mild it was for December. I could just about see Emily and the others further up the road, and could hear the echo of her familiar laugh as she came to a stop, looking behind her.

'Hey, Molly, is that you?' Emily shouted at the top of her voice.

'Aye, nothing wrong with your eyesight, pity about your memory,' I teased.

'Oh, I see you have company. Sorry for leaving you behind. I'll chat to you tomorrow.'

I sensed Emily's cheeky tone in her voice. I could

picture her making fun of my companion.

'You're okay, no bother,' I yelled back to her.

Emily and the others continued walking until they were soon out of sight.

Usually this area would be incredibly dark but tonight the stars twinkled like glistening diamonds in the black velvet sky and the moon shone luminously, so bright it lit up the path in front of us. I'd always found it pleasing to gaze at a clear moonlit night, watching the stars in the galaxy; they are a curious sight. I remember as a child lying in bed as the brightness of the moon would sneak its way through the gaps of our flimsy curtains, filling the bedroom with a mysterious light. Occasionally I would creep out of bed and peer at the stars from my bedroom window, and sometimes sit until the early hours of the morning, imagining different shapes and pictures unfolding before my eyes. I smiled secretly to myself, content with my walk home after all, completely forgetting about my aching feet.

Suddenly, without warning, a rough hand grasped my arm and dragged me through an opening in the trees, bringing my wonderful daydream to an abrupt end. Fear surged through me as I was being thrown into the field. I felt myself panic, like never before. I could feel his cold eyes staring defiantly through mine. My mouth tried to scream, but it was useless. I tried to wrestle him off. This too was just as hopeless. I was unable to speak no more than a mumble and unable to move from the weight of his frame on mine. His shoulders were taut as this demonic man overwhelmed my weak body. No longer were the shadows in the moonlight romantic and relaxing, they had suddenly become creepy and frightening as this evil brute attacked me.

After what seemed like eternity, but in reality were only minutes, he eventually backed away, disappearing without a word, leaving me humiliated in a cold, damp field, alone and terrified. I spent the next few minutes trying to get my bearings, my body numb with shock. How could someone do such a thing to another person? I felt sick to the pit of my stomach.

I began crawling my way through the long grass, digging my hands deep into the soft, moist soil, gathering the filthy mud in my fingertips, whilst I tried desperately to find my way out onto the pathway. My mind was in turmoil whilst I frantically searched the bushes to find the opening.

Faint laughter echoed in the distance causing me to jump. The giggles got louder as they neared. I felt sick again, my head began to spin and my heart thumped loudly as I tried to hold my rapid, trembling breath so as not to be found; I couldn't cope with someone finding me in this shameful state.

Soon the happy group passed by, their chuckles getting fainter as the group headed off into the distance.

A nasty thought suddenly sprang into my mind; maybe he's still lurking about. Perhaps I should've called out for help from those people, but they were now long gone, swallowed up into the night. With the fear of him still being about, I couldn't chance leaving this sordid place just yet. Like a fly trapped in a spider's web, I had no choice but to stay put.

The strange sounds in the wooded area caused chills to run along my spine. The minutes crept by slowly. I curled myself into a ball and wept bitterly, wishing I was safely in my bed and hoping my mother wasn't awake, wondering where I could be.

Unable to stand the sounds of the horrible night noises, I ventured out onto the dirt path and ran bare-foot, clinging firmly to Sadie's shoes and not looking behind me until I neared the familiar row of houses to our home. I quickened up my strides, not wanting to be outside for a second longer.

My mother would keep the back door unbolted when she knew we were out, and I prayed she hadn't got up in the middle of the night to secure it thinking that we were safely back. Panting and gasping for breath I finally made it home and was relieved to find it unlocked. Quietly, I slipped into the silent house. I quickly secured the door and leaned against it sobbing, my heart pounding. A diminutive light flickered in the living room from the oil lamp that she left on for us coming home. I made my way through the kitchen and into the living area, removing the lantern from the table before entering the hall. A small mirror hung in the hallway; I stopped and moved closer to examine what damage had been done to my face. My ghostly reflection stared back against the soft glow from the flame. There was a small cut to my upper lip and scratches to the right side of my face. Mud covered my cheeks and hair. My legs and back ached all over. Tearfully I tiptoed up the stairs, praying that my presence wouldn't wake anyone. I managed to undress without stirring the others and stuffed the tattered clothes into a corner under my bed, knowing they would be safe there until such time when I would get a chance to get rid of them. A small basin of cold water and a bar of soap I'd been using earlier remained at the foot of the bed. Whilst I washed the mud off, my teeth chattered as the cool water came into contact with my skin.

I climbed into bed and lay in the darkness trembling. My mind reeled over the events that had just happened. It didn't feel real. Trauma like this can sometimes feel like a nightmare rather than like reality. I'd just been through a girl's worst fears. Never had I felt so humiliated and full of terror. The horrible flashbacks entered into my thoughts every time my eyes closed. I remained awake.

By morning I'd decided it would be best to pretend I had flu so as I wouldn't have to get out of bed until my wounds healed.

For the next few days I remained in bed, burying myself under the blankets, pretending to snooze whenever anyone came to visit. I wasn't ready to face the world and couldn't bring myself to talk to anyone. My mother would come up every so often to ask if I wanted anything to eat or drink. I would mumble a few words back to her as she gently stroked my hair.

Most of the time I spent hidden away I didn't sleep, my mind haunted with horrible images of that brute and the frightful experience he'd put me through. The slightest of sounds would cause me to jump and my eyes burned with the vast amount of tears shed.

Eventually the pain turned to anger and my mind was

15

made up that I wouldn't let this evil destroy my life. I decided to get up and try to get on with my life, promising to forget about the incident; after all, it wasn't me that should be ashamed. I wished for the beast to be haunted by what he'd done. Every morning as he opened his eyes I hoped that it would plague him throughout each day, and that *he* may have the nightmares, not me. I would no longer allow myself to be troubled, the matter would be blocked out of my mind and the misery brought to an end.

'Molly, you are pregnant, aren't you?'

Doctor Devlin's words broke the lengthy silence, causing me to step back into reality. His frown deepens and it's clear he pities me by the way he looks into my eyes. My mouth begins to twitch as I fight back the tears. I can't keep this up; why can't I be strong, like I swore to myself I would?

Warm tears flow freely. 'Aye, maybe.' I hear myself reply as I fumble with the sleeve of my jumper. 'Please don't tell anyone. I don't want my family to know yet. I'll tell them when I'm ready.'

I get up and proceeded to walk towards the door, leaving Doctor Devlin astounded. He watches me leave the room without a further word.

Whilst walking home the reality of my situation begins to sink in. If Doctor Devlin's prediction is correct, the reality is the horror isn't quite over yet, in fact, it's only just beginning!

Chapter 2

'Dear God, please help me,' I whisper aloud, my body trembling as I pause for a moment before entering the house, trying to collect my senses, sweat dripping from my temples. 'Be strong, Molly O'Connor, be strong!'

My clammy hand turns the door handle and I walk straight through the living area and into the kitchen in a trance. Pots of potatoes and cabbage boil on the range, and the strong aroma of bacon rashers fill the air, but the kitchen is empty.

From the steam-covered window my mother is barely visible, kneeling on the ground, dipping the dirty clothes into a basin of water and scrubbing them clean, humming her usual cheerful tune as she carries out her chore.

My gaze falls on the clock; it's ten-past five, the others will be returning from work soon. Should I tell her now? Would it be better to wait for the rest of the family? No! I need time to think about this, the whole truth can't come out, it will destroy my mother.

Fear invades my thoughts, and memories of my father at once spring to mind.

As a child, like many children, the darkness terrified me. Each night before going to sleep I had to check under the bed, just to ensure there were no monsters waiting to pounce on me in the middle of the night.

My father would smile, tuck my long, chocolate-brown hair behind my ears and whisper: '*Molly, there's no monsters*

17

under your bed; nothing will ever hurt you, as long as I'm about, I'll always make sure of that!'

His reassurance helped to diminish those horrible thoughts in my young mind and I grew up remembering his words, however, right at this very minute I have everything to fear and my beloved father is no longer here to reassure me.

A lump forms in my throat, tears sting my eyes, watching my mother and how happy she looks. She's had her fair share of hardships. Memories of growing up flood my mind. My content childhood was practically transformed overnight to a difficult life, a life of struggle and poverty, full of ups and downs. I'm one of three children; Sadie being the eldest, next in line is my brother Donal, then I.

Kate, my mother, is known for her gentle voice and warm smile. Her beautiful, sparkling lavender-blue eyes are set in an almost perfect face.

Never did I hear her speak angrily or harshly to anyone; now and again she would say, '*Love must be sincere, hate what is evil but cling to what is good and always share with those in need.*'

She certainly practices what she preaches; she adores her children, despises gossip, and she doesn't entertain anyone that rips apart another person's character, but the thing that has stood out about her the most over the years is her kind, loving nature to others. She has never turned a blind eye to a needy soul, in fact, if anything, she goes out of her way to help people, even if that means doing without herself.

On many occasions, whilst peeling the potatoes for dinner, she would come up behind me and say in her utmost polite voice, *'Molly, love, never count the spuds, put on an extra few, for you never know who might knock at the door feeling hungry.'*

Sure enough her predictions were often true; no sooner would we sit down to our meal but a visitor or beggar would arrive at the door, and the spuds and butter would be served to the hungry being.

My mother's cousin Myra lost her husband quite suddenly to pneumonia, leaving her devastated and facing the future bringing up seven young children on her own. After the death my parents helped her as much as possible, often cooking them their dinner and looking after the younger children for her each Saturday.

Over the months it was clear that the heavy burden was really getting poor Myra down, the stress and strain became evident in her personality, she was clearly struggling to keep her family together. Myra landed at our door one afternoon in a distressed state, with only the two youngest of her children, the one-year-old twins Charlie and Anna. On this particular day it wasn't her dinner she wished for, instead she pleaded with my mother and father to take her two little ones as she could no longer cope either emotionally or financially.

Without hesitation they agreed. We treated them like they were our very own brother and sister. I was six at the time, Donal was just approaching his eighth birthday and Sadie was nine. We later discovered that Myra's other children were adopted by other relatives. The broken-hearted Myra turned to alcohol and never returned for any of her kids.

My mother is a trained midwife and worked full time until she had Sadie. Whilst my father worked hard as a weaver, my mother was kept busy with looking after us, maintaining a house, which was immaculately clean, and growing her own vegetables in the back garden.

She is a great cook and would bake scone bread and pancakes practically every day. If she is not baking, she is usually found scrubbing the house from top to bottom. Our home is the tidiest house in the row, and we certainly have the cleanest toilet – you can smell the bleach before you get a chance to open the door!

'Mrs Mop, will you sit yourself down, sure those floors are that clean you could eat your dinner off them,' my father would joke.

We were a happy, content, family until suddenly, out of the blue, our world fell apart when tragedy struck our perfect household. Just less than a year after Charlie and Anna joined us, my father took ill and tragically he died from a heart problem. It was a devastating time.

Although I was only a child, I was wise enough to know that my mother's own heart had been broken, no matter how good she tried to cover up her devastation or smile through her sadness, we knew she missed him terribly. But regardless of how much hurt she felt, she ploughed on with life for the sake of us.

The first Christmas without him was cold, not only because the temperatures had plummeted, but because the warmth that he brought about had been cruelly taken from us. It was chilling to the bone to be without him, and Christmas has never been the same with him gone from our lives.

Every Christmas since his death I still feel the same emptiness. I missed him sitting by the open fire in his favourite armchair chanting carols as the cheery inferno roared up the chimney, with the logs crackling and the flames dancing in the hearth, and the smell of my mother's homemade soup brewing in the kitchen, whilst we perched at his feet, listening to him telling us a story before we bowed our heads to say our family prayers.

On that first Christmas without him, the snow lay thick all over the countryside. I remember thinking unbearable thoughts of my beloved father lying deep in the ground in his cold, dark coffin. It was a horrid feeling.

Christmas morning came and we had no food except for some homemade scone bread and some delightful, plump, juicy oranges. I recall how we gathered around the huge open hearth, the logs crackling and the flames dancing, but no father and no smell of soup. As we sat on the rug, getting our bony bodies warmed by the fire, we tucked into our delicious fruit. The juice ran down our arms and we lapped it up with our tongue, not letting a single drop go to waste. The only sound to be heard was the crackle from the logs. From the corner of my eye I caught sight of my mother observing us scoff our fruit into our mouths and on down to our hungry stomachs. It suddenly dawned on me that she was not eating any herself.

'Here, take some.' I pushed a few segments into her hand.

'No, I'm not hungry, you eat it, love.' She smiled, replacing the fruit back into the palm of my hand.

'Go on.' I pleaded.

'No, Molly, honestly I would rather you eat it, darling.'

She had not eaten anything all day, and now she was refusing a share of my food. She loves us all so much, she would rather go hungry herself than take a bite to eat from her children. I finished the remainder of my treat with a pang of guilt.

Later on in the evening, my father's parents had arrived to wish us a happy Christmas. They lived in the town and owned a few grocery shops. Obviously my mother was too proud to explain to them that we were struggling since my father had died.

'Did you have a nice Christmas dinner, Kate?' I heard my grandfather ask her in the kitchen.

'Oh yes it was lovely, we had ours early today.'

Why would she tell him a lie? My mother is never one to tell lies – she is always far too honest for deceit. This made me feel angry, we hadn't had anything to eat – apart from the scone bread and fruit – and by the look of things we wouldn't be eating dinner tonight. There wasn't a morsel of food in the cupboards. It was clear she would never explain that she faced such bleak poverty. I was also wise enough to understand he would be furious if he knew the truth that we were going hungry, and after all, he has plenty. I decided to take it upon myself to inform him exactly how things were by pulling him aside at the first opportunity and innocently explaining the circumstances of our life, without giving much thought to the fact that I was going behind my mother's back and perhaps letting her down, but all I could think of was how to help her in some way.

My grandfather held my face in his huge hands and gently whispered, 'Thank you, darling, for telling me, you're a good girl, Molly. Now, I need you to do me a big favour. Can you make me a promise?' His eyes widened.

I nodded my innocent head in agreement.

'I don't want you to tell your mother that you have just told me those things, okay? It can be our secret.' His face brightened with a smile.

I nodded once again.

'Great, Molly.' He playfully ruffled my hair.

It suddenly became apparent that my mother might be upset with me for telling him. I kind of wished then that I had kept my mouth shut.

Less than an hour after my grandparents had left, my grandfather returned with a huge basket filled with all sorts of delights: there were mouthwatering cream cakes, biscuits, sweets, bread, jam, flour, eggs, cooked ham, chicken, beef, potatoes and a variety of vegetables.

'Can you believe it, Kate? We walked out earlier without giving you our gift. Happy Christmas to you all! Hope you enjoy your treats!' He beamed as he placed the huge hamper on the kitchen table.

My mother looked shocked.

'Well, sir, what can I say? This is very kind of you.' She paused, too stunned to speak as she gazed at the groceries. 'Thank you, sir, I appreciate this. Thank you so much.'

'You're very welcome, Kate.' He grinned before turning to me and secretly winking.

After he waved us goodbye, we made a run for the kitchen, almost tripping over one another in the process. We peered at the variety of food with excitement, the hunger pains waving through our tiny bodies. In no time, my mother had prepared the food and we sat down at the table to a rather late Christmas dinner, fit for royalty. It was well worth the wait, and boy we were ready for it. We scoffed mouthfuls of grub until we could eat no more.

I went to bed that night with my stomach full and feeling like a stuffed Christmas turkey.

From that day on, my grandfather would bring down a hamper for us on a weekly basis. The guilty feeling soon vanished as I watched my mother's spirits lift. Perhaps I had done the right thing after all.

In all my years, that was the only time I went behind her back; after that incident I never kept anything from her and swore I never would again.

'Ah Molly, good to see you're back, love. I'll get your tea served in a minute.' My mother stood up and proceeded to hang the washing on the line. 'I'll be in soon, almost finished, darling.'

Her voice startled me. Suddenly a shudder shoots through me like a massive bolt of lightning, tremors pulsated through my veins, sending the blood to rush to my heart. '*Never kept anything from her, swore I never would again*' rattled in my brain. Well, at least not until now!

Chapter 3

I shiver and pull the blankets closer to block out the chilly air. The weather is so cold for early spring, it feels more like a winter morning. I shut my eyes tight, desperately trying to get back to sleep.

My stomach churns and a wave of sickness surges through me. I groan at the thought of having to get out of bed again.

I steel myself, throw the blankets aside and swing my legs out. My bare feet meet the coolness of the floorboards whilst tiptoeing past my sister, trying not to waken her. Sensing her stir, I know it's too late; the creaks of the old boards have disturbed her.

'Is that you, Molly?' Sadie sits up and rubs her eyes in the darkness. 'What's the matter?'

My only goal is to get out of her sight as quickly as possible, and so, without answering, I swiftly exit the room and shakily make my way downstairs and outside to the wooden outhouse; at the end of the garden my delicate body is violently sick. I'm trembling from both the cold and the sickness. I try to clean my mess up as much as possible, which isn't easy with no running water. I lean against the door and sob; life is tough.

I manage to make my way upstairs again, hoping the curious Sadie has fallen back to sleep. To my dismay, her outline is vaguely visible, still sitting upright in the gloomy air, just as she was earlier.

'Are you all right, Molly?'

'Aye, I'm grand.'

I pull a face, knowing that Sadie can't see me clearly.

'You don't sound grand to me. I've heard you up early the last few mornings. You're looking terribly pale lately as well. Perhaps, you've a stomach ulcer. That sickness isn't good, something's up.'

Typical Sadie always thinks she knows best. I jump back into bed and get snuggled up. 'I'm okay.'

'You're not okay! You need to see a doctor!'

Although she isn't clearly visible in the dimness, I feel her eyes penetrating me. I groan and bury my head under the blankets.

I must have fallen back to sleep; my eyes open to find Sadie standing at my bedside, nudging my shoulder. I shield my eyes from the beams of sunlight squeezing through a gap in the flimsy curtains.

'Get up, you lazy so and so.'

'Would you not be a lazy so and so if you were awake most of the night?' I close my eyes, attempting to block out the annoying sunlight and my equally annoying sister.

'Come on, we'll be late for work, I'm not waiting on you today. I'm not keeping myself back.'

I fire back the blankets. 'Don't let *me* keep you back, head you on!'

Sadie remains hovering over the bed, her hands now firmly set on her hips, a look of defiance glaring in her eyes.

'Molly, every day is the same with you lately, we have to practically drag you out of your pit. Are you going to get up, or are you going to stay in your bed all day?'

27

'Stay in my bed all day? Now that's an idea!'

Sadie releases a sigh. It's evident she's getting more agitated by the minute.

'Okay, okay I'm getting up, you ol' moaner.'

I drag myself out of bed reluctantly, rubbing my hands through my messy hair and sighing at the thought of another day at work, wanting desperately to jump back in and curl up in the warmth. But if I went back to bed, there would be no getting me out of it today.

Sadie and I work together at Tillie and Henderson's factory. Employment for men in Derry is pretty scarce, but for women there's an abundance of jobs available in the shirt factories. The industry is thriving in our city and Tillie and Henderson's is the leading firm to be employed with. It's seen as a godsend to the poverty-stricken people of the city, and has encouraged the role of breadwinner onto the women of Derry. We are proud to have such a grand factory. Almost every girl in the area works for Tillie's.

The striking characteristic of the factory is the real family atmosphere it has acquired as a result of many families having maybe two or more family members working there. I've been employed at Tillie's for almost two years. The memories of my first day are still as clear as crystal, etched in my mind.

It's custom for teenagers to leave education around the age of fourteen; nobody stays in school any longer than they need to. As soon as my fourteenth birthday arrived, the overwhelming eagerness to enter the big bad world was immense. With Sadie already working at Tillie's, I was certain to get employment there too and start earning some much needed money.

My first day was quite a scary experience. The look of my new boss Liam Doherty was enough to terrify me. His eyes were striking, his hair combed neatly with not one strand out of place, and his shoes and clothes immaculately clean. My first impression of him was a fusspot, a man that took no nonsense; one look from this creature could put fear into me.

Goodness only knows what his impressions of me were. Mr Doherty looked at me from the feet up and back to my feet again, with his deep blue, quizzical eyes, that were just about visible under thick, bushy eyebrows.

'Hello there, I'm Liam Doherty, and you are?'

'Hello. My name is Molly, Molly O'Connor, sir.'

'Well, Molly, welcome to Tillie's.'

'Thank you, sir.'

His eyes fixated on the stranger before him: my long, wavy brown hair clinging to my bony face, soaked from the downpour of rain that I'd managed to get myself caught up in. My shoes were muddy, the result of galloping through fields with a thumping heart, reaching the bus stop just in time. He must have struggled to contain himself from laughing at the sight before him. I looked like a drowned rat, in a coat that was a size too big, drooping around my skinny frame, and to top it all off, it was missing a button.

He threw me a look of disapproval.

'I take it you're Sadie's sister, am I right?' he frowned.

'That's correct, sir.'

'Well, you've a hard act to follow, she's one of my finest workers, and I'll be expecting the same standards from

29

yourself.'

'Aye, of course, sir.'

'Now, Molly, let's go through some ground rules. You're probably aware that we're one of the biggest factories in Europe, manufacturing shirts like no other. Since Tillie's opened on 30th December 1856, the presence of this plant is a revolution that has put our city firmly on the industrial map. Why, you may think? I'll tell you why, because here at Tillie's we work, work, work! Working hard at all times is the first rule!'

'I'll work hard, promise. I'd never consider myself to be lazy, sir.'

'Good, Molly, you get nothing out of life being idle. Second rule,' he pointed a finger in my direction, so close he almost touched my nose, 'make sure you're on time. Latecomers will not be allowed into the workplace!'

It's known that if you're one minute late for work Mr Doherty would shut the door on your face. I certainly didn't want the door to be banged on my face, what with me being famous for always running behind time: late for school, late for dinner, late for Sunday mass, I'll probably be late for my own funeral!

'Okay, sir.' Nerves started to jangle in the pit of my stomach. It was clear this man took no nonsense.

Although he scared the wits out of me at the beginning, I grew to respect him and I sense the feeling is now mutual. One thing is for sure, if you work hard he'll leave you alone, and boy did I work my socks off! Mr Doherty respects hard workers. He's a fair boss to all. Nobody is treated with any difference.

I was appointed as a clipper, a job given to all new starters and a horrible, tedious one it is, I'm still waiting to be promoted! We're paid just half a crown to sit the entire day cutting loose threads from shirts before they are sent out. Not an enjoyable task, but there's no choice in the matter – someone has to do it. It's monotonous and extremely boring, but my family desperately need the money, and besides, I've left school with minimal education to do anything else with my life, something I regret now only two years later. Whilst at school I never really thought of anything else but getting out to work; looking back, my school days weren't as bad as I thought they were at the time.

The factory is nicknamed 'the sweat room', which is true to its name. Many a day the sweat would be lashing off us as we carried out our daily tasks; however, in the winter it's quite the opposite – it can reach freezing point. Most of the time we don't mind the extreme temperatures as the fun is always so good, it takes our mind off the cold and the heat. Some of the girls would break into a song to keep our spirits up, and it's always when we are least expecting it.

Emily is famous amongst the others for her silly songs. She often finds ways to have everyone in tears of laughter. On the hot summer days she will bellow out her famous tune, *'Oh I do wish I was down by the sea, where the seagulls they fly high and would shit right in your pie, where the seagulls they fly high, they fly high ...'* The girls would laugh and urge her for another tune, in which she needs very little encouragement. Emily being the show-off that she is never disappoints them.

31

Emily has been a friend of mine from a very early age, since we met at school. We are the best of buddies, but we're also like chalk and cheese. She loves being the centre of attention, whilst I hate it and would do anything to fade into the background. She's often full of jokes yet I can never remember one to tell. She's fun to be around, no matter how doom and gloom a situation is, she'll find a way to make me laugh, sparkling the dull moments as soon as she opens her mouth to speak.

Emily managed to get a job as a smoother. Having a friend as a smoother has its perks. For lunch most of the girls usually bring in homemade bread. Emily will use the hot irons to press the bread to make delicious toast, a great treat on the cold winter days. The hot toasted bread is a real indulgence, with the butter melting and trickling down our arms; it's mouth-watering.

Tillie and Henderson's stands proud on the Abercorn Road end of the Craigavon Bridge, and the magnificent building can be seen for miles across Derry.

From a distance, the sound of the factory horn can be heard. It screeches at ten minutes to eight every morning, wakening the city, and for this reason it has inherited the nickname, 'Derry's alarm clock'. The noise has the ability of sending the adrenalin pulsing through our veins; on hearing it we take to our heels, and dash towards the factory doors.

The first job of each day is the 'rat check', yes, the rat check! It's a must as the building is crawling with the dirty creatures. Our intruders make their way out from their hiding places during the night to rummage through the factory for food. It's custom for the girls to take their lunch at their work station, and as a result of this eating habit crumbs of food, such as fresh scone bread, often end up around the machines or on the floor. The disgusting beasts mainly munch on pieces of paper and fabric so the delicious, home-baked scone bread is a treat, and if there happens to be a smear of jam on it, they're in for a bonus!

The rats have become braver over time, the cheeky imps venturing out during the day. On one occasion Sadie put on her beautiful, new coat – that she saved for, for almost an eternity – only to discover a baby rodent chewing at the inside of the pocket. She let out a mighty shriek. We all jumped in fright. A furry head peeked out of the pocket, its minstrel eyes wide with fright; at once a bunch of crazy women sent out shockwaves of screams at the sight in front of them. The poor creature must've been scared witless at the drama that unfolded, without warning it leapt to the ground and scurried across the floor, before disappearing through a pile of boxes.

'The filthy beast! I can't believe it was in my good coat!'

Sadie wriggled herself out of the coat, her face crimson with rage. She marched across to the bin and dumped the garment into it, without giving the matter a second thought.

'How can I ever wear it again with that dirty thing crawling around the pocket, ahh it's so disgusting.'

'Ah, Sadie, wise up!' shouted one of the girls.

'Aye, catch yourself on, Sadie,' another called.

'Aye, it'll do you no harm, just give it a good wash, sure it'll be alright,' Emily tried to reassure her.

Soon everyone in the room began to giggle. I chewed on my bottom lip to prevent me from bursting into laughter at my sister, the drama queen, knowing only too well she wouldn't see the funny side of it. She shook her head, furious at everyone, before storming off towards the door, hating the joke being on her.

'Aaaaaagh, no, not another one!' Sadie cried.

She froze on the spot, her eyes wide with horror as another larger rat scampered past her.

'That's it, where's Mr Doherty when you need him? He's got to do something about this place!'

'Sadie, give over, stop making a drama out of it,' Emily joked.

'Well if the rest of you are happy to work with rats, work away. I'm not operating with that filth!' She flung open the door and dashed outside into the cool air, without a coat!

The girls exploded into fits of laughter. With Sadie gone, I could join them. I watched in amusement as Mary Deeny retrieved the expensive garment from the bin and squeezed into it.

'Hey this doesn't look too bad on me, what do you think, girls?'

Mary being a hefty woman, it just about reached her

shoulders. The girls began to chuckle yet again whilst Mary pranced up and down the floor, mimicking Sadie and pretending to fling the coat into the bin.

'Oh aye, have a good laugh.' Sadie's voice echoed throughout the room as she marched up to Mary, a stern look etched on her face. We were too wrapped up watching Mary, nobody had noticed her returning.

'Give me it back!' she demanded.

'Here, you can have it. Sure it's too big for me anyway.' Mary grinned.

Sadie snatched the coat from her. With caution she flung it over her arm, screwing her nose up at the same time, as if she was about to catch some kind of horrible disease. She finally had her beloved possession back. We should've known she would be back for it, knowing Sadie; she's famous to perform on impulse and then act sensibly once she calms herself down.

It was from that event that the 'rat check' was established.

Emily begins clicking a pair of scissors and kicking boxes as she passes, hoping to disturb any rodents that may be hiding.

I sat quietly at my work station. After yesterday's shocking news nothing feels real anymore.

'Anybody here like their tails trimmed? Or perhaps your whiskers might need a little clip?' *Snap, snap, snap* went the scissors, as Emily clicks them open and shut.

'Gees, you're making enough noise to waken the whole town, can you keep it down a little?'

'Molly, I have to make as much noise as possible to scare them off.' Emily rolled her emerald eyes.

'At this time of the morning?'

'Ah, Molly, what's up with you today? Are you in bad tune or what?'

I rub my tired head; it aches from major lack of sleep. I long to curl up into a ball and disappear for the day. 'The sound of those scissors is doing my head in,' I reply through gritted teeth.

'Ah, sure it'll help waken us all up. You look as if you could go back to your bed.'

'Aye,' I sigh.

Emily pokes her foot into a pile of fabric on the floor beneath my machine and out pops an enormous fat rat. Its body freezes for a few seconds; its chest heaves up and down, as its heart goes into panic mode. Before I know it, it has jumped right up onto my lap and then onto my workbench. The other girls release frantic screams. Their screeches echo around the room. I sit glued to my chair, unable to move an inch. Its dense black eyes fix on mine, but still I remain frozen to my seat.

Emily swiftly reaches for a huge piece of material and fires blows down upon the frightened creature, the rat dances about frantically in fear, whilst Emily flings the fabric in all directions.

Finally, it bounces back onto the floor and runs for its life, its nails scraping across the floorboards, before disappearing out of sight. I sit staring blankly into thin air, the commotion hasn't fazed me. It didn't bother me in the slightest. If only a rat was my biggest problem, but no, there's a bigger, two-legged rat and what he did to me, racing around my head right now.

'Molly, I can't believe you just sat there! That thing could have pounced on you at any minute.' Emily shakes her head in disbelief. 'Are you not aware that a rat in fear can go for your throat? I know a girl that was out walking one night when she was confronted by one, it sprang up and sank its claws into her neck, it was a whole handling trying to get her set free.' Emily released a sigh and shook her head, tossing her blonde locks to and fro.

I gaze at her speechless.

'Right girls, I think we need a wee puff after that ordeal. Let's go get a cigarette and don't worry about Mr Doherty catching us. I'll not be long in giving him a piece of my mind!' Emily clicked her fingers. 'Come on, girls, let's go.'

I stay fixed to my seat, unable to move an inch, the clatter and shuffling of chairs vibrate through the room as the others immediately follow Emily for a smoke.

'Come on, Molly, are you coming with us?'

I remain silent.

'No, in fact you *are* coming with us.' Emily returns and

pulls me up. I follow her out of the room in a trance.

I, just like many other girls, began smoking at a ridiculously young age, taking my first cigarette just before my fifteenth birthday. The only reason I started the habit was because we are allowed a five-minute break every two hours for a cigarette. It's a pathetic excuse for a break from our jobs, but one that many a girl embarks on just to get away from their sewing machines.

With smoking being an expensive habit, 'passing the butt' is a common custom amongst the girls. We take it in turns to buy cigarettes and share them at break times, with each girl taking a puff, then passing it on to the next; if you happen to be the last person in the queue you're usually blessed if there's anything left.

The smoke break is a chance for us to get caught up with the 'bars and the banter'. The jokes amongst the girls are always a good laugh.

Today I refuse my turn of the butt and my mood feels too low to enjoy the banter. I fold my arms tightly across my chest and lean my weight against the wall in a bid to prevent myself from collapsing; my legs feel like jelly and my stomach has begun performing somersaults, making me feel I could pass out at any minute.

'Gee, Molly, what's wrong with you? Our furry friend must've given you some scare. You're actually refusing a smoke.' Emily chuckles holding the butt between nicotine-stained fingers. 'It'll not go to waste,' she teases, as she inhales before blowing out rings of smoke.

I press my head against the wall and swallow hard. Suddenly saliva begins forming in the back of my mouth and beads of sweat have pushed their way out through my pores. My hands become clammy, the back of my neck feels sticky. I need to be sick.

With so much going on in my head I don't know if I'm coming or going. It won't be long until I'm the topic of the 'bars' and juicy gossip. I dread the suspicious looks and the talking behind my back, which will surely begin if they discover my news. My pregnancy will be the biggest headline to hit the factory. I know I have to try to remain tight-lipped for as long as possible.

One thing is for sure, they won't know the whole truth. The thought of my colleagues giving me sympathy makes me shudder.

'Molly, what *is* up with you today? You're not yourself at all. You're in a wee world of your own.' Emily nudges me, bringing me away from my thoughts. 'Did you hear what I just said?'

'What? No, sorry, what did you say? I'm just not feeling too good today.' I wipe the sweat from my forehead with the back of my hand.

'Friday? Do you remember what's happening on Friday? We're trying to sort out the plan.'

'What plan? What's happening on Friday?' I question, not caring what is happening. One thing is for sure, I'm not going out dancing with them. A night out is the last thing I need.

'Oh, Molly, your head is away with it today all right. I'll give you a clue – your sister.'

I look at her with a blank expression. 'I haven't got any idea what you're talking about, Emily.'

'Sadie's leaving on Friday. We're trying to organise her send-off! She's leaving to get married! Or have you forgotten that too?'

'Oh, that's right.' I wipe another layer of perspiration from my forehead.

Sadie is leaving to get married to Mark Burns. Mark is the son of a well-known businessman, his father being in the retail business. He is an absolute gentleman and our family adores him. We are pleased that Sadie has found herself a good man. Mark's father is retiring soon and Mark is taking over the firm. It's usual for women to leave their jobs if they marry a wealthy man and can afford to stay at home. Sadie is due to get married in a few weeks and so she's leaving work to begin a new life.

'Well, daydreamer, I'll run over the plans again, and listen carefully this time. As I was saying, as soon as we come back from our smoke break tomorrow afternoon, say about four o'clock, we'll catch her off-guard,' Emily whispers prior to taking a long drag of her cigarette. 'Molly, you and I will get the trolley and ribbons ready, and Mary will grab her. The rest of you do the usual. That okay?'

I nod in agreement, trying to look enthusiastic. 'Aye no

problem, we know the craic by now.'

It's common amongst the factory girls to give a girl a 'doing' before she goes off to get married. It's hilariously funny, but I guess a terrifying experience for the bride-to-be. It begins with getting tied up with coloured ribbons, well, not real ribbons but pieces of cloth cut up like ribbons. Next the girl gets covered in bright red lipstick, before being put into a large wicker trolley and wheeled around the factory. The rest of the girls rattle and shuffle their chairs, clapping and cheering as loud as they can. We then take her outside to tie her to a lamppost and douse her with flour and eggs.

The bride-to-be would be aware that she is likely to get a 'doing', and so she would be on her guard and extra careful towards the end of the week. We knew Sadie would try to clear off home early on Friday so the girls planned to catch her on Wednesday, when she would be least expecting it.

We stop again for a smoke break in the afternoon and Emily goes over the plans once more to the girls, who are barely able to hold back their excitement. Sadie is known to the factory girls as being a bit of a 'poser', and it's not hard to tell why they call her such names. She's never to be seen with a hair out of place and is often dressed in expensive clothes, with not as much as a speck of dust on her shoes. Her fussy nature is enough to drive you up the walls. The girls know that Sadie will likely go berserk at the thought of getting flour and eggs poured over her neat, shiny locks. They also know she will act the drama queen and so they are waiting on that day patiently. One thing is for sure – they will get a good laugh.

Wednesday afternoon comes. With a nod from Emily, the hefty Mary Deeny pounces across the room to Sadie's work station; before any of the rest of us know it, she has flung my delicate sister over her broad shoulder, like a flimsy, little rag doll and carts her to the waiting trolley. A shocked Sadie kicks and flings her limbs in all directions in an attempt to get free, but it is useless. Mary Deeny is built like a tank, it would take much more than our dainty Sadie to get free from Mary's strong grasp.

'You better put me down,' a horrified Sadie screeches. 'What the heck do you think you're doing?' Legs and arms kick about fiercely.

Laughter erupts from all directions.

'I mean it, Mary! You're soooooooo dead when I get you, you better put me down! Put me down, now!'

Sadie's voice is frosty and by the look on her face, she is just about to throw the biggest tantrum we have ever witnessed.

'Ah, ha, ha, ha, you and which army, princess?' Mary flashes a mischievous grin.

'Princess? Don't you dare patronise me.'

'Ah sure, it's only a bit of fun, princess.'

Mary empties her into the trolley with Sadie holding on to her tightly, white-knuckled and refusing to let go until one of the other girls forces her fingers away, sending her plunging in deeper. Her eyes peer out at the others, like a frightened animal that has just been caught in a trap.

42

Laughter and cheers fill the air again. Not only do they tie ribbons to Sadie's hair, but Emily makes up a mixture of eggs and flour and smothers them over her pretty locks. To our surprise, Sadie stops moaning and grins.

'Ah well, there's no good me fighting, I may as well get it over and done with.' She chuckled as they wheeled her from one end of the factory floor to the other.

I, on the other hand can just about manage a smile. My mind drifts off for a few seconds, as crazy thoughts of the situation I'm in race through my brain, sending my heart to thud against my ribcage. How I wish I was Sadie, getting pushed about in a trolley, with not a care in the world.

'Will you come on?' Emily drags me along, to join in with the fun.

Suddenly my eyes fill with tears. I swallow hard, trying to clear the lump in my throat; it is useless. It isn't long before salty tears trickle down both cheeks, seeping through my lips and falling onto my shirt.

'Ouch, for goodness sake what's up with you? Stop worrying, sure you'll find a good man one day yourself,' Mary announces with a curious look in her eyes, as she playfully ruffles my hair.

I stare back at her in disbelief. Does she really think I'm somehow upset, or worse still, does she think I'm jealous of Sadie? Aye, I'm jealous alright. I'm jealous not of our Sadie but of every female in the room in front of me. I want to shout from the rooftops at them all and ask 'why me?' Why did I have to be the one that was attacked? Why do I have to be the one that is left carrying his child? Why did my little, safe world have to be turned upside down? And why do I have to stand here and pretend that everything is alright, when the truth is I want to curl myself up into a ball and die somewhere?

It's evident that Sadie and I don't always get on well. She's forever trying to dictate to me, telling me what to do, always poking her nose into my affairs. The other girls know Sadie and I are sometimes distant with each other, but for heck's sake we're sisters. I would never envy my sister being happy. I'm pleased she has found a good man, someone that will take care of her. Right now I want to slap Mary across the face, but I know it's not her I need to take my anger out on, so I turn quietly away and dry my tears.

My lower lip trembles whilst I desperately try to shrug off Mary's comments. I attempt to clear my throat again, in a bid to defend myself, but it's useless; the tears well up for the second time, and I can once again feel the warm moisture rapidly stream down my cheeks.

'Oh, Molly, come here.' A gentle voice spoke amongst the silence and it is then that I realise that all eyes are on me, watching intensely. Emily makes her way over; she puts her arms around my shoulders, squeezing me gently. 'You'll be okay.'

'Aye, of course I will.' I sniffle and quickly try to compose myself. 'I know I'm just being silly, it's just that I'll miss our Sadie so much when she leaves the house.'

'Aye you're right you're being silly, sure I'll be over to

see you more times than enough.'

Sadie wipes a lump of gooey mixture off her lips and flings it playfully in my direction.

I try to squeeze a smile as the concoction lands on my cheek. From the corner of my eye I catch Emily watching me suspiciously. She knows I have just told a lie. The first thing that's raised Emily's suspicions is the fact I never cry much, and secondly it is only less than a week ago that I told her I couldn't wait to see the back of our Sadie!

Chapter 4

The door etches open and a smiling face peeps in. 'Is that a fry I smell?' Donal lifts his head and breathes in the strong aroma of bacon rashers and sausages. 'Hope there's some on that pan for me.' He grins as he steps into the kitchen.

'Of course there is, I got up early just to make you breakfast,' I smile back. 'It'll be ready in a few minutes.'

'Great! I'm starving, and a good fry is just what the doctor orders before a day's work.'

Donal removes the teapot from the stove and pours himself a mug of tea before taking a seat at the table.

I throw more rashers of bacon into the pan, in no time they are sizzling away.

'Gee that smells good, Molly.'

'Here, get tucked into this, breakfast won't be long.'

He smacks his lips at the sight of the platter of hot toast.

'Why are you up so early today?' he asks as he slathers a thick lay of butter on the toast; at once it melts. 'You usually enjoy a lie-in on a Saturday.'

'Ah, I couldn't sleep,' I reply, and crack an egg into the pan.

'What? Molly O'Connor couldn't sleep? Molly, you have to be joking.' He munches on his food.

I force a smile and place the plates of food on the table,

plates filled high with bacon, sausages, eggs, pudding and mushrooms. 'You make it sound as if I'm lazy.' I take a seat opposite him.

'No, you're not lazy. We all know you just enjoy your sleep too much. If the others hear you're up this early, they'll be thinking you're sick or something.'

His joke is enough to churn my stomach and put me off my food; if only he knew the truth!

'What's up?' he mumbles through a mouthful of toast. 'Why are you not eating?'

I toy with my bacon and eggs, pushing them around the plate with my fork, unable to eat a bite.

'What's wrong, Molly?' he pops some egg into his mouth. 'Your breakie will go cold.'

'Oh, I'm not that hungry after all.' My mouth freezes in an uneasy smile.

'Give it here then, it won't go to waste.' Donal reaches across the table and plunges his fork into a piece of bacon before transferring it to his plate. 'At least eat some toast before it goes cold too.'

'No, I'm fine; I'll give that a miss as well.'

'Molly, you need to eat something, it's not good going about on an empty stomach. There's no danger of me doing that.' He laughs and bites into a sausage.

There is something in his voice and a look in his eyes; I can't spoil it for him today. How can I break this news to him now? Such a weight of secrets plague my thoughts.

'Here, Donal,' I push my plate across the table. 'Take the rest of it.'

Throughout the years Donal and I have been like sticking plasters. We virtually did everything together and were rarely seen without each other. As well as being brother and sister, we were the best of mates; many people thought we were twins. With our deep, chocolate-brown hair inherited from our mother, our father's high cheekbones and almond-shaped blue eyes, similar height and build, it is easy to see why people would mistake us for twins.

Mother would usually send us to fetch fresh eggs from Mrs Flannigan's. We adored this chore and had many an adventure along the way.

Mrs Flannigan never seemed to take the same clothes off her. Her usual clothing consisted of a dull blue blouse, dirty, a whitish apron which had all sorts of stains on it, and a tattered skirt. She kept her hair tied back with a shredded ribbon. Her face had a grimy look about it as if it had never seen a drop of water, never mind a few suds of soap. Her cheeks were rosy red, like someone had just beaten her with a few prunes. She smelt disgusting: a mixture of turf, cows' dung and tobacco – not a pleasant combination. She hasn't changed much over the years. She is very rarely seen without her beloved cat Lucky tucked under her arm. Perhaps he should have been called Unlucky, for he lost an eye during a battle with another cat and walked with a limp.

As soon as we touched the rusted gate it creaked, and the sound would alert the geese and chickens that wandered about freely. Most of the birds would flee in different directions, but sometimes a few cheeky geese would stand proud, heads in the air, and their beady eyes would fix a stare on us. Some would make their way towards us and nudge at our legs as we walked through the filthy backyard. They didn't bother Donal, but I was terrified that they would bite me. As they tried to peck at my bare legs, many a time the thought would enter my mind to give one a good kick, to send it flying out of my way, but my sense of right wouldn't allow it. I hated her annoying little creatures. I feared I would fall over and land flat on my face in the disgusting backyard; if that ever did happen, well, all I can say is my toe would aim for the nearest feathered backside, conscience or no conscience!

Donal and I would creep into the hall of her home when she was busy getting the eggs. She is the only person that I know of that has carpet. Carpet is a fine luxury for the rich. The rest of us has to accept bare floorboards. Her home is wonderfully decorated with expensive ornaments and chandeliers but everything is coated with dust and it smells stale. A grand piano sits untouched in the living room. It is known that Mrs Flannigan is a fine pianist with a singing voice of an angel; not sure if that's true – I can't ever imagine her with a voice of an angel!

It is believed that her husband had an affair with her one and only friend when Peter was only a baby. Apparently they fled over the border to Donegal, but she remains tight-lipped about that matter. Perhaps there is some truth in it as she

49

has the bitterness of a lemon; something must have happened to make her so hostile towards others. She trusts no one and treats people with high suspicion. We have to give her the money first before she will exchange the goods. I find that amusing, as if we would be stupid enough to do a runner. After all, security is tight, we would have some battle getting past those geese! And knowing me, I would be *unlucky* enough to trip over her beloved Lucky!

'Who needs a guard dog? Just buy a few geese. They'll not be long in sorting burglars out,' I would whisper to Donal.

As a child, I hadn't much admiration for this lady. I saw her as a greedy old woman. Financially she was well off; she could afford to give people 'tick', which meant she would give you goods and you could then pay her at a later date. She would also give loans of money. 'Tick' and loans were only handed over once you signed her little black notebook. She added a ridiculous amount of interest on the loans, preying on the vulnerable, taking extra money from people who genuinely couldn't afford it. They got poorer and she got richer, that was just not fair in my eyes.

On the way to our errand we would pick wild blackberries from the bushes that lined the country roads, the only danger associated with this was the threat of getting stung by a bee or a wasp. After we gathered up the blackberries in a jar, we then took them back to our mother so that she could make delicious jam, which was a real treat smothered on a thick slice of scone bread.

During the summer months our trips to Mrs Flannigan's

were always so enjoyable. We would skip up the country roads under the scorching sun, the deep aroma of honeysuckle thick in the air. The delightful sounds of birds tweeting in the trees, and the buzz of the bumblebees busy gathering their pollen from the range of wild flowers that grew nearby, was music to our ears.

A much-loved game of Donal's was racing one another to see who could reach Mrs Flannigan's house first. He always won. Sometimes I would win, but he was such a bad competitor and huffed if I beat him, so to save arguments, I would let him succeed most of the time, not wanting to hurt his ego. I couldn't be bothered with his petty behaviour.

Our preferred hobby of all was collecting dead things. We would scan the countryside and pick up dead birds, hedgehogs, rabbits and even worms and bees. In fact any creature that we found that had breathed its last, we lifted up and carried home to bury in a nearby field. We then went on a search to collect pieces of wood to make a little cross to place above the grave. Each creature would be given a name before its burial. Donal had an old, rusty nail which he used to carve the name of the deceased onto the cross. Mother would watch us from her bedroom window in amusement as we bowed our little heads in prayer for the dead.

Sometimes we would venture into Mr Brown's fields. He is a local farmer who owns many acres of land, used for grazing his sheep and cattle. He is a small, stout man with not a hair on his head. He looks unruly and unclean at all times. He is also the grumpiest man I have ever met and is well known for his bad temper. Nobody likes him much. He has three daughters and they are all friendly, quiet girls; obviously they haven't inherited their father's personality.

If we were unfortunate enough to be caught trespassing on his property he would come running behind us, waving his stick in the air and threatening to slap our backsides.

Mr Brown had a small orchard of apple trees growing on his land, with an abundant supply of the delicious fruit. He knew this was the reason we were tempted to trespass on his property. If he caught us taking his apples he would go off his head. Two young children would easily outrun the plump, unfit man, and so we never feared roaming through his property to get our hands on the fruit, daring each other to go and fetch a handful.

I remember on one occasion it was my turn to get the apples when I managed to get myself stuck up a tree.

'Donal, Donal I'm stuck! Help me get down.'

I kicked my leg frantically in an attempt to free it from the branches but it was useless, the strong twigs were not willing to let go. I yelled through my tears.

Donal lay on the ground rolling about laughing and taunting me. I began to panic, without warning and without knowing what I was doing I opened my mouth and screamed and screamed and screamed. Donal, seeing the seriousness of the situation, eventually gave in and climbed up to help release my leg.

'Ha, ha look what we have up there! Is it two little birds

pecking at my apples?' A sarcastic voice came from below us. 'No, not at all, it's two little thieving shits!'

Mr Brown stood below us in his dirty boots and waved his stick in the air. He looked up at us with a scary grin on his face, his red face glowing with rage and his bald head shining like a spit-polished boot. Buster, his collie dog paused beside him waggling his tail to and fro.

'You little rascals! What do you think you are at? What have I told you about thieving my apples, and what do you brats think you're doing on my land anyway? I'll tell you what you're doing, you're trespassing! I hate trespassers!'

Mr Brown's words fired from his mouth. He had a sharp tongue, a tongue that could clip a hedge. His rage was developing more and more by the second. My panic soon turned to fear, adrenalin rushed through my veins.

'We're sorry, sir,' I heard myself reply helplessly. 'We're really, really sorry, sir.'

Donal took a fit of giggling.

'Sorry? You're right to be sorry, and what do you think *you're* laughing at, you little smart-arse?' He threw Donal an angry look before returning his scary face back to me. 'Now get down off my tree before I come up there and drag you down myself, and if I have to do that I'm going to put my dung-encrusted boot up your backsides, so far up you'll be spitting out cow's shit!'

He pointed a grubby finger in our direction, a finger that was decorated with a thick, dirty nail, the earth baked deep within it from the many years of farming his land.

Donal threw a sun-kissed leg over a branch in an attempt to go down, but accidentally put too much pressure on it, sending a spray of apples plunging to the ground below, directly on top of Mr Brown. To our horror, one of them bounced with such force off his bald head.

'Ouch! You little brats!'

Without warning Donal grabbed my arm. 'Quick, Molly, let's get out of here!'

He pulled me with him as he jumped onto the grass below. The adrenalin pumped through us.

'Run, Molly!'

'Go get them, Buster!' Mr Brown yelled as he gathered himself together and ran after us.

Donal dragged me along so hastily my feet barely touched the ground.

Our little legs galloped through the fields like a pair of racehorses. Never in my life did I sprint so fast.

We stormed through the orchard, jumped over a small wooden fence and into the field, running amongst the grazing cattle until we finally came to another wooden fence that led us onto the road, not once looking behind us. There was a strong smell of cow dung lingering in the air all around us and it made my stomach turn. Feeling that we were now safe, we both sat at the edge of the road gasping for breath. Buster caught up with us and the friendly pet began to lick my face.

'Oh no, he's following. Get up, Molly!'

Once again Donal dragged my arm and we set off for home, through the country roads, spurring the dust on the surface with our heavy boots. Our poor legs ached as we dashed as fast as we could, without stopping until we reached the front door of our house. Donal banged on the door until our mother opened it. We had just got our foot over the doorstep when firm hands lurched forward and gripped the two of us, holding us tightly by the collars of our shirts.

Mother looked at us in bewilderment.

'What is going on?' A look of shock appeared on her face as she met the red face of the unfit farmer. 'Mr Brown, what has happened to you?'

'These little brats have been stealing from my orchard, trespassing on my property. If that's not bad enough, they have only gone and hit me with my own apples!'

'What can I say, sir? I'm sorry, but I'm also extremely stunned. My children have never done anything to annoy anyone in the past and I can assure you, they will not be upsetting you again.'

She shook her head at both of us and looked at us with so much authority it made me feel ashamed.

'Say sorry. Do you two hear me? Apologise!'

We nodded in agreement, too afraid to lift our eyes to look at Mr Brown, who by now was puffing and panting; it sounded as if he was about to have a heart attack.

'I said, apologise to the gentleman.' She lowered her disappointed eyes.

'I'm sorry,' I replied nervously.

'Aye, me too, I'm sorry,' Donal chirped.

'This won't happen again. They won't be back on your land. I can assure you of that.'

'Oh you're right they won't. I never want to see the pair of them on my property for as long as I live.' He grabbed both of us by the ears and yelled, 'Do you hear me?'

We nodded once more without saying a word before Mr Brown clipped the pair of us around the lobes, gave Donal a quick kick up the backside and stormed off, leaving us standing in the hallway holding our stinging ears and looking sheepishly at our mother.

'I think you two better come in and sit down, you have a bit of explaining to do.'

We told her everything that had happened. She listened carefully before telling us off and sending us to our rooms. We were grounded for a week and ordered to remain in our quarters. Being held a prisoner was worse than getting a good beating, at least a few slaps was over and done with in seconds. The grounding was gruelling punishment, having to watch the other kids in the street playing and having fun. It did, however, give us plenty of time to think about what we had done. One of the things that struck me the most was my mother telling us that she had not reared us to steal. At no point before did I think we were thieving, we never looked at it as stealing, just young kids having some fun and stuffing ourselves with the delicious apples to curb our hunger pains. It made me appreciate that my mother was right. No matter what way we looked at it, we were robbing and causing a nuisance to an old man.

We blamed each other for our punishment. Donal gave off to me for getting us into the mess. 'If you hadn't have been such a cry-baby we wouldn't have got caught.'

'Well you were taunting me instead of helping me. It's not my fault, it's yours,' I fired back. There was no way I was taking the blame, after all, it wasn't entirely my doing.

'How's it my fault?'

'You're the one that always dares me to climb the tree. You made me go up.'

'It was your turn. I went up last week. Why did you cry so much anyway?' Donal screwed his face up. 'I can't believe you let out a massive squeal, you sounded like a pig being slaughtered!'

'Oh shut up,' I huffed.

The arguing went on for almost an hour and then Donal and I never spoke for almost three days. It was horrible.

For the majority of the week I sat perched on my mother's bed peering out at the other kids playing in the sunshine. The street was buzzing with activity. I longed to be out there too. Mr Hutton, our alcoholic neighbour, would stagger home late in the afternoons with his pipe protruding from his mouth and at the same time he would attempt to sing a song, to which we couldn't make head nor tail of. He sang the same tune night after night. The other kids were so used to him that they barely lifted an eyelid to his presence, until he retrieved his mouth organ and began to jump up and down in an attempt to perform a drunken Irish dance to the sound of his own dodgy music. It was hilarious to watch as the whole street would gather around and egg him on, with the kids stamping their feet and clapping their hands; with an audience he was in his element.

The highlight of the week was observing ' Nosy Nora' King. I laughed when I saw her standing at the end of her garden, eagle-eyed and listening carefully as two mothers up the street were engaged in an argument over their children.

Nosy Nora stood there, her brown hair swept back in its usual bun, shoulders taut, arms folded under her hefty bosom and chewing on her bottom lip, her brain taking in all the information it could. She is well known to over-exaggerate and blow matters out of proportion. I wondered what lies she would add to this matter; she is never short of a tale or two. Goodness knows what concoction of a story she would develop from this scenario. She knew everything about everyone, and nothing much went on in the street that she didn't know about. As soon as new information came to light she would make pathetic excuses to call into each of the neighbours, filling them in on any new juicy gossip.

My mother hated her coming into the house with information on other people's business. She had no time for her idle tittle-tattle. She warned us of the danger of chit-chat, explaining that scandal had no place in her home as it only destroys people's characters. Her usual saying was, *'Nobody has any room to talk about anyone else, everyone has their own skeletons in their closet'*. My mother never feared telling Nosy Nora exactly how she felt about her silly talk, and it was for this reason that Nosy Nora would always choose carefully what subjects to discuss in the presence of my mother, and when Nora engaged in blabbering in the street, my mother would often close the window to prevent the flow of gossip entering into our house.

It had been a long week stuck indoors and I certainly learned my lesson. I vowed I would never return to Mr Brown's again; it was safer to stick to picking up dead creatures. I also learned how stubborn Donal was. It was me that had to make the first move and apologise to him so that we could speak again. I couldn't tolerate the silence between us.

Once the week was over, Donal and I were back to our usual selves, collecting dead birds and climbing trees; of course, trees that were not on Mr Brown's property!

A loud knock on the front door interrupts my thoughts.

Donal glances at the clock, 'Gee, Molly, look at the time. That must be Sean O'Leary, must go.' He clambers from his chair, grabs his coat and peak cap before planting a loving kiss on my cheek. 'Thanks for the breakie, sis.'

'You're welcome.' My voice sails across the room as I watch him leave, and at once I begin to feel regretful for not

59

telling him about the pregnancy. An opportunity wasted.

Chapter 5

Sadie pulls back the curtains once more. A deep frown forms across her forehead at the sight of the burly clouds that have settled in the sky; thick, grey clouds that threaten to burst at any minute.

'Gee this weather does my head in! This would just have to be my luck wouldn't it? Why did we have to be born in Ireland? All it does here is rain, rain, rain. Why could I not have been born in some hot country?'

Uncle Mick smiles in amusement. 'You haven't stopped whining since you got up, girl. It's your wedding day. You're supposed to be happy! Sure aren't you marrying the man of your dreams? Speaking of that man of yours, does he know what he's letting himself in for, spending the rest of his life with you?'

'Oh get lost,' she looks over her shoulder to meet his eyes. 'He's one lucky man to catch me, and he knows it!'

'Lucky? Is that the fancy word for unfortunate?'

'Ah excuse me; if my memory's correct, you're still single, right?'

'And? What's wrong with that? I'm a bachelor and happy to remain that way.'

'You're single, Mick, almost forty-eight years of age and living with your younger sister and her kids, do I have to remind you? Why have you not found a woman for yourself, settled down and had children? I'll tell you why, because nobody would take you!' Sadie holds her hands on her hips, her body slightly curved to the right. She holds his gaze in a defiant stare. 'Isn't that right, Michael, dear?' Trying not to laugh, she chewed on her bottom lip.

'Nobody is *lucky* enough to catch a fine-looking chap like me. I could have my pick of women, but as I say, I'm happy, happy as a pig in mud and don't forget I only moved in here to help your mother look after you all after your father died. I don't need a girl. Sure all you are good for is moaning and groaning.' He holds his finger to his lips and stares at the ceiling, pretending to be deep in thought. His eyes squint, 'Oh, and cooking and doing the dishes. I suppose women are not bad at polishing boots either and ...'

Before Mick knows it, he has to make a swift dive, to avoid the missile that is flying through the air.

'You watch it, boy. You remember, men wouldn't be in this world if it wasn't for us women!' She flashes him one of her finest porcelain smiles. She's beautiful when she smiles.

'Gee, Sadie, I wasn't expecting to be hit up the face with a handbag! Sure I'm only winding you up, love. Mark is the luckiest man in Derry today.'

Mick steps closer and puts his arms around Sadie and presses a playful kiss to her cheek.

'Aye, it's about time something nice came out of that mouth of yours,' she teases as she looks out the window again and releases a huge sigh. 'Mother, did you leave out that Holy

Child of Prague statue last night?'

Mother continues smoothing the hot iron over Sadie's suit, humming delightfully, her thoughts a million miles away. The door from the living room that leads to the kitchen is ajar. I watch her curiously through the opening; her beautiful face reflecting contentment as she carries out her chore. It's evident she's ecstatic that her eldest daughter is about to get married. Like any mother would be, she's delighted her girl is marrying an ideal man.

'Mother, did you hear me?' Sadie calls again, getting slightly impatient.

She doesn't answer.

'Molly, will you ask her about the Child of Prague statue, or, if you like, you can go and look to see if she left it out.'

Like a puppy obeying my master I go to question my mother. She lifts her head from the ironing and lets out a gasp. 'Oh, Molly, I forgot about it!' She rubs her head and sighs. 'Oh how could I have forgotten?'

'Never worry. It's not the end of the world,' I reply in my best reassuring voice.

'It could be for our Sadie.'

We both laugh.

'Well, she seems in good mood. Mick is with her, they're in there winding one another up.'

It's a well-known tradition in Ireland – if you want the

rain to stay away on your wedding day, you must place the Child of Prague statue outside of the house the night before the wedding. Devotion to the infant Jesus is strong in Ireland. A special attachment to the Divine Child originated with the Carmelites in Prague at the start of the seventeenth century.

Nearly every home in Derry has a statue of the Child of Prague, and mysteriously nearly all of them have had to be mended as the hands have broken off. There is a great belief here, the more you respect Jesus, the more he will bless you and if you return the hands, then Jesus will bless you with peace. My mother adored her figurine; an old lady who lived next door to her as a child had given it to her.

I dread informing Sadie that the statue wasn't placed out last night; it's likely she will throw a tantrum.

'Sadie, she forgot to leave it out.'

No sooner have the words rolled from my tongue when Sadie bounces back with a mouthful.

'What do you mean, forgot to leave it out? That's it! It's bound to rain now. Our suits will get ruined and my hair will be a mess. Just look at those big black clouds. What kind of day is this for April anyway? It's springtime, where the heck is the nice sunshine?'

Sadie flings her arms up into the air and storms out of the room, almost knocking Donal over on the way out.

'What a nightmare!' Donal shrugs. 'That wee girl is never going to change.'

'Sure you know the kind of her, she's a drama queen.'

We both laugh and for a brief moment, I've almost forgotten about my dilemma.

'Donal and Molly, I'm not deaf, I can hear the both of you. And by the way, stop laughing at me!'

This was a foolish remark for Sadie to make. It makes us chuckle even more and Mick sniggers too; tears began to fill up in Donal's eyes as he giggles hysterically.

'Hey, Molly, do you remember the day you and Sadie were fighting at the top of the stairs? I think you might have been about nine or ten. What was all that about?'

A smile transforms my face as I recall the incident. 'Aye that's right, how could I forget that one?'

'What actually happened again?'

'I think we started fighting over the two stuffed teddies that our mother made for us. Do you remember mine had a red scarf and Sadie's a blue one, so that we knew our own?'

'Aye, that's correct. I do recall them; sure you wouldn't go out the door without yours. That's right, Sadie had lost hers and wanted your one, that's how the fight started, wasn't it?'

'Aye. I can call to mind her pulling the teddy from me whilst we were at the top of the stairs. I was standing facing the stairway whilst she was opposite. I pulled it back from her. Sadie began to pull in one direction and I pulled in the opposite and we went on like this back and forth for some time. The next thing I knew she tugged at the bear with a massive force, causing the arm to rip from its seams, sending her to topple backwards down about three or four steps. I clearly remember leaning over to grab her, to prevent her falling further, but she decided to slide herself on down, her head bopped up and down as she passed each stair. She then lay howling, and when our mother came running out to see what the commotion was about, Sadie accused me of throwing her down the stairs!'

'It was a good job Mick and I heard the both of you arguing. We decided to creep out to the hall to see what was going on. We witnessed it all, and we were able to tell the truth.'

'Aye and thankfully you did; I would've gotten a good telling off for that one. I probably would've been grounded for weeks.'

'It was after that we nicknamed her 'Drama Queen' wasn't it?'

'Aye, it definitely was indeed. She seems to be getting worse, Donal, as the years go on.'

'Ah well, maybe married life might just settle her down a bit,' he grins.

Without warning the living room begins to darken and outside appears to get duller. Suddenly the rain starts to drop, slowly at first, then it gathers speed until it parachutes down from the sky, so much so that everything outside is no longer clearly visible.

An angry voice shouts from upstairs, 'Oh, this is just not my day!'

Donal and I look at one another in amusement. We burst into a fit of giggles again, until a gentle flutter in my stomach startles me back into reality. My smile diminishes, fear sweeping through me at once. Just like the rat incident, I wish a bit of rain is all I have to worry about.

A few minutes later I peer at my reflection in the mirror, I'm dressed in a powder blue skirt, matching jacket and a cream blouse. I slip my feet into my shoes and as I lift my head up, to my horror I catch a glimpse of my expanding waistline: a tiny bump has formed. Whether I like it or not, this baby is growing at an alarming rate. I've been in denial for the past few weeks, refusing to look at my stomach and refusing to admit to myself that I am in this situation. My skirt feels uncomfortably tight, so much so I have to open the top button, giving me more room to breathe. My chest heaves at the release of my slow breath. I desperately hope nobody will notice.

'Molly, have you seen my bracelet?' My mother's question startles me.

Bracelet! My mind is at once flooded with thoughts of her heirloom. If only I'd never set my eyes on that thing, if it hadn't come off my arm, I wouldn't be in the mess that I'm in now. In fact, coming to think of it, I haven't seen it since that awful night. My mind reels over and over trying to figure out where it must be. It's no good. I can't recall where I've put it, therefore I decide to ignore her question.

Downstairs my mother is buzzing about like a bee trapped in a jar. I watch as she grabs her handbag and flicks a piece of fluff from Donal's suit as she passes him by. Thankfully she seems to have forgotten about the bracelet. The others are dressed and ready to go. It seems they are waiting on me. My gaze falls on Sadie. She looks stunning in her white, figure-hugging dress. Around her neck hangs a pearl necklace, a gift from Mark. She looks perfect. Soft, loose curls assemble delicately around her shoulders, and her swarthy skin glows against her frock. She looks radiant, I feel so proud of her. Sadie may be a 'drama queen' and a bit annoying at times, but she is still my sister and I love her dearly.

'You look amazing, Sadie, you're so beautiful,' I gasp. 'I wish you all the best for today and forever.'

I embrace her and hold her tightly for a few minutes. It's unusual for us to hug one another. She looks shocked at my compliments and even more surprised that I've shown her such affection. She smiles softly and puts her arms around me; for those brief seconds I feel so much love and warmth from my sister.

By now the rain has subsided and the sky is clearer, much to Sadie's relief.

'Right everyone let's go, Grandfather's waiting for us.' Donal ushers us towards the door. 'We need to go before Sadie. We don't want the bride arriving before us, do we?'

Outside we find him waiting patiently and Sadie's slightly irritated father-in-law-to-be. He's agreed to take Sadie to the church in his car, whilst my grandfather squeezes the rest of us into his vehicle. Very few folk have the pleasure of owning a car, and if you possess one you've plenty of money. We have neither, so getting transported in a vehicle is an exciting treat. We are like a bunch of kids all fighting over who is sitting in the front seat and who is getting the window seats at the back. In the end, my mother gets to sit in the front and Mick and Donal manage to get the window seats. Charlie and I are sandwiched in the middle, like a pair of sardines. Anna is fortunate enough to have got a lift with her friend's parents.

We pull up outside the red brick building of St Patrick's church; a small group of relatives and close friends are gathered in the porch, others stand smoking close to the neatly trimmed lawn. I spot my father's sister Aggie chatting to some family friends. I wave to greet her.

'Hi, Molly, how are you, love?' she grins and immediately makes her way over. 'Come here, give us a big hug. I haven't seen my favourite niece in ages. It's great to see you again, darling.' She gives me a tight squeeze.

'Hello Aggie, it's good to see you. Aye it's been a long time. I'll have to get a wee scoot down to you soon.'

'Of course you will, that'll be great. You all haven't stayed with us in ages. Next weekend, how's about it? Sure it'll be great craic, we've so much to catch up on.'

A huge grin appears on her chubby face, a grin so big it almost reaches her eyes. Before I can get a chance to answer or make any excuses Aggie begins looking around for my mother. It isn't long before she spots her amongst the crowd.

'Kate, come over here a minute.' Aggie waves her arms in the air, beckoning her to come over to join us. 'Molly's coming down to stay with us next weekend, isn't that right, Molly?'

Before I've had a chance to reply she continues, 'I want the rest of you down; it'll be a nice wee break for you.'

It is obvious from the astonished look on my mother's face that she's been caught off-guard. My mother knows it's no good trying to talk Aggie out of an idea; once she's made her mind up, there's no changing it. 'Ah it's a bit much for you, Aggie.'

'Not at all, don't be silly, I fitted you all in before in the past and I'll fit you all in now.'

'Well I ...'

'Well nothing, Kate, I don't want to hear any excuses.'

'Ah okay, I don't think I've any choice. I just don't want to be putting you to any trouble.'

'Trouble? Wise up, you're not trouble. We'll be glad of the company. We'll see you all next Friday.' She waves goodbye and follows her husband into the church.

'I didn't actually agree on going down to stay in Greencastle, you know the kind of her. I just suggested I'd come down sometime ...'

'Oh I know what she is like, don't worry about it. A wee break might just do us all the world of good, Molly.'

Father McGroarty steps from the church waving his arms frantically. 'Come on now folks get seated, we don't want to be hanging around out here when the bride arrives do we?'

We follow him into the chapel at once, likes lambs following their master. We quickly and quietly make our way to the pews and sit down. Emily comes in behind us and sits down next to me.

I glance around at the small crowd in the chapel. It isn't too difficult to distinguish our family from Mark's.

We're meekly dressed, clean and neat but nothing too fancy. Mark's family, on the other hand, appears outstanding in their grand hats and expensive tailored suits, together with shiny shoes and fancy jewellery. The men stand upright and walk into the chapel with an air of authority – you can tell they are men of importance – whilst the ladies stroll by with their heads held high, their noses stuck in the air, like there is no one like them.

'Oi, imagine having her as part of your family?' Emily nudges me in the ribs and rolls her eyes towards Mark's mother.

'Ssh, remember where you are.' I try not to laugh.

'Your Sadie will fit in with that crowd with no bother. She acts a right little snoot; she'll be grand with that family!'

'Sssssh, his toffee-nosed mother will hear you,' I whisper with a cheeky grin on my face.

Mark's mother is well known to be a very posh woman, one who looks down her nose at others. It's a wonder she even allowed her beloved son to marry our Sadie; then again, Sadie does appear a bit snobbish compared to the rest of us. Emily's right, Sadie will fit in with her in-laws well.

As the sound of the organ fills the chapel the crowd falls silent. Sadie enters the aisle, linked arm-in-arm with my grandfather. The place fills with aahs and gasps as she makes her way to meet Mark. He stands nervously at the altar watching her approach. His eyes twinkle as he gazes at his beautiful bride-to-be advancing towards him.

The wedding ceremony begins. I can't fully concentrate on the service, so many thoughts and images tumble about my mind. Butterflies form in the pit of my stomach.

Father McGroarty starts reading a verse from the bible and afterwards, in his homily, he begins talking about the power of love.

'My dear friends, as we gather today to celebrate the love between Mark and Sadie we must remind ourselves that love must be sincere. Never forget that love comes from God. Anyone who fails to love cannot be carrying out God's will, because God is love. God's love for us was revealed when God sent His only son so that we could be saved. We must never forget that Jesus suffered for each of us so that our sins can be forgiven. Therefore fill your hearts with love and I promise you this will bring you true happiness.'

My heart warms on hearing Farther McGroarty's speech. He truly has a wonderful way with words. My uneasiness settles.

Soon we make our way to the altar to receive the Body Of Christ, but before I kneel to receive the Eucharist, I catch a glimpse of someone familiar. Our eyes meet. My body freezes to the spot, my gaze locks on the coldest eyes I've ever seen.

Sweat forms on the palms of my hands and butterflies

rise in the pit of my stomach again. I feel clammy and uncomfortable. I haven't seen him since the night he violated me. What is he doing at my sister's wedding? How dare he show his face here today? He remains expressionless as he holds my stare. Father McGroarty clears his throat in an attempt to get my attention, causing me to jump. I don't know how long I've been standing glued to the spot; it must've been a pretty long time judging from the bewildered look on his face.

The beast's eyes are still on me as I feel the flutter of butterflies continue to move within my stomach. This time it isn't from nerves but from the travelling of his child within my womb. It suddenly hits me that I'm carrying this evil man's baby, a life that was conceived by such brutality. The thought repulses me. Suddenly I've an urge to vomit.

I make my way back to my seat hoping the sickly sensation will pass, it doesn't and so I have to escape. I dive towards the door, past a sea of curious heads as they watch me leave. Outside, vomit comes gushing from my insides. I press my shaking body against the stone wall and sob, feeling like such a hypocrite; minutes earlier Father McGroarty's reflection on love had inspired me, however all that I can feel right now, in my heart, is nothing but hatred and disgust.

Chapter 6

'Are you ready, or what? What's keeping you?'

'I'll be down now, Aggie. I'm just looking for a cardigan. Where the heck did I put it?' I rummage through my wardrobe frantically.

'Ah come on, sure you won't need it, it's a grand day today,' Aggie yells.

'Of course I'll need it, it can be right and breezy down your way and sure I hate the cold air.'

The truth is I want the cardigan to hide my expanding stomach.

'Ah you young ones, what are you not like? A good gulp of sea air in them lungs of yours will do you a world of good.'

'It's okay, I've found it, Aggie.' I run down the stairs, one arm in the cardigan and fumbling around for the other. 'You might be used to the chilly Atlantic breeze but we're not. You ol' biddies down there don't feel the cold,' I tease.

Aggie leans over and gives me a playful clip across the ear. 'You watch it, young lady, you're not too big for a slap from your aunt.'

Outside, Aggie's husband Paddy is waiting in his 'beat out banger' of a car. The loud spluttering of the engine fills my ears and the strong fumes invade my lungs. How the heck is that thing going to get us down there in one piece?

'Hello, Mr McAlister, how are you?'

I climb into the dusty back seat to join my mother,

Charlie and Anna. Donal has decided to give the opportunity of spending a weekend in Greencastle a miss this time.

'I'm not so bad, Molly, not so bad at all, and how are you yourself?' he pauses for a brief moment, but before I can answer him he continues. 'I've been looking forward to you lot coming down, it's well overdue, how long's it been? Gee it must be well over a year or so since you've been down to visit us, isn't that right, Aggie? Hi that's a grand day, the sun's fairly shining up there now, it's some difference from last week, but I see a wee cloud up there coming near us, let's hope it's not going to rain ...'

I peer up into the flawless sky and sigh deeply. I have forgotten just how much this man can talk. He never shuts that mouth of his. Mick has always said Paddy could *'talk for Ireland',* and he was dead right there.

The metal on the car rattles as the wheels bounce over every pothole and bump on the road. His car makes as much clatter as his mouth!

My mind drifts whilst Paddy rambles on. I can no longer concentrate on so much chat. These days I find it difficult to digest small talk, never mind anything else, having enough thoughts of my own going through my mind.

Before we know it we are past the border of Derry and entering the Irish Free State. We drive through the village of Muff. I shudder at the sight of the dance hall. I haven't been down here since the attack. We continue driving past Quigley's Point and Redcastle and onto a long stretch of road, until we finally come to the village of Moville. A few minutes later we arrive at our destination and come to a halt at their home, situated in the little fishing village of Greencastle. By this stage my head is pounding from listening to Paddy chatter on about anything and everything. Half the time my brain switches off, choosing instead to admire the overwhelming views of our journey; it is much more pleasant observing the roaming hills of Donegal than having my brain overloaded with information – the human brain can only take in so much when you're as tired as I feel today.

Aggie is obviously well used to his chit-chat. She doesn't engage in any conversation with him, instead she just sits in the front seat smiling as she looks out the window.

Paddy is a friendly man and I have to admit I have much admiration for him. For a man that lives in such a small location and spends most of his time at sea, he has such a great knowledge. As I glance around me at the breathtaking scenery, it almost feels like I've lived in this place all my life. I know so much about Greencastle from the numerous stories and tales that Paddy has told us during our regular visits over the years.

It was a pity that Aggie and Paddy were not blessed with children. They had been hoping for years that they would become parents and finally, after seven years of marriage, Aggie conceived a child, only to be hit with a massive heartache. Three months into the pregnancy she suffered a miscarriage. It was a devastating blow for them both but they continued to keep their spirits up, hoping that one day they might have a child of their own. They are now too old and they accept that being parents is not in God's plan for them. It is a shame because they would have made the most wonderful parents. They fussed over us, especially when my father passed away, and they loved us like we were their own kids. They would have cherished a child of their own, and besides, their huge house feels empty without the laughter of children to fill it. Perhaps this was one reason why they are always asking us down to stay, possibly to help create a family atmosphere about their home.

Their magnificent house stands on about four acres of land in Greencastle, County Donegal. This minute seaside village is situated on the east side of the Inishowen Peninsula at the mouth of Lough Foyle. Across the water, Magilligan Point is visible from their home. I have always found Greencastle to be a unique and interesting village, and the people here are adorable. The majority of the men support their families, working as fishermen in this bustling village, with fishing a thriving trade. Paddy is a fisherman and spends much of his life trawling the Lough Foyle, often bringing home fresh fish for tea, one of my favourite treats during our visits.

Their home is surrounded by beautiful gardens which they both take great pride in maintaining. The gardens are picturesque with charming flowerbeds and rose bushes. Positioned in the middle of the front garden is a pond with a variety of fish swimming about freely. To the left of the pond are huge cherry blossom trees. Many years ago Paddy had tied an old rope between two of the trees in order to make a swing for us; we enjoyed hours of entertainment on this new plaything. The front of their garden sweeps downwards facing Lough Foyle, while their floor to ceiling windows in the main dining area allows stunning views of Donegal, a site to behold.

As kids, Donal and I would sit for hours on end staring

at the magnificent coastline across Lough Foyle. I had fallen in love with Greencastle since those days and my admiration for this interesting place got stronger with every visit; it was always an ideal location for us as children for many an adventure.

My mother, Sadie, Charlie and Anna would stay at the house with Aggie. They would bake cakes or just relax about the gardens making daisy chains in the sun, whilst Paddy, Donal and I would go out and explore everything and anything within the village. My favourite place to visit was the castle. In fact, Greencastle's name comes from the castle in the area, which in turn is believed to have inherited its name from the green freestone with which it was built.

On one such visit to the castle I asked Paddy if he knew how long it had been built. Of course, Paddy, with his vast amount of knowledge, was able to give us a lengthy account of the history behind the castle.

'Ah, my dear, let me see now, how long ago was the castle built?' He rubbed his hand over his beard and he paused for a few seconds before replying, 'I'm nearly sure it was built in 1305, aye 1305 and according to my ol' grandfather – who had quite an interest in this masterpiece – it was created to provide a base for war manpower in the North West. The building was named 'Northburg'.

Donal and I sat amazed on the long grass outside the castle ruins, intrigued with Paddy's intelligence and knowledge.

'The Northburg, so that's its name?' Donal interrupted Paddy briefly.

'It is indeed or some folk like to call it Greencastle.'

'Who built it?'

'Well, Donal, it was the Red Earl of Ulster, Richard de Burgo, who established this castle.'

Hungry for further information, I pulled on Paddy's sleeve and begged him to tell us more. 'What else do you know about this place?'

'Ah sure I could go on and on. Let's see, well, shortly after the castle was built, I think it might have been ...' he paused to run his fingers through his thick, wavy hair, 'aye it was, I think about 1316, and it was then that it was first put to the test. There was a fleet led by Edward Bruce, they had set sail from Scotland with their goal of invading Ireland, and one of the first places they attacked was in fact Greencastle.'

'No way, what happened?'

'What do you think happened, Donal?'

'Don't know, haven't a clue.' Donal shook his innocent head, wide-eyed and eagerly awaiting Paddy's response.

'Well, Donal, they succeeded in taking it. Bruce was crowned King of Ireland in 1316 and he lost no time in capturing the castle. However, I believe it wasn't too long before he fell from power later that same year, and the castle was back in the hands of de Burgo. He later passed the magnificent building on to his grandson William. But an evil thing happened to William – it's said that in 1333 he was murdered and ...'

'What?' I gasped. 'He was murdered? No way!'

'Aye he was killed, and Norman power collapsed in the North West.'

'Who murdered him?' Donal interrupted.

'Not sure, some believe it was Sir Richard De Mandeville that killed him, they say that the assassination was an act of revenge for the death of William's cousin Walter Burke, whom William had held captive at Northburg the previous year. William didn't give him a morsel of food and left him to starve to death.' Paddy sat back, pulled out his pipe and proceeded to light it. Smoke and strong fumes of tobacco choked the air. 'Well, as it's said, if you live by the sword, you die by the sword.'

A shiver ran up my spine at the thought that someone had lost their life so cruelly just yards away from us. 'Paddy, that's so horrible, isn't it, Donal?' I looked in bewilderment from one to the other.

Donal remained silent, made speechless by all this intriguing information.

'That's not it all,' Paddy went on, inhaling the smoke from his pipe. He glanced around him, to ensure no one else was listening, and then spoke in a hushed voice. 'Rumour has it that William's sister tried to smuggle Walter food, but was unfortunate enough to be detected, and as a result was thrown over the battlements to the rocky shore below,' Paddy's eyes widened. 'What a horrid outcome for the sister!'

By this stage Donal and I were glued to the grass beneath us, hanging on to every little bit of information that rolled from Paddy's tongue. We were completely wrapped up in his intriguing tale.

'I can't believe that someone could be so mean to their sister.' Donal shook his head in disbelief. 'I would never do something like that,' he replied in a childlike fashion.

'Oh believe it, son, it's amazing how wicked some folks can be,' Paddy warned, sucking on his pipe.

'Is it haunted?' a worried Donal quizzed.

'I'd say it must be. Is it, Paddy?' I looked at him intensely, searching his eyes for the answer.

'Well I think I'll keep the ghost stories until another time.' He patted my shoulders gently and smiled softly.

I eyed him suspiciously. 'Ah, Paddy, just tell us, we promise we won't be scared.'

Paddy's lip curled into a cheeky grin. 'No, Molly, love, there'll be no ghost stories told today, and anyway, I haven't finished my story.'

Donal's eyes widened again at the thought of more information regarding the mysterious castle. 'Ssh, Molly, let him finish.' Donal elbowed Paddy and urged him to continue.

'Where was I?' he paused to scratch his scalp and inhale some more of the overwhelming tobacco.

His smoky breath fanned my face and my nose wrinkled.

'You just finished telling us about the sister being thrown over the side,' I replied eagerly.

'That's right, Molly,' he nodded a slow nod and his expression lit up again before continuing, 'the castle then fell into the hands of the O'Doherty's, but in 1555 Calvagh O'Donnell threatened their power by transporting an army of mercenaries from Scotland. He then tackled the building with a weapon known as the 'Gunna Cam', which means crooked gun. It is the reason the building now lies a wreck.'

'That's terrible, it's such a waste.' Donal shook his head in disgust.

'Aye it is, Donal,' Paddy agreed before continuing his tale. 'In the 1600s the castle became the property of Sir Arthur Chichester. He carried out some repairs and made it livable for troops. It was later leased to a man called William Newton, but by the year 1700 it was a total shambles.'

'Paddy, how do you remember all this?' Donal quizzed looking somewhat confused. It was a vast amount of information for a child to absorb.

'Donal, my grandfather would tell me this tale almost every night before I nodded off to sleep. It was one of my favourite bedtime stories.'

A smile crept across Paddy's face and a twinkle appeared in his eyes as he reminisced about the past. It was evident that he had fond memories of his grandfather.

'Paddy, you should write a book.'

'Well, Molly, maybe one day. I certainly have enough information in this brain of mine to write many books.' He tapped his head and laughed.

'You sure do,' I smiled.

'Right you two, it's getting late, we need to be heading back before Aggie sends out a search party!' Paddy got up slowly from the grass and placed his hands on the bottom of his back, to help straighten himself and gently pulled the two of us up by our arms. My legs felt stiff from sitting in the same position for so long, and my dress felt damp from the dewy grass.

We reluctantly followed, but I longed to hear more of

Paddy's exciting story. Something told me we hadn't heard all the tales about the interesting masterpiece. I glanced back at the mysterious fort. The sun was setting, disappearing behind the trees, casting a sprinkle of sparkling light on the ruin every time the trees swayed from side to side in the gentle breeze. I observed it for a while and almost thought I saw a shadowy presence move up on the battlements. A shadow, a figure, or perhaps a ghost? Goosebumps appeared on my arms. Maybe the castle *is* haunted, I thought; or perhaps it was just my imagination running away with itself. Either way, I bet Paddy has a lot more to tell about this place.

Just as I had predicted there is a slight chill in the spring air. I climb out of the car and wrap my cardigan tightly around me in an attempt to keep out the cold. The poignant aroma of turf and the salty air invades my sense of smell and I gulp in this delightful fragrance; it always makes me feel somewhat safe and content.

My mother whispers, 'I'm glad to see my girl smiling. You seem to have been a bit down in the dumps lately, Molly.'

I'm taken aback by her comment but try not to let her sense my surprise, 'Aye, my heart always was in Donegal. I suppose this place has the ability to make folk smile. Greencastle is so uplifting.'

Since learning I'm pregnant, I've desperately tried to push the truth to the back of my mind, putting on as brave a face as possible whilst around my mother, but still it seems she senses that I have been feeling 'down in the dumps'.

'You should have been a wee Donegal woman,' Paddy

adds.

'That would be nice, I could spend all day gazing at the Antrim coast.'

'Aye after you did your chores that is,' Paddy jokes. 'There's no time here for sitting about staring at coastlines,' he smiles softly.

I pull my bags from the car and follow the others inside the house.

'Sit yourselves down now and we'll have a nice wee cuppa. I've just baked a fresh apple pie especially for you, well, especially for Molly that is.' Aggie glances at me with a sparkle in her eyes. 'I know it's your favourite thing in the whole world, love.'

'You're right there, Aggie, sure isn't it the only reason I'm down here?' I smile and we laugh together.

'And there I was thinking it was watching the view of the Antrim coast and all that,' Paddy teases.

'Aye, well that too, but it doesn't beat our dear aunt's apple pie.' I flash him a cheeky grin, forgetting all of my troubles for a while, leaving them behind in Derry.

No sooner has Aggie placed a hot cup of tea in front of me from her finest china collection and a huge slab of steaming apple pie – still hot from the oven – it is gone, scoffed down my throat in a few seconds. Not once do I lift my head from the table to speak to anyone.

The room is filled with the clatter of cutlery hitting crockery as everyone tucks in to Aggie's fine food.

'Gee you're right about one thing, Molly, you do enjoy your aunt's cooking.' Paddy stares in shock at the empty plate in front of me. 'Hi, Aggie love, get Molly another slice of that pie.'

Aggie immediately places another enormous portion in front of me.

'Hey, Molly, you'll never eat all that. That bit there would choke a donkey. Give us half of it over here.' Charlie pretends to take the plate from me.

'Get lost!' I jerk the plate back and begin munching my way through the food. It isn't long before that has disappeared too and my tummy feels like it is about to explode. That will teach me for making an absolute pig of myself. I rub my expanding stomach. It begins to ache from the overload of grub.

Charlie teases, 'I think you could be doing with a good sleep after that.'

He's got it bang on target there; that's exactly what I want to do, but I decide it would be inappropriate to go to bed so early. If I go to sleep now they will have a hard job getting me wakened again.

'No, Charlie, I think I'll opt for a walk down by the pier instead. Does anyone fancy coming?'

The truth is I hope nobody will come with me. I want to be alone to gather my thoughts. I just ask out of politeness.

'Aye, I'll walk with you, Molly.' Aggie finishes drinking the contents from her cup. She rises from her chair and crosses the room to retrieve her coat from the coat stand in the corner of the kitchen.

The pier is only a few minutes' walk away and soon we are strolling along under the soft pink sky, the evening slowly setting in. I know from Paddy's many conversations that the pier was built in 1813 and is used as a tie-up for trawlers and salmon boats. It's from here that he leaves to fish each day. The waft of seaweed and fish hangs strongly in the air.

'I love the smell of this place.' I breath in a huge gulp of fresh air and taste salt on my lips.

'Do you know I barely even notice the scent nowadays, I guess I'm too used to it.' Aggie smiles as she swats away a flying insect.

'Aye I suppose you would get used to it, but for someone like me who isn't down here daily the smell is incredibly overwhelming.' I suck in the air slowly, allowing it to tantalise my nostrils.

We stop and lean over the moss-covered stone wall of the pier and watch a trawler in the distance creep slowly towards us. The delicate breeze carries the sound of the churn of the engines across the lough. The reflection of the sun glistens on the clear water. Suddenly, a few feet away, a black ball appears on the surface sending delicate ripples to cascade around it.

'What's that?' I ask, pointing to the mysterious object.

'Oh that's Bertie the seal, he's usually seen popping his head up now and again looking for food. The fishermen have him spoilt rotten. They throw down some fish to him daily.'

'He's a lucky one then, doesn't have to hunt for his own food, the crafty little sod.' I smile as I watch him bopping his head up and down and glancing all around him looking for his fishermen friends.

'Aye, why go looking when you can get it handed to

you,' Aggie chuckles. 'Isn't that right, Bertie?'

Bertie vanishes for a few seconds then darts his head up closer to us. He is now near enough that we can see his huge, dark, button eyes and long whiskers.

'I've nothing for you, Bertie son, don't be looking for food from me.' Aggie holds up her empty hands and shrugs her shoulders.

With that he cheekily turns his head and disappears again under the water.

We both laugh. 'He must have heard you, or perhaps he saw that your hands were empty,' I joke.

I catch a glimpse of Aggie smiling at me contently.

'Molly, you seem happy enough to me.' She looks at me lovingly.

Our eyes meet briefly before my gaze falls to the ground. I am shocked at her sudden remark. Without realising, I fall silent and begin to run my fingers along the moist stones of the pier until my fingers came to a halt at some carvings in the stone. A closer look reveals the words read 'Molly was here 18.7.32', below it in bigger writing it reads, 'Donal was 2!' We had scratched that on to the stones when we were kids after Donal found a rusty old nail. After we'd finished scrawling our statements, Donal put the nail into his pocket exclaiming that it would come in handy sometime.

'Look at this, Aggie,' I point out the engravings.

Aggie glances at it briefly. 'Ah, aye I see it.'

I can sense her interest is on me and not on what is written on the stone.

'Molly, darling, is there something up with you?'

I don't answer, instead I choose to raise my head from the stone wall and look into the distance. After a few minutes a seagull catches my attention. I watch as it sweeps downwards towards the water then swiftly flies upwards again with something in its mouth, before flying off once more into the distance. I wish I am that bird, free to fly off into the horizon.

The silence is immense.

'Your mother's worried about you.'

'What?' I ask.

'She's worried you're not acting yourself lately.'

Without knowing, my attention returns to the stone wall again. I begin to pick the wet moss from it with my fingernails and flick it into the water below, watching it fall as the wind carries it sideways into the cold waters.

'Molly, what's up, love?' Aggie puts a gentle hand on my face and strokes back wisps of my hair. 'Look at me, darling, you can talk to me.'

'What has she said to you?'

'She thinks you're a bit depressed and withdrawn lately.'

'I'm okay,' I lie, trying desperately not to make eye contact with her in fear that she might know I'm telling her a fib.

'Molly, I've noticed it myself too. You're not your usual bubbly self at all; and standing still at the altar at Sadie's wedding, I can't understand what that was about. *And* you went home sick without even attending the wedding reception. That just isn't you, is it?'

'I'm okay, I was unwell at the wedding, that's all.'

'Molly, you can trust me, if there's something bothering you, tell me and I'll help. Everyone's concerned.'

'Everyone!' I blurt angrily. 'What do you mean everyone? What has *everyone* being saying?' I raise my voice for the first time to my aunt.

'Molly, there's no need to be getting paranoid; others have just been noticing that you're very quiet, that's all.'

I grit my teeth. 'It's none of their business.' I march off in a temper. 'There's nothing wrong with me,' I yell over my shoulder.

'Molly, wait!'

I sense Aggie running after me. I stop and turn around.

'Listen, darling, if you say there's nothing wrong with you then that's fine, I'll not mention it again. However, if there is something bothering you, you know you can trust me. I promise I won't breathe a word to a single soul, I give you my word on that.'

Tears begin to stroll down my cheeks and the salty air stings my face. If there is anybody that I can trust I know deep down I can trust Aggie, and besides I have kept this secret from my family for long enough now. I have to talk to someone. I will explode if I have to keep this burden on my shoulders for much longer.

'There is something bothering me,' I cry.

'Do you want to talk about it?'

I nod.

Aggie beckons me to a wooden bench that faces the pier; it is used by the villagers to stop for a rest. Sitting down on the cool bench I stare into the emptiness in a bid to gather my thoughts; my tears escape, but no words come out of my mouth. I don't know how to tell her. I don't know where to start.

'Aggie, you have to promise me that you'll not tell anyone.' I search her eyes for a hint of assurance.

'Molly, I promise you, love.' She places her hand on mine and squeezes it gently. It feels warm and soft, just like her personality.

'Something really bad has happened to me,' I sob uncontrollably. Every fear that I've had bottled up inside me now comes out in the form of huge sobs. A waterfall of tears develops.

Aggie holds my hand tighter.

Through my sobs I manage to blurt out, 'I - I - I've been raped.'

It is now Aggie's turn to remain silent. At first she stares at me in apparent disbelief before nodding her head frantically, the tears welling up in her eyes.

'Molly, I'm so sorry...' she pauses. 'I just don't know what to say.'

Again we fall quiet. The only sounds to be heard are the waves gently lapping against the pier and the squawk of seagulls in the distance.

I break the silence and spill out the traumatic events of that awful night.

'Molly, you'll get through this. You're a strong person. You have to get it into your head that this wasn't your fault.' She takes my hand and rubs it gently. 'With every passing day you'll learn to deal with this and get that little bit stronger.

Molly, this is a terrible thing that has happened to you, but I know you will meet a good man one day and you will get over this. I promise you my lips are sealed. I'll not mention it again, but if you ever do feel you want to talk about it, well I'm here to lend an ear.'

'I'll never get over this.'

'Aye you will, darling. I can't even begin to imagine how bad you feel right now, an awful, tragic thing has happened to you. But I'll pray to God that you will find comfort one day and perhaps, who knows, God may give you the grace to forgive this person for what he has done to you.'

'Are you joking?' I announce sarcastically. 'You can get rid of that idea. I'll never be able to forgive him, not in a million years,' I sigh as I bury my head in my hands in disgust.

'Aye, I understand that you might feel like that now, but there will come a day when you will be able to move on and get on with your life.' Aggie puts her arms around my shoulders and places a loving kiss on my cheek. 'I'm here for you, darling, my darling, Molly, I promise. I'm here for you.' She rocks me gently in her arms.

My body begins to tremble and the sobs return. 'It's not as easy as that. I'm pregnant!' I blurt out.

Aggie releases her grasp of me and turns her face towards mine. She looks like she has been hit by a ton of bricks. Her mouth falls open speechless, her eyes widen and she stares at me in disbelief.

'What?'

'Aye, I'm pregnant.'

'Molly you have to tell ...'

'No way,' I protest.

'Molly, this is serious, you *have* to tell your mother and you need to go and report this to the police.'

'I will tell her when I need to about the pregnancy, but I am not telling her about the rape.'

To my surprise she agrees to respect my wishes.

'Molly, it's your decision, but take my advice because this will come out in the end.'

'Not if I can help it.'

'I'm here for you, love, whatever you decide. I'll help you in whatever way I can.'

'Thank you,' I sniffled.

'Come here to me, darling,' she says between her tears, and she reaches her arms out to me.

She doesn't need to ask me twice for a hug. I long for a cuddle and needed one now more than ever. I lean my head against her shoulder and weep bitterly.

A few minutes later we silently walk back towards Aggie's home. Neither of us can find anything to talk about. I feel relieved that I have shared my secret.

My mind is made up. I will allow the others to enjoy their weekend, but as soon as we return to Derry, I'll tell them about the pregnancy.

Chapter 7

The laughter from the kitchen directly below my bedroom echoes throughout the house. Father McGroarty has called in for his usual Sunday evening visit; his parents live next door to us. Every Sunday he takes the time to call with the neighbours after he sees his mother and father.

We have known him all our lives and have a special fondness to this kind, considerate man. He is treated like a family member but my mother still has to make a fuss when she knows he is coming, just like she would do with any priest that entered under her roof. Priests are seen as highly respected members of society, and so it is custom to ensure that the house is immaculately clean and the finest china cups brought out for the tea along with freshly baked scones.

Occasionally my mother buys in biscuits for his tea if she can afford it, of course, much to our dismay, we dare not touch them. Our tongues would be hanging out looking at the tempting treats and hoping that Father McGroarty would leave us some. No sooner were his feet out from under the table and out the door we would race over to the plate and scoff the leftovers, almost falling over one another in the process.

Father McGroarty would place himself down in his usual chair in the kitchen and sip over his tea. Mother, Donal and Mick would sit with him, chatting for up to an hour. Mick would have him in stitches laughing with his silly jokes. The atmosphere is always one of warmth and relaxation, and, occasionally, I would join them. However, tonight I decide to remain in my room, not being in the mood for jokes right now.

I decide that as soon as he has left, I will tell my family the shocking information. Now that the decision is made to break the news tonight, I can't wait to hear him go; this burden has to be removed from my shoulders.

I pace up and down the bedroom and rehearse my words over and over. It feels like my body is going to burst with adrenalin. My nails have been chewed away until there is nothing left to bite. Explosions erupt in my brain with the thoughts of what story to tell. The tension has been building up inside me since my trip to Greencastle, and, like clouds gathering before a storm, the tension is gathering; it's only a matter of time until this build-up bursts.

Since learning about the pregnancy I am unable to eat or sleep properly and my body shakes as soon as the thoughts enter my mind, which is almost all the time. My stomach is expanding rapidly and I constantly look pale and gaunt. It would only be a matter of time before others start asking questions.

'Well, folks, I'll love you and leave you. Thanks very much for the tea. It is lovely to see you both again. God Bless.'

'You're welcome, Father. We'll see you next week,' my mother replied.

'Where's your Molly at today, she's usually about for the craic?'

'That's a good question. I think she might be up the stairs; if she is she's been very quiet, perhaps she's fallen asleep.'

I creep out of the room and stall at the top of the staircase, waiting patiently for him to leave.

'Tell her I was asking for her anyway, Kate, won't you?'

'Aye, Father, I will. Perhaps, Father, you could do me a favour?'

'Of course, what is it?'

My mother lowers her voice to a whisper. I can barely make out what she is saying.

'It's Molly. I'm worried about her.'

'Molly? What's the matter with her?'

'That's a good question, Father, I'm not sure what's wrong with her at the minute. There's something up, I can't put my finger on it. I just don't think she's herself right now.'

'Kate, if I'm honest, I have noticed. I don't want you worrying too much. It's probably just a teenage thing. Teenagers can be funny at times.'

'Aye, I know that, but I also know Molly, it's not like her to be so withdrawn.'

'Would you like me to have a wee word with her?'

'If you don't mind, that would be great.'

'No chance!' I whisper. 'I'll be avoiding him like the plague!'

'Will do, take care and sure I'll look forward to seeing you next week.'

'Thanks, Father.'

'No problem at all, Kate. Try not to worry. I'll say a wee prayer for her.'

I need more than a prayer, any chance of a miracle, Father? I sigh leaning my head against the staircase.

The moment that I have both longed and dreaded has

95

finally arrived. I inhale a gulp of air into my lungs and try to gather myself together for the onerous task ahead; this will not be easy but it has to be done. The front door opens again causing me to almost jump out of my skin.

'Hi, what's the craic?' Sadie chirps cheerfully as she and Emily enter the house.

'Hello, Emily, I think Molly's asleep but come on in and I'll get you a cuppa.'

'Thanks, Mrs O'Connor, I'd love a wee cuppa.'

'Right, that's it,' I whisper. The main people are now in the kitchen and so I have to get on with it. 'No time like the present. Please help me, Jesus.' I drag myself downstairs reluctantly. 'There's no going back now, Molly O'Connor!' I whisper under my breath.

'Oh there you are, Molly, I'm just putting on a cuppa for Sadie and Emily, fancy one?'

'Aye please.' I nod at my mother without looking at the others.

I sit down at the kitchen table. Minutes later she places a cup of steaming hot tea in front of me. I take a few sips of the warm liquid and when I glance around at the others, it is evident how happy they all look. My stomach sinks at the thought of upsetting any of them. 'I've something important to tell you all,' I blurt out rather too quickly before falling silent again.

My mother has sensed the solemn tone of my voice. 'What's up, Molly?' she asks whilst studying my reactions.

There is a lengthy awkward stillness as the words catch in my throat, and for a while I find I am unable to speak. The silence is so immense in the kitchen, so quiet, I can hear the clock on the whitewashed wall in front of me ticking, the sound of the pendulum as it swings from side to side rings in my ears.

Mick places his cup down and looks at me intensely. 'What's the matter?' he leans over the table to remove a biscuit from the plate and proceeds to dunk it into his drink, before shoving it whole into his mouth and swallowing it down with a huge gulp of tea.

I hang my head in shame unable to answer his question. The adrenalin and the courage that I have managed to build up all day has vanished in a flash, leaving a weak, shattered little girl in a helpless state. I at once feel like the loneliest person in the world, and an overwhelming desire to get up from my seat arises, an urge to run out the door and keep running as far away as possible; that's where I want to be right now, as far away as possible!

My mother breaks the silence. 'You look annoyed at something. Whatever it is it can't be as bad as you think.'

She places a hand lightly on my shoulder. Our eyes meet; my heart breaks. I try to speak but no words come out.

'Can it, love?' She smiles sweetly as my stomach churns. 'My darling, what is the matter? Molly, you're a terrible worrier, you are always the one out of all my children that seems to fret about everything.' She pauses to release a little laugh and strokes my hair. 'Over the years the one thing that I've learned the most from life, is that worrying and fretting over things is useless, it only leads to despair. Anxiety is no good for the health, Molly. There's always an answer to problems.' She sounds reassuring. 'So what is it that you are concerned about, dear?'

Again I cannot speak.

'Aye your ma's right, Molly, there's always a solution to everything,' Mick manages to say through a mouthful of biscuit.

'Molly, we've all noticed you've not exactly been yourself for the last few weeks. It's probably not as bad as you think. Tell me what it is.'

I pause for another while, taking in everything that she has just said. All eyes are now fixed on me waiting for a response. Against my will, tears roll from my eyes. Now more than ever I really do want to run away. I feel like a mouse trapped with nowhere to go, with all these humans watching me intensely. I have to tell them now. There is no way I am going to get out of it.

'I don't think there's an answer to this problem,' I sniffle. I lift my eyes so that I am now looking directly at my mother and completely ignoring the others. I manage to mumble out the words that I know only too well will break her heart. 'I'm having a baby.'

The words come out like a slap up the face, one of those mighty slaps that leaves a fierce, fiery red stinging mark on the skin.

She loses her smile and develops a solemn expression. I at once wish I could take my words back.

The tables are turned. It is now time for the others to look troubled as the news sinks in, each of them digesting my unexpected statement. Mick, who is just about to dunk another biscuit into his tea, freezes holding it just above the cup, his mouth opened wide to speak, but no words managing to spill out.

Mother steps back from the table, clutching at her chest as the blood clearly drains from her face. 'What?' she asks aghast.

Sadie remains perched on her chair, her knuckles clinging tighter to the cup in her hand, her eyes fixated on me, terror and fear clearly visible in her expression.

Emily has a shocked, disbelieving look spread on her face.

Silence closes in around me, it grips me so tight I feel suffocated, like the air is being squeezed from my lungs. I want to begin shouting random words to loosen its hold, but I can't speak and so it just grasps tighter. The kitchen is suddenly too small and crowded for this topic. It feels like the walls are closing in on me. I want the ground to open and swallow me up.

A sudden bang from Donal's fist as he slams it down hard on the table fills the room. 'You're what, what do you mean you're having a baby?' he questions, his face red, set ablaze with rage, salvia comes shelling out of his mouth like gunfire.

Donal shouts with such fury, anger that I have never experienced from him before. He frightens me, catching me off-guard. His reaction scares me and clearly startles the others.

'You can't be, you're only sixteen for crying out loud ...' His voice fades and his face turns a stranger colour as his pulse rate shoots through the roof. 'Who is responsible for this?'

'I, I can't ...'

'What do you mean you can't, you can't what? Don't mess around with us, Molly!'

'I'm sorry, I ...'

'Sorry? Sorry is not the word I want to hear.' His voice gets louder and more intense by the second. 'You better tell us what *bastard* is responsible for this.' He hurls his cup across the room. The lukewarm tea spills through the air before it slams against the wall behind me, the mug exploding into sharp pieces that scatter in all directions around the kitchen floor. Stains of tea cling to the wall. I duck to avoid the missile in fear of what is going to come next.

'Stop!' Mother raises her hand. She stares at Donal in utmost shock. The expression on her face says it all. There is no need for words. She is disgusted with us both right now. 'Don't speak another word. I will not have that kind of violent behaviour in this house. Do you hear me, Donal?' Her eyes are full of hurt.

Sadie looks as disgusted as my mother is, although she does have her usual judgmental expression splashed across her face. I'm not sure if that look is etched on her face because of me, or as a result of Donal's behaviour.

Mick hangs his head in deep thought, obviously too shocked to speak. My attention turns to Donal. I stare at him, wide-eyed and scared out of my wits. His chest heaves up and down in a rapid rhythm, his eyes pierces through me.

Donal's crystal blue eyes narrow and eye me with suspicion. 'Well, what have you got to say for yourself? You have the cheek to spring us with this kind of news and then just sit there in silence!' He again shouts, his voice getting louder and louder before smacking another blow of his fist on the table. 'Answer me, Molly!'

I have to glance away. I can't even look at him when he is this mad let alone answer him.

'How did you get yourself into this mess and who's the father?' Donal leans over the table. He is now so close I can feel his breath on my cheek. His eyes remain narrowed, his chest still heaving rapidly. Like a volcano about to erupt, he is about to explode at any second.

I begin to sob, feeling emotionally vulnerable. I can't deal with the fact that Donal, my best friend throughout my life, is now reacting so harshly to me. I'd mistakenly convinced myself that he would be my rock through this, but how wrong I'd been. Never at any point did I think he would react so furiously. He bangs his fists down again on the table with a huge thud making me jump and sending the plates and cups rattling.

'For the last time, Molly, who's the father?' he snarls, so close to me I can see his saliva hissing through his teeth.

'Please, leave me alone. You're scaring me,' I cry through streams of tears. The roaring and shouting becomes unbearable.

'I told you to stop, Donal. Stop right now!' Mother yells with such authority that he immediately obeys her command. 'Will you give Molly a chance to talk and stop shouting at her, what good is yelling going to do? Can you not see that she's upset enough?'

'Okay, let's hear it, Molly,' Donal replies with a tone of

sarcasm in his voice as he returns to his chair.

I remain tight-lipped, still refusing to look at him.

'Well, Molly, in all my days, I've never expected you to come out with such news. I'm disappointed with you ...'

'Disappointed? What kind of word is that? Ashamed or disgraced would be more appropriate descriptions,' Donal interrupts. 'It's an absolute scandal!' He rises again from his chair and points his finger directly at me. 'You're a disgrace, a disgrace to yourself and a disgrace to this family.' His face turns crimson again with rage, his words fire from his mouth like sharp daggers that pierce my heart. To add final insult he announces with a glare of defiance in his eyes, 'You're no sister of mine, Molly O'Connor!' He spits his words as though they are tainted with poison.

He lifts his coat that is slung over his chair, throws me a withering glance and marches out the back door, slamming it so fiercely behind him it causes vibrations to shake through the kitchen.

The atmosphere is uncomfortable, tense and frightening. I guess I naively underestimated the effect this bombshell would have and the impact it would have on my family. The awkwardness seems to last forever, until my mother finally lifts the cups and starts placing them into the washbasin before she begins to scrub them vigorously, her thoughts a million miles away. She stares blankly out of the window into the backyard. She then tries to busy herself tidying up the kitchen, avoiding eye contact with the others and trying her best to disguise the tears that have begun to fill up in her beautiful, gentle eyes. A few tears escape and trickle down her delicate cheeks before dropping on to her apron and disappearing into the fabric. I long to gather up her tears like precious pearl drops, long to put my arms around her and hold her close to me, and I desire to take away the pain and the agony that I have caused her. My thoughts are so wrapped up in my mother; I haven't noticed the others leave the kitchen.

I sniffle and try to clear my throat, 'I'm sorry I've upset you.'

Without turning around to face me, she replies in a slow, quiet voice. 'Go to bed, Molly. It's getting late.' She continues scrubbing at the spotlessly clean table. 'I'm tired. We'll deal with this matter tomorrow.'

She leaves the kitchen without glancing in my direction and goes upstairs, leaving me alone again with my thoughts and emotions in turmoil. The lack of eye contact from her is unbearable. I would have rather that she shouted from the rooftops like Donal had done. Seeing her hurt like this is a bitter emotion to deal with. I knew if she was aware of the true story she would ache even more. I can't allow myself to break her heart further. I will deal quietly with the truth and suffer on in silence. I would rather my family look at me in shame and have all sorts of accusations thrown at me than her to know the truth. If she only knew what that evil animal did to her daughter it would put her in an early grave. He has destroyed my life and, by the looks of things, he has destroyed my family bond forever.

Chapter 8

I find myself walking down a small country road, the destination unknown, but I continue my journey. It is not long until the road begins to creep upwards, getting steeper and steeper. I gaze at the magnificent alpine trees that decorate both sides of the road. They are so huge it seems they almost touch the fluffy clouds that hang delicately in the deep blue sky above.

The road continues to twist and turn with no clue as to when it will come to an end. The only sound to be heard is the chirp of hungry young birds in the distance, demanding to be fed. The sound is music to my ears in these mysterious, serene surroundings. The more steps I take, the closer I get to my unknown destination. Suddenly the road becomes more like a dirt path that leads up a huge mountain. The desire to continue fills my heart, and so on and on I go. The further I walk the more I leave the built-up area behind and the hustle and bustle is now substituted by an eerie, chilling silence.

The dirt track becomes rocky; my feet slip as the stones move with the pressure of my body weighing down on them. I begin to feel tired and my mouth feels parched. A flower at the side of the track catches my attention, distracting my thoughts from this desolate place; its beauty is a sight to behold. I bend down to breathe its sweet smell. My senses are overwhelmed by its delicate aroma.

My thoughts are lost briefly, unaware that someone has crept up behind me until he grabs me tightly. One strong arm wraps around my neck while the other covers my mouth, he holds me with such force. I try to open my mouth to scream but no sound comes out. I struggle until my body can fight no more. It is useless, his strength overpowers me. Desperately I attempt to pull his fingers away from my mouth, but fail miserably. I begin to fight again, struggling in a frenzy to free myself. With every bit of strength left in me I manage to swing my head round and at once my eyes fix on my attacker.

I awake flinging my arms around frantically, fighting against emptiness, my body soaking with sweat. It takes a few seconds to realise it has been another nightmare. Night after night these images come back to haunt me, so much so that I hate going to bed for fear of seeing his cruel face while I sleep. The dreams feel as traumatic as the attack itself, leaving my body shaking with terror, forcing me to relive the horror of that night time after time.

'It's only a dream,' I mumble. 'He can't hurt me anymore.'

I use the sleeve from my nightdress to dry my wet temples. I glance in the direction of Anna's bed. She sleeps contently, snuggled under her blanket; thankfully I haven't woken her. I rest my throbbing head on the sweat-dampened pillow and force my eyes to close in an attempt to get back to sleep, but it's useless; his disgusting face keeps appearing in front of me. The reality is I'm no stranger to nightmares. Each day his actions gnaw at my thoughts, then at night he creeps into my dreams. Each night I see him in many different forms, and with a thousand diabolical expressions etched on his evil face. This is possibly something that will remain with me for the rest of my life, and this angers me.

I can't allow myself to lose sleep over the matter; I will have to try to get back to sleep. I toss and turn for some time before becoming aware of mumbling from the kitchen below. It is unusual for anyone to be up so late, and besides I thought everyone had gone to their beds. I decide to get up to check out who is downstairs. Making my way out to the hall and tiptoeing down a few stairs the voices become clearer and I recognise them as my mother and Mick. My ears immediately spring to attention on hearing my name, and so I creep further downstairs and into the living room to listen to what is being said.

'Kate, you have to agree, this is the only thing we can do. Molly can't bring up a child. She's only a child herself for crying out loud. Will you at least think about it?' Mick's voice sounds desperate.

My mother doesn't answer. It's obvious she is pondering over his advice.

'Kate, think about it, you need to consider what's best for Molly and what's best for the family.'

My heart begins beating rapidly. What the heck is he talking about? The idea of being sent away to some horrid place to have this baby in secret springs to mind; these thoughts cause me to shudder. It's too much to take in. Panic starts to take over me. There's no way my mother would agree to this.

I feel my eyes widen and my heart race. I'll run away quicker than get locked up!

Horrible stories have often been told in the factory about girls being sent away to have their babies in secret. These girls are kept hidden from society rather than bring shame to their families. It's a massive sin to have a child outside of marriage and girls that get pregnant are seen as being filthy and are treated as outcasts. Perhaps I would be able to accept being sent away if I was guilty of doing something wrong, but given the fact that I am an innocent victim, I will do everything in my power to prevent being dispatched to some cloak and dagger destination. It's no secret of the gruelling lifestyle that girls are faced to endure at these locations. Many a story has been told from the other girls at the factory of what happens at these awful places. The girls describe in great detail the fate of those poor, unfortunate girls being punished solely because of the shame they've brought on themselves. Falling pregnant out of wedlock in Ireland is almost seen as a crime as equivalent to murder, and the girls are treated like criminals. I have heard how animals are treated better than these poor girls. Anger forms within me; I am no criminal and I will refuse to be treated like one. I will not allow myself to be in a situation where girls are forced to carry out tedious tasks, fed little food and in return attacked mentally and emotionally. I will not put up with that.

A volcano erupts within me and before I know it, red-faced and seething, I barge through the kitchen door, flinging it open so fiercely it bounces off the wall behind and springs back, almost hitting me in the face. Startled, my mother and Mick stare in shock.

'I'm not going,' I spit raising my finger and pointing it directly at Mick, 'do you hear me? I'm not going and you can't make me, Mick,' I announce hysterically, my body shaking.

'Going where? What are you talking about, Molly?'
Mick looks confused.

'You're planning on sending me away aren't you? Stop treating me like I'm some kind of stupid idiot. I know exactly what you're at Mick ...'

'What?' he frowns.

'You are not sending me away!'

'Sending you where? Molly, you've lost me,' he shrugs.

'Wherever the heck you're planning on leading me, don't lie to me, Mick.' My voice begins to get louder by the second as my temper flares. 'I heard the pair of you talk about sending me away to have this baby in secret. I'm not going ...'

'Now hold on a wee minute, you've got the wrong end of the stick, Molly, we didn't say anything about sending you away, did we, Kate?'

'No.' My mother shakes her head and smiles. She swallows and her smile tightens.

There is an uncomfortable silence whilst I struggle to gather my breath. Mick pulls out a chair from the table.

'Take a wee seat and I'll explain things.' He nods at me to sit, but I refuse to move. 'I'll tell you what our plans are.' His tone softens and he looks to my mother for support.

She fixes her worried eyes on him. A peculiar look develops on her face. 'Our plans? I haven't agreed to this, Mick.'

'I know you haven't and that's fine, but at least let me talk it over with Molly first. Take a seat, Molly. Kate, will you make us all a wee cuppa?'

My mother at once removes herself from the chair to

make the tea, meanwhile I make my way to the table and sit down facing Mick, wondering what the heck is going on and what he's about to say. One thing is for sure, it must be pretty serious.

I can't look at him, instead I watch as my mother removes the teapot from the stove and pours the tea into the cups. She turns around and looks at me briefly. I notice that her eyes are filled with tears. She blinks them away furiously. My heart breaks at the thought of causing her so much pain.

She places the two cups of tea in front of us, but doesn't join us. Instead she leans against the wall, sipping slowly at her tea and staring into thin air, her thoughts a million miles away.

Mick shifts uneasily in his chair. He takes his cup, holding it tightly in his hands before lifting his head to look at me.

'Your mother and I were discussing how young you are to be having a baby, not even to mention that you're unmarried and have refused to tell us who is responsible.'

Mick pauses briefly before taking a gulp of tea and glances over my shoulder to my mother who is still somewhere in space. He places his cup on the table and looks at me from under his bushy eyebrows.

'I know somebody who may be able to help you, somebody who I'm sure would be able to take care of girls like yourself.' He presses his lips firmly together and smiles gently. I can tell it's a false smile. He rubs his face wearily and permits a stillness to develop between us.

I feel I should say something to interrupt the uneasy silence. 'What do you mean take care of girls like me?' My eyes pierce through his. 'I'm sorry for being so ignorant. I don't know what you're trying to say, Mick.'

'Well, I mean ...' Mick grips the cup tighter and gazes into it. He proceeds to scratch his bald head for a few seconds. He slugs back the remainder of his tea. Without lifting his eyes to make any sort of eye contact he takes a deep breath and continues. 'What I'm trying to say, Molly, is there's a way out of this mess. We can arrange to have it sorted.' His voice sounds bright and cheery.

'Sorted?' I reply. 'What do you mean?' I listen intently for his response.

'I mean we can arrange to get rid of it. It won't take long and I'm sure it'll all be over before you know it. You won't have to worry about it again.'

'What do you mean by *it*? Are you referring to the baby that I'm carrying?'

'Aye, sure it's not a baby yet.' He throws his head back and releases a false laugh.

Speechless, I look to my mother, she refuses to make eye contact, and is still in a world of her own.

He drums his fingers on the table, waiting patiently for my response.

'Mother?'

There is a deathly stillness. I feel hugely confused and frustrated.

Mick finally speaks after the long silence. 'What do you think, Molly?' he sighs, sounding impatient now.

I turn my attention back to Mick. 'Get rid of *it*, as in kill *it*? Destroy *it*? Do away with *it*? You mean kill the baby, Mick,

110

is that what you're trying to say?'

'No, no, no. it's not killing, sure it's not a formed child yet, it's just a bunch of cells and stuff.' He threw me another one of his false smiles.

'I, I don't know what to say.' I feel like slapping him but I grit my teeth and hold back.

I look at my mother for some kind of reaction but her expression is stone cold. It's difficult to guess what she is thinking; she has obviously been swayed by Mick. She begins to clear the cups from the counter but regardless of how much action or noise she creates, she can't run away from the uncomfortable tension.

My initial reaction to the idea is sheer horror; no matter how much hurt and anger I feel within myself, I know deep down that ending the pregnancy is the wrong thing to do, not to mention the fact it's a mortal sin.

Mick couldn't be farther from the truth, there's no way that getting rid of this baby will solve my problems. Nothing can undo the fact that I've been raped. Having an abortion is likely to cause more dilemmas. I wouldn't be able to live with the guilt of ending a life, regardless of how that life was conceived. There's no way I can agree to this. I could never imagine that my good, catholic mother is even listening to such a suggestion, let alone thinking about it.

'I'm not doing it.' I shake my head in anger.

'Now listen here, I'm only thinking of what's best for you, young lady.' Mick speaks with an unusually aggressive tone. 'You haven't even thought this through yet, at least sleep on it.' He gives me a frosty look.

'Mick, I don't have to think about it, or sleep on it for that matter, no doctor or whoever you have in mind is coming anywhere near me to rip this baby to pieces,' I reply hysterically.

I've already had my fair share of violation as a result of the rape. I am not prepared to be violated again.

'Do you want this child? Is that what you're saying? Is it, Mo …'

'No, that's not true!' I interrupt. Of course I did not want it. It was the last thing I wanted. 'I'll give it away.'

'Oh, give it away, will you? Sure that'll solve all your problems, won't it?' I have never heard him talk with such hatred in his voice. 'Look at your poor mother. You're breaking her heart and she's worried sick. Does she need this mess right now? Do you not think she has enough in her life to deal with without you adding to it, you selfish little brat!' He spits the words from his mouth with such anger, his blood boiling and his temper flaring by the second. Rage fires in his eyes.

His behaviour scares me, but I have to stand up to him on this.

'How dare you speak to me like that?' I yell back. In all my years I have never raised my voice to him, always giving him the utmost respect at all times. 'No, I do not want this baby, but I also do not want to kill it. I'll give it up for adoption.'

Like a crack of a whip he fires back, 'Suit yourself, you little whore.'

'What did you just say?' I narrowed my eyes.

I lift my cup and without waiting for his answer or giving it a second thought I throw the tea over him. Lucky for him the tea has cooled down.

He jumps to his feet, about to shout again when my mother interrupts. 'That's enough. You'll wake the whole house with your shouting and roaring, in fact you're likely to wake the whole street!'

She looks upset, her chest heaves up and down and her face turns crimson. We both fall silent and Mick sits back down again.

'I'm sorry, Mother, but I can't believe you above all people aren't standing by your faith. I refuse to listen to this suggestion of Mick's, never mind contemplate it.' I throw him a look of disapproval.

'As I said earlier I haven't agreed to anything. Right now my mind won't allow me to think straight. I just don't know what to do.'

I look into her eyes and reply in a softer tone. 'Mother, I know you aren't thinking straight, if you were you wouldn't allow the destruction of a life. I know you wouldn't.'

'Oh, Molly, I don't know, is it a life or is it just a bunch of cells like Mick has said? Maybe it wouldn't be a bad thing to do after all. Having this baby will destroy your young life.'

She comes over and sits at the table. She places her head in her hands and releases a huge sigh. After what seems like eternity she lifts her head and looks straight at me.

'What do *you* want to do, Molly?' Her eyes soften but her face is filled with sadness.

I pause, absorbing her sad expression. I can't let her

down.

'Okay, I'll do it.'

'Good on you,' Mick punches the air. 'You're doing the right thing. Trust me, Molly, you won't look back, you're making the right choice.'

I ignore Mick's comment. I want to scream at him choice? What choice has the poor child got? I'm sure it would choose to live.

'I'm doing this for you, Mother,' I reply, ignoring Mick.

'Is that what you want, love?'

'No, Mother, it's not what I want, but as I say, I'll do it for you. If it keeps you happy then I'll agree to it. But, I can already feel this baby move, surely it would be wrong to end its life, and even if it is just a bunch of cells, this still ends up a life. We were all a bunch of cells once.'

'Gees, Mick, my head's done in. What am I saying? Molly's right, what am I even thinking about this for? Taking a child from the womb is wrong and I won't allow it.'

'Kate, Molly's in a mess, she needs to get this matter dealt with!'

'As far as I'm concerned this discussion is over and done with. I mean it, Mick, it's over and done with.'

'It seems the pair of you have made your minds up.' He slumps in his chair, his battle lost.

'Aye, Mick, that option is finished with.' My mother purses her lips.

Mick gets up to leave.

'Don't come crying to me when your life's all mucked

up, girl, you have your chance to fix it now.' He points a finger at me. 'Don't leave it until it's too late.'

'Wait, Mick, stay and hear what I have to say. I think Molly's right in everything that she has said. We can't send her away. I wouldn't hear of that and we can't make her get rid of the baby – it wouldn't be right, I couldn't have that on my conscience. It just leaves one more idea.'

Mick raises his eyebrows. 'What other alternative is there?'

'Well, I've been thinking about this all night and I'd like to suggest that *I* bring up the child.'

'What? Kate, you're mad!'

'I'll pretend to everyone that I've adopted another baby.'

'You're off your head, that'll never work out. Can you really see that working, Molly?'

'I don't know. I suppose it could,' I shrug.

'It will not work out, listen to me, it will not work out!'

'Aye it will, Mick, I'll make sure of that.'

'Make sure of it! How the heck will you make sure of it, Kate?'

'Calm down, Mick,' Mother says quietly.

'You're letting her off too lightly. You should be demanding to know who's got her into this mess and let us go and sort him out instead of walking on eggshells around her,' Mick replies through clenched teeth.

My mother looks at me then back to Mick. 'That'll be sorted out. Molly will tell us in her own time. I've reared other children that weren't mine and I can do the same for this one.

115

We will pretend that the child belongs to another cousin of mine,' she looks into my eyes, 'but I'm warning you, young girl, this mustn't go any further than these four walls, if you want to keep your dignity then you'll have to remain quiet.'

I nod in agreement.

'Are you two forgetting one thing? How do you plan to hide a pregnant girl? In only a few months' time she'll be like the side of a house!'

'We'll deal with that when it comes the time. Molly, you'll have to lock yourself in that room of yours or maybe we can arrange for you to go and stay with Aggie and Paddy. I'll speak to her about it and I'll speak to the rest of the family.'

Again I nod in agreement. I don't care what arrangements she wants to make, as long as she is happy with them.

So the matter is finalised. I will have the baby and keep it quiet from the neighbours and their chin-wagging gossip; my child will then be handed over to my mother to rear. That suits me fine, I think. The whole matter will be kept hush-hush.

Chapter 9

The following weeks roll by, with every fleeting day similar to the one before. The relationship between Donal and I has become unbearable; he refuses to engage in any friendly conversation, and speaks only to hurl abuse or to question who the father is.

Since the pregnancy has come to light everyone has started treating me differently, none more so than Donal. His initial reaction shocked me, but his behaviour afterwards is perhaps the most hurtful of all. The others act strangely, but I suppose it's not surprising given the fact that I have landed them with such a bombshell. I can deal with their actions. Donal, however, is just downright hateful. He comes home after finishing his shift working on the docks at the Derry quay, and takes up his seat at the table as the family gather round for dinner. I bid him good evening as I always have done, but to my dismay he acts as if he hasn't heard me; I have suddenly become invisible to him.

We rarely see each other in the mornings. He will be away to work before I get out of bed. After dinner he will then go and gather water from the well, or collect some turf for the fire, before retiring to his bedroom to read his books. Apart from when we gather to eat our dinner, the only contact I have with Donal is when we occasionally pass each other on the stairs or on our way to use the toilet. When we do meet, I look at him for some kind of communication, even a little eye contact would do, but he refuses, often keeping his head low and again treating me like I'm invisible or some kind of outcast in the family. This emotional torture is tough.

This treatment from my beloved brother is hard to deal with, but I guess I've no choice but to accept it and get on with life. It's funny how your thoughts and feelings can change about someone practically overnight. After weeks of this abuse I decide that if he is going to act in such a hateful manner I will be as cruel back, so when he speaks to me I remain silent, or just get up and walk out of the room, without making eye contact with the brother that I once was so close to. The lack of response from me enrages Donal even more – he detests being ignored. If there is one thing in the world he hates the most, it's being disregarded, especially when he's waiting for an answer. If he'd have stood by me, I would've told him the truth; we never had secrets.

I no longer look up to him. He's no longer worthy of my admiration. His selfish actions have caused me so much hurt in the space of just a few weeks.

Mick has not been much better. He speaks only when he needs to. It's obvious that he's still seething with me for refusing to go along with his idea of getting rid of the child. He's made it crystal clear that he's not happy with my decision to continue with the pregnancy. Sometimes I will catch him looking at me in disgust, but I try not to let him bother me too much.

Charlie and Anna act like nothing much has changed. The matter is no big deal to them. I suppose they're too young to understand anything different.

Surprisingly, my mother hasn't mentioned anything since the night I heard her and Mick discussing the matter in the kitchen. I have, however, caught her eyeing my stomach suspiciously from time to time. She treats me as normal as she possibly can, although it's evident that the sparkle in her has dulled. She has also not mentioned anything more about me staying with Aggie. I was hoping that she would bring up the subject so that I could tell her that Aggie is aware of my plight, however I find the less said about my situation the better. I get the feeling the rest of the family must feel the same, but I know it's only a matter of time before the subject comes up again; after all, it's impossible to brush a matter like this under the rug.

Emily has become a tower of strength. I spilled the truth to her one morning at work. She's such a great friend. I had to be honest with her, and besides there have never been any secrets between us. If there's anyone I can trust it's Emily. She was so furious when she heard the news, and blamed herself for not waiting on me after the dance. But Emily's not to blame for this mess. She wasn't to know I was in any danger.

Sadie hasn't been seen much at home since her marriage, not a bad thing either. When she does visit, I'm usually upstairs, glad not to have to talk to her. Sometimes she will come to my room but I pretend to be asleep. She's the last person I need to hear giving me a lecture. It's not clear what her thoughts are regarding the situation, and I honestly don't care. I have taken enough of her judgmental and dictating character all of my life. Sadie is likely to be longing for the opportunity to give me a good telling off and waiting for the chance to come down on me like a ton of bricks. I don't want to listen to her. In fact the further away she is from me at this time in my life, the better. However, the annual retreat is commencing tomorrow so I know I'm bound to bump into her at that. I dread it; my stomach feels sick at the thought of meeting her.

The retreat is held in all parishes during the first two weeks of May each year. Ladies attend on the first week and the men come along on the second. Anyone over the age of fourteen is required to attend. The churches are filled to capacity during this time; they are practically packed to the doors.

We attend St Patrick's church in Pennyburn and each year the crowds get bigger at this event, so much so that extra seating is placed inside the chapel in every available space, and loads of people that are unable to get a seat are required to stand inside and even outside in the church grounds.

Mass is celebrated each morning at six-thirty, with sermon and devotions taking place at seven-thirty in the evening. Hail, rain, or snow, we are required to be there each day. Luckily, the weather is usually fine this time of year, not too warm or too cold, and this year is no different. It's lovely, typical May weather, nice and sunny, which is just as well; it's a lengthy trek each day to get to the church.

Every year the ladies in the street meet at quarter to six in the morning and again at quarter to seven at night to make the half-hour walk to the church together. Nosy Nora will mingle in with everyone, making sure she gets a chance to talk to us all at some stage in the journey. The intriguing thing about Nosy Nora is her unique way of getting information from folk without them even noticing. She has it mastered.

We are just about to leave for the first morning of the retreat when my mother whispers in my ear, 'Watch what you say to Nora, you know the kind of her.'

'Aye I know.' I have already decided prior to the warning that I am going to try to avoid her at all costs.

Each morning and evening I deliberately try to steer clear of Nora, which is not the easiest of tasks, but somehow I do succeed not to get into deep conversations with her. I usually manage to end the conversation with her by saying, 'Do you smell alcohol?' This question is enough to scare her away.

Nora is well known to enjoy a wee tipple of whiskey or brandy, or basically anything she can get her hands on. She likes to hide the fact that she enjoys a drink and she naively believes that nobody can tell when she's drunk. It's easy to know if she has been knocking back a few shots: her round, chubby cheeks usually turn crimson and her eyes glisten like stars in a cloudless night sky, not to mention that she's inclined to talk faster and a waft of alcohol will almost knock you out if you are standing close enough!

The retreat finishes in church on Sunday at three o'clock in the afternoon. Sadie has been getting a lift to and from the chapel with her new husband, and so I've managed to avoid getting into any deep conversation with her too, however she's arranged to meet with us to walk to church for the closing of the retreat. I'm dreading it. I had an awful feeling that Sadie's arranged this just so she can get a chance to talk with me properly.

Sunday arrives. What a glorious day it is, the sun is

glistening brightly, not a cloud to be seen in the clear blue sky, giving an instant, uplifting feeling. We gather at the end of the street, all dressed in our finest Sunday best, hair combed neatly and our shoes well-polished. Sadie appears, dressed in a pretty pink suit with matching shoes, as usual not a hair out of place. I suddenly feel frumpy and fat squeezed into my old clothes. With my baggy blouse draped loosely over my skirt to disguise the undone buttons, I look a mess compared to my sister. She smiles over at me nervously, revealing her pearly white teeth. I sheepishly smile back.

I watch with horror as Sadie makes her way over to me as the group set off in the direction of the church. She links onto my arm, taking me by surprise, and we walk together in silence for a bit. It feels strangely comfortable, and for the first time in my life I feel so much at ease with her.

'How are you doing, Molly?'

'I'll be okay.'

The truth is I don't feel okay, but I have to put on a brave face.

'It mustn't be easy for you.'

Sadie sounds concerned.

'No, it's not at all easy, but as I say, I'll be okay.'

'Aye, I know you will, you're a right little fighter. I would've crumbled under the stress of everything by now.' She whispers in a sympathetic tone, 'It's not the end of the world, Molly, you'll get through this.'

'It feels like the end of the world to me. I'll never get through this.'

'Aye, Molly, you will.'

Nosy Nora's ears must have picked up on some of our conversation. It's not long before our discussion is interrupted with her presence.

'What's the story with you two lassies, what are all those whispers about?'

She playfully elbows Sadie in the ribs, and squeezes her way between the two of us, separating us in the process and sticking herself in the middle.

'Right then, girls, tell us all the bars,' she giggles, looking from me to Sadie before her beady eyes fall on me again. 'What's going on?'

My mischievous streak takes over me and I can't help but want to wind her up.

'Well, you would never believe the juicy gossip Sadie and I have been talking about.'

I lean closer to Nora and watch in amazement as her eyes widen, she's ready to burst at the seams as she eagerly awaits my news.

Nora rubs her hands in excitement. 'I like the sound of this, what is it, Molly?'

Sadie looks at me, horrified at the thought of what I am going to say, she lowers her eyebrows, a signal for me to keep my mouth shut. Sadie should know me better, I'm not that stupid. I'm just looking to have a bit of fun with her.

'Gees, Nora, I really don't know if I should tell you. You would need to promise not to tell anyone.'

I observe her eyes widen more and try not to laugh.

'Ah, Molly, I promise you, sure I'll not tell a single soul. I promise it'll go no further.'

'Are you sure you'll keep to your oath?'

'You know the kind of me by now, there's one thing about me; I keep to my word.' She crosses her heart with her finger. 'Cross my heart I give you my word.'

I lean closer to her again; the smell of alcohol is overwhelming. I whisper quietly, 'Well, since you have assured me you won't tell anyone, I'll trust you.'

Nora's eyes dance with excitement. 'Aye, I promise you, Molly. Now go on tell us the craic!'

'Nora, you're not going to believe this but ...'

'What? What is it?'

'Do you believe in leprechauns, Nora?'

'Leprechauns? Well I do indeed. I know most folk don't but there must be some kind of truth in them, there's certainly enough stories in Ireland about them, but what have they got to do with the juicy gossip?'

'Well, Nora,' I continue, 'I have heard that leprechauns are out hunting for drunks.'

'Ah, no way.' She looks at me with such innocence.

'Honestly, Nora, some even had the nerve to enter our back gardens.'

'What do you mean?' she shrieks in a childish tone. 'Gees, you're having me on.' She frowns.

I struggle not to laugh.

'Sssh, you'll scare the life out of everybody if this secret gets out.' Sadie points a finger across her own lips. I can tell that she too is having difficulty keeping herself from laughing.

I don't know what is funnier, my stupid story or the

thought of Nora spreading it round the neighbours with her extra bits added to spice it up a little.

'Aye, can you believe it?' I reply with a serious look on my face.

'Actually, I can believe it, Molly. I always said it's just a matter of time. I knew this would happen one day. The cheek of them!'

I release a small snigger, I can't help myself. Sadie turns her head in the opposite direction to have a chuckle, her shoulders jerk up and down now and again. Poor Nora is so traumatised by my tale she hasn't even noticed the smirks on our faces. I have to bite down hard on my bottom lip to prevent from erupting into a fit of giggles.

'Now listen, head you on over to the others now before they suspect something's up, and remember, Nora, don't mention a thing to the them,' I warn with a serious expression plastered over my face.

'You're right, Molly, I'll do that. Listen, girls, I'll have a wee proper chat to you after about this.' She winks.

'No bother at all, we'll talk again after mass,' I respond.

'That was some laugh. It's a sin poor Nora believes every word of it,' Sadie grins with amusement.

'Aye,' I reply nodding my head. 'I can't believe she fell for that one. Well, Sadie, that'll give her something to chew over for a while. How long do you think she'll keep it a secret for?' I grin.

'I'd say she'll tell the others on the way home, after the retreat. She won't be able to keep it to herself for much longer than that. She's probably dying to explode right now.'

'Aye you're probably right, Sadie, that's if she doesn't blabber it out before we reach the church.'

'Aye, she'll not be able to hold that tongue of hers for long enough.'

We giggle for a little longer before Sadie turns to me with a more serious tone in her voice. 'I'm going to be here for you, Molly, no matter what you need, you only have to ask.'

Sadie takes me by surprise. Winding Nora up has almost caused me to forget about my troubles for a few minutes. Looking into Sadie's eyes, it's evident she genuinely means every word.

'Thank you, that means a lot to me.'

'Not at all, Molly, we're sisters. I care about you. I just want what's best for you. I don't blame you for not agreeing to Donal and Mick's plan; after all it's easy for men to suggest to just get rid of it. It's not them that have to carry a child in their womb and...'

'What? Did you just say *Donal* and Mick's plan?'

'Aye, it was them two that came up with the idea of ending the pregnancy.'

'I had no idea that Donal was in on that as well, I thought it was only Mick that was up for that idea.' I shake my head in disbelief. 'I can't believe he was behind it too. Do you know something, Sadie? That's just another insult from him.'

'I'm sorry, Molly, I didn't realise that you weren't aware of that. It was actually Donal that came up with the idea. Please do me a favour and keep this to yourself, I don't want any trouble.'

'Don't worry, it's not your fault. I really should've

known that he was behind it. I can't believe he's such a coward; he couldn't discuss the matter with me. He had to get Mick to do his dirty work! Don't worry, I won't be saying anything to him, I can't stand to look at him these days let alone talk to him. He's let me down so much.'

'Molly, I know they've both been really cruel to you, but it's just their way of dealing with it. I'm sure they'll come round to things soon. You and Donal have always been so close, in fact, I used to get jealous and often felt left out because I wished I could have had the same strong bond that you two had. Donal will change in his own time.'

'It doesn't matter if he does. He's hurt me so much. I don't think I can ever be the same to him again, Sadie. I honestly believe that the damage is done.'

'He'll come round. I'll talk to him.'

'No, no I don't want you to talk to him. Please don't.'

'Are you sure? It might help if I have a word with him.'

'No, he'll not listen to you, you know the kind of him, he's stubborn and besides he'll just think you're interfering.'

'Okay, but I don't want you to worry.'

Our discussion comes to a halt as we near the church. With only minutes to spare before the service, we hurry inside and make our way to the last remaining seats at the back row. Unfortunately I have no choice but to take a seat beside Nora who is in deep thought, her eyes fixated straight towards the alter and not even turning once to see who has sat beside her.

I sit down on the wooden bench and feel a surge of relief sweep through me. Sadie has been a tremendous help in assisting to lift some of the burdens that I had felt bound down with. It's strange how people can react differently to trials and difficult situations. The people around you can often surprise you by their reactions. I had never expected Sadie to treat me kindly, whilst, on the other hand, I had never expected Donal to treat me so mean and cause me such pain. One valuable thing I've learnt from this whole mess is not to judge people or assume how they will respond, you can never tell until faced with a situation. Donal's sneakiness has shocked me.

It isn't long before the church is filled to capacity. The rows of heads in front of us are bowed low as they pray before the service begins. The rattle of the rosary beads and the shuffle of feet are the only sounds to be heard.

I nudge Sadie and whisper, 'Do you think she's still traumatised?'

'Looks like it.' A grin spreads across her face.

'Gees I hope I haven't scared her.'

'She'll be okay, Molly.'

'Should I tell her after mass that I was joking?'

'Nah, let her go, she'll have something else to occupy her mind soon, she's a bit tipsy, she'll forget about your story.'

Mother lowers her eyes at us, a look of disappointment appears on her face. I know what she is thinking; she detests anyone talking in church, she sees it as disrespectful.

Sadie and I fall silent and look sheepishly away.

Suddenly Nora sits upright and attempts to act respectable. She looks a little tipsier now than she had done earlier. She must've had another drink somehow. The smell of alcohol hangs in the air. My goodness, I think she's about to receive the Body of Christ with alcohol in her system – surely that can't be right? I at once feel sorry for her. For someone to have to drink like that, they must have their own problems hidden, locked up in their closet. Maybe that's why she gossips so much; maybe she's trying to escape the reality of her own life. Perhaps she likes the idea of highlighting other people's affairs so that the attention doesn't land on her. As I wait for the service to begin I say a silent prayer for her, and pray also that my own family problems will be solved somehow. I need a miracle.

Father McGroarty takes his position at the altar and soon the service commences. He begins to preach about the power of prayer.

'When you pray you will know peace, for without prayer there is no hope, and therefore no peace. My friends, all of us here today will face trials in our lives and have our crosses to carry. Each and every one of us will, at some point, taste the flower of pain and isolation; it may be from sickness, poverty, losing someone dear to us. Let me tell you, that when it is your turn to feel like this, or to suffer in one way or another, your only comfort will be in prayer, for the Lord allows us all to suffer in one form or another, as suffering can bring out the best in people. It allows you to look at life in a different way, and to look at Him more closely than material things or worldly longings. So I tell you my dear friends, your rosary is a precious tool. I challenge you all to take up praying on your beads and let them be your introduction to the heavenly staircase. Pray, pray, pray and you will find peace, for the Lord refuses nothing from a sincere heart. I tell you all, ask and you shall receive, seek and you shall find, knock and it shall be opened to you!'

I have never been so fixed on a speech. It almost feels that his words have been written especially for me, and I again begin to feel more at ease. His sermon sinks deep into my heart and I vow I will try to pray through this difficult time; after all, what other options have I got and what have I got to lose?

As always during the ceremony, we are requested to renew our baptismal vows and renounce the Devil whilst holding a lighted candle.

'Now, my dear friends, I will ask you to stand and renew your baptismal vows.' Father McGroarty grips his candle in his hands.

At once we shuffle to our feet, in obedience to the priest's request.

Father McGroarty will normally create an atmosphere of faith. He begins to raise his voice loudly, setting an intense scene as he commences the vows, asking us: 'Do you renounce Satan and all his works and all his empty promises?' His voice echoes throughout the church, ensuring those gathered at the back and standing outside hear this important part of the service.

To all of the questions we answer, 'We do,' in a loud, determined tone as we hold up our burning candles in the air.

Nora struggles to stand upright, clutching tightly to the candle in her hand. She must have got overexcited by the atmosphere of the loud voices of the crowd as she points her candle higher into the air than normal and shouts loudly: 'We do, de eff with the ol' bugger,' she slurred. 'Satan has been trying to take over the world, but now the leprechauns are coming to try next!'

The congregation tries not to laugh and I can't help but smile as I glance at Sadie and we both burst into a fit of giggles. I have to pinch my nose and cover my mouth in an attempt to keep myself quiet. My mother would be disappointed at us for behaving in such a manner in church and so I try my best to compose myself.

Poor Nora, she must have had one brandy too many! Leprechauns? Now where did she hear that one from?

Chapter 10

'Morning, Emily.'

Emily looks up from her machine. 'Ah, morning, Molly. You look in good form today, what's up?' she replies, smiling as she places the fabric onto the hot metal and presses down firmly with her weight. Steam fills the air.

'I'm grand. We had some laughs yesterday at the retreat.' The thought of the events from yesterday brings a smile to my face.

Emily is a Protestant; she doesn't attend our church, but she's more than familiar with the retreats as I often chat about them. I fill her in on what Nosy Nora said at church the day before.

'Oh dear, I can't believe she done that. She'll be rightly showed up this morning. She won't be able to show her face around the street the day, that's for sure. You Catholics are mad in the head.'

'Are you joking? She'll be round all the neighbours, including my mother, telling them. My mother's going to go mad if she finds out it was me that made up that story, I may leave the country!'

'Molly, you are so dead.' Emily giggles. 'You'll just have to deny everything.'

'Aye I'll have to worm my way out of it somehow. Can you imagine what she will say if she only knew it was me? If I hadn't told Nosy Nora that ridiculous story she wouldn't have made such a scene during the ceremony. My mother didn't crack a smile in church yesterday; she would be offended at something like that.'

'Aye you're right. I know the kind of her. She takes her religion serious.'

'She does indeed.' I nod my head in agreement. 'If looks could kill, Sadie and I would've dropped dead on the spot, she was raging at us for sniggering.'

'Oh, I can imagine her face.'

I remove my coat and sit down at my machine.

'Sadie and I had a little chat about things.'

'Oh dear, the chat that you've been dreading? How did it go?'

'Actually, you won't believe this, but it went really well. She offered her support and was so nice to me. I can't believe it myself.'

'That's good, Molly, but it does surprise me though.'

'Aye, me too. It just goes to show you how wrong you can be about people, doesn't it?'

'Aye, you're right there. You need all the support you can get right now, so take whatever she has to offer. What's the story with your Donal, any change with him?'

'No, he's still acting the same. I found out yesterday that he was the one behind the ending the pregnancy idea,' I whisper.

'No way! I guess that doesn't surprise me,' Emily shrugs. 'Don't worry about him. He'll come round at some point.'

'Aye that's what Sadie said, but I'm past caring about him,' I sigh in disgust. 'Right, enough chit-chat, I need to get started on these shirts.' I pick up the scissors to begin my work.

'Ah sugar, I've just cut my finger.' I hold up my forefinger; blood streams from it and begins to fall down onto the bundle of fabric on the table.

Emily makes her way towards my workstation. 'Gees, Molly, that looks like a nasty cut you have there. You'll need that seen to.' She grabs a piece of cloth and wraps it tightly around the wound, holding pressure on it in a bid to stop the bleeding. It isn't enough to keep the blood under control, and quickly it seeps through.

Soon a group of colleagues gather around us to see what all the fuss is about. On hearing the commotion Mr Doherty pops his head out from his office and, on seeing so many of the girls not working, he marches over.

'What the heck is going on here? Why are you all standing about doing piss all?' He pushes his way through the group of girls, a frustrated expression etched on his face.

I hold up my finger, covered in a blood-soaked rag. 'I've cut my finger, sir.'

He rolls his eyes and shakes his head furiously. 'Molly, did nobody ever tell you that you'll never be a cutter in this factory until you cut your precious little finger?' And with that he walks away. He stops to look over his shoulder. 'Will the rest of you lot get back to your machines right now!'

'What? The cheeky...'

'Ah, don't worry about him, Emily. He's obviously in a bad mood.' I wrap another rag around my finger and try my best to get on with my work.

Later that day Mr Doherty returns and stands over me, eagle-eyed and watching me closely. I've worked at a much slower pace today as a result of the throbbing pain from my wound. The bleeding has eased off slightly, but the pain is intense. As a result of my slow rate I have a small backlog of work. He looks at me suspiciously and eyes up the bundle of material waiting on the floor. Beads of sweat roll down my forehead and trickle down my cheeks. How the heck am I going to get that lot finished, I think?

'Not much work done here today, Molly, looks like you've done more chatting than anything else.' He breaks the silence and points to the floor. 'How are you going to finish that pile before the end of the day?'

I'm sick and tired of taking nonsense from him and from everybody else lately.

'I'm not planning to finish it today, sir,' I reply sarcastically, without lifting my head from my machine, refusing to give him any kind of eye contact. 'You know fine well that I cut my finger this morning and you also know that I'm no laze about that stands around gossiping all day. I'm a hard worker.' Answering him back is a dangerous gamble that anyone can take – it's sure to get you your marching orders. I can feel the tense atmosphere as the other girls fall silent whilst eavesdropping on our conversation. Their machines stand still. There is not a sound to be heard.

'Get into to my office now,' he commands in an angry tone before he turned on his heel and storms off in the direction of his office.

I jump up from my seat and follow him in a rage. 'You're dead right I'll get into your office,' I grumble, my temper reaching boiling point.

How dare he speak to me like that? I'm going to give him a piece of my mind. I march across the factory floor through a sea of whispers from the others. He holds the office door open and before he gets a chance to invite me in I storm in, slamming the door behind me in the process.

Mr Doherty takes a seat behind his desk and his eyes pierce mine. 'Molly, I will not be spoken to like that.' His voice has a tone of such authority. 'Do you understand?'

My body begins to shake with anger. 'And neither will I.' I stare at him defiantly. 'How dare you speak to me like that?'

There is a deathly silence and I wonder what is coming next. He raises his fist in the air and bangs it on his desk sending paperwork to fly in different directions, causing me to almost jump out of my skin.

'Who do you think you are, young lady?'

I don't know where my courage came from, perhaps it's the surge of pregnancy hormones, but somehow I manage to fight back.

'Sir, how dare you speak to me like that! How dare you bang your fist on that desk! I'll tell you exactly who I think I am. I am one of your hardest workers who has never left any backlog of any description in my life since the day and hour that I have been employed here. I work my butt off for you and your stinking factory, working in appalling conditions. The heat is so unbearable these days we almost feel like we're going to pass out; and what about the rats, the pests that you have chosen to ignore, it's a disgrace the way you treat us.' I stop to take a breath of air before continuing, 'I have had an accident at work this morning and I have as good an excuse as any to have a backlog of work, but you haven't listened to me today, have you?'

He sits in silence and appears somewhat taken aback by my sudden outburst.

'You didn't even ask me how I was at any point today. My finger could have been hanging off for all you care.'

Mr Doherty throws his head back and laughs. 'Your finger is hardly hanging off now is it?' he says sarcastically. 'You had a wee cut, Molly, sure we have all had wee cuts.'

'Good job it hadn't fallen off, for my boss wouldn't have given it another thought. Would he? And before you decide to sack me for standing up to you, I'm resigning from my post as from now, this very moment!' I blurt out before I know it, my face ablaze with anger.

'Molly, I can't have you talking to me like that, especially in front of the other girls. If they see you getting away with it they'll think they can do the same, and I can't have that. Do you understand where I'm coming from?'

'Do you understand the meaning of treating others like you would like others to treat yourself?'

'I'm sorry, I don't know what you mean.'

'I mean exactly what I say. If you don't want me to speak to you in public like that, don't you think you should have refrained from communicating so abruptly to me in front of others? You showed me up in front of my work colleagues and you made me out to be some sort of lazy girl. You know fine rightly I'm not idle.'

'Yes, you're right, you're not.'

'You embarrassed me in front of my friends.'

'I didn't mean to.'

'And what about the amount of times you've banged the door shut in the faces of workers just because they're a few minutes late for work? I've seen you close the door and leave good workers standing red-faced in the pouring rain getting drenched, just because they're a few minutes late for work. Come off it, sir, that's no way to treat people. It's not on. It's just down right hateful. It's not fair.'

'What's not fair, a black cat's hair?' he sneers trying to make fun of the matter.

'Am I supposed to laugh? Oh sorry ha, ha that is sooooooooo funny. You're hilarious.'

'Molly, I call that punctuality. It doesn't do them any harm. I'm making sure they're aware they should be on time for work that's all. It's called good management.' He shrugs his shoulders dismissively. 'There's nothing wrong with that, Molly.'

'No it's not good management! It's mean and it's nasty; those girls work their butts off for this factory, and if someone is a few minutes late for work they shouldn't be treated so badly. Some of them women have young children, and I've heard stories of those children being sick or being awake during the night for various reasons, and as a result the poor mothers end up sleeping in for work, and the worst about it, they do all they possibly can to get to their jobs, just so that they're not short in their wages at the end of the week, to make sure they're able to put a dinner on the table for their kids. As I said, it's not on. A good manager would not treat their workers

138

so badly.'

'As I say, Molly, I call it ensuring punctuality.'

'You can call it what you like, I call it bullying!' My voice rises a decibel.

The expression on his face changes, obviously taken aback with my latest comment.

'I'm no bully,' he replies in a defensive manner.

'No? I certainly think so, and I'm sure I'm not the only one to think that you're a bully; and it's part of the reason why I'm resigning. You ask any of the girls out there and I can guarantee they'll all say yes. You've a cold heart of stone. I can't handle somebody who treats others so coldly.'

'Ah, Molly, don't be so hard on me, I'm not that bad, am I?' He pouts his lips like a child that has just got scolded.

I raise my eyebrows and he smiles sheepishly.

I hold out my hand to shake his, 'I'll bid you good day, sir.'

Mr Doherty holds my hand, refusing to let go. 'I admire your courage, Molly. I guess you're right in everything you've said. I suppose I've been getting away with it for too long. Sometimes people spend so much time observing the faults of others they can actually ignore their own flaws. Thank you for pointing mine out to me, Molly.' He releases my hand and smiles before opening a drawer and reaching inside: he displays a homemade chocolate muffin. 'Here, accept this as a peace offering, Molly. I was saving this for my afternoon tea, but I think you should have it.'

'So there *is* a soft side to you after all?' I tease as I lean over the desk and accept his gift.

'Ssh, don't go around telling the others, I can't have them thinking I'm a pussycat in a wolf's costume now can I? I guess I'll see you at work tomorrow then, Molly, will I? Eight o'clock sharp, I don't want to be banging the door in your face now.'

'Thanks for the muffin, but I'm still not coming into work tomorrow.' With that I walked towards the door. 'Good day, sir, take care.'

He smiles with a confused look on his face. 'You're a stubborn young lady aren't you?'

No, I'm just pregnant and need an excuse to leave, I think. 'Aye I suppose you could say that. Some say I'm a bit like my brother Donal, he can be a right stubborn boy when he wants to be.'

'Oh I see, so it runs in the family then. Sorry I haven't had the pleasure of meeting him. Well, Molly, if you ever change your mind you're always welcome back, and if it's any benefit to you, you are one of my best workers here.'

'Thank you for your compliment, sir.'

'I don't say sorry often, but when I do say it, you can be sure it's straight from the heart. I'm sorry, Molly, and you're right about everything you've just said about me. Perhaps sometimes people need to hear things they don't want to. I promise I won't shut the door in anyone's face again for being late; I guess I never looked at it like you explained it to me.'

'Aye I guess the truth can be hard to face.' If anyone knew that, I did. 'Don't we all want to run away from the truth at some time in our lives?'

'You're right. Are you still going to leave then?' His

eyes soften and his voice sounds sweeter.

'Aye, it looks like it,' I sigh. 'But, you never know, perhaps I'll be back one day. Goodbye, sir.'

I pierce my lips together and try to squeeze out a smile before walking out of his office and out onto the factory floor again through a midst of peering eyes and whispers. I grab my coat and sling it over my shoulder before making my way to the front door.

I overhear someone say, 'She must have been sacked, she was in there ages.'

I stop in my tracks and turn to face the girls. 'No, I haven't been sacked, but you're right, I'm going, I'm leaving.' I turn on my heel and make my way to the door, stepping outside into the glorious sunshine as Emily and the girls watch on, too stunned to speak.

A river of tears fall from my eyes as I walk down the street. Working in the factory is the only thing that has been keeping me sane these days!

Chapter 11

The summer months whizz by, much quicker than any of us could have imagined. Since leaving the factory I remain at home, passing most of my time hidden away in my bedroom. It's more like a prison for me, spending practically most of the day staring at the four depressing walls of my cell, or gazing into space, or curling myself up into a ball on my bed. Occasionally I sit by the window and just look out into the back garden or to the sheep that graze in a field behind our yard. Now and again I would wander into my mother's room where the view is much better.

As each week passes, my fear grows and so does my bump. The baby is due around the of end of September; the closer it gets to that dreaded time, the more my fears develop and run riot in my brain. It's difficult to think straight.

The first day of September is a warm and sunny Friday, but people don't seem to have that uplifting, happy feeling today that usually accompanies the glorious sunshine. There is a sense of unease felt by everyone as a result of the war raging in Europe, and the people of Ireland fear the worse. Doom and gloom seems to be etched on every face.

A wireless radio is our key means of keeping informed of what is happening around the globe. There's a scarcity of wirelesses and news from around the world is difficult to obtain, so it's times like this people welcome any news from Nosy Nora, regardless of its authenticity. One thing that we're sure of: if there's something important to hear then Nora will be aware of it, and she won't fail to ensure the street hears about it. Mick has a wireless, so at all times we are kept informed of any new developments regarding the war. Many of the neighbours will call into our home to listen to it with Mick, and, much to my dismay, I have to dive to my room, confining myself to my cell until they leave, in order to make sure no one gets a glimpse of me heavily pregnant.

Today the house is packed and the atmosphere is tensing up by the minute. I decide to sit in my mother's bedroom to watch the activity out the front. Everyone seems that little bit more on edge today. Their panic proves correct. I watch as Nosy Nora runs through the fields holding her skirt high, revealing a washed-out, tattered petticoat. She looks like some kind of ghostly apparition flowing in the distance. The sight of her alone is enough to scare the wits out of folk. A few of the neighbours had gathered at the bottom of the street only a few minutes earlier.

Nora wails like a banshee, 'Hitler has invaded Poland! By five o'clock this morning five cities had been set ablaze in Poland. I'm telling you, it's only a matter of time. Believe me, you mark my words, boys, we'll be next!' Panic-stricken she dashes quickly past them, not stopping for her usual good old chinwag.

On hearing the commotion, Charlie comes galloping into the room. 'What's all that screaming about, Molly? What's going on out there?'

'Oh, what do you think? It's only Nosy Nora making a mountain out of a molehill as usual, pay no heed to her.'

Charlie peers out the window next to me and rolls his

eyes.

'Look at that clown, what's she not like, Charlie?'

We observe in amusement as Nora rounds up her children one by one, ushering them to follow her into the house. We lean further out of the small, open window to get a better look and to hear the commotion.

'Come on now, wains, get into the house. Come on now all of you, get in, quick.' She shoves them into the garden gate, almost knocking them over in the process, terror clearly evident in her voice.

'Ah, Mammy, gone leave us alone, we're playing hopscotch and it's my turn to do the hopping,' little John, the youngest of her sons, protests as he steps backwards, moving away from her. He kicks and flings his arms as his mother scoops him up under her arm and marches along towards their home. 'Put me down, put me down!'

'Hopscotch? The only hopping you'll be doing is hopping in that door, before them Germans gets their hands on you, do you hear me, boy?'

John's bottom lip curls up as he struggles not to cry.

Charlie shakes his head in disbelief. 'What the heck is she at? You would think a bomb is going to drop any minute from the sky, and blow us all to pieces, the way she's reacting.'

'It's the kids I feel sorry for the most, she has their wee heads done in. I'm sure she's frightened the life out of them, talking to them like that. Oh, Charlie, look at wee John, he's about to sob.'

'Would you not cry if you had to live in the same house as that mad hatter?' Charlie giggles.

I smile. 'Cry? I'd be bawling my eyes out!'

The men on the street don't seem to find this latest information as amusing as Charlie and I. In fact, if anything, they actually look to be quite shaken by the latest news.

'Look at them poor souls, Charlie. She has frightened the life out of them poor creatures too.'

'Aye, they look like they've seen a bleeding ghost. In saying that, she frightens the life out of me; the sight of her alone is enough to scare the daylights out of anybody.'

We both snigger at the thought of the drama she's just created.

'The ol' scaremonger – anything for a drama!' Charlie replies through his laughs.

Meanwhile the men on the street gather in deep conversation, solemn expressions etched on their faces. Have Charlie and I missed something? Surely not.

The news of the war has clearly caused a stir with the locals. The rest of my family are very much interested in the goings-on around Europe, but for Charlie and me the news doesn't bother us; as far as we are concerned, wars are fought in faraway lands. Who wants to bother about a little place like Northern Ireland when there are bigger fish to fry? Besides, with the birth expected in a matter of weeks, I have enough of my own problems to be worrying about.

'Tell the ol' mad hatter to hide away up there, out of the way of everyone. She's sure to be safe up there from the Germans!' Charlie lifts his finger and points in the direction of Grianan Fort, visible in the distance.

I peer at the great stone masterpiece, the origins of the

site is said to date back as far as 1700 BC. It's one of Ireland's greatest circular forts, standing seven hundred and fifty feet above sea level. 'Mick took us up there once when we were kids,' I announce proudly. 'It's a great spot. It's so high off the ground and it's ideal to view the surrounding lands and the water below. You can see for miles around.'

I pause, recalling fond memories of the day Mick took us on a trip to explore the fine building. Donal and I had nagged him for months to take us to see the fort; eventually Mick gave in, warning us that we had a long walk ahead of us. My mother packed a lunch, consisting of homemade pancakes and fruit, before we set off on our journey. Mick was right; we walked for what seemed like days, through fields and stony dirt tracks, until we finally stumbled onto the heather and mossy marshland that lay below the splendid fort. I remember my first thought as I peered up as a small child of how big it actually is when you are up close to it. It's only ever a speck on the horizon from our home.

Donal and I ran on ahead of Mick to peep through the holes in the dry stone walls, with the hope of finding some ancient treasure. To our dismay, we found nothing but creepy-crawlies and spiders. Once we entered inside we discovered a flight of narrow stone steps, allowing us to climb to the top of the mighty building. Here a breathtaking sight of the Lough Swilly stretched for many miles before our eyes. Dominating the horizon to the northwest were the Glenveagh Mountains, with Muckish and Errigal – the highest mountains in Donegal – standing proud in the near distance.

I was so intrigued by the beautiful sight in front of me

146

that I hadn't noticed Donal and Mick setting off to explore some other area of the amazing fort. When I turned around to speak to the others I suddenly found myself alone, surrounded by nothing but a creepy silence. At once an eerie feeling swept over me. Donal had once said that the place was haunted; suddenly it felt as if eyes were watching me through the gaps in the stone walls. It wasn't long before I scampered down the steps, almost falling over myself in a frantic search for the others. Looking back on the incident now it was amusing, and probably just a child's mind running away with itself.

'Aye, I've heard you can see some spectacular sights from up there.' Charlie leans on the windowsill and gazes at the black speck on the horizon.

'You'll have to get up there sometime; you were too young when Mick took us. Mick informed us its full name is Grianan Aileach. He claims the name is from the Irish language, meaning the Stone Fort of the Sun.'

'Aye, I'm sure Mick told me that too.' Charlie nods in agreement. 'In fact, he also said that legend has it you're advised not to whisper a secret within the walls of the fort as everyone will know.'

'I've never heard that one. But, legend has it, you're not to whisper a secret in front of Nosy Nora, or else every living creature in Derry will know!'

We both burst into a fit if giggles. The sounds of our laughter echo through the street. We laugh so hard any thoughts of wars, bombs, Germans and babies are as remote as ever. As far as we're concerned, the war won't affect Derry. Our wee, humble town will carry on as normal whilst the rest of Europe is plunged into turmoil. Sure, the Germans probably don't even know our little island exists. Nothing for us to worry about! Or is there?

Chapter 12

September 3rd 1939 is a date not to be forgotten, a day my life changed forever.

I am abruptly awakened from my sleep shortly after midnight, with twinges of pain coming and going. They aren't too bad at first, and the pain is bearable. These twinges continue throughout the entire night. It never crosses my mind that I might be in labour; the baby isn't due for another few weeks, and in my naivety I think it is nothing to worry about.

Morning comes and the pains are still there.

I lie in my bed feeling tired and exhausted from my sleepless night. The discomfort is now becoming a great deal more intense, lasting much longer, and, to make matters worse, the spasms are arriving much more frequently.

'Arrggggggh,' I release an almighty scream, unable to hold back any longer. 'Mother, help me!' It is useless; she and Mick were listening carefully to the wireless. 'Arrgggh Mother, please help me!' I yell again, stumbling out of bed and crawling towards the door on my hands and knees. At this point the pain feels immense. Again, screaming out unable to hold back, 'Arrggggh.' My screams are so loud and so intense someone is bound to hear me now. I bang my fist against the floorboards before falling on the rug.

'Arrgggh.' I thump my fists forcefully against the floorboards once more, as another intense pain shoots across my lower back. 'Help!'

'Molly, is that you? Are you okay?'

My mother dashes up the stairs, to find me rolling on

the wooden floorboards in agony. 'Oh, darling, let's get you into bed.'

'I can't,' I manage to say through gritted teeth, the discomfort shooting through my body with such force.

'Mick, Mick,' my mother yells from the top of the stairs. 'Mick, get Doctor Devlin.'

Mick's full attention is on the wireless and the person speaking.

I let out another scream as the pain hits again.

'Molly, listen, love, I'll be straight back. I'm going to get some help.' She dashes out the door and shouts from the top of the stairs again. 'Mick, did you hear me? Will you go and get the doctor and do it quick!'

'What for?' Mick comes bounding up the stairs as my mother returns to my room.

'For Molly, she's in labour ...'

'I need to push. I can't hold back any longer, my body won't let meeeeeeeeeeeee ...'

'Molly, the baby is coming, take a deep breath.' Mother sighs as she rolls up her sleeves. 'Mick, get some towels, quick, before you go.'

Mick hands her the towels before disappearing out of sight.

I can't refrain any longer and find the urge to push with all my strength. With one final scream and one last thrust, digging my fingertips deep into my mother's shoulders, the screams of a newborn echo throughout the room. The pain at once stops. My head rests on the cold, wooden floorboards, damp hair clings to my sweaty face. The reality of the situation is too much to contemplate, nothing feels real. I want to close my eyes, to sleep and wake up later to find it is all just a horrible nightmare.

'Molly, it's a little boy,' Mother whispers softly as she cradles the tiny bundle close to her chest. He wiggles his naked body in her hands, kicking and flinging his delicate limbs about as he screeches loudly.

My eyes fix upon the small infant moving about in her arms. Suddenly reality strikes me. I have just given birth to a living child. Thoughts of how he was conceived almost make we want to throw up, the memories of his evil father come flooding back. My thoughts are swiftly interrupted as the door flies open and in dashes Doctor Devlin, followed by Mick.

Mick stares at the baby. 'It looks like you don't need me here,' he announces, sarcastically, before turning on his heel and making a quick exit.

Doctor Devlin takes over and within minutes he delivers the afterbirth. 'I got the easy job; it looks like your mother got the harder task. Let's get you into bed, Molly.'

He looks at me with that same look on his face that he gave me months earlier. Is it a look of sympathy, a look of shame, or perhaps a bit of both? It's difficult to tell with Doctor Devlin; he is such a professional man, never giving away any signs of what he's really thinking, a difficult man to read.

The baby's screams pulsate through my brain. I want to scream at my mother and Doctor Devlin to get lost, get out of my sight and to take that thing with them, to allow me to go to sleep! As if sleep can solve my problems – fat chance of that – but right now my body needs some rest.

I struggle desperately to fight back the tears, but, adamant that I have cried enough, there will be no more tears falling from these eyes.

'Well, my work's done here. Is there anything else I can do for you, Molly?' Doctor Devlin sounds caring.

'No thank you,' I whisper quietly, barely audible.

'Are you sure?'

'Aye, I'll be okay.'

'Doctor Devlin, thank you so much for all your help, it's very much appreciated. However, there is one more thing that you can do for us.' Mother pauses and looks at him with pleading eyes. 'We would be grateful if you didn't speak about this matter to anybody. Molly has been through so much, we've decided that I will bring this baby up as an adopted child. Nobody needs to know the truth that the boy is Molly's.'

His usual frown sets in his forehead. 'I see.' Doctor Devlin looks towards me, waiting for me to comment. 'Well, it's entirely your business; if that's what you've decided, I'll give you my word. I don't discuss my patient's private affairs with anybody else. This is your business, no one else's.' Again he stares through me. It's clear he wants me to say something, however his lips remain sealed.

'Thank you again. I'll walk you to the door.' My mother smiles at him softly.

'No need to, Kate, you stay here with Molly, I can see myself out. Now, if you need anything at all, you know where to find me.' Doctor Devlin walks towards the door and steps out onto the hallway before looking back over his shoulder. 'Molly, are you sure you're okay?'

152

'Aye.' I nod, hoping he would just hurry up and go, so that I can crawl under the blankets and disappear forever.

'Good. I'll be off then, but remember if you need anything just ask.' He nods his head before turning towards the stairs.

'Goodbye, thanks again for everything.'

'You're welcome, goodbye, Kate, goodbye, Molly.'

As soon as the doctor leaves my mother begins to wash the baby before she dresses him and wraps him up gently in a blanket. 'What would you like to call him, Molly?' She brushes her lips over his soft cheeks.

I don't answer. My mind in a deep trance, my emotions once again in turmoil, and for the second time today, struggling to fight back the tears from escaping my tired, sleep-deprived eyes.

'Molly?'

My gaze turns towards the two of them and I watch as the little infant pushes his tiny hand in and out of his mouth, in a bid to suckle his fist – missing the aim most of the time – his head moving frantically from left to right searching for his target. He has the most beautiful, huge, blue eyes, set in a round, chubby, angelic face. His pink, creased skin looks soft and delicate to touch, and his dark, sticky hair is thick and it's clear it will be curly. He is the most beautiful baby my eyes have ever seen.

I should be proud of him and should love him. My heart wants to love him with every beat, like any mother would want to adore their child, but my mind is telling me otherwise. From the second that Doctor Devlin announced the news to me I didn't want him, and still don't want him now. He shouldn't be here. He should never have been born. How is it possible to accept this child, when already I am reliving that night, all those months ago, every time my gaze falls upon him? It would be too difficult to put those thoughts out of my mind, when here, in front of me, is the result of that horrific attack. It makes me feel sick that this beautiful baby has been created out of such an evil act. The more my eyes look at him, the more my stomach churns, the more I hate his father and the more I resent this tiny, innocent baby.

'Molly, did you hear me, what would you like to call him?'

My mother snuggles him close to her and caresses his cheek with so much sweetness and tenderness, you would almost think she had just given birth to him herself. Already she loves him.

'Take him away!' I hear myself reply. 'Take him away from me!' My voice grows louder.

She lifts her head and looks on, both shocked and surprised. 'What?' she questions in a confused tone of voice.

'I don't want him, so just take him away from me.'

'Molly, he's your son, you shouldn't say things like that.'

'No, he's your son not mine! Isn't that the plan? I don't want to have anything to do with him. Get him out of my sight. Take him out that door now and take him as far away from me as possible!'

'Keep your voice down, Molly. Maybe you should hold him for a while. It might help you to bond with him.'

'No! No I don't want him. You decided you would bring him up, so you keep him. I'm having nothing to do with him, not now, not ever! If you don't want him, give him away to someone that does. It doesn't matter to me where he goes.'

'Molly, I'm disgusted that you're even thinking like that, let alone talking like that. You don't really mean it.'

She shakes her head in disbelief. She looks heartbroken.

'I mean it alright.' I sit upright in the bed and pull my knees up close to my chest, resting my chin on my knees and stare at my mother stubbornly. 'I've never felt so strongly about anything in my whole life. He's yours now, so have him, and as far as I'm concerned you can keep him, give him away, whatever. I don't care, and as far as I'm concerned, I never will!'

'Molly, I'm doing you a favour by bringing him up as mine, I don't know what else to do. Have you any better ideas? I've done my best to support you through all of this and all you can do is shout and roar cruel things. You haven't even got the decency to tell us who the father is. Any other mother would have walked away by now and left you to deal with your own mess.' She stares at me, a look of disappointment spread on her face before continuing, 'Who is the father, Molly? Don't you think he should be told he has a son?'

'You wouldn't understand.' I rub my tired eyes and turn my gaze away from her, not wanting to get into this conversation right now. 'I don't want to talk about him. His father will not be notified that he has a son because he doesn't want to know, he'll only deny that the child is his anyway, so let's just leave it at that!'

She releases a disgusted sigh. 'Aye, well that's fine. It seems to me that this poor child has two parents that don't want to know about him, doesn't it?'

I can sense the disappointment in her words; her tone of voice says it all. We had never argued over anything in the past, and it saddens me that we were bickering with one another now. 'I'm just tired that's all. I'll hold him later, please, just let me rest now, I need to sleep. I'm not in the mood to argue with you.'

The child releases a mighty scream. I cover my ears and try to block him out.

'He's hungry, Molly, he needs your milk.'

'No chance!'

'Now then, Molly. Take him.'

She holds him out to me. I freeze.

'He needs his food, Molly. Quickly now.'

'I - I can't,' I cry and tears stream down my face. No way on God's earth can I allow a rapist's child near my body.

'The baby will suffer if it doesn't get nourished, Molly.' She moves closer.

Though its pink creased face looks as innocent as a cherub, I would rather chew a mouthful of wasps than let him near me. The thought of him touching me makes me feel as dirty as on the night his father violated me.

'I'm sorry,' Mother says. 'But the child will die if you don't feed it, Molly. I will bring this little boy up as my own, I promise you that. But I don't have any milk to give.'

Despite my tears and pleas to God, the baby is in my arms and suckling before I can realise. I understand what she is

156

saying, that its immediate needs can be brought by none other than me. But it's still hard to nourish a rapist's child. I close my eyes and wait for it to have its fill, and in my mind I take the long walk to Grianan Fort, eating the fruit and pancakes mother packed for me.

'Take him now, he's finished.'

My mother nods without uttering another word and leaves the room, with the baby contently sleeping in her arms. I close my heavy, tired eyes and at once drift off into a deep sleep.

I wake up later to find the room in silence and darkness. My sense of time is way out. The sound of chatting coming from downstairs and the faint cry of a baby at once remind me that I have given birth earlier, causing a shudder to run along my spine.

'Oh Mother of Jesus protect us all!'

It sounds like my mother screeching from the kitchen below. It is an unusual statement for her to make and at once it stirs me. I tiptoe downstairs; the living room is empty. The others are gathered in the kitchen, listening to the wireless with such interest.

I open the door of the kitchen and find the family huddled together hanging on to every word that is broadcast from the wireless. Each of their faces appear to be frightened and the air is heavy with tension.

'Ah don't worry too much, it might not affect us,' Sadie tries to reassure my mother placing her arms around her shoulders and hugging her gently.

They are all so fixated on listening to the breaking news

157

that nobody has noticed my presence in the room.

'What's the matter?' I question, interrupting the silence.

Startled, Mick turns to face me. 'What's the matter?' He pauses. 'Our peaceful existence has just ended, and I'm not talking about the arrival of baby Shane.'

'Baby Shane? I'm glad you've decided on a name for him.' One less thing for me to worry about, I think.

'I'm talking about the news that's just after been declared.' He pauses again for a second before continuing in a serious tone. 'We're now involved in the World War.'

Chapter 13

Since the birth of baby Shane I have slipped deeper and deeper into depression. My life has been turned upside down. Nothing could have prepared me for the emotional hurricane that has taken over my mind, leaving me feeling a sense of emptiness and complete uselessness; it's horrible beyond imagination. It sure is a dark and lonely world.

For me to acknowledge Shane is out of the question. It's difficult to bring myself to be near him. I've tried to look at him, but each time my eyes fall upon him I can see a miniature version of his evil father; when I feed him I have to turn my eyes away. To me, he's always in the way, a nuisance that constantly makes me feel sick every time I hear him cry or see his face. The fact is my life will never be the same again.

During the pregnancy I had blocked out the fact that this situation is real, not once thinking of the effect that this new addition would bring about, or how I would manage seeing the baby in the flesh. The truth is, now that Shane is here, and here to stay, it's difficult to cope with.

My mother is wonderful. She does everything for him that a mother should do. She wraps him up every night and rocks him to sleep, singing him soothing lullabies, just like she had done with each of us. She knows exactly what to do to chase away the tears. She sure is an expert in the field of bringing up children. I admire her strength and patience and even envy her in a peculiar way, wanting so much to be like her, but unfortunately I don't have her special traits.

Mick often refers to her as 'Derry's very own saint'. It's

easy to see why he calls her this. She truly is a tremendous woman. Since our argument shortly after the birth, she never got angry with me again. My cold hostility towards Shane doesn't perplex her. She's never once asked why I feel like this or pressured me to feel any different. She seems to accept that I want to distance myself; perhaps she has hopes my feelings will change one day.

'You'll come round in your own time, Molly,' she will remark.

'I don't want to come round to anything. I'm okay the way I am.'

'You're young, darling, you've still a lot of growing up to do, but you will one day,' she promises with a gentle smile on her face.

My mother by no means complains as she goes about her duties, taking on the role once again of motherhood to someone else's child. None of the neighbours raised an eyebrow seeing her with a newborn baby, and thankfully Nosy Nora was too caught up in the war to bother about anything else. However, my gut feeling is that Father McGroarty has his suspicions – perhaps he knows the truth. My mother, under no circumstances, could tell a lie to a priest. It would eat her inside having to deceive her neighbours, but there's no way that she could deceive Father McGroarty. She respects him too much and she also trusts him one hundred percent. It doesn't bother me if he does know, but I decide it is best to keep my distance from him and so each week when he pays a visit I retire to my room.

With it being difficult to face the family, it's easier to

spend my time in my prison cell, hiding away from the rest of the world, just like during the pregnancy. I rarely help around the house, rarely go as far as the front door, and often go for days without washing myself or brushing my hair.

The news of the war and its effects on Derry is another thing that dooms my mood; it affects everyone in some way or another. Only weeks ago Charlie and I had joked about the war and thought everyone was taking it too seriously. How wrong we were. Folks had every right to be fearful, and my feelings and fears are now with everyone else's. At 11:15am on Sunday 3rd September 1939, shortly after I had given birth, Neville Chamberlain established that fear when he informed the nation that a state of war now existed between Britain and Germany. As Northern Ireland is part of Britain, the people have taken that information seriously. We are now on high alert. The next morning's headlines in the daily papers proved terrifying reading: 'Hitler plunges the world into war' and 'German bombers just two hours flying time from Ulster'. With headlines like that, it's enough to make us fear the worst.

It's a nightmare, with the news of war holding everyone's attention. The panic felt throughout the rest of Europe has now landed on our own doorsteps, and a considerable level of disruption in wartime is unavoidable, much to the stress of all. Soon after the news of war was made known as a threat to us, a blackout order was imposed. In order to make Derry invisible from the air, a strict blackout was deemed necessary at night. It's crucial to extinguish all street lamps and drape our windows with black curtains so as not to allow any light to escape. We are allowed small hand torches, but they only give a limited amount of light. I detest the dark and always have done from a young age. The blackout is one of the most difficult aspects of the war to have to deal with; it's dismal, and we have to endure this tedious exercise every night of the week, but it's a small price to pay for our safety. Air raid wardens patrol everywhere, ensuring this rule is taken seriously and adhered to fully.

Exactly four weeks later from the day the blackouts were imposed, petrol rationing followed. The introduction of this rationing means there are fewer cars on the roads. Because Sadie lives a few miles from us and depends on her husband to drive her to visit, her visits have become less frequent, which is a pity, Sadie has been a tower of strength over the most difficult months of my life. The sound of her voice from downstairs is enough to make me drag myself from my bedroom. Aggie and Paddy also prefer to stay in Greencastle. With the Republic of Ireland being free from the threat of war, many people that live there are discouraged to venture into the north of Ireland due to the fear of bombs landing or the dislike of the blackouts. This lack of family contact only adds to my sadness. I long for their company more than ever before.

With leaving the factory so abruptly I hadn't given myself time to think about buying anything in for the baby, and to be honest it didn't cross my mind to save for bigger items, such as a pram. My mother was disappointed at first when she heard that I'd resigned from my job.

'How can you be so irresponsible, Molly?' she sighed, a disappointed look etched on her face. 'What are you going to do now for money? In case you've forgotten you've a baby on the way, and whether you like it or not, babies cost money!'

'Sorry, Mother, I just didn't think about prams and stuff.'

It wasn't long until she came round to the idea.

'I suppose it's a good thing that you left your work when you did, Molly, you're expanding by the day. It's probably best you're not at your work, after all. You would've had to leave sooner or later.'

Just before the baby arrived my mother arranged to get a loan from Mrs Flannigan in order to purchase a secondhand pram. She agreed to pay her back a few shillings a week, with interest of course.

That selfish woman infuriated me. 'Do you have to ask that ol' bag for the money? She's taking the piss out of people charging interest in a time of such hardships.' Anger rose within me.

'Molly, don't refer to her like that, where else will I get the cash from?'

The old stingy sod is still raking in the money during hardships, and the interest she adds is an absolute disgrace. She keeps track of her loans in her little, black book: all payments made, missed and overdue payments are carefully tracked, and everything is kept up to date. If an installment is skipped it's recorded and added to the next week, with extra interest.

My mother is struggling to pay the weekly fee but she is making sure that Mrs Flannigan gets her money when it is due. It was agreed that once the baby was born I would get a job and pay her back, but right now getting a job is the last thing on my mind.

Soon autumn arrives. I awaken one morning to the scent of freshly baked scones and homemade soup. The delightful smell has drifted upstairs, filling my bedroom with the mouth-watering aroma. It smells so good it sends my stomach into spasms, rumbling with the temptation, longing for the meal to be ready and waiting patiently for my mother's call.

'Molly, your lunch is served, you coming down?'

'Aye I'll be down now.' I jump off my bed.

Downstairs Shane lies fast asleep in his pram, a hand-knitted blanket from Aggie is tucked around him keeping him snug and warm. As I pass him by I steel a split-second to gaze at his angelic face. He looks peaceful as he lies contently sleeping. His delicate, chubby, miniature hands are curled up and pulled up close to his cheeks, as if he is about to engage in some serious boxing. His skin looks so soft. I find myself reaching out to stroke it but I am stopped by the sudden bang on the front door. The noise startles me. My mother goes at once to open it and is greeted by Donal arriving back from work. I jump slightly and I am taken aback as my eyes meet Donal's briefly. The brother, sister relationship between us was destroyed beyond repair – it is clear he despises me. The silence between us is now a normal way of life. It bothers me, of course it bothers me, but I refuse to let him see how much it is affecting me. We are both aware the matter makes our mother unhappy. She has tried on many occasions to get us to speak, but it is of little use; he is adamant that he is not going to give in.

I quietly sit down at the dinner table without striking up any conversation with the others. As usual, the less said the better. I've distanced myself so much from them I no longer feel part of the family unit. The sad thing is, I no longer know what to say to any of them these days.

Donal appears more agitated than normal, and suddenly the soup isn't as tempting, and my appetite is lost again.

Mick has his wireless on in the background, his ears listening closely for any news regarding the war situation. Since war has been declared he has listened to the wireless for hours on end, using all his spare time to gather as much information for the neighbours as possible. I am happy to have the radio on; at least it's a distraction from the uncomfortable atmosphere.

The family eat their meal in silence. I try to force the food into my mouth.

Donal is the first to break the silence. 'I've got something important to tell you all,' he announces in a serious tone, looking around at each of the others, but as always, avoiding eye contact with me.

My mother appears startled. 'I've had enough important news to deal with this year.' She dips her spoon into her soup and stirs the contents about, without glancing up, 'Not sure if I can take anymore.' She plunges her spoon into her bowl of soup again so fiercely the contents spill out onto the linen tablecloth. 'What is it, Donal?'

Mick leans over to turn his wireless down. 'What's up with you, boy?'

The group's attention is now fixed on Donal.

He clears his throat and looking directly at Mother he announces: 'I've joined the army. I'm leaving to go to war.'

165

Chapter 14

As the saying goes, a picture can say more than words; the look on my mother's face, from this latest, devastating news, said it all. There's no need for any comments. It's clear she's not happy.

'Is nobody going to say anything? Are you all going to sit there, looking like a bunch of dummies?' Donal's eyes dart on each of the members around the table, meeting mine only briefly.

It is a cold, heartless, statement to make. Donal is certainly not the same man that he was this time last year. He's changed so much in the space of a few months.

He was never one to show any interest in the army, he enjoys his job too much at the docks. Surely he wouldn't want to leave that all behind, to take up a completely different focus in life, and besides, he is too much of a 'home bird' to leave. As youngsters we would tease him and call him names, such as 'mammy's boy', for he would follow her everywhere and cry if she was out of his sight.

My mother, on many occasions, would say, *'Donal, you'll always be attached to my apron strings'.*

As the years went on, Donal even joked that he would never leave his family home to marry a girl, his famous statement being, *'There's no way any woman could match my mother's cooking'.*

In fact, Donal can't visit Aggie and Paddy in Greencastle without feeling homesick, so how he had planned to survive thousands of miles away, in a strange country, amongst raging war and confusion with people he didn't know, baffles me, and surely the others thought the same.

Mother breathed a huge sigh and swallowed her tears; her eyes are saddened. 'Why, Donal? Where did this notion come from?'

'Sean and I talked about...'

'Sean O'Leary! Are you having a laugh? So it's that ol' clown that's planted these crazy thoughts into that brain of yours,' Mick interrupts shaking his head in disagreement and disbelief.

Sean O'Leary is Donal's friend from the docks. Ever since they met they've been the best of buddies. Sean is known to be a bit of a 'head case', a 'scatter brain' that seldom takes anything in life seriously, the news he's going to join the army too is laughable to say the least.

'Somehow, Donal, I can't imagine the Sean boy fighting for his life, or saving others for that matter, that madman couldn't beat snow off a rope!' Mick sneers. His lip begins twitching ready to burst into laughter at any point. 'What the bleeding heck does he want to join the army for, is he hoping to become some kind of hero?' he throws back his head and laughs aloud.

Donal doesn't seem to see the funny side of Mick's comments.

'I know he can be a bit of a 'loose cannon' but at other times he can be really responsible, and anyway it's not that

167

crazy an idea, army life is a good starting point for any man. It wasn't just Sean's concept, other men were talking about it too, but they backed out at the last minute. We've been discussing it now for weeks.'

'I'm not surprised the others dropped out, they've obviously seen sense. This is a crazy plan! You're mad, Donal, you've lost your marbles, boy!'

Donal sighs with disgust, 'Mick, I'm going ...'

'Stay here, please, Donal,' Anna pleads softly. She has been sitting listening carefully to the matter. Anna, being the shy member of the family, is not one to give an opinion or make proposals, preferring at all times to just go with the flow with whatever the others agreed on, whether she likes it or not. But when Anna does make a suggestion, it is always something worth listening to.

Donal appears taken aback by her plea. He replies in a quieter tone, 'Anna, sweetheart, I need to go. I'll be okay, love, I promise.' He turns his attention back to Mick. 'As I say, Mick, it'll be a good starting point.'

'A good starting point? Donal, come off it, what's the chance of you coming back alive? Sure your life is just starting.'

'Mick's right, Donal,' Mother says. 'What is the chance of you coming back alive? Don't put yourself in danger, you only get one stab at life, don't squander it!'

'Ah, Ma, you're just worrying too much, it's natural for you to be concerned. I want you to look at this as being the best experience that I could get in my ...'

'Mother's right, we only get one stab at life, Donal,' I

interrupt without giving it a second thought.

I know as soon as I have my words out that I shouldn't have got involved in the conversation. I at once want to take them back and fade away into the background.

Donal turns his head so that he can look at me directly, and with piercing eyes he stares right through mine, giving me such an uncomfortable, cruel look, a look that says, 'how dare you make a comment when you have already ruined your life,' a look that says, 'I haven't been talking to you, Molly, you're nothing but a piece of dog's waste clinging worthlessly to my shoe,' a look that reminds me of his words, *'you're no sister of mine'*, a look that says more than a million words.

I glance away from him and his uncomfortable expression, his stare remains fixed on me for a few seconds longer, his eyes penetrating my soul, before he turns his attention back to mother.

'Anyway, Mother, as I was saying, don't worry about me. I've been assigned as a peacekeeper. Trust me, I'll be okay,' he sighs pushing his bowl of soup away from him.

'A peacekeeper? Oh you'd make a wonderful peacekeeper, wouldn't you? It would fit you better if you made peace at home!' Mick throws him a look of disgust.

'Listen, all of you, no matter what you say, none of you will change my mind. I'm going and that's that!' Donal lifts his peak cap and places it firmly on his head. He stands up from his chair, flings his coat over his shoulder and darts towards the door. 'My mind is made up, I'm going, and that's final!'

The vague hum in the distance of a train's engines creates a stir amongst the crowd. The small gathering listen vigilantly as the familiar sound gets louder with every inch it draws nearer. The wind carries the echo through the air to our ears.

'Look, I can see the train coming.' Anna pulls on my sleeve and dances up and down with excitement at the sight of the huge train charging down the track. The ground rattles beneath my feet.

It isn't long before other children in the group cheer and clap frantically. Moments later the train pulls up beside us. It comes to an abrupt halt, sending vibrations through the track. Steam puffs from its funnels and an overwhelming smell escapes from its engines, filling the air with its strong, choking fumes.

The dreaded time has arrived, the moment for families to say their farewells to their sons, brothers, fathers, husbands, as they leave to go to war. Their relations know only too well that there is a possibility they may never see them again. The atmosphere is tense. I watch as relatives hug their loved ones or grip them tightly, not wanting them to board the train and wanting to save every precious, last second they have with them. The expressions on their faces show evidence they want to freeze time, not wishing another second to tick by. Others hold hands or kiss cheeks, before waving their farewells. Some share a last joke prior to their final goodbye, whilst mothers cling to their precious rosary beads, praying silently for the protection of their sons.

Mother whispers in Donal's ear, 'Take care, son. I love you, my darling.' She puts her arms around him and fixes a chain around his neck from which hangs a beautiful, silver

Miraculous Medal. 'That's been blessed already by Father McGroarty. It will keep you safe from danger.' She smiles lovingly at her son.

'Thanks, Ma.' Donal clutches his medal and plants a kiss on it before embracing her. He gives her a huge hug and kisses her on the cheek. 'Goodbye, Mother, and remember, don't be worrying about me, I'll be okay, I promise you I'll be fine.'

'I love you, Donal.'

'I love you too, Mother.'

He then turns and gives Mick, Sadie, Charlie and Anna a cuddle and wishes them well. Aggie and Paddy have travelled up to see him off. He embraces and kissed them too. Mother dabs a tissue at the corners of her eyes.

Without warning a strange darkness sweeps over the place. The sky becomes laced with black-bellied clouds filling the horizon. The burly clouds move closer above us and lie thick and heavy in the sky, like they are just about to give birth to a serious downpour. There was a feeling earlier that it was going to rain, and it looks even more threatening as the skies grow murkier by the second. The strong Atlantic wind takes up force and sweeps our hair in all directions; the icy gust is sharp and freezes our cheeks, evidence that winter is creeping in. An unexpected flash of lightning lights up the sky, followed by a mighty crackle of thunder. The clouds burst open and the rain pelts down, seeping through our clothes and soaking our hair.

A slight panic rises amongst the others. The men cut short their goodbyes and rush to take shelter in the train. Rain bounces off the metal vehicle in an aggressive manner. The weather reflects our moods: cold, dark and damp.

Goosebumps form on my skin. I shiver. Strands of soaking wet hair cling to my face. 'Goodbye, Donal.' I choke back the tears.

Donal nods, 'Aye, take care.' He dashes over towards mother, gives her a quick, final hug and kiss. 'Right, I'm off before I get drenched.'

He turns and runs off towards the train, and before boarding he glances over his shoulder and waves briefly. No hugs, no kisses for me or Shane, not even a handshake; my heart wants to explode with pain. How can he be so cruel? I desperately wanted him to give me a cuddle.

Donal takes up his position beside the window and smiles gently at my mother. Sean O'Leary sits beside him, waving frantically at his family as if he is going on some kind of a holiday. He looks like a kid with no sense, about to go on a school trip; how the army accepted him is beyond belief.

The train door shuts with a loud bang, the engines begin to roar again, and soon it is pulling off. Women pull out their handkerchiefs and wave them in the direction of their loved ones, whilst the train chugs off into the distance.

I stand with my hands stuck firmly into my pockets and watch until it is a black dot on the horizon, until the vehicle and its passengers have been swallowed up in the distance. I silently pray to the Lord to protect Donal, but, most of all, to mend our relationship. It will need a miracle to melt that stubborn heart of his.

The last thing I wanted or expected from Donal was him leaving without us speaking. I had hoped we would have sorted things out before he had left, longing above all that there would be no bad feelings between us, but that was not to be.

A spine-chilling thought enters my mind. What if there is a chance that we may never see him again?

Chapter 15

The hurt I felt as a result of Donal's hostile behaviour, in time, turned to feelings of anger, as each day passed without any contact from him; this anger grew stronger by the day, until it began to bubble inside me like a volcano, waiting to explode at any minute.

My feelings towards him could be compared to a bag of potatoes. We all know what becomes of a bag of spuds in time, the longer they stay in the sack, the more they will rot and decompose, and in time, turn smelly, soft and gooey. The smell from these rotten vegetables is disgusting. That's what my feelings for Donal are beginning to feel like: rotten and disgusting.

I had honestly thought that if he couldn't talk to me face-to-face he might find it easier to release his feelings in written words, but as time went on it seemed he couldn't bring himself to do that either. My dear brother Donal is nothing more than a coward now in my eyes, a weak, pathetic man that couldn't face his problems and deal with them like the rest of us, and like a coward, he ran away when the going got tough. This makes me more furious with him. The biggest problem in my life is, surprisingly, Donal and his childish, cruel behaviour.

I begin to see every aspect and everyone around me in a completely negative manner. It is difficult to see things any differently, after all, there's a raging war in Europe, our lives have been turned upside down, a rapist is running loose and to top it all off my brother has disowned me. The rest of my family carry on as normal as they can, but underneath their false smiles they must see me as some kind of filthy girl, who slept with her boyfriend and got herself pregnant! They probably think I'm not telling them who the father is because they feel I want to protect his identity, maybe, even worse, perhaps they think I'm still in love with him. Little do they know I hate every inch of his sleazy, creepy body. Little does anyone know that some days my anger builds up within me so much it makes me want to find him, beat him round the head with the nearest thing I can get my hands on and to slap him around the face, pull his hair out from the roots, spit into his eyes; and each time my eyes fall upon his child I want to pull my own hair out! I long for the day when I can stop feeding him. Little does anyone know the demons I face as soon as my eyes open, and it doesn't stop when they are closed to go to sleep. No, the monsters certainly don't stop to allow me rest, they like to work overtime at night, invading my dreams with all kinds of horrid images.

My mother has started to irritate me; she's always smiling, always content, never letting any hardships or trials get in her way of her happy, positive attitude. She carefully hides the fact that she's missing Donal, but we know behind her cheerful smile she's breaking her heart over his departure. Her chores continue to be completed with a song or a little hum to herself. She goes about looking after Shane without a complaint. Perhaps I'm jealous of her; I want to feel happy and content in my life, but all I feel each day is depressed.

There's no escape from my misery, nowhere to run. Every new day is a constant battle and nobody has any idea what my life is really like. It feels like my body is trapped in some kind of dense, dark hole, and no matter how much I try to dig myself out, I just keep sinking deeper and deeper into it. I feel my life is worthless.

Often I look at Shane and think to myself what the heck was going on in my mind when I settled to let my mother bring him up. I should've given him away at birth, or perhaps even agreed to ending the pregnancy as Mick had suggested; it certainly would've been an easier way of escape.

I gaze at the four dreary walls in my cell, my brain feeling like it is going to crack. The walls begin to feel like they are closing in on me, and so I decide to go down and sit in the living room. Mick is curled up on the settee with Shane asleep in his arms.

Ironically Mick, being the one that was so determined on me having an abortion, is now the one person – apart from my mother – that dotes on and loves Shane the most. He treats him like he's his own son, fussing over him, cuddling and showering him with love and attention at every opportunity. He will give off to me for not showing the baby any affection.

'Hello, Molly. It's good to see you out of that room of yours,' Mick beams.

I take a seat near the window. 'Hello, Mick.'

Shane stirs, yawns and opens his eyes. I sigh and stare out the window into the distance.

'Molly, Shane's awake, would you like to hold him?' he questions gingerly.

'No.'

'Go on, just for a few minutes.'

'No, Mick!'

'Why are you so distant from this child?'

'Why do you keep asking me the same questions? Leave me alone, Mick.'

'Pull yourself together, Molly. You should pay more attention to this wee man, he needs you, and while you're at it, pay attention to yourself! Have you looked at yourself in the mirror lately?'

I turn to face him. 'Get lost, Mick! I didn't come down here to listen to you giving me a mouthful!'

He waggles a finger in my direction, 'You behave yourself, young lady. Don't speak to me like that.'

I bury my head in my hands and release a slow, exhausted sigh. I'm sick and tired of my family, I think.

'I'm serious, Molly, you've let yourself go! Get a wash and take Shane out for a walk in his pram, it will do you the world of good. You need to do something for him.'

His advice is as welcome as sour milk in my porridge!

I lift my head to look at him again and then roll my eyes. 'You all seem to be doing a good enough job without me and will you stop doing my head in, I'm tired of hearing the same old phrases over and over! Nothing changes. It's the same rubbish that keeps coming from your mouths.' I shake my head frantically, mimicking the others, 'get yourself together, Molly, give Shane some attention, Molly, get out and get some fresh air, Molly, and take Shane with you, you look a mess, Molly, brush your hair, Molly, cheer up, Molly. I'm sick and tired of hearing it all!'

'Well, it's the truth, isn't it?'

'Oh, piss off, Mick, and stop tormenting me!'

'What did I say to you about talking to me like that? You're getting too big for your boots! We're only trying to help you.'

'You can't help me, Mick, nobody can.'

'We can help, Molly, if you let us try, but you're shutting us out of your life. You don't listen to a word any of us say.'

'Aye, actually you're right, you can help, you can help by leaving me alone!'

Mick's tone softens. 'Molly, you're making a deliberate attempt to build a wall between yourself and the rest of this family. I understand you're feeling a bit down in the dumps but ...'

'A bit down! Mick you have no idea how I'm feeling. Maybe if you all looked closely enough you would see that my life is falling apart! But no, you're all too wrapped up in your own little worlds to notice that I'm hurting badly, I'm more than a bit down! I hate myself and I hate Donal and it is all because of that little ...'

'Now you hold your tongue, don't say another word.' Mick points his finger directly at me. 'How can you be so cold, young lady? You are one fortunate girl! Can you imagine how different your life could have turned out if your loving mother had decided to turn her back on you? I never thought I would see the day that Molly O'Connor has a heart that has turned stone cold.' Mick shakes his head, a disappointed expression etched on his face.

'I can't make myself love him. I can't help it if I don't

have any feelings for him, can I? He's as welcome in my life as a wasp is at a picnic!'

'Molly, that's a terrible thing to say! Do you know something? I care for this child more than you and that shocks me. But my attention will never replace the love from a parent, every child needs to be adored by its mother, no matter what the circumstances are, but at least some affection is better than none at all. I don't think you can honestly say you don't love him, I think you've just locked that heart of yours up and can't find the key to open it again. My advice to you is to free it, for you'll get nowhere in life with a closed cold heart.' Mick pauses to bounce Shane up and down on his knee. The child releases a happy gurgle, a huge smile spreads across his delicate face. 'Trust me, Molly, you'll get nowhere with a sealed heart.'

I turn my face away, not wanting him to see me cry. Mick is right, my heart needs to be opened to Shane but I don't know how to do that.

'I'm going back to bed, Mick, I didn't come down here to fight with you.'

Back upstairs my mind reels over everything he has said. How can I show Shane love, when I don't even love myself anymore? I loathe myself to a point that each night, when getting into bed, I pray I don't wake up the next morning. And when daylight comes, my immediate thoughts are, God no, not another day, how am I going to face another rotten day? I long for God to permit me to breathe my last, but He doesn't seem to be listening to me either and so I have no choice but to battle on.

179

Shane's cries can be heard upstairs, I have to hold back with all my strength from shouting, 'Shut up, you little brat!'

I hold my hands over my ears, desperately trying to block out his annoying screams and fix my stare on the picture of the Sacred Heart of Jesus. 'Why, Jesus, did you allow him to be born, why, why, why? Why did you have to be so cruel, allowing a child to be conceived through rape? Don't you see I've suffered enough without having to ache further?' Tears begin flowing from my eyes at an alarming rate.

Thoughts of ending it all suddenly pop into my head and, once those thoughts are planted in my mind, there is no getting away from them.

I go to bed later that night with the idea of ending my misery still rooted in my mind. I get very little sleep. I try to block out this negative idea, but it is useless. I toss and turn all night, feel too hot and kick off the blanket, then feel too cold and want to cover myself again.

The more I reflect about suicide the more it feels like it is the best thing to do. These thoughts grow stronger.

From then on every day when I wake, the idea of killing myself is on my mind, and each night I battle to sleep with the notion whizzing through my brain. It seems like an easy way out of this dull, depressing black hole.

If I just end it all now, the pain will be over once and for all, and given the fact that I can't bring myself to love Shane, surely he will be better off if his mother is out of the picture. Aye, it will be easier for him, healthier than growing up feeling unloved. I will be doing Shane a huge favour. I won't have to feel like some kind of filthy girl. Donal will no longer have to be uncomfortable around me and perhaps he can come back home, much to everyone's delight. I could end it all and just go to sleep forever. My family won't realise at first that I am doing them a good turn, but they will know in time. Aye, it will be much better if I am out of the picture. Sure I don't even feel I belong here anymore anyway, and the advantages of me being dead far outweighs the advantages of me being alive. My mind is made up: I will end my miserable life somehow. All I need now is the courage to do it.

Chapter 16

Dear Ma,

How are you? I trust you're keeping well. I hope you
didn't get too wet that day we were leaving. It's been a long
time since we have seen rain like that! I've been thinking so
much about you all since arriving here and I thought I would
drop you a wee letter, to let you know I've got here safely. So
you can stop your worrying now, you can put your rosary
beads down and blow out the holy candles! I know the kind of
you; I'm sure you will be worrying your wee heart sick until
you've heard from me.

Well, Mother dearest, you'll be glad to know that I'm
doing great, no, actually, great is a strong word, I'm doing
okay. I would be lying if I didn't say I'm pining for you all. I
do feel very homesick more times than enough, but I have to
keep telling myself that I'll see you all again someday and that
I may as well make the most of this experience in my life. I
have to give myself time to settle. I think I've made the right
decision by coming out here. I'm already feeling like a true
grown-up. It's amazing how much you have to grow up when
you're away from home (especially when you miss your ma so
much, not to mention your ma's delicious cooking!) You don't
realise until you're away from something how much you can
yearn for it, and how much you take things and people for
granted when they're around you each day. I do miss home and
I want you all to know you are always in my thoughts and in
my prayers.

I have to admit, Mother, life in the army is great but it's

no easy task. It's definitely not the place for the idle souls! The first few weeks were probably the hardest, getting used to being away from Ireland and not seeing the familiar faces daily. And then there's the whole thing of getting used to so many different people, not even to mention the strict rules and regulations that must be followed – this does take a bit of getting used to! I've met some really decent people out here; we're all in the same position so we understand how each other misses home and our families. I've made great friends out here and we look out for one another, however, I have to admit I've met some nasty characters also, but they don't bother me too much. The food takes a bit of getting used to. As I write this letter, I can just imagine the aroma of your good ol' homemade soup, your scone bread and donuts, oh, how I long for your cooking again, (how am I ever going to survive? Ha, ha!) My mouth is watering at the very thought of your baking and my stomach is growling like a caged animal!

Tell Mick I was asking for him and you can also tell him I said all that giving off about Sean O'Leary is wrong: Sean is a tower of strength to me and to everyone else out here. He's been amazing and acting so responsible. Don't get me wrong, he's still a bit of a prankster and head case but he's been great. His jokes and witty stories gets the day in and lifts our spirits. In fact, maybe joining the army is just what he needed. Maybe it's just what I needed too. I have a feeling that this encounter will be a life-changing adventure for us.

Well, Mother, I must go now. You take care of yourself, don't be going and burning our house down with all those holy candles!!! Only joking, keep lighting them for me, (I know you will anyway). I have a feeling I'm going to need them. Tell Aggie and Paddy I send my love. You're forever in my thoughts, Ma!

Love you always,
Donal

Chapter 17

This new wartime atmosphere is one of apprehension and uncertainness felt amongst one and all. With the safety measures of the blackouts put in place, people expected this inconvenience to mark their daily lives. As another precaution, air raid shelters have been scattered throughout the city and numerous notices have been issued giving folk advice on what actions to follow during an air raid or gas attack.

We have been given gas masks by the local authority. As a rule we have to carry these ugly protectors with us at all times, yet nobody in the country bothers; perhaps we think we're untouchable. The city folk take theirs with them pretty much every time they leave their homes. They're rarely seen without them. Gas attack posters have been stuck to almost everything in the city – lampposts, walls, and shop windows – with official instructions on what to do if there's a gas attack. God forbid if there is one, but at least we're well educated to deal with it.

Mick arranged to have an air raid shelter built at the bottom of our back garden. Mother went along with the idea to keep him happy, although she isn't too bothered about having one. If a siren goes off, Mick ensures we have our gas masks on and we are all safely in the shelter. Here we remain in the dark, with our small torches, until it is thought safe to return to the house.

Mother refuses to leave the home; instead she sits praying with her rosary in front of the Sacred Heart picture, her eyes shut tight, throwing herself deep into concentration, the only light being a blessed candle. '*If the man above wants me he'll take me, no shelter is going to stop that,*' she says, with such faith in God. '*For one thing we're all sure of is death, there's no running or hiding from our last breath.*'

The shelters are merely iron cages covered in concrete. Mother's probably right – I'm sure they wouldn't survive a direct hit, however, they could probably protect the occupants from things like shrapnel.

Food has become scarce as the war takes its toll, so rationing books containing tokens have been introduced. The vouchers have no monetary value, they're basically a means to ensure everyone gets their fair share of what goods are available. Unfortunately the measly supply of coupons each month has to cover items such as clothing and towels, as well as food.

Mother came up with a great idea for the flour bags that she obtained from the bakeries: she bleached them until they became snow-white, and used them for sheets for Shane's bed.

The first food products to be rationed were bacon and ham; sugar, tea and margarine followed. Fruit – both tinned and fresh – has become almost unobtainable, as has dairy products such as cheese and cream.

Christmas 1939 is over in a blink and the beginning of 1940 isn't welcomed with the usual enthusiasm a new year brings. The new year is just another depressing year beginning, nothing new about it. It only drags along all the hardships of the previous one.

Nothing is changed much in my life, except for the depression now having a firm grip of me. I accept my problems aren't to be swallowed up in the past year; no, my issues are here to stay. There's no feelings of 'out with the old and in with the new', it's more like 'out with the old and in with the worse to come'! Each day the thoughts of suicide grow stronger, but I battle on hoping one day I'll wake up and feel normal again. I long for that moment to come, but it sure is taking its time.

Early 1940 begins and it becomes necessary for the government to issue coupons for clothes. This affects women more than it does men as silk stockings are extremely scarce. Sadie whines constantly about this; she adores her silk stockings. Spirits, cigarettes and even hair clips become difficult to find.

The Ministry of Health begins to produce leaflets to educate people on how to cook healthy meals. It's important, due to the scarcity of food, that none of the vitamins and minerals are wasted in what items we can get our hands on. Mother is on the ball at once; she ensures we are given appropriate meals to keep us healthy and she continues to do so; cooking healthy meals is not a problem for her. With my mother growing her own vegetables in the back garden it means that we are lucky enough not to have to face the scarcity of these either. She grows the most beautiful potatoes, carrots, lettuce, tomatoes, parsnips and – my favourite of all – strawberries. Her strawberries are delicious; many of the children in the street knock at the door looking for a handful of the tasteful fruit. Picking the fruit and vegetables from the garden and scrubbing off the hardened soil is about the only task that I enjoy doing these days.

Being in the allotment has a tremendous soothing effect; it's great for helping me to forget about my troubles briefly and to keep the thoughts of suicide at bay. Mother has a wonderful rose bush set at the back of the garden. She had planted it shortly after my father passed away. It was a few years after his death I learned from her, as we sat in the back garden whilst she went about her gardening, that she planted it in memory of him. It had helped her to come to terms with his death, and, whenever she felt alone or sad, she would go outside to catch a glimpse of the rose bush, and at once it felt as if he was still near her. She told me it soothed away her troubles and brightened up her day. My eyes filled with tears as she told me that story; ever since that day, the beautiful plant, with its charming blood-red, velvet petals took on a new meaning for me. I also didn't know until that day, that the rose was his favourite flower of all.

We're lucky to live in the country. We're better off than those living in the city. At least we have an abundant supply of eggs and milk from Mrs Flannigan, but the old sod exploits the situation by increasing her prices, thus driving the poor and needy folk to borrow more on 'tick'. With her interest on her loans being so high, people are constantly in debt to her. The selfish woman loves it.

I lie on the sofa with my hands folded behind my head and gaze at the ceiling.

'You look down in the dumps, Molly. Why don't you go out for a walk? I'll come with you,' Mother suggests.

'I don't feel like it, not today.'

188

'Ah, come on now, Molly, you need a bit of fresh air. You've been cooped up in this house for months. Why don't you take Shane out in his pram and fetch some eggs whilst you're out.'

I no longer go on errands to Mrs Flannigan's. My mother has become custom to my different excuses to get out of this duty. The days of turning this chore into an adventure are long gone; a distant childhood memory of two innocent children playfully going about their tasks is over, those sun-filled days of mischief and laughter have ended. Mother tries constantly to get me to go, but nothing she says will encourage me otherwise.

'No way, it's too far to walk, and besides, I've got a terrible headache.' It's my usual excuse for not wanting to leave the house.

'Okay, well, take a walk down the street. It'll do you good, fresh air's great for a headache.'

I release a slow sigh. 'Right, I'll take a walk down the street.'

I shift to the end of the sofa with the intentions of getting up, but I don't move any further.

'Great, I'll put on Shane's coat. Although it's spring, it's still a bit nippy...'

'No! Don't bother, I'm not taking *him*, I want to go on my own.' I jump off the sofa.

My mother's face freezes.

I generate my way to the front door and make a quick exit before she demands me to take him. I take a walk down the bottom of the street and watch the sun shine in an azure sky.

The sweet aroma of the countryside air reminds me that spring has been born, a season I love. The sound of baby lambs in the distance is like music to my ears. All around me I'm surrounded by such natural beauty.

My thoughts are lost and my mind is set free as I envelop myself in the beautiful environment, but this doesn't last. It's not long until I can imagine people watching me. I hate the thought of people staring. I'm now so paranoid with the idea that my secret is no longer undisclosed. Deep down I know I'm being stupid. If anyone in the street had any suspicions that Shane is my son, it would've been all over the place by now. The news would've been the juiciest bit of gossip to hit the neighbours in a long time. I'm just being silly, I battle with these beliefs every day, but I can't escape from the paranoia, and so after a few minutes I quickly turn around and head home.

My mother stares at me as I enter the living room. 'You didn't stay out long.' She eyes me suspiciously.

'No, I changed my mind.'

'I'll tell you what, Molly, let's get ready. We'll go to Greencastle today instead of tomorrow. How do you fancy that?'

Life has got tougher since the war broke out, with cigarettes being so scarce we have no option than to smuggle these across the Donegal border. Mick can't do without his cigarettes but I have cut back on them immensely, in fact I have lost interest in smoking as well as everything else. We're fortunate enough to live so close to the border of Donegal, and with the Republic of Ireland free from the war, smuggling items across the border is rife and easy with careful planning.

Each week intrepid souls gather at the end of our street and, with Mick usually leading the way, they then cycle across the border into the 'Free State', passing the Customs House, armed with a list of goods requested by their families and neighbours.

Aggie and Paddy were soon involved in this new way of life. When they come to visit they bring along special treats like chocolate, sweets, biscuits and – my favourite treat of all – brandy balls, which are impossible to get in Derry these days. But, because of the war, Aggie hates coming up and so my mother and I have no choice but to go down to them to stock up on the essentials.

My face lights up with a smile. 'Aye, let's go to Greencastle.'

'It seems to me visiting Aggie is the only thing that puts a smile on that pretty face,' Mother grins as she cups my chin in her hands and kisses my cheek.

We make it our business to visit Greencastle every fortnight. The bus takes us to Moville; Sometimes we walk the short distance into Greencastle, or Paddy usually picks us up at Moville and drives us to their home where we're greeted by Aggie who has the tea brewing, awaiting our arrival. The tea is always accompanied with a full Irish fry consisting of crispy bacon, fresh fried eggs, a mountain of mushrooms and proper delicious sausages. The sausages back in Derry have tasted awful since the food scarcity. I don't know exactly what they're putting into them, and perhaps it's just as well, but they don't taste the same. A fry is not a fry unless there are a few slices of freshly baked scone bread; there's no shortage of newly baked scone bread at Aggie's home and we're allowed to lash on the butter. No need to skimp on it down here, we can have as much of it as we like. We feel like royalty as we dine at Greencastle. After tea is finished, apple pie or cream cakes follow. It's a good job we're not trying to lose weight, for this is no place to diet! Aggie's home is definitely a no-diet home; eat as much as you like, when you like, is her motto in life, and it's evident in her expanded waist line and round, chubby face.

Each visit to Greencastle flies by so quickly. We leave to return home in the evening with our bellies full and our pockets bulging with all sorts of goodies.

Today Greencastle looks so beautiful. There's a sense of peace everywhere.

After lunch, Paddy and I take a stroll down to the fort; we walk around the ruins for a while before heading in the direction of the pier to watch the fishermen return from their day's work. As I watch the men emerge from their boats, I have an overwhelming feeling to jump off the pier and plunge myself into the water, and never return.

My eyes feel glued to the murky water below us. The thought of ending my life runs rampant in my mind. I drag my interest away from the sea. There is lots of activity about the area today. In an attempt to free myself from my urges I fix my attention on the men gathering up their brown fishing nets. I watch as they carefully place them on the grass opposite the pier to dry, they then return to their vessels to gather the lobster pots.

Paddy, sensing my sadness, places his hand on my shoulder and says, 'Molly, is there something wrong? You don't seem to be yourself today.'

My goodness, where's Paddy been for the past year, I think. I want to scream at him, telling him I haven't been myself in ages! I want to drown in that water! His face radiates happiness, the beauty coming from within his soul; I could never be rude to this wonderful man and so I hold back my anger.

'No, Paddy, I'm not myself today.' I stare into the sky and watch the flight of seagulls, squawking, screeching and diving over the water. 'I'm just feeling a bit tired, that's all.'

He smiles, his face full of gentleness. 'Let's get you back then, love. I'm feeling drained today myself.'

We arrive back at the house and we're greeted with my mother, standing in the doorway, gazing into the distance, her delicate frock clinging to her body as the gentle wind sweeps in from the sea.

'Good to see you back, we're just about to eat,' she smiles and follows us into the house.

'Ah there you are, just in time for tea,' Aggie announces as we step into the cosy kitchen. She rolls up her sleeves and places on her oven gloves before removing a pie from the range; it's polished like a pair of boots, shinning bright.

The table is covered with a white tablecloth and is laid with gleaming cutlery and matching china cups, saucers and plates, all with the same blue floral design on them. A bowl full of tempting red apples sits in the centre.

I lift my head and sniff the air. 'Something smells good.'

'Aye,' Aggie's round, chubby face breaks into a smile. 'I've baked you a chicken pie.' She places it on the counter and removes her gloves before taking a knife and cutting into the thick pastry.

My stomach rumbles. I hadn't realised how hungry I was until the aroma of the hot food invades my nostrils. I take a seat at the table next to my mother and wait patiently for my dinner.

Aggie places a plate of potatoes, peas, carrots and an enormous piece of pie in front of me. 'Get tucked into that,' she playfully pinches my cheeks. 'That will put colour to those cheeks of yours and some meat on those bony arms. Isn't that right, Kate?'

'Aye, she doesn't eat much these days,' Mother answers.

'She won't be leaving her good ol' aunt's without a full belly. I'll make sure of that.' Aggie waves a finger in the air and grins again.

I return the smile and begin eating the delicious dinner, and, to the surprise of all of them, I finish the lot.

'My goodness,' Paddy releases a hearty laugh. 'Don't eat the pattern off the plate, Molly!'

The laughter is infectious; Aggie and my mother chuckle along with him. Surprisingly I can't help but join in too.

'Hurry up with the dessert then!' I giggle.

From the corner of my eye I catch my mother looking at

me contently. I suppose it's been a very long time since she's witnessed me laugh.

After dinner I sit on the lawn and watch the sun set in the sky, its soft reflection glinting on the calm waters of Lough Foyle is soothing, and I shudder at how close I was to jumping into it earlier. I honestly think if Paddy wasn't with me today, I would have plunged off the pier. My body would be floating about in there right this very minute.

'Molly.'

I glance around and see Paddy waving.

'We're leaving soon. The bus is due to arrive shortly, love.'

'Okay, Paddy, I'll be up now.' I turn my attention back to the scenery before my eyes. 'I hate leaving. Oh how I wish I could stay here forever,' I whisper to myself before heading back to the house.

Before departing, my mother wraps Shane in his blanket and stuffs make-up, stockings and shoe polish in beside him. I kiss Aggie goodbye and follow my mother and Paddy to his car.

'See you again soon, Aggie,' I wave from the car. 'And thanks again for the food.'

'Ah you're welcome, pet,' she returns the gesture. 'Take care and safe journey.'

Paddy drives us back into Moville and chats to my mother about the war; my mind is too confused to engage in the conversation. I can feel darkness creep back into my thoughts.

'See you again soon,' he announces with a smile as we

climb out of the dusty car.

'Thanks for everything today, Paddy, take care and God bless,' my mother replies.

'Thanks, Paddy,' I force a smile.

'You're both welcome and, Molly, make sure you get a wee sleep when you get home, pet.'

'Aye, I'll definitely get a rest.'

'Okay, I'll see you soon.' He leans out the window and blows us a kiss.

I blow him one back before getting on the bus and my heart sinks as I leave this beautiful part of the country.

On reaching the Customs House a stern-looking custom official demands to board the bus for an inspection. My heart skips a beat as we wait nervously for him to get off. He prances up and down the aisle, eyeing each individual suspiciously as he passes.

Now and again he comes to a halt, holds his chin high and squints his eyes. 'Anything to declare?'

The passengers sit quietly, looking as guilty as sin and shaking their heads, signalling that they have no goods on them.

'They're not going to declare anything, what a stupid question. It would be so silly if they made all that effort to obtain the goods to have to give them up now,' I whisper with an amused grin on my face.

'Ssh, Molly, please keep your voice down, love.' My mother places her finger over my lips.

The official isn't fooled; he knows there is smuggling going on and he easily picks out the awkward-looking ones and ruthlessly requests them to hand over their items. I observe how they reluctantly give in with a sheepish look on their faces and a silly excuse as to why they have the goods in their possession. No excuses are accepted, and items are confiscated immediately. Everyone has a sour expression on their faces; it's clear they can't stand the man but then again, he's only doing his job.

For some reason the official doesn't question my mother. Maybe she looks too sweet and innocent to be a smuggler. A good job he didn't question her, she wouldn't make a good liar, she isn't exactly a professional in the field of telling fibs. Although she does surprise me; never did I think I'd witness her breaking the law, but perhaps maybe she and others don't see it like that. People see it as a means of surviving and my mother is no different. Wartime has released a lawless streak in folk, my mother being one of them!

Chapter 18

Today, since early in the morning, my soul has been in dense darkness. I gaze critically at myself in the small compact mirror in my hand. I look the way I feel: a mess. The reflection staring back is barely recognisable. My dark-rimmed eyes are unable to hold the gaze of myself and so I quickly dart them away, only to have them drawn back to the mirror like some kind of magnetic force. Perhaps it's curiosity wanting to know if it's really me looking back. The crystal blue eyes that once sparkled are now dull and sunken, accompanied by dark circles. My skin that was once smooth and flawless is dry and flaky; the rosebud lips that were once plumped and moist are now cracked and appear chapped at the corners. My hair is tatty and unruly. I look like a tramp.

'My God, how did I come to this? Molly, you're a broken soul,' I whisper.

The hate I have for myself is evident in my appearance. I've let myself go and it shows in this horrible manifestation. The reality in the reflection only adds to the misery I've become accustomed to.

'Why hasn't somebody said something?' I murmur through gritted teeth. Then again, they did say, I just haven't listened to them. My family has become familiar with my erratic behaviour. I suppose they aren't too sure how to handle me. They continue daily to tiptoe around me, careful not to upset my feelings. In my fragile state I will often fly off the handle at the least of things, and so the others just get used to my new personality.

I've become terribly paranoid and agitated and feel the need to isolate myself from everyone else, without being aware that I am doing so. There is a constant need to get away from them all and escape. Nobody understands me. Emily doesn't know how to cope with my moods either and so I've distanced myself from her too. As time is going on, the Molly everyone knew is being swallowed up with self-hatred.

I feel like an animal caged by my own thoughts, with nowhere to go and no one to talk to. My hands feel bound by heavy chains, my heart pierced beyond repair.

'I hate you.' I sigh at the image, pulling the compact closer to my horrid face until my breath mists the glass. I wipe it clear with the sleeve of my cardigan and screw my nose up at the thing looking back. 'You look pathetic!' I yell, grinding my teeth until my jaw hurts. I stick my tongue out and make horrible gestures to the person on the other side, not really aware of what I'm doing. 'Do you hear me? I hate you, I hate you, I hate you so much!' My hand shakes violently. The compact slips from my trembling grasp and hits the floor with a crash, causing it to shatter into pieces.

I throw myself onto my bed and wail loudly. It's a good job there is nobody at home, my shrieks would have frightened the life out of them. My mother has taken Shane out for a walk in his pram to catch a bit of fresh air and hasn't yet returned.

My hands grip the crocheted bedspread that Aggie crafted many years ago. Unable to control my sobs the tears stream down my cheeks, soaking the wool of the blanket. After a while I get up from the bed and fall on to the floor, shaking and hysterical. I start crawling towards the broken mirror, intending to select the spikiest piece of the glass. I don't know where the idea came from, and without a second thought I roll up the sleeve of my cardigan and glide the sharpest end of the glass slowly up and down my arm, ripping at my skin until blood becomes visible. It oozes from my torn skin, trickling little by little, then more rapidly, down my arm and onto the floor.

It feels quite odd. The pain from my wounds seems to strangely replace the pain that I've been feeling over the past months. I'm enjoying every second of it. By no means did I imagine that the physical pain could somehow cure my emotional pain, but right now it does.

Images from the night of the attack come flooding into my mind, and with every rip of my skin and each drop of my blood spilling onto the floor, the awful memories of the attack appear to flow away too.

I take the piece of glass into my other hand and begin the same procedure, running the instrument along my other arm. Rhythmically the sharp weapon flows up and down my upper limb, this time with much more force and intensity. I cover my elbows, my arms and down round my wrists. The blood pours from the many wounds, staining my clothes, but I don't care. With every cut I perform, another little bit of my hurt escapes from my mind and my heart. I want to let it all out. I have to. I need to release every emotion that has been locked away for so long. This is for the best. I know I'll feel so much better when I have finished. I will feel on top of the world soon. Then I can flutter my wings and fly off, disappearing into the horizon, as free as a bird, no longer caged by the pain.

After a short time my body feels weaker and weaker until I can no longer hold the glass to perform anymore trauma. I just want to go to sleep; aye everything will be okay once my body takes a break. I lay on the ground in a pool of my own blood. My exhausted body needs to rest.

I close my eyes, immediately drifting off, flapping my wings, free as a bird, just as I've imagined.

Freedom at long last.

'Rest in peace, Molly,' my low voice mumbles.

Chapter 19

The sound of the front door opening causes me to stir. I try to lift my head but the room keeps spinning. The hum of voices entering the hallway sails to my ears.

'Mrs O'Connor, that pram looks heavy; let me help you in with it.'

'That's great, thanks, Emily.'

'Gees this pram is heavy, how do you manage it?'

'Oh I'm used to it; mind you, I don't know how I'm going to cope if this wee man keeps putting on weight. He's gaining the pounds at an alarming rate.'

'Sure that'll be your fine cooking, won't it?' Emily laughs. 'If I lived in this house I'd be the size of it!'

'That's what it is, Emily. Speaking of cooking, I'll put you on a cup of tea, I've just baked some fresh pancakes this morning. Do you fancy a wee cuppa?'

'Sounds good! I'd love one.'

'Molly must be still upstairs, go on up and I'll call you when it's ready. Will you tell her to come down? She needs to get out of that room.'

'I'll not be long in dragging her out of her prison,' Emily laughs.

She enters my bedroom. 'My goodness, Molly! Molly, Molly can you hear me?' she grabs my shoulders and begins to shake me. 'Molly, can you hear me! Kate, you need to come up here! Kate, Kate! I need you up here!'

I try to open my eyes.

My mother dashes upstairs with the baby still in her

arms. 'What's wrong, Emily? Oh my God, what ...' Mother covers her mouth in shock, the blood draining from her face. She hands Shane to Emily and lifts me into her arms. 'Molly!'

I try again to open my eyes but they feel so heavy, as if a ton is hanging from each eyelid.

'Who did this to you, Molly?' she questions in a soft, worried voice.

Emily scans the floor, her attention drawn to the shattered glass scattered at her feet. 'It looks like she did this to herself.' She shakes her head in disbelief. 'Oh my God, I know she's been feeling down but I didn't think she felt this bad.' Tears fill her eyes.

'Molly, can you hear me? Answer me, Molly!' Mother yells hysterically.

I flutter my eyes but can't speak. Every bit of energy has been drained from my body.

'Oh, thank God, she's alive! She's trying to respond!'

My mother nods towards the bed. 'Put Shane down, he'll be okay.'

Emily places the baby on the bed close to the inside and puts a pillow beside him so that he won't roll off.

'Emily, love, please get me a sheet from the cupboard in the hallway.'

'Aye, of course.'

'I need you to get me a basin of water. Will you also get me a cloth from the second drawer in the kitchen? Thanks, dear.'

She returns minutes later, her arms full of everything that my mother has asked for.

My mother removes my bloodstained cardigan. She begins to soak the cloth in the water and gently dabs it over my wounded arms, wiping away the blood slowly, so as not to cause me to suffer anymore unnecessary pain. I wince as the cold fabric makes contact with my skin.

'You'll be okay, dear. I'm almost finished.'

With all of my strength I try to keep my eyes open.

Emily stands behind my mother, watching in silence. It is clear from the look on her face she feels my pain. I conceal my head on my mother's shoulder, refusing to look at either of them. I know they are devastated at seeing me like this, the broken girl in front of them.

My mother's nursing background comes in handy once again. She knows exactly what to do. Her caring, tender instincts are still with her after all these years allowing her to handle the situation perfectly.

'Oh I forgot, I need a towel. You'll find one in the same cupboard out there.'

'Sure, Mrs O'Connor.' Emily once again disappears and comes back seconds later with a towel.

My mother pats my arms until they are dry, then takes the sheet between her teeth and tugs on the fabric until it rips into pieces, expertly wrapping them around my arms to bandage them up. She splits the ends of the dressing and ties it around my wrist, so as to prevent the fabric falling off. 'Isn't that better, love?' She takes my chin in her hand and tilts my head so that our eyes meet. She looks at me with so much love.

I nod sheepishly before my head returns to the downwards position again.

204

'Now I want you to listen to me carefully, Molly. You mustn't do anything like this again. Do you hear me, darling?'

Again I nod in silent agreement, too broken to make eye contact, too traumatised to speak.

'Molly, if you ever feel like doing something terrible like this again I want you to talk to me. You can talk to me about anything, Molly, don't be afraid. I want you to know that I'm here for you, darling.' She removes her own cardigan and wraps it around me, helping to put my arms into the sleeves. 'Let's get you out of this room. We'll go downstairs and get a cuppa.'

'You two go on down, I'll follow in a few minutes. I'll just get the room sorted out and I'll bring Shane with me.'

'Thanks, Emily, that'll be great,' Mother replies.

Downstairs, we sit on the sofa. She cradles me in her arms. 'Molly, I promise you I'll help you, darling, but you must also help yourself. You must tell me if you ever feel that you are going to harm yourself again. Will you do that, Molly?'

'Aye,' I reply, my voice a mere whisper.

She plants a soft affectionate kiss on my forehead. I bury myself in her arms and begin to weep bitterly. I cry so hard, every emotion I have been feeling comes flooding out with the tears.

'That's it, let it all out, love. Let go of whatever is bothering you. I know you need a proper cry. You've been bottling up your feelings for far too long. It's time to release it all, once and for all. Everything will work out, I promise you, love.' She rocks me gently in her arms.

205

I see images in my mind of all the good things she has done for me, how could I have been so selfish? Thankfully, by the grace of God I have been saved.

My tears develop into sobs.

'This won't happen again, I promise you that, there won't be a next time. I'll make sure of that, Molly.'

Next time I could kill myself, I think. There mustn't be a next time!

Chapter 20

Donal continues to write, explaining his adventures and how much he's enjoying his new responsibilities. Mother regularly sits by the window, her hand clutching back the curtain as she watches for the postman, eagerly waiting to see him enter our garden or hear his familiar knock on the door, and when he arrives she stops everything to rush outside to retrieve the mail. We don't get post that often, so when we do, it's more than likely to be a letter from Donal.

With a beaming smile she runs her fingers across the familiar handwriting on the envelope, before childishly ripping it apart to reveal its contents. She looks over it, silently to herself first, then sits at the kitchen table and reads it aloud to the rest of the family.

I can't share in the same excitement as the others when correspondence is received from Donal. In the beginning I did, but as each letter arrived it contained a joke or a reference to other members of the family such as '*Is Paddy still talking for Ireland?*' or '*Is Aggie still snorting snuff?*' At other times he might ask how such and such is keeping but, surprise, surprise my name or Shane's is never mentioned. It's almost as if we aren't part of the family anymore. We've been erased from his memory and it seems I'm the only person that notices. Nobody has said a word about this characteristic of his letters, or then again perhaps they have noticed and decided it's better not to say anything to me.

Some might think I'm being silly, but the fact he

doesn't acknowledge us has angered me so much. For me, it's as if he has never gone away, he may as well still be here, ignoring us continually. My blood boils at the thought of my brother. I long to shout at him, grab him and give him a good shake for being so stubborn and hateful, but with him being miles away I can't, so I have to store this rage up inside, with all the other resentment and thoughts that have taken root and grown inside me over the past year. The fury is eating away at my insides; it's soul-destroying.

Today I decide, upon rising from my slumber, that I won't let anything bother or perplex me – especially Donal – as it's no ordinary day: it's my birthday, and I have made up my mind to take everything into account that Emily said after I'd almost killed myself. Emily told me that life is worth living and if I let go of the demons that are haunting me, I'll feel much better. She also said that I should make a firm commitment to attempt to get myself together. It's much easier said than done, it will be hard, but I know deep down I must try. I've promised her and my mother that I will never stoop so low.

Today an urge of excitement rushes through me, a feeling I normally feel every year on my special day. I bounce out of bed bright and early and hurry to the window to yield back the curtains, allowing soft morning sunshine to invade my room. A row of clothes flap freely in the gentle breeze on the washing line.

On entering my mother's room I find it empty. Her window is slightly ajar, permitting the cool breeze to freshen the air. I pause at the window for a few seconds, my eyes falling on the roaming hills of Donegal in the distance. It sure is a picture to behold. A blackbird flies by and lands itself on the wooden fence at the end of our front garden. It delicately bobs its tail and opens its throat to sing a delightful morning tune. I feel good for the first time in ages and vow to try and remain in high spirits.

From the corner of my eye I catch a glimpse of the postman standing with Nosy Nora, his body language giving out clear signals that he hasn't the time to stand about chatting. His head moves up and down now and again, and with every nod he takes a step backwards trying desperately to get away from her clutches. Nora doesn't appear to notice the distance that has developed between the two of them. She continues talking like mad, her jaw going up and down in a fast pace until finally the postman lets out a sigh. 'Well it's been nice chatting to you, but, Mrs King, I really must be off now. At this rate I'll never get any work done.' He pulls back the arm of his jacket, to take a look at his watch. 'I'll chat to you later.' And before she has a chance to argue or say another word he turns his back on her and begins to make his way towards our house, whistling happily as he reaches into his bag to pull out the mail, cautious not to look behind him in case she nabs him again.

I dive downstairs, taking two steps at a time, just reaching the front door before my mother. Today's the only day of the year that I receive any mail. Each year Aggie sends a handmade card, on my birthday, from her and Paddy. She loves arts and craft; she always decorates the card in such a beautiful and creative manner.

'Morning,' I gasp, red-faced and slightly out of breath.

209

'Morning, love.' A friendly set of eyes greets mine. 'Someone's eager to see me,' he chirps, looking somewhat surprised.

'Aye well, I'm eighteen today. I guess I'm still like a big kid and I can't wait to open my birthday card. It's the only one time of the year I get anything from you.'

'Oh it's your birthday! Happy birthday! I hope you enjoy your special day!' He smiles handing me two envelopes before disappearing down the pathway.

My hands tremble. The familiar writing almost jumps from the envelope sending my blood to pulse through my veins and pump into my heart at an alarming rate. My eyes scan over the writing again and again in utter disbelief.

My mother remains standing in the hallway, her apron covered in flour. She has obviously gotten up early to bake my cake. Every year, for each of us on our birthday, she makes a yummy cake, loading the cream into it until it is pouring over the sides of the sponge, then decorates it with sugar icing. It's tradition for the family to gather around the table after dinner to sing 'happy birthday', before getting tucked into a cup of tea and a slice of her finest baking. Afterwards we are normally seen licking our fingers and running them around the plate to gather any remnants of crumbs and cream. Not a single bit of her cake is wasted; it's much too good to spare. We can't get enough of it. And, if it's your birthday, she always gives you a second helping whilst the others watch in envy as the birthday boy or girl gulps the last piece of cake down their throat.

'What's up, love, who are the letters for?' My mother wipes her hands on her apron as she peers over my shoulder.

'They're both for me.' I hold up one, 'Well, I know this is from Aggie. I think the other is from ...' I look over the familiar text again before quickly ripping open the envelope. 'This one is from Donal!'

'From Donal?' Her eyes dance with excitement.

'Aye, Donal,' I reply in awe.

'Read it out, love, what does he say?' She flashes me a huge satisfying smile.

I take a deep breath before continuing aloud, my hands still shaking. *Happy birthday, Molly! I really do hope you have a good one. Have a lovely day, you deserve it. Thinking of you all.*

Love Donal.'

My mother's hands settle on my shoulders. 'That's great, pet.'

I turn, clutching my card and sob into her arms. I feel as if I'm floating off the floorboards. It's wonderful. This is the happiest day of my life.

Chapter 21

As a result of the ongoing war, the once quiet docks of Derry's quay now bustle with activity. This is currently the most important base for the Atlantic, with warships lined down to Lisahally. At the docks the ships are stationed up to four abreast; for some seamen to get to their vessel they have to cross two or three others.

The city is now flooded with thousands of mariners on the streets. There are all nationalities – French, Canadians and Americans – much to the delight of the local ladies, not too much for the men. When these pretty sailor boys are in town, dressed smartly in their suits, spit-polished boots and their hair neatly in place, the scruffy local lads never get a look-in with the women. The Derry men aren't amused with the new talent invading their streets; the females, on the other hand are enjoying every bit of it. The girls get themselves dressed up and go for walks in and around the city just to get a glimpse of the new handsome men, and perhaps, if they're lucky enough, they might even get asked out for a date.

When the sailors get time off from their duties they hit the streets of Derry, lavishly spending their money. Many of them are known to flog tobacco and alcohol off their ships. Derry has become a major zone for smuggling; it's so easy to do so. The forces flog just about everything, bar their ship!

Since my humiliating, crazy, antics a few weeks ago, my mother and Emily have started doing everything in their power to help me. Looking back at the incident I've no idea why I went into such a rage at the time, why, on that particular day, thoughts of suicide had invaded my mind so much. I never want to find myself in such a dark place again. I'm now willing to accept their help in order to get myself back to as much normality as I can. I don't want to feel trapped in my own body anymore, steeped in so much self-hatred and feeling lonely and desperate. I could no longer carry on the way I'd been, my emotions were spiralling out of control, so when Emily suggests we take Shane out for a walk in his pram one sunny Saturday morning, I decide not to jump into refusal but to accept the invitation. In my mind I tell myself it will help both myself and the baby.

We walk for what seems like miles and chat about everything and anything. Emily cracks a few jokes on the way, bringing a smile to my face. Getting out into the sunshine and filling my lungs with the glorious fresh air reminded me of enjoyable days gone by.

'Here, Molly, take this,' Emily suggests as she steps away from the huge, bulky pram and beckons me to grasp the handle. At first I hesitate, but again I try to persuade myself it will benefit us both and so I give in and take over pushing the baby.

I clasp my hands around the metal handle and for the first time since his birth, I push him along, feeling slightly awkward and somewhat paranoid as we walk, baking under the warm sun.

'Molly, I know it's going to take you a while to accept him, but you'll get there with the proper help and support,' Emily smiles softly, sounding reassuring.

I shrug my shoulders and roll my eyes to the sky above.

'Do you know something, Molly?'

'What?' I ask drearily.

'Your feelings towards that wee man lying in there are the root of your problems.'

I release a huge sigh. 'Don't be silly, Emily. How do you work that out?'

'I'm not being silly. I truly believe if you can begin to accept Shane and learn to love him, in time you'll begin to realise what a special child he is.' Her emerald eyes twinkle.

I ponder over her words. 'Maybe, Emily, I need to love myself again first.'

She looks taken aback by my reply. 'What do you mean? You don't hate yourself, do you?' she questions aghast.

'Aye, I loathe myself! Each time I look in the mirror I feel sick, my head spins and my stomach ties itself in knots.'

'Really? Is it really that bad, Molly?'

'Of course it is! Why do you think I did so much damage to my arms? I did it because I examined myself in the mirror and I didn't like what I saw. I just lost control.'

'Oh dear, Molly, you mustn't feel like that.'

'I try not to,' I sigh.

'Please don't hate yourself, love.'

'Aye, I know I shouldn't and I am trying not to.'

'And don't hate Shane.'

'Emily, I don't hate Shane! Hate is a very strong word. Do you know something? I can't understand why God allowed me to get pregnant after what I went through. Why burden me with a child and all the hardships that come along with him? Emily, I don't get it. I just don't understand God!'

214

'He obviously has a plan. Nobody knows what that plan entails. We just have to accept what's put in front of us.'

'Do you think the rape was part of God's plan?' I reply in a frosty tone.

'Of course not! Don't be so silly, Molly. The rape was an act of evil, conducted from the man below,' she points a finger to the ground.

'Sorry, I'm just feeling confused. I don't know why God has allowed a child to be born through rape. It isn't fair.'

'I can understand why you feel like this, believe me, I've tormented my own brain trying to figure it out. You might think my idea crazy, but I really do believe the reason God blessed you with Shane is to help you cope with the situation.'

'What?'

'Look at Shane as being a wonderful gift that'll help you accept what happened has happened. It can't be undone. You've got to learn firstly to love him, secondly to forgive his father and thirdly, get on with your life.'

'Now you really are being ridiculous,' I snap back, without realising how sharp my tone sounds. 'How can he be a gift? Nobody can expect me to look at him in that way! It's easy for you to say that, but in reality it's much harder for me.'

She appears hurt by my outburst.

'I'm sorry for snapping at you …' I pause before continuing in a softer tone. 'I've been punished enough. I certainly don't need a child to remind me every single day of his father. You might not want to hear this, but Shane is certainly no gift in my eyes!'

'I do understand, you're right. It's easy for me, but I

promise you, Molly, you'll feel much better if you open your heart to love him.'

'Aye, so everyone keeps saying.'

'Molly, listen to me, you've stored up too many bad and negative thoughts in your mind and nobody can blame you for that, but trust me, if you can replace all the negative thoughts with positive ones, you'll feel much better. Not only will it do you a world of good, but it'll also profit this special little boy.'

'Did anybody ever tell you you're wasted slogging your guts out in a factory? You're a genius, coming up with all these ideas!' A hint of sarcasm is evident in my voice.

'Ah well, you never know what the future holds for me,' Emily jokes and tosses her blonde hair. 'Well what do you say, will you give the child a chance?'

'Emily, you don't understand,' I exhale helplessly.

'Okay, okay, I don't understand what you're feeling and I can only imagine what you're going through, but I do know you much better than anyone else, and it's clear we haven't seen the true Molly in a long time. The true Molly doesn't have a heart of stone. She has a heart of gold, and somewhere in it you'll have love for this wee man.' Emily draws back the hood of the pram and a round, chubby face beams back at her. 'There's a seed of love in there and I'm going to do all in my power to water and nourish that seed until it blooms and bursts with adoration for him. Isn't that right, wee man? He needs you as much you need him and...'

Emily is interrupted by a shriek and a giggle from Shane as he points to a dog a few yards away. He lifts up his hand and rubs his thumb and fingers together frantically, kicking his legs about with excitement, 'Ga, ga,' he yells. He watches as the dog follows its owner down a lane until they're both out of sight.

Emily leans over the pram and peers at the innocent child. 'Do you like the doggy? Where is he? Where did he go?' She pinches lightly on his cheeks, 'You're a little cutie, isn't that right, darling?' Shane continues to smile and gurgle. 'Aye, you're trying your wee best to talk to me, isn't that right? Well it won't be long till you're chatting away.'

'How far are we walking?' I wipe the beads of sweat from my head. 'I'm exhausted.'

'Not much further. I was thinking perhaps we could go into town to catch a glimpse of the new talent. I've heard them Yanks are drop dead gorgeous. What do you think?'

'What do I think? I think the less I see of men the better! I should've known there would be blokes involved, you're man mad, Emily.'

'You never know, Molly dear, we might be lucky enough to meet some rich Yank that'll sweep us off our feet.' A cheeky grin appears on her face and her eyes dance with excitement.

'I certainly do *not* want to meet a Yank to sweep me off my feet! I reckon a fella in my life is the last thing I need.'

'No, not at all, I believe it's quite the opposite. In fact, getting you a man is the second part of my plan for your recovery.' She throws me a sunshine smile and her face lights up.

'Absolutely no way, I'm not letting you find me a

man!' I remove another layer of sweat from my forehead and sigh, 'Emily, you don't understand what I've been through. How can I possibly trust anyone after all that's happened? Are you for real? Anyway, what man would want someone as fragile as me? I'm a mess and I'm being totally honest here.'

'Not all men are tarred with the same brush,' she waves a finger in the air.

'Aren't they?' I shrug.

'Of course not, Molly, you know that. Trust me, Molly, there's a good one out there somewhere for you.'

'Right now I don't think much of men. Most of the ones I've came across have let me down.'

'Aye, you're right, most of them, but not all of them. You need to learn to accept that not all men are the same. As I said earlier, getting you a man is the second part of my plan.'

'So you're an expert all of a sudden.' I stare into Emily's eyes, searching for a response. I can feel myself getting irritated by her 'think positive' theory.

'You don't need to be so sarcastic,' she snaps back. 'I'm only trying to help you to stop seeing things in such a negative light, that's all. I'm going to help you. I don't care what it takes, I'm going to keep trying. You'll ruin your life if you don't start listening to those that care about you.'

'Listen, I don't want to get into an argument with you.'

'We're not arguing, I'm just telling you how it is. You're trapped in a world of your own. Whether you like it or not, you're going to have to do something about it, but at least you're not on your own.'

I stare in a daze into the crystal blue sky. 'I'm sorry. I

know you're only trying to help.'

'No bother, I know it's not easy.' She smiles softly. 'Listen, buddy, we're going to get through this, okay?'

I nod and smile back. 'Okay, if anyone can improve things, it's you. I'll go along with your plans. It's not as if I have much to lose.'

'Great.'

'I trust you, Emily. I haven't been too easy to be around lately, but I promise you I'll give it a try. I'm still not too sure about the men side of your plans though.'

'Ah to heck with the men, we girls will do just fine without them.' She throws her arm around my shoulders and hugs me gently. 'However, I still wouldn't say no to a nice hunky navy man and if you don't want one, sure I'll date the both of them. I'll just meet them on different nights.'

I can't help but smile at her.

Just a few feet ahead boats of all sizes line the docks, stretching along the River Foyle. The waves dance about in the murky waters, sending a swirl of white froth to lick against the vessels.

As a security measure the defence forces installed an anti-aircraft system to protect the docks, using a ring of immense, helium-filled barrage balloons, anchored with huge steel cables. These mighty balloons float about a hundred feet above the ground; the purpose of this is to prevent the enemy bomber planes from flying low over the docks. The silvery grey balloons are visible from miles away.

'Emily, those ships are an amazing sight.' My eyes widen.

219

'Aye, look at the big balloons bobbling away in the air. My goodness there's a lot of activity going on, the place is buzzing with the forces ... ' Her voice trails as she eyes a group of sailors emerging from their grand ship, looking smart and sophisticated in their immaculate uniforms and spit-polished boots. They turn to walk in our direction.

'Hey look, they must be Americans. They must be going for a walk on their break,' Emily announced with excitement.

'Aye,' I reply unenthusiastically.

She nudges me in the ribs. 'Now that's what I call talent. My feet are aching but to heck with it, no pain no gain. I'll tell you, Molly, it's worth it just to get a glimpse of these hunks.'

'What are you not like?' I laugh.

Emily frantically fixes her hair, pouts her lips and holds her head high as she walks straight and proud towards the group of men.

'Good afternoon, ladies,' a tall, dark-haired young man greets us in a strong American accent. He removes his hat and bows his head. The others do the same.

'Hello there, how are you doing?' Emily chirps back, with her equally strong Derry brogue, batting her eyelashes and flashing a flirtatious smile.

'Very well thank you, ma'am,' one of them answers before they continue on their journey.

'Oh my goodness he's gorgeous, isn't he? My poor heart has just missed a beat,' Emily belts out rather too loudly, not caring that they aren't out of earshot. 'They sound like

Americans, oh I love the Yanks!'

'Hey, excuse me, ma'am.'

We both stop and turn around quickly. The American that had spoken earlier sprints towards us, holding a tiny bootee in his hand. 'I think your baby dropped this,' he looks at me and smiles. 'Does this belong to him?'

I stare at the familiar blue bootee that my mother had knit only weeks ago. 'Ah, aye it is thanks. I hadn't noticed it gone.'

The handsome sailor bends down to place the footwear back on Shane's foot. 'Isn't your mom lucky I found it then?' he beamed at the child.

'I'm not his mother!' I quickly interrupt, my face ablaze.

'Oh, I'm so sorry. I just assumed that you were his mom, but then again I guess you're probably his sister right?' He holds out his hand. 'I'm Karl, Karl O'Brien. I'm from the USA, but you've probably guessed with a name like O'Brien I've Irish blood in me,' he jokes. 'I'm sorry if I've insulted you.' He beams a smile radiant as a summer's day.

I accept his warm handshake. 'It's okay,' I return the smile. 'I'm Molly O'Connor, and this is my friend Emily.'

'Hi, Emily it's nice to meet you.'

'Are you off duty today?' Emily queries.

'Yeah we sure are. It's great to get out and about when we're off. We get to meet such friendly people. There's one thing I love about you Derry folks, you're all so easy to chat to.'

'Aye, we're not a bad bunch, sure we're not, Molly?'

221

Emily nudges me in the ribs again, almost knocking me off my feet in the process. 'What do you usually do to pass the time, Karl?'

'We normally go for a stroll then make our way to get some food. I've heard there's a great place near Foyle Street for fish and chips, we'll hang out there for a while today then go to one of the dances tonight.'

'Ooh that sounds good,' Emily announces as she eyes up his smart uniform.

My attention is drawn to his shiny shoes – they shine so much I can almost see my face in them!

Karl turns his interest towards me, his aqua-blue eyes fix on mine. They're the most beautiful eyes I've ever seen. Like a magnet with metal, my gaze holds his. 'Hey, if you girls are going out later, call into the Corinthian Hall if you can.'

'Ooh, we were just saying only minutes ago that we should go there tonight, isn't that right, Molly?' Emily lies.

I remain silent.

'Isn't that right, Molly?' she lands another strong nudge in my ribs, stirring my attention.

'Aye, aye that's right.'

'That's great! I'll see you there.' Karl flashes me another grin, revealing his perfectly white pearly teeth, shining bright against his sun-kissed, swarthy skin. 'Perhaps I'll get the pleasure of a dance with you, Molly.'

'Aye, of course,' I find myself replying without thinking.

'Fantastic! I'll see you there. Hey, I better catch up with the other guys. I'm looking forward to our date tonight, Molly.'

With a wink of his eye he turns and sprints off towards his colleagues.

We stand briefly in silence for a few seconds. 'Hey, Molly no bother to you,' Emily mimics Karl's American accent. 'What were you just saying about men, you can't be bothered with them and all that? Did I hear the words dance and date get mentioned?' A cheeky grin creeps across her pretty face.

I raise my hands to my head. 'Oh gees, Emily, what have I just gone and done? How did I manage to get myself into this one?' Butterflies begin to develop in the pit of my stomach.

'You've just went and got yourself a date by the sounds of things. It wouldn't be anything to do with his good looks and charming manner? Perhaps that's how you've got yourself into this one?' She grins again, 'And the best thing about it? I didn't have to arrange the *date*, you did so yourself!' she laughs.

Panic at once develops within me. 'No I can't go. I can't do it, Emily.' I shake my head frantically as the palms of my hands suddenly felt sweaty. 'I'm not ready to date just yet, Emily. I can't meet him. Look what happened the last time I trusted a man.'

She rolls her eyes. 'Calm down, Molly, of course you can meet him. It's only natural for you to feel nervous. Everything will be okay, and besides, I'll be there too,' she replies in her finest reassuring voice.

'No, I'm not going. We've only just met the guy, we've no idea what he's really like. I'm not going and that's that!'

223

'Calm down, the place will be buzzing with people. I promise I won't leave you.'

'I'm not going!'

'You're going and that *is* that, even if I have to drag you there kicking and screaming!'

Emily's choice of words turn me cold. I think about pointing out that she was at the last dance too, and was of no help when I was dragged – kicking and screaming – into a field and torn apart forever. But that is still the bitter me, Emily is not to blame. I push those silly thoughts away.

'Okay, I'll go.'

Chapter 22

I slip into the crimson dress, just one of the many outfits Emily has brought for me, and glare at myself critically in the mirror, unhappy with the image looking back. 'I don't feel comfortable in this one either,' I shake my head. 'No, it's just not right, Emily.'

I unzip the dress and wriggle out of it, before slinging it on top of the other clothes which lay scattered on the bed.

'For goodness sake, Molly, I've never known you to be so fussy. What's wrong with it?' Emily questions, shrugging her shoulders and shaking her head in disagreement. 'I thought that one looked the best on you, put it back on,' she pleads. 'If you ask me, you're just making excuses not to go out tonight,' she points a finger in my direction. 'I've told you I'll be dragging you there even if I have to take you kicking and screaming.'

I wish she wouldn't use that phrase; it sends shivers up my spine.

'They'll be no excuses tonight, Molly.' A smile dances in her eyes.

I inhale a deep breath and stare at my scar-covered arms; the wounds have healed but the pinkish marks are still visible. 'Emily, I need something with long sleeves. I'm not going out displaying these.' I hold both arms up in the air and sigh helplessly. 'Look at them, the sight of these are enough to make anyone cringe.'

Emily flashes a sympathetic look. 'Aye.' She nods. 'Sorry, I almost forgot. The marks are a bit noticeable at the minute, but listen, don't let those scars get you down, they'll fade soon. I can understand why you want to cover them up,' she replies, trying her best to sound as reassuring as possible. 'Oh, I'm just remembering, there's a black dress in the bag. It has long sleeves.' She leans over the bed, and reaches into the bag, to reveal the black, knee-length dress.

'It's perfect.' I slip it over my head. 'Will you give me a hand to do up the buttons at the back?'

Emily bounces off the bed. 'Aye, sure.' She fastens the buttons of the dress and takes a step back to examine me.

'Now that is absolutely gorgeous on you, you look fantastic. Trust me, Molly, you really do.'

I observe myself in the mirror again, this time pleased at the reflection staring back. The dress fits like a glove. 'Aye, I like this, it's much better and doesn't reveal as much flesh as the last one.'

Emily rolls her eyes. 'Well, are you going to settle for this then?'

'Aye, I'll wear it.'

'Thank goodness for that. I was beginning to worry that the dance would be over before you get out the door, and poor Karl will think he's been stood up, won't he?' she giggles.

The thought of Karl sends butterflies rising within my stomach. 'Karl!' I gasp, covering my mouth. 'Oh no, Emily, I nearly forgot all about him.'

'Forgot about him? What do you mean? How could you forget about those beautiful blue eyes, raven-black hair, chiseled cheekbones and firm masculine body, not to mention that dazzling smile and ...'

'Oh stop it, Emily. Seriously, what am I getting myself into?' I bury my head in my hands. 'I don't think I'm ready for this just yet, and besides you're right, Karl is a very handsome man. Sure he can get any girl, what would he want with someone as plain and troubled as me?' I sigh helplessly.

'Molly, stop putting yourself down! If you keep thinking like that, you'll never be ready to date a man. You're a lot more pretty looking than you think. I saw the way he looked at you; he's as much attracted to you as you are to him.'

'The very thought of meeting him frightens the life out of me, it scares the wits out of me, Emily.' I pause as my eye catches sight of myself in the mirror and suddenly I don't feel as comfortable as I had done just minutes earlier. 'I'm not sure about this.'

'I'm not going to keep repeating myself, you'll be grand, and besides, I'll be right beside you and the place will be packed with people. We're going to have some fun tonight.' Emily lifts up the hairbrush and runs it through her silky hair. 'I can't wait to check out his good-looking mates.'

I watch her pouting and posing in the mirror behind me and can't help but smile. 'Okay, we'll give it a shot,' I reply before applying a thin layer of lipstick.

'Great! Is that us ready to go then?'

'Aye, let's go before I change my mind.'

My mother is busying herself as usual in the kitchen, cleaning up the aftermath of the family dinner. She pauses at the sight of us. 'Oh goodness, Molly, you look absolutely gorgeous. I haven't seen you look so good in a long time. You're beautiful, darling.' Her face fills with happiness.

'Thanks, Mother.'

'Emily, you look terrific too.'

'Oh, thank you very much, Mrs O'Connor,' Emily beams as she twirls around a full circle and strikes a pose, her skirt swinging to and fro, swishing from side to side. 'We're not bad looking, when we wash our faces, are we?' she jokes.

'No, not bad looking at all.' Mother throws her head back and laughs. 'It's great to see you two going out. Molly, you've been stuck up those stairs for long enough. Enjoy yourself tonight, love.'

'I will,' I reply nervously.

'Make sure you do. You don't sound too reassuring. Please have a good time. You need a bit of fun, Molly.'

'Oh, we will, I'll make sure of that, Mrs O'Connor,' Emily interrupts.

'I'm sure you will,' Mother grins, nodding her head in agreement.

'Okay, I'll try.' I plant a soft kiss on my mother's cheek before leaving and waving her goodbye.

Butterflies flutter again through my stomach, almost making me feel sick, as we enter the Corinthian Hall. The soft, ruby-red carpet, lining the foyer feels like walking on sponges. The thick, luxury floor-covering cushions our every step. The long foyer leads into quite an impressive ballroom, which has a magnificent marble floor and marble pillars. It's clear to see why the navy men are attracted to this particular dancehall. The Americans are known to be a step ahead of everybody else; this place suits them down to the ground. It sure is first class. To the left side of the room there is a sweeping staircase that

228

curves at the top and leads to a balcony which surrounds the entire room.

The balcony is lined with handsome gents all dressed from head to toe in their military uniforms, especially washed and pressed for the occasion, and looking quite smart and sophisticated. They have a bird's eye view of the dance floor below as their jaws, going a mile a minute, chew on gum.

'Hey, this place is very swanky, isn't it, Molly?' Emily nudges me in the ribs.

'Aye, you can say that again, very posh indeed.' My eyes roam about the fine hall.

'I can see what the girls mean about this place.' A grin appears on Emily's face as she eyes the talent of young men around her.

My attention falls on the huge glistening chandelier at the centre of the high, raised ceiling. The crystals sparkle all around the room. The sweet music is soft, and not too loud like the other dances. At least here you can have a conversation whilst the music plays in the background.

The men tap their feet gently in time to the enjoyable beat, whilst the ladies move elegantly from side to side, their skirts and dresses swaying to the tune. The dance floor is empty, the night still young. I imagine it won't be long till the floor is filled as the evening rolls by.

'Oh, listen, Molly, there's my song, 'Run Rabbit Run' on. I love that tune.' She lifts her arms up into the air and begins shaking them about, in time to the music.

Soon the dance floor fills. A sea of heads bob up and down in rhythm to the melody. By the looks of it, Emily isn't the only one that enjoys this particular track.

Emily begins to sing to the chorus, shaking her hands up and down and dancing on the spot.

Everyone starts singing. It must be popular, I think. How sad am I? I haven't even heard the song, until now.

The surroundings have a safe and comfortable feeling about them. I feel happy that I've come here after all. As I observe others having a good time it makes me realise how much I've cut myself off from society.

'Molly, look, there's Jimmy McDaid,' Emily whispers, pointing over to a group of people standing in a corner. The rest of the group are noticeably from Derry; they stand out like sore thumbs, and they haven't acquired the same sophistication as the young Americans.

'I can't believe any Derry man would venture into a place like this, sure they have no chance of getting a woman with all these Yanks about,' Emily jokes.

'Aye, exactly.'

The skinny, clumsy Jimmy McDaid, looks so much out of place and appears slightly awkward, and his friends much the same. He has been a friend of ours from our school days; he hasn't changed at all, still the same Jimmy by the looks of things.

'Oi, don't bother looking over at him,' Emily warns, a serious expression on her face. 'We don't want that crowd coming over to talk to us; they'll only spoil our chances with the Yanks. If he and his friends come over, we'll never get rid of them.'

I can't help but burst into a fit of laughter as Emily

drags me by the arm and trails me along to the other end of the dance floor. My smile is soon wiped off my face when we practically fall into Karl and his friends. We must have seemed like a right pair of clowns. We quickly try to straighten ourselves up and act respectable.

'Hi there, girls. I was beginning to think you weren't going to show up.' Karl flashes a cheerful smile; at once my heart melts.

For some reason, he looks more handsome now than he had done earlier. 'Hi, Karl,' I reply, red-faced and slightly breathless.

'Have you just arrived? I've been looking out for you two all night.' His face shines with another smile, bright and warm as a sunny morning.

My head is telling me to stay clear from men, as concerns echo in my mind, but my heart is directing me to Karl. I can't help but like him. I knew from the second I clasped eyes on him that there was an attraction between us.

'No, we've actually been here for a while,' Emily answers whilst she eyes up his companion and flashes him a flirtatious smile.

'Hi, I'm Steve. What do you think of this place? It's pretty awesome, don't you think?' he returns Emily an equally flirtatious grin.

'Oh you're dead on there, and the talent's not bad either,' Emily beams.

I cringe at Emily's comment. She often doesn't think before she speaks.

Karl's aqua eyes dance at Emily's remark before

beckoning us to join him at a table behind him. 'Hey, girls, I want you to meet some of my colleagues and their partners.' He slips his arm through mine, sending shivers through my body. It's a strange feeling, but nice all the same.

We follow him to a table full of laughter. Everyone at once falls silent as they catch sight of Karl, eyes piercing through us as we join them. He introduces his friends one by one, but, after the fourth person, my brain doesn't register their names; there's just too many of them to remember.

The men are Americans and all work onboard the same ship as Karl. The ladies are much too posh to be local girls, and their eveningwear is intriguing.

Many of the girls haven't removed their mink and silver fox fur coats, and I notice all of them have their claw-like nails painted bright red. It's evident from their jewellery that it's worn in a competitive fashion. They're obviously trying to outdo one another, with the most outstanding, and expensive items, dangling from their ears, draped from their necks, or wrapped around their wrists.

Jimmy McDaid springs to mind; it seems he isn't the only one that appears to look like a fish out of water. Emily and I are like two poverty-stricken Derry girls who have wandered into the wrong place amidst such glamour and riches.

I no longer sense we belong here and feel silly for coming. Again thoughts that I am not good enough for Karl rise in my head. Surely he can find himself a much more glamorous girl, like his pals. I eyeball the door, wanting to escape and run a mile from here.

Karl puts his arm around my shoulder, and gently pulls

me closer to him. He appears to be proud that I'm standing next to him.

I can see Emily eyeing up the ladies. She's probably thinking to herself that she will have to get one of those fur coats. She'll end up borrowing the money to have one by the end of the month; by that time the weather will be too warm for fur, but, knowing Emily, that won't stop her.

The music begins to slow down and in time the dance floor fills with couples slow dancing intimately together, embraced in their loved one's arms.

'Would you like to join me for that dance you promised?' Karl whispers softly in my ear.

'Ah… of course.' I smile nervously, with thoughts of running away still on my mind.

Emily winks and throws me a reassuring smile, as Karl takes my hand in his and leads me onto the dance floor. We embrace each other and begin moving slowly, in time to the music. I find myself transfixed in another world as I peer into his eyes. His warmth and his musky scent make me feel safe and content again. His silky hair brushes against my cheek. It feels enchanting.

'Are you having a nice time, Molly?'

'Aye, I'm having a great time.' My nerves have now settled. It feels like I belong in his embrace.

'Good, then you'll have to let me take you out on a proper date.' Karl raises his eyebrows, and tilts his head slightly to the right. 'What do you say?'

My heart wants to explode with joy.

'Aye, I will,' I answer, hoping he won't notice how

timid my voice sounds.

The song ends much too quickly.

'Thanks for the dance.' Karl lowers his head and plants a kiss on my cheek, sending the blood racing through my veins.

With the night going by in a flash, it isn't long before the music comes to a halt and the bright lights switch on. Karl holds out my jacket and I slip my arms inside.

'Molly, I would really like to see you again. You didn't sound too sure when I asked you earlier. I don't want to make you feel under pressure. If you don't want to go out, just say.'

'Of course she would like to see you again,' Emily pipes up before I get a chance to answer him.

'Oh no, don't think that, I would love to see you again, Karl.' I flash Emily a look of annoyance; the truth is I can't wait to see him. I didn't need Emily to answer for me.

'Excellent! I'm off duty next weekend, do you fancy going to see a movie next Saturday?'

'That sounds great, Karl. I'd love to.'

'Hey, Emily maybe you and I could join them,' Steve suggests.

'Oh, Steve, you've got yourself a date.' Emily's eyes twinkle.

Karl gives me another kiss on the cheek, before bidding us goodnight. 'I'll see you about quarter to three, outside the picture house next Saturday.'

'Okay, see you there, Karl.'

I climb into bed that night and lie staring at the ceiling, a smile of contentment spread on my face. I've had a wonderful night.

A wave of excitement rushes through my body at the thought of my next date with Karl. Roll on Saturday. It can't come quick enough, I think, as I close my eyes and drift off to a deep, relaxing, peaceful sleep.

Chapter 23

Crowds queue outside the cinema, eagerly waiting to get inside. We walk along William Street, our eyes darting in all directions in search of Karl and Steve, but, to our dismay, the two men are nowhere to be seen. The huge double doors fling open, and at once the hordes of people are swallowed inside.

'I think we've been stood up.' A disappointed look spreads over my face. I can tell by Emily's gloomy expression that she feels just as distraught.

Emily sighs. 'Aye, it looks like it, doesn't it? Are you sure we got the time right?'

'Karl said quarter to three, the film starts at three.'

'And are you sure we were to meet here?' Emily looks doubtful.

'Aye, definitely,' I chew on my bottom lip and sigh, 'well I'm sure he said to meet him here.'

'It's just going on three o'clock. I won't be surprised if Steve stands me up, I don't think he's that bothered anyway, but I'll be shocked if Karl doesn't show. He seemed genuinely interested.'

'Ah well, as I said to you before, I'm used to men letting me down. I'm annoyed with myself for allowing him a piece of my heart. To be honest with you I couldn't care less if they come or not, maybe it's not meant to be.'

'Well I care, I'm so mad. I really wanted to see the film!' Emily crosses her arms and sticks out her bottom lip.

'Aye, I wanted to see the movie too, but to heck with it. We'll see it some other time.'

I can't help but laugh at the sight of Emily; she looks so childish.

'Has someone tickled your funny bones? What are you laughing at?'

'The look on your face, you look like a child that has just been told off,' I giggle.

'I feel like I'm going to start crying like one!' Her face splits into a smile. 'I hear Clarke Gable plays a fantastic role in this flick. Ah he's so handsome, I love watching him on screen. Never mind a date with Steve, I want to see Clarke Gable!'

My mouth twitches into a snigger again. 'Ah, why doesn't that surprise me?'

'Molly, have you any money on you?'

'What, me? Are you joking or what? I haven't two shillings to rub together!'

'Ah well, we'll have to come back next week, I'll make sure we see 'Gone with the Wind' with or without Karl and Steve, and speaking of those two, I'd like to knock the wind out of them for ditching us! A good kick up the backside, that's what they need.'

'No better girl to do it!' I giggle.

'Oh you're dead right there. Come on let's go then, we've wasted enough time.' Emily shrugs and begins walking away. 'I'm not hanging about here like an idiot. Nothing annoys me more than getting stood up – it's hard to swallow. They're a bunch of ...'

'Hey girls, wait up!' a memorable voice yells.

We both stop in our tracks, and as we do we catch sight of the two familiar men running towards us. My eyes come

237

alive at the sight of seeing him again.

'Oh, thank goodness you're still here,' Karl panted. 'I'm sorry we're late, we were held back by the boss. He wanted to discuss a few things. Were you two about to give up?' He raises his eyebrows and his face breaks into a friendly grin.

'I thought we were stood up there for a minute, and aye, we were just about to head home,' I answer, relieved that they have appeared after all.

'I'm so sorry, Molly.' Karl takes my hand and squeezes it gently. 'It won't happen again. And if it does, you make sure you wait,' he teases before planting a kiss on my cheek.

'Karl, we need to get in here before we miss the film. Let's hope we can get a few seats together,' Steve says as he ushers us inside.

The cinema's prospered during the wartime. With the seating capacity stretched to the limits, it seems many accept this as a means of escaping from the chaotic mess the rest of the world outside is plunged into.

A sea of heads silently wait for the Saturday matinee to commence. We shuffle our way inside and scan the rows of seats, hoping to get four together, but, unfortunately, none of us could find four empty.

'Hey, look, there are two there, and another two a few rows in front,' Karl whispers, 'they'll have to do.' He gently takes my hand and leads us in the direction of the vacant seats. We sit down in the soft, comfy, cushioned chairs, whilst Emily and Steve dash to grab theirs, a few rows in front.

Karl reaches inside his pocket and pulls out a bag of

sweets and some chocolate bars.

'Brandy balls! They're my favourite,' I gasp.

'I thought you would like them, honey.'

His soft tone makes me feel secure in his company. The lights go out and the place is shrouded in darkness, the room fills with silence, until the film flashes on the screen before us.

The film captures my attention at the beginning. The main character, Scarlett O'Hara, reminds me at times of myself. Scarlett was sixteen, a widow and pregnant, and later gave birth to a baby boy.

Karl's masculine arm brushes against mine as he reaches over and takes my hand, holding it in his. I marvel at how smooth his skin feels. My mind whirls, barely able to concentrate any longer on the storyline. All I can think about is how lucky I feel to be sitting next to this handsome gentleman. I don't care what happens to Scarlett, or what the world is getting up to outside; I enter into a land of dreams. Whilst everyone else in the cinema loses themselves in the midst of the movie, I'm falling in love with Karl. Falling in love? What am I thinking? I've only just met him, but it's true. I can't believe it myself, but I'm falling head over heels for him!

The picture show comes to an end and the lights switch back on.

'What a film! That was amazing, what did you think about it, Molly?'

My daydream ends. 'Oh, what? Ah, aye, it was great, it was brilliant, fantastic,' I stammer.

'Did you think it would end like that? It wasn't how I expected, it was awesome. Whoa, I'm definitely surprised.'

'Ah, surprised, aye me too,' I lie in agreement. Little does Karl know I've spent most of the time daydreaming and haven't the foggiest idea what he is talking about.

'Let's go and get something to eat, what do you fancy, honey?'

What do I fancy? I fancy Karl O'Brien, fancy him like crazy, I feel like replying, but manage to refrain. 'I don't mind, I'll let you decide.'

'How about fish and chips from Greasy Bertie's? To be honest, I'm getting addicted to the food there, it tastes so good.' Karl licks his lips and rubs his tummy. 'I'm not sure how good it is for the waistline though,' he jokes.

My eyes run over his toned body; not much wrong with that waistline, I think. 'That sounds good to me.' I turn to Emily and Steve, 'Is that okay with you?'

'As Clark Gable said in the movie *"Frankly, my dear, I don't give a damn".'* Emily giggles.

'That was a great scene,' Steve replies. 'I loved the way he just walked away from her and stepped out into the foggy air. It was wonderful.'

'Aye, it was very dramatic,' Emily turns to Karl. 'Karl, I'm starving, I'll eat anything, and besides, Greasy Bertie's is our favourite chip shop too.'

'Okay, that's that sorted, to heck with the waistline,' I grin.

'Yeah, to heck with it, and besides, we'll not be long in walking it off when you meet me tomorrow for a stroll, isn't that right, Molly?'

'Another date, Karl?' I smile flirtatiously.

'Yeah, it sounds like it, doesn't it, Molly O'Connor?' he flirts back, slipping his arm around my waist and leading us down William Street towards the chip shop.

We're not the only ones to opt for fish and chips; the queue outside is halfway down the street. We stand waiting for what seems like ages, but I don't mind. It doesn't bother me. Other girls eye up Karl and I feel proud to be with him, linked arm in arm.

Inside the chip shop my stomach grumbles with the aroma of battered fish in the air. My mouth waters as I watch the lady sprinkle salt and vinegar on our food before wrapping it up in newspaper.

We leave and eat as we walk the lengthy distance towards my home. Evening is starting to creep in.

'I don't know about you but I think we may have walked that overload off today, never mind our plans for our stroll tomorrow.' Karl throws his head back and laughs. 'Gosh Molly, you do live miles away.'

'It'll keep you fit,' Emily teases, as she stuffs the last remaining piece of greasy fish into her mouth and licks the salt from her fingers.

Karl raises his hands in the air, 'I'm not complaining, but it's a good job I enjoy the exercise.'

'That's my home up there.' I point to the row of modest houses in the distance.

'Thank goodness, Molly, I don't think my legs can take anymore!' Steve sighs and rolls his eyes, 'and to think we have to walk all the way back!'

Karl stops and turns towards me. He slips his arms

around my waist. My legs feel like jelly.

'Will I meet you here about three o'clock tomorrow?' His mesmerising eyes gaze into mine.

'What, here?' I question, slightly taken aback.

'Yeah, is that okay with you?'

'Aye, it's just that it's quite far for you to come. Shall we meet halfway?'

'No, it's okay.'

'I really don't mind. It's not fair you having to walk such a long distance.'

'No, don't you worry about me, I'll get here on time somehow.'

'Fine, if it's okay with you, I'll meet you here then.'

'Great, see you tomorrow, honey.' He plants another soft kiss on my cheek before heading off with Steve.

From the corner of my eye I catch a glimpse of Nosy Nora leaning against a lamppost, her arms folded under her hefty bosom. She squints her chestnut eyes suspiciously as we draw nearer. 'Who are those boys, Molly?' she questions, in her usual prying tone. She chews on her bottom lip, her eyes examining me closely as she waits patiently for an answer.

'Oh, those boys are our boyfriends, Nora,' Emily answers. A false smile emerges on her face, as we pass.

I can feel her eyes watching, burrowing right into us.

'That'll give her plenty to talk about,' I whisper, giggling.

Chapter 24

I finish drying the last of the dinner dishes and place the cloth on the counter before making a dash for the door. During my quick exit I almost tumble Anna over as she enters the kitchen. 'Oh, I'm sorry, dear.' I reach out my hand to grab her and prevent her from hitting the ground.

'It's okay.' Anna straightens out her skirt. 'What's the big hurry, Molly?'

'I'm supposed to be meeting Karl,' I puff.

'Karl? Who's Karl?' she shrugs.

I don't register her question. I'm too interested on trying to get out the door.

'Karl is Molly's new friend,' my mother replies.

I draw back the curtains and glance down the street; my eyes catch a glimpse of the familiar figure waiting patiently at the bottom of the street. My heart skips a beat at the sight of him and it lurches from my chest, landing somewhere in my throat.

I run my fingers through my hair and make my way out the door, stopping only briefly to bid good day to Nosy Nora. No doubt she's seen Karl and has called in to find out about him.

I pass a few girls on the street. They stand whispering together and looking in the direction of the handsome stranger, his presence causing a bit of a stir amongst the locals. He is now leaning against a lamppost.

Karl straightens up as I approach. 'Ah, there you are, Miss O'Connor,' he frowns, pulling back his sleeve and peering at his watch, a smile slowly creeping across his face. He leans back slightly, rocking on the heels of his spit-polished boots, folding his arms across his chest, glee dancing in his eyes. 'I take it you're getting your own back for yesterday.'

'Oh, I'm sorry I'm late,' I reply slightly out of breath. 'I promised my mother I would help her with the dishes.'

'I'm only kidding with you. We'll say that's us even then.' From the centre of his face a smile emerges, spreading across his face and developing a sparkle in his eyes.

'No, no, no.' I shake my head slowly. 'I wouldn't call it even; I'm only ten minutes late, if my memory's correct, I think Mr O'Brien was almost fifteen minutes late, was he not?' I laugh. 'He almost caused us to miss the film, did he not?'

'Oh?' Karl shrugs. 'Well as long as your memory is good, that's the main thing. I like a girl that will keep me on my toes,' he laughs.

I glance around me and only then do I notice we are alone. 'Ah, where are Steve and Emily?' I look up and down the street, but they are nowhere to be seen.

'Steve and Emily?' Karl looks puzzled.

'Aye, where are they?' I question, my nerves beginning to get the better of me.

'I'm not sure where they are today. They didn't say anything to me about coming with us. Did they say anything to you? I thought it was just you and I, and besides there's only enough food here for two.' He grins, holding up a small bag. 'I thought we could go for a picnic.'

Although Karl's voice is echoing somewhere in my brain, I can't register what he is saying, his words tumble about, not making much sense. I struggle to believe that I've arranged to meet him without telling Emily; how could I have been so stupid? Me above all people? I should have been more careful. Now that we're alone together, it suddenly feels like my safety net has been taken away, and all sorts of fears begin to take over my mind. Terror sweeps through me as my body is plunged into a panic attack.

'Molly, did you hear what I said?' Karl grasps my hand. 'Molly, are you okay? You look pale and... Molly, you're trembling.'

I want to run to security, and my eyes scan the street. My attention is drawn to Nosy Nora, standing at the end of her garden and leaning on a broom. Now and again she will swoosh it back and forth, pretending to be hard at work sweeping the dust away, whilst all the time observing all around her. Mother mustn't have given her enough information for her to stay.

'Molly?'

Emily's words spring to mind '*not all men are the same.*' I have to give Karl a chance, and besides, what are the chances of lightning striking twice?

'I'll be okay, Karl it's just ...' I swallow hard. 'I don't know what came over me.' I wipe my sweaty palms on my skirt and inhale a deep breath through my nostrils, then release the air slowly from my opened lips. The inside of my mouth has become like fur and my tongue almost stuck to the roof of it. I have to get myself together; the key to releasing myself from this alarming feeling is to try not to panic further, to keep as calm as possible. Again I breathe, slowly through my nostrils and out from my mouth, through my nostrils and out my mouth, until finally my heart settles and the panic eases.

'Listen to me, Molly, we don't have to go if you're not feeling up to it.' Karl's eyes fill with concern. He genuinely appears worried. 'I think I should take you home.'

'No! No, I'll be okay, and besides, you've walked all this way. The least I can do is join you for a picnic,' I reply in a reassuring voice, breathing in another gulp of air as I desperately try to pull myself together.

'Molly, only if you're sure you're feeling up to it, I don't mind if you're not well, we can rearrange it for another day.'

'No, I'll be fine, honestly, I'm okay.'

'Well, only if you're sure.' Karl's face brightens with a smile.

'I'm positive.'

'Okay then. Where does that road lead to?' He points his finger in the direction towards Muff, and my heart begins to pound again. I've avoided that area since the attack, and there's no way on this earth I'm going to give in today.

'What?' I stammer, my voice shaking again.

'Down there.' Karl continues to point down the dusty dirt track. 'Shall we take that route?'

'Absolutely not!' I reply, much too abruptly. 'There's a field just up behind my house, it's ideal for a picnic.' My tone softens. I decide to play it safe; the pasture overlooks my home, and with it being popular with folks out for a Sunday stroll, there's always a guarantee of someone being about, at least that way we won't be alone together.

'Great, shall we go?' Karl holds out his arm, 'I'll follow you, Miss O'Connor.'

It's a glorious day, ideal for eating outside. The sun is shining in a cloudless sky, there's a light breeze in the air and the temperature's perfect. We walk up past our row of houses and the group of girls that are still watching him. Nosy Nora is now inside her home; she hovers near the window and holds the curtain back with her hand.

'I bet she'll be straight back up to our house for information on you,' I joke.

Karl hasn't a clue what, or who, I'm chatting about. He shrugs dismissively. 'Who are you talking about?' he quizzes. 'I'm lost.'

'Oh sorry, don't mind me. I'm just babbling on about the street's main gossiper. Her name's Nora, but we've nicknamed her Nosy Nora. She lives just over there, the house with the kids playing outside.' I nod my head towards her home.

'I see her now, and I can tell why she's called Nosy Nora: if she bends any further out of that window she'll be in the street,' Karl laughs, shaking his head in disbelief.

At the top of the street there's a dirt path which leads onto the field. Just as I had predicted, there are other people about. Some are walking their dogs, whilst others are out for a stroll to pass the lazy, Sunday afternoon, romantically holding hands. We continue walking until we reach the top. Countryside is visible all around from where we stand.

'Whoa, you sure did pick a great place for a picnic. The view is spectacular.' Karl stands, his hands sunk in his pockets

247

as his eyes observe the scenery in front of him, his head moving in all directions absorbing the beauty.

'Aye, it's nice here. I've always enjoyed coming up to this place as a kid. I can't remember how long it's been since I was last up here, mind you, it's been a while.' I sit down on the soft grass. The field around us is lined with small daisy buds, just waiting for the right moment to greet the sun's rays.

Karl remains standing a little longer. The roaming hills of Donegal and Grianan Fort lie ahead in the distance, whilst the River Foyle is visible from behind us. 'This place is fantastic, it's so peaceful and there's so much greenery.' Karl finally sits down, and reaching into his bag he pulls out some lemonade, sandwiches and fruit.

'Thanks.' I take a sip of the cool liquid, my sense of fear quickly fading, and soon I begin to feel at ease again.

'There are plenty of people about today. I take it this area's popular with the locals.' He takes a bite from his sandwich.

'Aye, the locals come here often, but this area also attracts people from further afield too. It's here that Amelia Earhart landed her plane in 1932, and ever since it has attracted all sorts of visitors.'

'Amelia Earhart,' Karl pauses and runs a hand through his dark, silky hair. 'I've heard of her.' He places his hand under his chin. 'She was the first lady to fly non-stop across the Atlantic, am I right?'

'Aye that's correct, and her plane came down right here in this grassland. It's thought it crashed as a result of having to endure strong northerly winds, icy conditions and mechanical problems. I remember someone saying it took her something like fifteen hours to make the journey. She was lucky to be alive.' I took another sip of my drink.

'Did you see it land?' Karl queries sounding intrigued.

'No, but I heard it alright. We hadn't a clue what the noise was about. I can remember running up here and seeing the aircraft. I was more interested in seeing a plane in reality than anything else. It was my first time seeing one so close.'

'Poor Amelia had just crashed her jet, after flying almost fifteen hours in treacherous conditions, and all you wanted to see was the plane?' Karl teases as he leans back and folds his hands behind his head, stretching his legs out onto the long grass; he rests contently, breathing in the fresh countryside air.

I laugh. 'Aye, kids don't think of the reality behind events like that, do they? They're just interested in what amuses them.' I nudge him playfully.

'That's true.' Karl pulls me gently towards him and presses his lips against mine. It feels magical. All my fears vanish with the touch of his soft, moist lips.

After a while we sit upright, I rest my head on his shoulder and we watch in silence as the sun sets against a pink sky.

'I have to admit I love Ireland, it's such a beautiful country, Molly.'

'Aye, I guess it is. Didn't you say your ancestors were Irish?'

'Yeah, my father's family,' Karl nods.

'Oh right, whereabouts?'

'They're from Donegal, a little place called Greencastle, or so I'm told.'

'Greencastle!' I gasp.

'Yeah, do you know it?'

'Of course I do, it's only a few miles down the road. I have an aunt and uncle that live there. We go there and see them often.'

Karl's eyes sparkle. 'That's amazing. I must get a trip down there to visit sometime.'

'Aye you will, you'll like it, it's a wonderful place. You'll have to meet my uncle Paddy sometime. If there's anyone that will know anything about your ancestors, Paddy McAlister will,' I laugh. 'He knows everything about everything.'

'Great, I'm looking forward to meeting him. I feel excited about this.' Karl rubs his forehead and sighs. 'Molly, I could stay here all day with you in these glorious surroundings, but, I hate to say, I really need to be getting back. It'll take me about an hour to get back to the ship.'

'Aye of course, the afternoon has passed so quickly.'

'I've enjoyed today, it's been so relaxing.' Karl leans closer to me. 'Molly, I've only met you a few times but I feel as if I've known you all my life.' He looks deep into my eyes. 'I would like to meet you again, soon.'

'Aye, I'd like that, Karl,' I find myself reply as I gaze into those mesmerising eyes.

Karl leans closer again and places his hand under my chin, tilting my head towards his he kisses me again. My heart melts as his soft lips caress mine, every nerve in my body tingles. It feels wonderful, so much so I don't want the moment to end.

We walk down the field hand in hand until we reach the street. My mother and Nosy Nora are standing at our front door. 'Oh, there's Molly now, we were just talking about you, Molly,' Nora yells, waving her arms frantically in the air.

'Oh, I bet you were,' I sigh under my breath. 'She's probably been back in with my mother since she saw us earlier,' I mumble.

'You're kidding me?' Karl whispers.

'No,' I reply. 'Like I said earlier, she would be straight up like a shot to hear all about you. She'll want all the juicy gossip.'

'Molly, come on, bring him up so we can get introduced to your new man,' Nora shouts all over the street, much to the dissatisfaction of my mother who clearly doesn't appear to be happy with her manner.

'Look, she's calling us, perhaps we should go and talk to her for five minutes. It would be rude not to,' Karl suggests.

'No way! Talk about being shown up.'

'Ah, just for a few minutes. Come on.' He gently pulls on my sleeve.

'Okay,' I shrug as we walk towards them. 'Oh, Karl, please don't pay any heed to her, goodness only knows what she'll come out with. That tongue of hers is a dangerous tool.'

He looks at me with amusement. 'Don't worry, Molly, I'm only interested in meeting your mom anyway.'

I'm taken aback by his statement. Butterflies sweep through me once again at the thought of him wanting to meet

251

my mother. Is it a symbol that he must be serious about us? Perhaps I'm looking too much into it; regardless, his words feel comforting.

My mother smiles as she watches us approach. She bounces Shane playfully in her arms whilst he pulls on her hair. Nora's eyes roam from Karl's head to his feet, in her usual prying manner, taking in every detail.

'Hi, Mother, hi, Nora,' I nervously turn towards Karl. 'This is Karl, Karl this is my mother Kate, baby Shane, whom you've met before, and our dear, friendly neighbour, Nora.' I smile at Nora, through gritted teeth.

'Hi, nice to meet you both.' Karl shakes their hands in turn.

'Well, Karl, that's a fine uniform. Are you a Yank or what?' Nora folds her arms under her hefty bosom and runs her eyes slowly from his face to his feet and back to his face again. 'What are you doing away out here?' she pries.

'Yes, I'm from America, and I came here to meet Molly.'

'Aye well, I can see that, but I mean, what are you doing in Derry?'

'He's here with the navy, Nora, and his ship is docked at the quay,' I interrupt hoping to distract her. I roll my eyes in frustration at her comments. My mother flashes me a look of disapproval; she detests this habit of mine.

Karl leans forward and takes Shane's hand. The baby wraps his grasp around Karl's finger and holds it tightly. 'Hello there, Shane. That's some grip you got there, young man.' Shane releases a loud giggle and lets go of Karl's finger. He kicks his legs frantically to and fro as Karl tickles him gently under the chin. 'You're a happy chap today, aren't you?' Karl ruffles Shane's curls and he laughs some more.

'Well if you ask me, I don't see any point in you two going out, sure he has to go back to America. What's the point in wasting your time? You'll only end up breaking one another's hearts.' Nora lifts her finger and points it straight at Karl. 'You mark my words, boy, there will be hearts broken.' She presses her lips firmly together and shakes her head, in a matter of fact fashion. 'You have to head back home one day, sunshine.'

The cheek of the woman, I think.

'You never know, maybe Molly will come back to America with me, Nora,' Karl replies, with a grin on his face.

My mother raises an eyebrow in a curious fashion.

Karl holds his hands in the air. 'I'm only kidding, Mrs O'Connor. I'll just have to stay here then, but we'll deal with that matter when it comes to it.' He smiles, revealing his perfect, gleaming white teeth against his swarthy, sun-kissed skin.

'Good, you almost gave me heart failure there,' my mother smiles.

'Aye, you Yanks are good craic. You sail in one day and sail out the next and leave the poor women behind to pick up the pieces,' Nora interrupts, and as she speaks the strong smell of alcohol chokes the air.

'Nora, that's a bit harsh,' I reply, in defence of Karl. I'm beginning to get more and more irritated by her silly comments.

'True,' Karl nods his head. 'Then again, if fate has brought us together then fate will keep us together.' He winks.

'It's time you were heading on home now, Nora. I have to get the tea ready and I'm sure your kids will be looking for theirs,' my mother suggests, before turning her attention to Karl. 'Would you like to join us for something to eat?'

'No thanks, Mrs O'Connor, thank you for the offer.' Karl draws back the sleeve of his jacket, and glances at his watch. 'I really ought to be getting back to the ship before they send out a search party for me, but I'll take you up on that offer the next time.'

'Yes, please do. Goodbye, Karl, and it's been nice meeting you.'

'Goodbye, it's a pleasure to meet you. Goodbye, Nora, take care.'

'Aye, I'll see you.' Nora lowers her eyes in a suspicious manner.

'I'll walk you down the road. I'll be back in a few minutes, Mother.'

As soon as we are out of earshot Karl says, 'She sure is a curious little lady.'

'Aye, you're right about that, she is indeed. I'm sorry about the way she spoke to you, it was embarrassing.'

'Don't worry about that, it's not your fault. I don't pay much attention to people like her and anyway, as I said earlier, I've had a great day today. I've enjoyed your company, Molly,' he grins.

'Aye, I've enjoyed yours too.'

He places his arm around my waist and we stroll further

down through the country roads. The sun is now well settled in the sky as evening begins to creep in. Karl leans forward and kisses my cheek. 'Now that I know where you live, I'll be popping in every day I'm off duty.'

'Good, I'll be waiting for you.'

'I'll see you next week then, same time, and same place. You've walked far enough; you need to be getting back soon, your mother will have your tea ready.'

Before I can answer I feel his delicate lips on mine again. It feels wonderful. I belong in his arms.

'I'll see you soon, Molly.'

He gives me a gentle hug and we linger together, enjoying the moment.

'Aye, okay.' I watch as Karl heads off down the road and disappears into the distance. I can't deny it; I'm falling in love with him, whether I like it or not. I find myself transfixed by him, my history almost forgotten about, only my future important.

I no longer fear my past; my future takes on a new set of fears. Nora's words haunt me. Is Karl capable of breaking my heart? How will I handle it if I lose him? These thoughts burn in my brain, but I decide to brush those feelings to the back of my mind; after all, as Karl said, we'll worry about that when the time comes.

Chapter 25

A year goes by Karl and I grow closer by each passing day, to the point that we become inseparable. He smothers me with love, but he doesn't suffocate me, he lets me breathe too. We continue to go to the Corinthian Hall and to the cinema, and have many long walks in the countryside. We even manage a few trips to Greencastle. I feel secure with him; like a turtle that welcomes the waves, only then is it safe. I'm fortunate to have met such a wonderful, thoughtful man.

It is on our first trip to Greencastle, as we stand embraced by the sea, that Karl declares his love for me. I admit to him that I feel the same. However, the moment is spoilt when he catches a glimpse of one of the scars on my wrist. When he asks what it is, I lie and tell him I fell into some barbed wire as a child. I hate telling him fibs, but know there is no other choice. I don't want to risk losing him. No matter how close we have become, I can't tell him about what happened and why such unsightly blemishes cover both my arms. I make sure to wear a cardigan everywhere I go; the marks are not as red but they're still there, reminding me of that terrible day when I inflicted so much damage on myself.

I can't tell Karl. There's no point in opening old wounds. It would be too risky; there's no way I can allow the truth to spoil what we have. It isn't worth it, and besides, we are content now. I won't permit myself to return to those dark, lonely days.

My family adores Karl. They can tell he's a good man and they see how happy we both are. At first when I introduced him to them, I felt on edge, my nerves were wrecked, worrying that someone would reveal one of my many lies. My mother had informed the rest of the household about my suicide attempt – the others were on high alert but just like the pregnancy, they never mentioned it. I'm glad; it means they are unlikely to let the secrets slip in front of him. I'm sure they are just as eager to keep my secret quiet.

Paddy was delighted when he heard that Karl's ancestors were from Greencastle, and of course, he knew all about the O'Brien clan just as I had predicted. He filled Karl in on his relatives' background, describing how the O'Brien's had been a well-known fishing family and popular amongst the locals. He went on to explain that he remembered Karl's grandfather, David O'Brien, and described him as being an intelligent man who had his sights set higher than spending his days trawling for fish. David had ambition to do something challenging with his life; it was this desire that drove him to flee Ireland for a better existence in America.

Karl was elated on hearing this information, and even more so when Paddy informed him that David's brother, Colm, was still alive – the only remaining O'Brien member living in Greencastle. Colm is an elderly man in his late seventies, but is still as fit as a fiddle and occasionally he finds the energy to join Paddy for a spot of fishing.

When Paddy introduced Karl to Colm it was a touching moment. It was moving to witness the tears of sheer happiness in their eyes. Colm's sun-damaged face, from the many years of exposure at sea, lit up on seeing his young relative, his eyes twinkling with delight. Over time the two men have got to know one another with us visiting Greencastle as often as we could. Karl even managed to join Paddy and Colm at sea whilst I stayed and cooked dinner with Aggie. I had pulled Paddy aside and made him promise to ensure he didn't mention the secret in front of Karl.

Normally, over the Easter period Aggie and Paddy come to visit us and stay for a few days, before heading off back to Greencastle. However, this Easter they were doubtful with the war intensifying. They felt safer at home; even though it's only a few miles down the road, they may as well be a million miles away. The South of Ireland is still untouched by the conflict.

Mick wouldn't hear of it. He managed to persuade them to come and reside with us as usual by reminding them that there is nothing to worry about, and explaining that Derry remains untouched since war had been declared here over eighteen months ago. It was therefore agreed that they would come and stay with us until the Wednesday after Easter; I'm sure they agreed out of politeness more than anything else.

My mother loves this special time of the year, and was delighted to hear Aggie and Paddy had decided to join us after all.

After Sunday Mass we return home. Karl isn't on duty until six o'clock so he accepts my mother's invite to have dinner. Mick and Paddy sit around the kitchen table telling stories whilst the rest of us listen, intrigued by the tales and adventures that both men got involved in when they were younger. Karl encourages them on to tell more; he loves hearing about their antics.

On Easter Tuesday night my mother, Mick, Aggie, Paddy, Charlie and Anna were downstairs. My mother had just put Shane to bed at about seven thirty, much to Aggie's dismay. My mother has him in a routine; she doesn't want to spoil that. Aggie, on the other hand dotes on him and longs to keep him up later, but with him being cranky it is best he gets his sleep. I retire to my room shortly after tea. No sooner have I entered my quarters when a loud noise zooms overhead.

'Molly!' Mick shouts. 'That's a German plane, not a British one!' Apparently he can tell by the sound of it.

The adults run outdoors to investigate the curious aircraft. The sound of a commotion develops in the street and so I decide to rush downstairs and follow them. Outside, all of the neighbours are in a state of panic.

'Did you see that, folks?' Nosy Nora shrieks in an over-dramatic tone. 'There's a parachute with a bomb attached to it and it's heading towards the ground.'

I roll my eyes. 'That's most certainly a lie,' I whisper to Mick. He doesn't answer; he is too transfixed on Nora's statement. I sense he is frightened.

'Oh Sacred Heart of Jesus help us this night!' Aggie prays whilst she blesses herself looking up at the sky. 'I knew it, Paddy, we should have stayed where we were. Don't say I didn't warn you!'

'Listen, Aggie, don't let Nora scare you, she's away with the fairies half of the time,' I giggle. Aggie, just like Mick, doesn't answer, and certainly doesn't see any fun in my words, her expression remains fearful.

'Let's go folks!' Mick announces, and before we know

259

it he is ushering everyone inside, panic evident on his face. A deafening explosion rumbles through the air. The contents of our house tremble. It isn't long before the sound of a second explosion erupts.

'Oh my goodness,' Aggie screams, 'Kate, what are we going to do? They're going to bomb us out tonight!' Her body is shaking.

'It's okay, Aggie, calm down,' my mother says in a soft reassuring tone. 'Molly, go upstairs please and bring Shane down here to us.'

I run out of the room and upstairs to fetch the baby. Much to my disappointment he isn't amused with being pulled so abruptly from his peaceful sleep. He rubs his tired eyes and screams a deafening screech in my eardrums, only adding to the tense atmosphere.

Back downstairs Aggie is becoming a nervous wreck, her tension begins rubbing off on the others. They appear as scared as she sounded.

'Right, let's get everyone into the air raid shelter, quick. Is everyone here?' Mick scans the room and when he is happy that we are all together, he urges us towards the back door. 'Kate, you're coming too whether you like it or not, I'm not leaving you behind!'

My mother nods and comes behind with candles, food and blankets. I still have Shane in my arms, and once we are safely in the shelter I sit with him on my knee and cuddle his tiny head into my chest, rocking him gently until he stops crying. I haven't held Shane for this long. Part of me still doesn't allow myself to acknowledge him. I have opened to him quite a bit, but I'm not fully there yet, too scared to accept him, a section of the barrier I had built in the early days remains standing.

When the war was first announced I'd been too young and naive to appreciate the seriousness of the whole affair, but after tonight it's now time to stop burying my head in the sand and to accept that life is changing. We can do nothing to prevent this. It's times like these that the fragility of life can be tested, and it does make me think deeper about how important family and friends are in my life. They can be here today but gone tomorrow. I kiss Shane's forehead and hold him closer to me, wanting to protect him; perhaps it's a maternal instinct.

Much of the night is spent awake, with the others listening for any sounds or disruption. I must have eventually nodded off. I awake to find a blanket draped around me, and Shane snoozing on my mother's lap.

With the sun's light squeezing into tiny spaces between the entrance, and the familiar sound of birds chirping outside, it's evident daybreak has arrived.

'Mick, wake up. I think it's safe to go back into the house.' My mother taps him on the shoulder.

He stirs, then springs to his feet. 'What? Did I fall asleep? Is everyone okay?'

'Aye, Mick, you dozed over for a while, and don't worry, we're all fine.' Paddy smiles.

We are no sooner back inside the house, when someone bangs on the door.

'Who the heck is that at this time of the morning? We're not used to this nonsense back in Greencastle,' grumbles

Aggie. It's not like her to be so moody. She was clearly still affected by the bombing episode from the night before.

'I'll go and see,' I said. On opening the door, Nosy Nora almost knocks me over as she barges her way past in a somewhat confused and hysterical manner. She must be on the drink again, I think to myself.

'Molly, you have got to help me,' she pleads, turning to face me and pulling on my sleeve. It was only then I notice how pale she looks.

'What's the matter with you, Nora, are you okay?' I query, my smile fading.

Nora pauses as she catches her breath, before continuing. 'No, Molly, I'm just after hearing Messines Park has been bombed, and as you know, my ma lives there.' She rushes on into the living room and breaks the news to my stunned family.

My body freezes in shock. Fear begins surging through me. I know Nora's mother lives there as she lives next door to Emily. Emily would often joke that Nosy Nora got her prying traits from her own mother, as she's also the eyes and ears of their street.

'Will one of you come with me? I need to see my ma,' Nora pleads with tears streaming down her face.

'Let's go, Nora. I have to see if Emily is okay, I'll go with you.'

'No, Molly, I think you should stay here, it could be dangerous.'

'Mother, I can't, I want to see Emily, and besides, Nora needs someone to accompany her.'

'Right, very well, but I'm coming with you then.'
Mother passes Shane to Aggie and dives to get her coat.
'Aggie, will you be okay with him, just till I get back?'

'Of course, Kate,' she agrees, but from the look on her
face she appears as if she wants to run away home, never mind
stay in Derry a second longer.

In no time we are out the door. Messines Park is about a
thirty minute walk away but we race through the fields for a
short-cut, trenching through the long blades of grass, climbing
over fences, weaving through all sorts of wild bushes on the
way until we were minutes from our destination.

I sprint ahead of my mother and Nora with a feeling my
heart has suddenly been placed in my throat.

'Molly, wait, we can't keep up,' Nora yells in the
distance.

I continue on, not stopping until, some minutes later, I
finally arrive at the bombsite. Broken glass lays strewn
everywhere and debris is scattered all over the street. My heart
sinks on seeing so many of the houses badly damaged. My eyes
scan the crowds of people in search of my friend, but she is
nowhere to be seen.

I spot Father McGroarty talking to an elderly man. He
catches sight of me and waves, and at once he squeezes his
way through the crowds of people to make his way over. By
this time my mother and Nora arrive, both of them sounding
out of breath.

'Molly, what are you doing here, love?' He places his
arm gently around my shoulders.

'Have you seen Emily, Father?'

'Emily?'

'Aye, my friend Emily, she lives in this street.'

'Oh yes, I remember her now. Sorry, Molly, I can't recall seeing her, but I'll ask around and let you know if I hear anything.'

'Father, what about my ma, have you seen her? Oh gees, I'm worried sick.' Nora clutches her chest and her eyes fill with tears.

'Nora, she's fine, she's over there.' He points to his left at a crowd of people. 'She's been treated for shock, but other than that she's okay.'

Nora takes to her heels and heads off.

My mother sighs at the destruction around her. 'It's unbelievable that anyone would want to carry out such evil on innocent people. Father, what happened? We heard two explosions, was the street hit by two bombs?'

'No, Kate, the street was hit by a landmine and a second one fell near our church.'

'What? Near the church? Oh my goodness, is the building damaged?'

'Yes, it's slightly harmed but it's still standing, that's the main thing. Thankfully nobody has lost their lives down there. I wish I could say the same for here.' He presses his lips together, shaking his head he looks sadly at the ground, a grim expression takes over his face.

'What do you mean, Father?' I ask. 'Who's dead?'

'I haven't been given all the names yet, but I know a total of thirteen people have lost their lives.'

I don't need to hear anymore. I run towards Emily's

house pushing through everyone in my way.

My heart leaps at the sight of some policemen standing outside her front door.

'You can't pass here, love.' The police officer holds out a strong arm and stops me in my tracks.

'Officer, I need to get in to see my pal,' I plead trying to push his arm out of my way.

'Sorry, I can't let you pass, it's not safe.' He grasps my arms firmly.

'Let go of me! I need to get in, please let me in.' I start to struggle in an attempt to free myself from his vice-like grip. 'Let me go!' I manage to release myself from his grasp and with all my strength plunge my way forward.

The taller of the two officers stands in my way and holds out his arms preventing me from going any further. 'It's not safe. I'm sorry, madam, but you can't pass,' he repeats in a tone of authority. 'And besides, there's nobody in there.'

'What do you mean there's nobody in there? Where are they?' My eyes roam the area, stopping at the sight of Emily's bedroom window; her curtains blowing freely in the breeze, the glass completely gone, and no sign of her anywhere.

Chapter 26

'Molly.' A gentle hand taps me on the shoulder. I spin around and come face to face with Father McGroarty. He looks at me softly, and with a sympathetic tone I hear him say, 'I've just been informed that Emily is amongst the injured, she's been taken to the hospital.'

'Oh thank God she's alive! But is she going to be all right?' Tears burn my eyes.

'I'm not sure how serious her injuries are, but I've been told she's not critical.'

'Father, I need to get over to see her.' I turn and run off towards my mother, with Father McGroarty following me through the dust-filled air.

'Oh, Molly, I've just heard about Emily. It's terrible.' My mother shakes her head in disbelief.

'I have to get to her. I can't stand not knowing if she's going to be alright or not, it's just horrible,' I cry.

'Molly, you can't go now, you won't get in. I've been told she isn't long away. The medical staff need to treat her.'

'Father McGroarty is right.' My mother puts her arms around me. 'We're best to wait a few hours and then we can go.'

'Come down to the parochial house, I'll make you a cup of tea and some breakfast. I'll drive you to the hospital later.'

'Thank you, Father, but I wouldn't want to put you to any bother. I'll get Sadie's husband to take us.'

'No not at all, Kate. I won't hear of it. I would love to help you, and besides, I want to visit the injured anyway.'

'Well okay, only if you're going that way,' she agrees.

The crowds in the street soon disperse. People begin to make their way into different houses. For some of them, their own homes were destroyed or too dangerous to return to and so they have no option but to go to their neighbours' dwellings. Others are forced to leave the street, to join family and friends in different parts of the town.

'There's one thing you can say about the Derry folk: when there's a crisis, or a time of need, there's no shortage of good citizens to pull together to help.'

'True enough, Kate,' Father McGroarty nods in agreement. 'It's sad in a way that sometimes it takes a tragedy like this to bring us together, but you're right. Things like this can bring out the best in people. Let's go, I'll get a pot of tea on. You've always been good to me, now I would like to return some kindness to you,' he smiles.

'Okay, I think we could be doing with a cuppa after all.' My mother slips her arm around my waist. 'Come on, Molly, let's go, darling.'

Inside the parochial house Father McGroarty urges us to sit down on the cosy, velvet sofa whilst he goes to make us tea. My body sinks into the comfortable chair and I rest my aching head against the soft cushion. A surge of guilt travels through me, with feelings of Emily alone somewhere in the hospital. Silently I pray she'll be okay.

The holy pictures, scattered on the walls in front of me, interrupt my thoughts. Every nook and cranny in the room holds something of a divine nature. My attention is drawn to a huge picture of Jesus on the Cross. His Mother and Veronica are below, looking up at him and weeping. Blood seeps from each of his wounds and drips onto the ground. His face portrays the agonising suffering of his passion, but his eyes are so soft and warm as he gazes mercifully from the cross. The dark, mahogany frame is expertly carved with such beautiful detail. Next to it is a huge, gold-framed picture containing the Blessed Virgin Mary with the infant Jesus in her arms. She's clothed in some kind of greyish-blue garment which has a hood covering her head. Her eyes seem to pierce my soul, eyes that appear to watch my every movement. Her gaze makes me feel uncomfortable.

'Do you like that picture, Molly?' Father McGroarty questions. I hadn't noticed him return. He pulls over a small coffee table and places a cup and saucer in front of me, accompanied with a plate full of toasted bread and some biscuits.

'Ah no, I'm not sure I do.' I have blurted out my thoughts before I knew it. My mother looks mortified with my sudden outburst. 'I feel like she's watching me,' I reply timidly.

He gives me a smile. 'Oh you've hit the nail on the head there, Molly. She's observing you alright; she's watching over you. You've nothing to be afraid of. That picture is an image of the Mother of Perpetual Help: anything you need help with, say nine Hail Mary's for nine days in front of the image and I'm sure she'll come to your aid,' he smiles confidently.

'My goodness, you're such a man of faith. I've too many problems; somehow I don't think a few Hail Mary's will sort them out.'

My mother's expression jolts from frosty to frozen. She clearly isn't happy with my comment. She buries her head in her hands as her face turns crimson. Oh dear, I've put my foot in it again, I think.

'Okay, but I prefer the picture of the crucifixion. Jesus looks so compassionate in that one.' I point to the beautiful masterpiece. 'There's something eye-catching about it.'

'I have to admit that's one of my favourites too, Molly. It's hand-painted, and I've been told it took longer to carve the frame than it did to paint the image. That portrait has been in my family for many years. My grandfather gave it me when I decided to join the priesthood.'

'It's beautiful,' I reply before taking a sip of the warm tea. I digest every detail of the fine art.

'It is in indeed,' my mother remarks. She passes the plate of toast to me. 'Molly, have a slice.'

'No thank you, I'm not hungry.'

'You should try to eat something. Who knows when you'll get a bite to eat, you're not likely to get anything at the hospital.'

The hospital, how could I have forgotten? My thoughts have been so far distracted with all the chat surrounding the pictures, it has almost escaped my mind why I'm here in the first place.

'Molly, your mother's right, you need something in your stomach.' Father McGroarty holds the plate under my nose. I look at him sheepishly, accept a slice, and reluctantly take a bite, not wanting to offend him.

'Do you know, Kate, it must've been the grace of God

that saved the church from being bombed.'

'Aye, true enough, it could've been easily destroyed. It would've been an awful disaster if the bomb had ruined it.'

'It would have been a shocking loss surely. Can you imagine the devastation to the parishioners if they got up this morning to find they had no church to attend? It would have destroyed them. Mass is so important to people, particularly during times like this, and it's times like this that folk pray more. They've no one else to turn to, and, with a need to turn to someone to be fulfilled, they turn to God. You need prayer in your life.'

'You're right. It doesn't bear thinking about,' my mother nods in agreement.

'What a tragedy for all those people that lost their lives. I do hope their souls rest in peace. Then there's the unfortunate people that have lost their homes; may God protect their families and comfort them in their loss.' Father McGroarty bows his head in a prayer-filled moment.

'It makes you think, Father, it makes this evil war all so real, when it lands on your own doorstep.'

'It does indeed, Kate.'

'You never know what's round the corner.' My mother sips her tea slowly.

'No, that's true, you never can comprehend what's going to happen next and you by no means expect such a catastrophe to happen so close to home.'

I sit quietly on the sofa, unable to string two words together to participate in this conversation. My attention is drawn again to the picture of the Mother of Perpetual Help.

270

'Help Emily,' I whisper under my breath, as I feel the eyes from the image penetrate my soul again. 'That's all I ask you for, please help Emily.'

Chapter 27

It's common to hear folks comment on how they hate hospitals. It's understandable – after all, they are for the sick – but I enjoy the hustle and the bustle and watching people dashing around carrying out their important tasks. I used to dream, as a child, of becoming a nurse. The idea of helping people intrigues me, especially caring for the older generation. The elderly folk pull on my heartstrings, especially when they get to the stage of not being able to look after themselves. The majority of them probably worked hard all of their lives, bringing up children or putting all their energy into their careers. Most of us are destined to grow old, and may even need care one day ourselves, so at a very young age I decided to become a nurse specialising in caring for the elderly. It wasn't until my teens that I realised I would be useless in this profession. With having a fear of needles, it became clear I wouldn't get very far. This concern was enough to put me off my childhood dreams.

The strong smell of the disinfectant, lingering in the air, is another reason for my love of hospitals. The aroma is so powerful. It seeps into clothes and clings to hair. I can recall as a youngster leaving the infirmary with my mother after visiting a relative; all day I pulled on strands of my hair and held them close to my nostrils to get a waft of the distinctive scent. I absolutely loved coming here, but today, however, I'm one of those who detest the sight of it. I dread what kind of state we will find Emily in.

Once inside the building, it's clear just how depressing

the place actually is, with its flaky, whitewashed walls and dull, gloomy atmosphere adding to the somberness. Today the site is packed with people coming to and fro, buzzing with activity, obviously an effect of last night's bombing. People look sad and are evidently in a state of shock and confusion. They dash frantically about, not stopping to meet or greet anyone in their path.

I observe one lady wailing into the arms of a group of men and women.

'Oh dear, that poor soul, she must've received bad news.' Father McGroarty sounds concerned. 'I'll be back in a minute. I want to see if there's anything I can do for her.'

Her howls create a sense of panic in myself and other passers-by. I feel my legs buckle and a feeling of faintness sweeps over me.

A familiar face in the crowd approaches us. 'Molly, it's good to see you, love.' Emily's mother smiles, a look of strain etched on her face.

'Mrs Wilson! How is Emily, is she okay?'

She nods her head slowly. 'Aye she's going to be fine. She's blessed to be living; she's a few broken ribs and a punctured lung, but thanks be to God, she's alive, and that's the main thing.'

'Oh thank God for that,' I sigh with relief, 'a punctured lung? That sounds pretty serious though.'

'Aye it is, Molly, but sure she's in the best place, she'll recover in no time. Our Emily's a fighter.'

I smile. 'Aye, you're right there. What ward is she in?'

'Ward three. I'm going home now to see the others. I've

been up all night. I'm dreading seeing what state the street is in.'

'How did Emily get hurt?' my mother questions.

'She'd been standing by the window, fixing the blackout curtains, just before the bomb hit. The glass and part of the wall came in on top of her.'

'My goodness, she's very lucky she wasn't killed!' my mother replies.

'Aye, she is indeed.'

'Is the house badly damaged?'

'It is but, Mrs O'Connor, I'm not worried about the house. Sure it's only bricks and mortar; we'll have it sorted in no time.'

'Listen, you're all very welcome to stay with us until you get yourself sorted, I'm sure we can fit you in somehow.'

'Mrs O'Connor, thank you for the kind offer. My sister has room at her home. I think we're going to stay with her for a while, but thanks again for the caring gesture.'

'It's the least I can do. You know if you need anything at all, don't be afraid to ask.'

'Thank you. I appreciate your goodwill.'

'I'll leave you two to chat. I'm going to head on up to see Emily. Mrs Wilson, I'll see you later, take care.'

'Okay, Molly. God bless and thank you for coming over.'

'Wait, I'll come with you.' Father McGroarty follows. 'I'm going to start with ward one to see if there's anyone I know there, then I'll make my way up the rest of the wards. Tell Emily I'll pop in to see her later.'

'Okay, Father, that I will do. Did you find out why that woman was so upset?'

'Yes, sadly she's lost her daughter. Emily will probably know the girl, they live a few doors from her family.'

I cover my ears, 'Oh, don't tell me her name. I don't want to have to break that news to her, not today above all days.'

I climb the three flights of stairs until I come to ward three, by which time I'm slightly breathless. I glance around the corridor, hoping to catch someone's attention, but everyone appears too busy to stop, each of them wrapped up in their own tasks. After a few seconds I catch sight of a tall, slim girl, peering into a file in her hands.

'Excuse me.'

She looks up and smiles, 'Yes?'

'I'm looking for Emily Wilson. Do you know what room she's in?'

'Sorry, I'm not sure. You'll have to ask the matron, she's just in there.' She points to an open door to the left of the corridor.

'Thank you,' I reply. I rush to the room, but before I get a chance to knock a short, plump woman, comes charging out, almost bumping into me in the process, with a face as cold as stone – quite the opposite from the first lady I spoke to.

'Hello, can you help me? I'm looking for Emily Wilson.'

The pint-sized matron freezes, fixes me with an icy stare. She remains glaring through me, like I have horns on my head. 'Can't you see I'm busy?' she grumbles, pushing past and strutting off down the corridor, almost tumbling me over as she passes.

'Why do people have to be so rude?' I whisper under my breath.

'Hey, pay no heed to her.' I hear a voice from behind speak softly.

I spin around to be met by the first girl I spoke to.

'I've just found out that Emily is in room L. It's down at the bottom of the corridor.'

'Oh, that's great. Thank you for your help.'

I gallop down the corridor with so much eagerness I don't notice the grouchy matron leaving one of the rooms, her arms filled with medical equipment. We run straight into each other, causing her to plummet to the floor and sending bandages and needles flying into the air. She falls to the ground, flat onto her face. Her uniform has gathered up around her waist revealing off-white coloured bloomers. The doctor that was following her struggles to prevent himself from laughing aloud as he bends down to help her up. I can hear some nurses sniggering in the background.

'Oh dear, I'm so sorry,' I say awkwardly. I kneel down to lift her bits and pieces off the ground. 'Are you okay?'

From the look on her face, it's enough to alert me that she's most certainly not okay.

She snatches the bandages from my hand. 'You stupid so and so! Don't you know you should look where you're going?' She runs her free hand down to flatten the front of her uniform, her face cherry red with embarrassment and anger. 'You're a silly...'

'I'm sorry,' I reply sheepishly.

I glance back at the doctor, who is still desperately trying not to chuckle. I can see him chewing on the inside of his cheek in an attempt to hold back his giggles.

'I should throw you off my ward!' She barges, lifting her finger and pointing it so close to my face she almost touches my nose. 'You need to watch where you're going, young lady. I wouldn't think twice about throwing you out on your ear!' She storms down the corridor before disappearing into another room.

The young doctor smiles sympathetically and rolls his eyes. 'Pay no heed to her. She's a grumpy old woman. Don't worry, her bark's worse than her bite.'

A fierce head appears in the corridor. 'Doctor McDowell! Are you coming or what? There are patients waiting to be assessed.'

'Yes, I'll be up now.'

She turns and marches further up the corridor; it's only then that we both notice that the back of her skirt is caught in her bloomers.

We laugh together. 'Should one of us tell her?' I ask.

'Nah, I think we'll let her find out for herself,' the doctor grins. 'I must go before she explodes up there.'

After speaking to Emily's mother, my nerves have settled down slightly. I expect to see her sitting up and having a bit of banter with the staff and the patients. My expectations are dashed upon entering the room. I'm not prepared for the shock of seeing her; she lies in her bed, attached to different machines. A drip has been fixed to her arm, from where

277

intravenous fluids are being transferred to her body, and an oxygen mask covers her bruised face. She looks pale and gaunt.

'Hi, Emily,' I whisper before planting a delicate kiss on her forehead and trying my utmost best not to sound too worried.

She looks at me and tries to smile. She lifts her hand to remove her mask, and at once releases a painful groan. Her chest rises and falls rapidly before she manages to reply, 'Hi, Mo ...'

'You don't have to speak, don't bother saying anything. You're struggling to breathe at the minute.' I lean over and place the breathing apparatus back around her mouth. 'I'll just sit here and keep you company for a while, I'm in no hurry to get back home. I'll do all the talking today, you can just stay in that bed and listen to me ranting on for a change,' I tease. 'That'll be a first, Emily Wilson quiet for more than ten seconds.' I laugh.

Emily's eyes light up, she can't help but grin.

I take her hand in mine and, in a more serious tone, I continue. 'You gave me an awful fright. I thought you were a goner for a while. My nerves have been wrecked since hearing about the bombing.

'Looking back over the past year, I don't know how I would've gotten through the darkest parts of my life without your help and support. There's no way I could've coped if we'd lost you.'

'I was ... sc ... scared,' she managed to say.

'Oh, I'm sure you were; you stared death in the face.

That must've been frightening for you.'

She squeezes my hand.

I sit with her in silence, knowing she's happy with me just being here. She nods off to sleep for a few minutes and when she wakes she appears content that I'm still here sitting in the same position.

'Go on, have a nap, buddy. I'll stay with you.'

She smiles and closes her eyes before drifting off to sleep once more. She certainly is a true friend to me. It takes a good pal to put up with the nonsense that I've put her through: my heavy depression, the awful mood swings and constantly snapping at her. The worst thing of all is that I couldn't see for myself at the time just how much a treasured possession she is to me.

Emily has been there for me when I needed her the most. It's now my chance to repay her.

Chapter 28

Emily soon gets her strength back, and slowly but surely she returns to the bubbly girl we all know and love. She has to remain in hospital for almost four weeks. I journey to and fro every day on Mick's bicycle to visit.

Today Karl and I have arranged to take her to the Saturday matinee, which of course means I have to wear my cardigan with the tight-fitting arms. Most of the scars have faded away, but those that remain look like they're here to stay.

We arrive early and thankfully we manage to get seats together. Each of us is excited to see the much talked about film, Doctor Jekyll and Mr Hyde.

'Molly, you do know this is a horror film, don't you?' Karl places his hand on mine. 'I know you don't like scary movies.'

'Aye I know it is, but I've heard this is a great show, and besides, I do enjoy Spencer Tracey. He's a brilliant actor.'

'Yeah, he's awesome. He's the main lead, isn't he?'

'He sure is,' Emily pops a sweet in her mouth. 'I'm looking forward to it. I hear it's really creepy.'

'Oh no, maybe I shouldn't have suggested this movie after all.'

'I'm sure you'll enjoy it, Molly, it's based on the story by Robert Louis Stevenson. I read the novel just last year. I hope the film is as good as the book; I enjoyed reading it so much I couldn't put it down,' Karl replies as he places his arm around my shoulder and plants a soft kiss on my cheek.

'Karl, I know I'll be burying my head in your arms for

most of it.'

'Ah, Molly, you can bury your head in my arms anytime.'

'Oh here we go, the two lovebirds have started. You know, I do love being a gooseberry!' Emily rolls her emerald eyes and sniggers.

'Ah what? What are you talking about?' Karl questions as an amused look appears on his face.

'A gooseberry, stuck in-between the pair of you! You two don't need me tagging along everywhere you go; the pair of you should be smooching in the back row,' she pauses, 'oh, it's been a long time since I had a good canoodle in the back row.' She throws her head back and giggles. 'Well it's been almost a year, since that friend of yours, Steve, dumped me for that toffee-nosed snob who flung herself at him at the Corinthian.'

Karl sighs. 'Ah, Emily, that's his loss.'

'Karl's right, and don't worry about tagging along with us, we've plenty of time for that. And besides, we wanted you to come with us or we wouldn't have asked. Don't worry, we'll be smooching away to our heart's content later.'

Karl raises his eyebrows and slips his hand in mine. 'That sounds good to me.'

Emily lifts her finger and points it straight at us. 'Listen you two, don't be going and getting all lovey dovey on me now. I'm warning you both!'

'What? Emily you started it!' I protest in humour, whilst Karl begins planting kisses over my cheek.

'Sssh! Will you all shut your big mouths, don't you

know the film is about to start? You young ones, anything for a carry on!' A not-so-amused elderly lady, sitting in front of us, turns around to give us a good telling off. 'Now shut your fat gobs and let me hear the film in peace!' she growls as she snaps a huge piece of chocolate from a bar in her hand and shoves it into her mouth.

She curiously reminds me of an old headmistress of ours who took no messing from any of us. We daren't cross her path at school. A closer look reveals she is in fact the same woman. A shudder runs up my spine as I recall on many an occasion getting strapped across the hands or back of the legs, most of the time for the silliest of reasons. As a youngster I was terrified of her.

'Emily,' I whisper, 'look, it's Mrs Friel.'

Emily opens her mouth in shock and makes a face behind the old teacher's back.

We sit for the remainder of the film as quiet as mice, too afraid to speak, and besides we are so engrossed in the storyline none of us wants to talk to each other. As soon as Doctor Jekyll drinks the potion that turns him into the evil Mr Hyde, allowing his dark side to run wild, the hairs are standing on the back of my neck. I don't bury my head into Karl's arms as I'm so immersed in the movie; not wanting to miss a second of it.

The picture show comes to an end and the lights switch on.

'Hey, I thought you two wanted to cheer me up, that scared the wits out of me!' Emily giggles. 'I'm only joking. I have to say I enjoyed it.'

'Good,' Karl replies and pretends to wipe a layer of sweat from his forehead. 'So we don't have to bring you back next week then? We don't want you to feel like a *gooseberry* do we?'

Emily playfully pushes him, 'Oh get lost you.'

'I'm only kidding, you know you're welcome to come with us anytime.'

'Aye I know, and thanks, guys.'

'You're welcome,' I smile.

'Right,' Karl rubs his hands. 'Let's go and get some fish and chips.'

'Sounds good to me,' Emily beams.

After leaving Emily at home, Karl and I walk hand-in-hand towards my house. Nerves begin to form in the pit of my stomach.

'What's up, Molly? You've gone very quiet.'

'Oh, Karl, there's been something niggling and gnawing at the back of my mind now for weeks.'

'What is it, honey?'

'Well ...' I stare into the distance, 'there's been no contact from Donal in a while, which is unusual for him. I've been trying to put the idea out of my thoughts, convincing myself that I'm just a compulsive worrier, but now as the weeks roll by and still nothing from him, I'm starting to panic. I'm growing really concerned that something has happened to him.'

'Molly, don't worry. He's probably so busy he might have forgotten to post the letter; I've done the same myself,' he smiles.

'Aye, you're probably right, and knowing our Donal that's something he has done.'

At the front door, I kiss Karl goodnight and watch him jog down the street until he is out of sight.

Inside, my mother is sitting at the kitchen table, sipping tea and clinging to her rosary beads. I sense something is bothering her this evening, but, as usual, she does a great job of covering up her emotions. She's so good at hiding her inner feelings she should've been an actress I think, observing her brighten and smile as she catches sight of me.

'Hi, love, where's Karl?' She takes another drink of her tea.

'He's gone. He's back on duty tomorrow morning.'

'How was the movie, dear?'

'Aye, it was great, we enjoyed it and Emily seemed happy to get out of the house for a while.'

'What did you watch?'

'We went to see the same one that Mick saw last week – Doctor Jekyll and Mr Hyde.'

'Oh, I hear it's spooky, don't think I would like it.'

'To be honest I didn't think I would enjoy it, but I have to say, it's the best film I've ever watched.'

'That's good. You like spending time with Karl, you and him have grown very close.' She stares at me in silence for a few uneasy moments.

Why has she changed the subject so quickly? Instantly I can almost read her thoughts. She must be thinking I better not get myself into trouble again. Paranoia engulfs my brain and rage at once pumps through my veins. It seems that no matter what I do I'll never be able to escape my history. It isn't fair. I want to scream my anger across the table, but hold back.

After a few minutes, sensing the awkward silence, she leaps from her chair and makes her way towards the teapot. 'Would you like a cuppa, love? It's still warm enough and there's some fresh scone left.'

'No thanks, I'm okay.'

Her statement has upset me, and together with the worry of Donal on my mind, it's the last thing I need. As much as I try to free myself from the past the reality is I'll never be able to, and if anything has happened to Donal the pain of living without making amends with him will be an unbearable weight to carry.

'Are you sure? Sit down, love, have one with me. I'll make you something else to eat if you don't fancy scone.'

'No! I don't want anything. I'm not hungry, and besides, we picked up some fish and chips earlier.'

'Are you sure?'

'Aye. I'm going to my bed, I'm tired.' I retire to my room, disgusted with myself and my mother. I could feel her eyes on me as I left the kitchen, but I didn't look at her. She had hurt me badly. She may as well have taken a knife and pierced it through my heart, opening the old wounds.

Alone in my quarters, tears begin to flow. I cry silently into my pillow before falling off to sleep.

Next day, after Sunday Mass, I lock myself away for most of the day, not wanting to face any of the others.

I awaken early on Monday morning to the sound of chatting from the wireless downstairs and the chirping from birds in the nearby trees, letting me know they're up and I'm not. As I draw back the curtains, the glorious sunshine immediately fills the room. My attention is drawn to my mother in the garden below; she's digging out some weeds from the flowerbeds. A solemn expression is etched on her pretty face. She takes great pride in keeping her patch well maintained, but she also tends to busy herself about her shrubbery when something is bothering her or when she feels under stress. I watch her for a while and observe how she digs the spade deep into the soil and tosses it about in a careless fashion, clearly out of character for her. She must've sensed that someone was watching her. She moves around and peers up at me. Our eyes meet briefly for a few seconds before she turns away and reverts her attention back to her task. This makes me feel uncomfortable, and only adds to the anger that I'd felt the previous night. I decide to go down and confront her.

Outside I'm greeted with the soft, warm breeze, the sparrows singing in the trees and sheep bleating in the distance. Bees swarm about, gathering pollen from the vast amount of colourful flowers that decorate our garden.

I can feel the tension. 'Mother, what's the matter with you?' I spit my words out, interrupting her thoughts.

Without raising her head she answers, 'Nothing, dear.' Again, she sinks the spade into the ground, penetrating it deep into the earth and throwing it sloppily about.

'Don't nothing me!' I snap back. My words sound cruel and hostile.

She turns her gaze towards me, looking shocked and

confused at my sudden outburst which has surprised both of us.

'I know what's bothering you,' I continue. 'You're worried about the relationship I'm having with Karl, isn't that right?' I accuse, my temper flaring up within me, to the point I almost forget who I am speaking to. I didn't realise I was going to yell until it was coming out of my mouth.

'No, Molly, you're wrong.' She shakes her head in disagreement.

'Aye, I know you are!' I snarl. 'It's easy to tell when something's bothering you. What are you afraid of? Are you scared I'll land myself in bother again and leave you to bring up another one of my offspring? You think I'm a filthy, evil girl that goes around ...'

'Stop!' She holds up her hand. 'You pause right there, young lady.' She raises her voice slightly and points her finger at me. It's my turn now to feel stunned and speechless whilst she speaks with such authority. 'Why don't you let the whole street know your business?' she lowers her voice to a whisper. 'It's been hard enough to keep your secret, and here you are shouting it out all over the place.'

I lower my head in shame at my paranoid outburst. Her words have just brought me down to earth with a bang.

'You're right about one thing; the notion of you getting into trouble again did cross my mind. Aye it has, and there's nothing wrong with that, but I've had to sweep those thoughts to the back of my mind because, Molly, I have to trust you. I also know deep down that you regret your actions. I don't believe you'll make the same mistake again.' She pauses to gather herself together. I can tell she doesn't want to cry, if she starts it's likely she won't be able to control all those tears that have been stored up over the years.

'I'm sorry, I won't get into trouble again.' My shoulders slump in shame.

'You would be a very foolish young girl to do so. I don't believe our family could handle another matter like that. You've seen what it's done to Donal. The scandal has destroyed him, and your relationship with him has been damaged forever. Molly, you've acted selfishly in the past and I've been here for you to help pick up the pieces. I've stood by you and supported you through the worst stages of your life. I've helped you to return back to some kind of normality. In a way I'm glad that you've met Karl, he's a wonderful young man. He's very decent. I want to see my children happy, and not sad or hurting. As a parent, I feel the pain more when my children are suffering. I would gladly exchange places with my kids and take on their hurt rather than see them miserable; it's what any loving and caring parent would do. In fact I would die for each of you.' She pauses and lifts a strand of my hair that had blown across my eyes and places it neatly in place. 'I love you, Molly, but I think you need to stop being selfish and thinking of yourself. My worries have nothing to do with you and Karl.' She swallows hard and gazes into the distance for a few uneasy minutes. 'If you want to know the truth, I'm worried sick about Donal. I don't know if you've noticed, but I haven't received anything from him since he wrote to you on your birthday.'

Her words hit me hard, like a punch in the face. She has knocked the wind from my sails.

I'm disgusted with myself. How could I have been so self-centered? I wish the ground would open up and swallow me into it.

'You're right. I'm so sorry. I have noticed he hasn't been in contact, and to tell you the truth, I have been concerned too, but I have tried to put it out of my mind.' I reach over and take her hand and give it a squeeze. 'I'm sure Donal will be okay. Karl said he's probably forgotten to send the letter.'

She embraces me and holds me in her arms. 'Donal will be fine, love, I promise he will be just fine.' She rocks me gently in her arms. My mind reflects on her words, and as always she brings peace to my heart.

'You hit the nail on the head, when you referred to me as being selfish. How could I have ignored your pain? It's been difficult enough for me but it must be so difficult for ...'

'Ssh, love, don't worry, I understand. Anyway, I'm sure he's okay. I've been storming Heaven with my prayers, I'm certain someone up there's listening to me.' She holds the same loving smile on her rosebud lips regardless of her mood.

A loud bang on the front door startles us. 'I'll get it, Mother, you stay here.'

I jump to my feet and make my way inside the house. On opening the door I come face to face with a smart-looking telegram boy. My heart skips a beat. The lad smiles sheepishly. My mind goes into turmoil; I recall Mick mentioning that the nickname for telegram boys is 'Angels of Death' since the war began, because they only usually come to notify the relatives that family members are either killed or missing in action. Seeing the look on his angelic face I know he's here with bad

289

news.

His eyes fall to the ground, then quickly dart back to meet my gaze. He opens his mouth and blurts. 'The Ministry of Defence regrets to announce that Lance Corporal Donal O'Connor is missing in action, feared killed. Letter to follow.'

Chapter 29

My body freezes. His words float about my brain as I try to take in the news.

'There must be a mistake. Donal's not dead!' I cry in disbelief, shaking my head to and fro, slowly at first then picking up speed, until I'm moving it frantically from side to side. 'No, no, no, no. He's not dead!'

'I'm sorry, ma'am, I'm so sorry for your loss,' the Angel of Death mumbles before stepping backwards to retrace his steps and make his way swiftly down the street on his rusty bicycle, without turning his head. He soon disappears out of sight. With his job complete he clearly wants to get away as quickly as possible.

There's no way I can break this news to my mother now, especially after our argument. This latest blow will break her heart, perhaps even destroy her forever. I walk towards the back garden in a trance. I can hear the sweet sound of her humming a Glen Miller tune. I pause at the kitchen window and watch her for a few minutes. Her mood has changed. She appears cheerful now as she digs at the flowerbeds. She looks too happy, I can't spoil the moment, it would be unfair. Right now isn't a good time, but, then again, when is a suitable point to spring an announcement like this on her?

I decide not to return to the garden; it will be too difficult to face her. I won't be able to look into her eyes and act normal. Instead, I retire to my room in an attempt to gather my thoughts. As I lie on the bed staring at the ceiling above, the news suddenly hits me hard. My body trembles and warm tears start to trickle over my cheeks, forming a pool on my pillow. I haven't felt this bad in a long time.

My mind reels unable to accept that Donal could possibly be gone. 'There's no way! He couldn't be,' I cry. My tears flow like a waterfall.

I spring upright. 'Maybe it's a mistake,' I whisper. 'Aye, it had to be an error.' After all there's been no body found yet, to prove that he's deceased. The telegram boy did say 'feared dead', he didn't say he's definitely dead. I jump off my bed. I'll go and chat to Emily, I think. Downstairs, my mother has begun to peel the potatoes for the evening's dinner and is still humming the tune from earlier.

'Who was at the door earlier, love?' she questions with a smile.

'Oh it was only a beggar,' I lie, hiding my tear-stained face. I peer out the window and chew on my bottom lip, hoping she won't sense the deceit in my voice.

'Oh, we haven't seen any beggars about now for weeks; hope you found something to give them, Molly.'

'Aye, I gave him some bread and eggs,' another fib rolls from my tongue. I hate being dishonest. 'Are you finished working in the garden?' I query in an effort to try to change the subject.'

'Yes, it looks well with all the weeds gone.'

'It does indeed. I'm going to take a run down to see how Emily's doing. I'll take a loan of Mick's bicycle. I don't feel like walking today.'

'Okay, tell Emily I said hello.'

I make my way to the front door, without looking at my

mother, feeling relieved to be out of her sight for fear that she will notice that I am telling her a string of lies. I jump onto Mick's bicycle and I'm just about to cycle away when the sound of the front door opening stops me in my tracks.

'Molly, you haven't eaten anything yet. Do you want me to make you a sandwich before you go?'

'No I'm fine thanks, I'll get something later,' I call over my shoulder.

'Okay, love, I'll see you for dinner.'

I cycle to Emily's as fast as my legs can move. The street has improved since the bombing a few months earlier, although some households remain unfixed, their doors and windows still boarded up. Some families haven't yet returned; the memories of losing their homes and having to rebuild them is perhaps much too painful, and then there's those that have sadly lost loved ones. Who knows if they'll ever find the strength to come back here.

I come to a halt at Emily's front gate and stop to gather my breath. Emily is sprawled out on an old, wooden chair basking in the sun's warm rays.

'Hi, Molly,' she grins.

I rest the bicycle against the fence and open the gate, fighting back tears as I make my way up the garden path. My legs feel like jelly.

'Hey, a girl's got to get herself a good tan,' she teases as she watches me approach. Her smile quickly fades as she detects something is wrong.

'Molly, what's up, love? You look as if you've just seen a ghost!' She flashes me a weak smile.

I sit down on the lawn beside her and peer up at the beautiful, blue sky. I can't find the words to tell her.

'Molly?' Emily squints against the strong sun.

'You're not going to believe this,' I sigh. 'I've just been informed by a telegram boy that Donal's missing and feared dead. He said a letter will follow.'

'What?' Emily covers her mouth with her hand. 'Oh, Molly, no way! No, it must be a mistake.' She shakes her head in disbelief.

'I haven't told anyone yet. What am I going to do?'

'Molly, I, I don't know what to say.' She jumps off the chair and sits down on the grass. 'You haven't told your mother?'

'No, I couldn't tell her. Maybe I should wait till teatime, when all the family are together to inform them at the same time? Or maybe I should just talk to her before the others come in? Then again, I was thinking perhaps I should just ignore it and hope that it's all been a huge mistake.' I search her eyes, looking for an answer.

She shakes her head. 'No, Molly, I don't think you should ignore it. After all, didn't the telegram boy say a letter would follow?'

I bury my head in my hands. 'Oh dear, aye, he did say that. Oh, Emily, what will I do?'

'Well then, you really must discuss this with your mother before that letter arrives. It'll be better to hear news like that coming from you. I can't imagine the shock she'll get when she opens that mail.'

I run my hand over my tired eyes and forehead, and

groan. 'Why does life have to be so cruel? It seems as soon as I get over one hurdle there's a higher one waiting for me. You're right; I'm going to have to break it to her.'

Emily places her hand on my shoulder. 'Do you want me to come with you?'

'No, it's better if I go myself, I need to tell her as soon as possible.' A boulder formed in my throat and tears develop in my eyes. 'What was I thinking? I should've disclosed this information to her straight away. I'm such a silly...' Tears escape and roll down my cheeks.

'Oh, Molly. Don't cry, love.' She places her arms around my shoulders.

'I need to get home.' I bounce to my feet. 'I'm going to head off, Emily. I don't know what came over me, I shouldn't even be here. I really ought to be with my mother.'

'You've had a terrible shock. Listen, if there's anything I can do for you just let me know.' Emily reaches for her shoes and places them on her feet. She links her arm around mine and walks with me to the gate. 'Molly, I'll be thinking of you.' She gives me a hug before I get back on the bicycle and cycle out of the street.

The possibility of Donal being alive is slim; he would never leave it this long to get in touch. I feel selfish for leaving my mother alone and can't wait a second longer to get back to her. I should never have left in the first place, but I panicked and didn't know what else to do. Determined to get home as fast as possible, I push down hard on the pedals. Minutes later I arrive at the front door and pause outside before entering. 'Dear God, help me once again,' I whisper. This will be the hardest thing I've ever had to do.

Thankfully my mother is alone, sitting on her favourite spot on the settee, reciting the rosary in silence. On hearing me enter the living room she lifts her head and nods to acknowledge my presence, although she doesn't speak. She never talks whilst praying and doesn't like being interrupted during her moments with God. I sit down beside her with a need to get this over and done with; she has a right to know about her son.

'Mother, I've got something to tell you,' I murmur, my voice barely audible and my body trembling with nerves.

She turns her attention towards me, blesses herself and places her wooden rosary beads on her lap. 'What's up, love?'

My mouth becomes so dry it feels like a fur boot. It's difficult to speak. 'I lied to you earlier.'

A puzzled look spreads over her face. 'What do you mean?'

'There was no beggar at the door earlier.'

'No? Who was it then?'

'I don't know how to tell you this.' I hesitate, shaking now more than ever. 'It … it was a telegram boy.'

Her eyes widen, 'Donal! It's Donal, isn't it?'

I nod. I can no longer speak, my lips feel glued together and my throat parched. I observe how her top lip curls a little. The next few seconds will haunt me for the rest of my life.

I am still watching her when the most awful high-pitch shriek erupts from her mouth. She howls as she springs to her feet, clutching her chest, her rosary beads fling across the room. She wails fiercely as she makes for the front door and runs out onto the street. The terrible noises sound like an animal being shred to pieces in the wilderness. It goes on and on until all the neighbours emerge from their homes to investigate the commotion.

Her cries transform into screams, as she begins to yell over and over again. 'My son, my son, what have they done to my Donal?'

Never in all my life have I witnessed such emotion from my mother. I run to her, and arrive at her side along with a few of the neighbours. She gives a final shriek and collapses into my arms.

Chapter 30

Karl's aqua blue eyes scan the walls of our living room; his attention is drawn to the portrait of Donal, Sadie and myself.

'That's a lovely picture. You're all very young.' He gazes affectionately at the artwork.

'Aye, my father sketched it about a year before he passed away. Drawing was his favourite pastime.' Recalling the memory warms my soul.

'Your innocent faces portray a happy family life,' he replies as he flashes me one of his charming heart-melting smiles.

My eyes fill with tears. 'Aye, we were happy, especially Donal and I. We were very close.'

'I picked up on that, from the many stories you've told me.'

'Karl, we were inseparable. I can't believe he's gone.' A tear escapes and trickles down my cheek. 'I'm going to miss him terribly.'

Karl pulls me closer. 'Molly, I wish I could take away your pain.'

I sniff and wipe my cheek with the back of my hand. 'I'll make us a cup of tea. I know we planned to go for a picnic today but, if you don't mind, I'd rather stay here. I'm not in the mood to go out.'

'Of course I don't mind. We'll go another day. I'll make the tea, you sit where you are.' He bends down to stroke my hair back from my face. 'Do you want me to make you something to eat?'

'No, I'm not hungry, just a cuppa thanks.'

'Molly, you really need to eat something, it'll keep your strength up.' Karl smiles sympathetically.

'No, Karl, honestly I'm okay.'

'Fine, I'll not force you,' he replies, his tone soft and understanding.

I sit alone in the sitting room whilst he leaves to make the tea. It's difficult for me to accept Donal's gone, and it's equally hard not to blame myself for his death. Of course it's my fault: if it wasn't for the way our relationship turned out, and the atmosphere at home, Donal wouldn't have felt the need to run away, to escape from the situation. If only we had sorted things out before it got as far as it did, maybe things might have worked out differently.

It seems a gloomy cloud looms over me, a cloud of misery and misfortune, that affects my life and everyone else close to me, and so the urge to lock myself away again becomes overwhelming. I can feel my mood slipping into darkness once more, and this frightens me. I can't return to those days, and I mustn't allow the depression to get a hold of me for a second time.

My brain feels like it is being split into two sections. Part of it wants to plunge myself into self-destruction, permitting me to give up on everything and everyone around me, including saying goodbye to Karl. The other part is telling me how blessed I am to come through what I did with such fantastic people to help me along the way, and what a long way that was. Those folk were there when I needed them the most and I will never forget that.

To take a step backwards now would hurt my mother. She's suffering enough without me adding to her worries. She has been my rock through the hardest times. I need to be strong now more than ever, for her sake. No matter how bad I feel right now, life must go on, and, regardless of how thorny the path in front of me is, I must continue my journey, looking ahead at all times.

I catch a glimpse of Karl through the half opened door between the living room and the kitchen. I drink in the sight of him, absorbing how handsome he is and my heart twists with emotion, goodness only knows what he sees in me, surely he could do much better. I observe how he delicately removes the teapot from the stove; he moves with such ease in our home, it feels like he's part of the family. He pours the tea into the cups and immediately wipes up some spillage from the counter. A comfortable feeling overwhelms me; he's a good man and I'm so blessed to have him. Fortunately for me, he entered my life at the right time. Karl is unaware that he's helped me to learn to live again. He gave me a focus in life, a new road to take when I had felt cornered in a dead end.

I return my gaze to the family portrait. Almost at once a nervous feeling plunges to the pit of my stomach; our relationship isn't entirely based on honesty. It's unfair keeping the secret of Shane and the attack from him.

He loves and trusts me. I adore him dearly, but I can't stop thinking that I'm holding back my ability to cherish him fully because of the secret I'm hiding from him. Two people that love one another shouldn't hold secrets. They should know each other better than anyone else. No relationship can thrive or survive if it's based on dishonesty. A lie will always raise its ugly head in the end. Deceiving Karl has riddled me with guilt. It's forever in my conscience and I desperately yearn to tell him the truth. I've lived with these fibs for long enough, but the fear of how he will react scares me. Confused and in turmoil my mind is filled with mixed emotions, scattering into every available space in my thoughts.

'Molly, your tea is going to go cold.' I have been so preoccupied by my dilemma, I hadn't noticed Karl had come in from the kitchen and is sitting beside me again on the settee.

'Oh, Karl, if only you knew the half of it,' I sigh, taking a gulp of the lukewarm tea and raising my eyes to the ceiling.

'I know this is a difficult time for you, Molly.' Karl takes my hand and holds it gently in his.

I glance at him and as soon as my eyes meet with his, I know instantly; I can't allow myself to deceive such a decent man any longer, even if it means losing him. He doesn't deserve to be lied to, and besides, I've let this go on for long enough. Never in my wildest dreams did I think we would've grown so close and fallen so deeply in love, and now that we have, it's time to be truthful with him.

'Karl, I need to tell you something.' I chew nervously on my bottom lip. My heart begins thumping in my chest. 'I haven't been fully honest with you and I'm sorry.' I pause and try to think of what to say next. 'You'll probably run a mile from me, and who could blame you.'

He shakes his head in confusion, 'Molly, I'm not sure I want to hear this if it's that bad.' His expression is blank. He's mystified by my words.

I breathe in a mouthful of air before continuing, 'I've lied to you for long enough.'

I stop again and watch him frown, a look of bewilderment mixed with fear sweeps across his face. 'Karl, something terrible has happened to me, something really bad.'

'What? What is it, Molly?'

'I've been attacked. I've been raped.' The words are out; there's no going back now.

'What?' Karl shouted. 'When? Who did this?' Anger quivers in his voice.

'It happened just over a year before I met you and it doesn't matter who did it, I don't want to talk about it,' my voice croaks as my eyes begin to gear themselves up for more tears, but I manage to hold them back. 'Emily and Aggie are the only two that know. I haven't told anyone else. I couldn't bring myself to notify the rest of my family, just like I couldn't disclose this to you. I hope you understand my reasons for keeping this to myself.'

Karl holds his head in his hands. His face turns crimson. He takes a deep breath. 'I'm shocked. You've hit me with two bombshells today; first Donal, and now this I, I don't know what to say, Molly.'

'I'm sorry, but there's a third,' I reply timidly.

He lifts his head and looks at me. The muscles in his jaw jerk. His chest heaves up and down rapidly, a look of disgust etched on his face. 'What?'

'Shane, he's...'

'He's your son?' Karl searched my eyes for an answer, his mouth gaped open like a goldfish.

I stare at him, not knowing what to say.

'He's your son, isn't he?' he nods.

I turn my gaze away, directing my attention instead to the floor, too embarrassed to look him in the eyes.

'Molly?'

'Aye, he is.'

'Shane's your son,' he repeated, shaking his head in disbelief and looking as if he had just swallowed a fly. 'Shane's your son!'

'I'm sorry, Karl. I should've told you by now, but I couldn't bring myself to do it. I'm so remorseful, and as I said earlier I'll understand if you leave me. I've kept it from you because I never predicted us to be together so long and certainly didn't expect to fall in love with you, and now that I have, it's not fair to keep this from you any longer.' I wipe away a tear. 'Sorry for wasting your time; you could've met a girl that doesn't have such baggage, and I'm sorry I've prevented you from that.' I babble on through the tears.

Karl pulls me closer. 'Molly, I'm not going to leave you. I love *you* and don't *want* anyone else,' he whispers. 'I understand why you didn't tell me.'

'You're not angry with me?'

'No! I'm fuming mad with the scoundrel that did such an awful thing to you.' Karl grits his teeth and punches the air with his fist. 'If I get my hands on him, I'll show him what a coward he is.' He lowers his head. 'Molly, I'm not ashamed of you, if anything I'm proud of what you've came through, but I can't understand why you didn't tell your family. Who do they think Shane's father is then?'

'They haven't got a clue because I refused to declare this, and they seem to have accepted that I'm not going to tell them. They've swept the matter under a rug, well, all except Donal. He never forgave me, and now that he's dead I have to live with the fact my brother and I never made amends,' I cry bitterly.

'Molly, come here.' Karl places his arms around me, and as I fall into him I begin to cry my heart out.

'So, that's the reason there was conflict between you two? I've always wondered what went wrong.'

'Aye,' I nod through the sobs. 'Donal never forgave me for bringing shame to myself. If only I'd told him the truth.'

'Molly, Donal did forgive you, he wouldn't have sent you a birthday greeting if he hadn't forgiven you. You have to believe that.'

'Maybe you're right, but that was the only time he acknowledged me. He ignored me in all of his previous letters.'

'It still proves that he was thinking about you.'

'Aye, but Karl, he's still going to his grave thinking his sister is ...' the bitter tears returned with such force.

'Molly, don't, you can't beat yourself up like this. You have to let those thoughts go. If you don't, you'll drive yourself insane. You need to speak to the police. You mustn't let this person get away with what he did. Not only has he damaged you, fathered a child that he doesn't know about, but he's also ruined your relationship with your brother. You also need to be honest with your family.'

'I'm unable to bring myself to do that, and besides, they have been through enough. They now have to deal with losing

Donal. There's no way I can cause them any more grief.'

'Okay, I understand that, but you must still report the matter to the authorities.'

'No way!' I shake my head.

'Molly, this is serious!'

'Karl, I can't, please understand that.'

'You mean you're going to let him get away with his crime, leaving him a free man so that he can attack again?' Karl replies in bewilderment.

'He might not,' I protest.

'Molly, be realistic! A monster like that will almost certainly strike again, if he hasn't done it already, especially if he thinks he's got away with it with you!'

I feel the old stirrings of anxiety in my gut and my whole body begins to tremble. What if Karl is right? What if he does assault another girl? I couldn't live with myself if that happened.

'I'm sorry, but right now I'm not strong enough to deal with making a statement. Maybe someday, Karl, but now is not a good time.'

'Okay, maybe in the near future then.'

'There's one last thing I need to tell you.' I remove my cardigan and display my scars. 'I didn't fall into barbed wire; I did this to myself.'

'Oh my ...'

'I'm sorry for the lies, I promise I'll never be untruthful to you again.' Tears escape and run uncontrollably down my cheeks. Karl pulls me closer to him once more, his familiar scent and warm embrace is so comforting. We sit together in silence for a few minutes.

'Molly, let's go for a bit of fresh air. I think we both can do with that walk after all.' He pulls me gently to my feet and slips on his jacket before linking his arm around my waist. I go with him reluctantly.

After a few minutes in the country air I soon realise he was right; the fresh air quickly helps to lift our spirits. We climb up the steep path behind my house and enter the "Amelia Earhart Field".

We sit ourselves down on the soft grass and absorb the magnificent scenery as we have done so often in the past; only this time we both remain silent, pondering over the events of the day.

Karl places his arm around my shoulders and whispers, 'Do you know something, Molly? I'm proud of you, honey.'

I throw him a surprised glance. 'What?'

'I'm proud of you for having the strength and courage to tell me the truth. It must've been difficult for you. I guess you're suffering terribly with not being able to tell the others.'

'Aye, but I try not to think about it any longer. It's in the past where it ...' A small, black, velvet box stops me from continuing. I watch as it slips from Karl's pocket and hits against a rock, protruding from the grass. The impact causes it to open a little. 'What's that?'

'What?'

'That, it just fell from your jacket pocket,' I point at the box.

'Oh it's ...' Karl's face turns slightly red. He leans forward to pick up the object and with a sheepish grin he shrugs his shoulders. 'Oh dear, oh dear, oh dear. I guess the surprise is spoilt then.'

My heart does a somersault in anticipation of what is coming next.

'Well, since you've seen it, I may as well carry out what I had planned to do today,' Karl nervously replies. He gets down on one knee and opens the lid to reveal a beautiful solitaire diamond ring. It sparkles and glistens in the sun.

'Molly, I'd intended to ask you today, but with the sad news of Donal I decided to postpone it. However, now that you've seen the ring, I may as well go ahead. I know today isn't the greatest day to ask you but ...'

Karl looks deep into my eyes and takes my hand in his. 'Molly, I love you and I always will. I'd like you to be my wife. Will you marry me?'

Needless to say, I almost faint!

Chapter 31

Despite her heartbreak, my poor mother continues with her life. She cried herself to sleep that night and continued to sob as she lay in bed throughout the next day. But she's a fighter and so she got up the next evening, dried her eyes, and came down to face the rest of us. Once the tears had stopped, that was the end of them. Life must, and will, go on.

She throws her energy into what she does best: being a mother, carer and cleaner. Her efforts are thrust into looking after Shane, cooking for us and ensuring the house is spotless. In fact, half of the time there's no need to clean our home, or tidy the garden, but perhaps it's her way of dealing with her loss.

Her sparkle is gone. No matter what kind of false face she puts on, it can never hide the pain. She gets her fair share of suffering, more so than other folks, but handles hardships well, believing that suffering is a gift from God. She is often heard saying '*Jesus saves one of his precious thorns for those dear to him, allowing them to share in his passion.*' This latest thorn is sure to be the sharpest.

Hurt through physical pain can always heal, however, emotional injuries can leave bigger scars that will fade, but will never go away. My mother has emotional wounds that bring with them the memory of losing her young husband, my pregnancy, and now losing her beloved son Donal, her only blood son. Charlie and Shane are as precious to her as her own children, but the reality is she never gave birth to them, and although she loves and treasures them, we know she doesn't hold the same bond with them that she has for Donal, the bond that comes only with childbirth.

Lots of tea and sympathy from the neighbours are helpful in a way. She appreciates their concern, but what good is that? It can't bring Donal back, and it certainly won't heal her broken heart.

Father McGroarty visits her daily since hearing the news; his words bring her little comfort, but I know they will remain in her memory, and perhaps one day, when the shock is over, his guidance might be a benefit to her.

Seven days have passed since the telegram boy paid his visit. My mother waits patiently to receive the letter that he promised would follow. She remains each day by the window, staring out to the street in anticipation.

'Can I get you a cuppa?' I sit beside her on the sofa and observe how terribly pale she looks today.

'No, Molly, I'm fine,' she replies in a hoarse tone.

She places one hand across her chest and the other she uses to cover her mouth, as she explodes into a fit of coughing.

'That's an awful cough you have, you really should be in your bed.'

'Don't worry about me, I'm fine.' She forces a smile, but her eyes can't conceal the sorrow.

'You know, you don't have to hide your pain. It's okay to cry.' I place my arm around her shoulder.

'Crying is a waste of energy, Molly. No matter how many tears I release, nothing will bring back my son.'

'Aye, that's true, but it can make you feel better. Trust me, a good cry will help.'

'I feel numb, I don't want to weep. I'm in limbo, not knowing if Donal is dead, and, if so, how he died. Deep down, I know that he's gone, there's no other reason for him to stop writing to me. I want him found and returned to us; not having a body to bury and a grave to visit is unbearable to think about. I need his remains back home, to give him a proper burial. I won't rest, Molly, until that's accomplished.'

I'm touched by her strength. I can feel my eyes water and I try to compose myself. Not wanting to blubber in front of her, I leave the room to return to my bedroom.

The familiar rattle at the front door causes my heart to skip a beat. As much as I have longed for this letter to arrive, I've also dreaded it coming. It will finalise the fact that Donal is gone from our lives forever. I want to jump into bed and hide under the blankets, but change my mind; my mother needs support today more than ever, and so I reluctantly make my way back downstairs.

'Hello there, Mrs O'Connor. How are you doing today?' the postman beams, oblivious to our turmoil, but his smile shrinks when he witnesses the painful appearance on both our faces. 'You look as if someone died, surely things aren't that bad.' He releases a hearty laugh, trying his best to cheer us up.

I want to scream at him for his stupidity, but, in the presence of my mother, I stop myself.

'Well, I hope this letter from Donal cheers you up a bit, I know you wait patiently for his correspondence.' He flashes a grin again before offering the letter to my mother.

I roll my eyes, 'Donal! It's not from Donal, you fool ...'

310

'Molly! Watch your manners.' Her hand quivers as she retrieves the envelope from him. 'I'm sorry for her outburst, but my son is ...' Her body trembles and she pauses, 'Donal, is dead.' She shakes her head in disbelief. 'He must have written this before he passed away.' A tear rolls from her sad eyes and trickles down her cheek followed by another one, and another, and another, until they escape from their prison and fall uncontrollably.

'Oh, Mrs O'Connor, don't weep, please don't cry. I didn't mean to upset you.' He reaches into his pocket and pulls out a handkerchief. 'Here take this, it's clean.'

'Thank you,' she sniffs.

'I don't know what to say to you, except I'm so sorry to hear that. I'd no idea.' He removes his peak cap and places it across his chest. 'Donal was a great young man, I'm truly remorseful for your loss.' He replaces his cap back on his head and looks awkwardly at both of us.

'Thanks, and I'm sorry for calling you a fool.'

'Oh, don't worry about that. I'm the one that needs to be sorry.'

The poor man leaves looking terribly embarrassed.

My mother stares at the familiar handwriting. Donal's bold scrawl jumps from the tear-stained envelope. 'The postman is right, Molly. It's definitely from Donal!'

Chapter 32

My mother clutches at her chest once more, and I watch in horror as she begins coughing with such force.

'I'm worried about you.'

'I'm okay,' she gasps. 'Oh, my ribs hurt.' She looks at the letter in her hand and releases an exhausted sigh before running her fingers across the seal and opening it.

'Is it any wonder, that cough has been tormenting your lungs for the past few days. You need to see ...'

A sudden cry from Shane stops me. 'I'll get him.' I race upstairs.

Shane's angelic face brightens as he observes me entering the room. A weak smile forms on my face. I can't help but feel guilty. Little does the poor child know how much I once detested him.

'Molly! Come down here, quick!'

I pick up Shane and dash back downstairs. 'What? What is it?'

'Here, read this.' She hands me the letter.

'Hello Mother,

I've heard the rumours that I'm supposed to be dead, well, assumed dead. They've told me they've even sent a telegram to inform you of my disappearance. I hope it hasn't reached you yet, and, if it has, you can bin it (that is if you're still living after that kind of news!). Well, Mother, you can breathe again because I'm still alive (well, just about!).

I got myself injured and separated from the others; there

was chaos and everyone began to run to safety, but I was unable to get away and I passed out. The next thing I knew, I awoke being peered at by an elderly couple. They took me in and nursed my wounds as best as they could until they managed to get me proper medical treatment. I'm so grateful to them both. I'll tell you all the details when I see you.

Well, now for the good news. I've just had surgery on my leg and I've been told I should be home in the next few weeks. I can't wait to see you all!

Take care, see you soon.

Love,

Donal.

I read over the note again, the words barely seem real. I feel as though I'm in a dream, just waiting to wake up at any minute to find that no letter exists.

My mother raises her eyes to the ceiling and shouts, 'Lord, thank you, thank you so much!'

I turn and look into her eyes and together we scream aloud with joy. She throws her arms around me and we dance about on the spot like two children.

Mick enters the room, 'What's going on?' he looks at both us, bewilderment etched on his face.

'You're not going to believe it, Mick!' I screech. 'Donal's alive, and he's coming home!'

Chapter 33

Our family gather around the dinner table that evening and we eat our food with joy in our hearts. It's wonderful to see such bliss in their faces. 'Listen, folks, I've got some more good news for you all.'

My mother throws me a curious look. 'I like the sound of this.' She smiles before covering her mouth with a hankie and coughing with such force.

'I'll tell you in a minute, I just have to nip upstairs first.'

I remove the sparkling ring from under my pillow and slide it on my finger. It fits perfectly. I smile to myself; it's been such a long time since I felt this happy, I'm pleased that I can now show it off to the family.

I race downstairs, my heart thumping with excitement. Since immediately accepting Karl's proposal, I've chosen not to wear the ring; it didn't feel right in light of the circumstances. But now the confirmation has arrived that Donal's okay, it's time to parade my treasured possession to the world and to announce the wonderful news.

I enter the kitchen, my face beaming with delight and I'm surprised to find Sadie has arrived.

'I've just heard about Donal. Oh, Molly, I'm so thrilled. Thank goodness he's okay. Mick was just saying that you've some good news too. What is it?'

I hold my left hand up in the air, and at once the room fills with gasps as my diamond glistens in their eyes.

'You're getting married!' Sadie screams. 'No way?'

I nod, grinning from ear to ear.

'Molly, come here!' Sadie embraces me in a breathtaking hug. 'It's about time that man of yours got his act together!' She throws her head back and laughs. 'Ah, sis, I'm over the moon for you!'

I watch as my mother's already joyful expression seems to bloom with shock or with bewilderment, I'm not sure, but it's a look that pleases me. I witness the gleam in her eyes and my heart warms.

'Molly, I'm so proud of you.' My mother's eyes are filled with tears. 'Darling, you've made me the happiest woman in Derry right now.' She swallows back her tears. 'My heart is ready to explode. This day can't get any better!'

'I'm glad to make you feel happy for a change.'

Mick sets his plate aside and gets up from the table. He shakes my hand and gives me a kiss on the cheek. 'Good on you, girl. You've met a great man. Karl's one in a million, and he's welcome in this family.'

'Thanks, Mick.'

Charlie looks up from the table, 'Congrats, Molly. Mick's right, Karl's one of the best.'

Anna makes her way over and puts her arms around my waist. I glance down at her, her innocent face gazes into mine. 'I'm happy for you but I'll miss you when you leave the house. I'll not have any sisters left here.'

'Oh, Anna, you're going to make me cry. You'll always have us. I'm not going to move to America, don't worry.'

'America! I never thought of that! Oh, Molly, you won't leave us, will you?'

315

'No, Mother, don't fret. Karl and I have already discussed that. I've told him I'm too much of a home bird – I could never leave Ireland. He's finishing his time in the Navy soon, and has said he doesn't mind us finding somewhere to live here when we're married.'

'Oh, thank the Lord,' she smiles, before her lungs are thrown into turmoil again as the awful cough returns.

The excitement is interrupted with her condition; she appears to be getting worse.

'Kate, I've noticed that splutter irritating your lungs, especially over the last few days. It's taking its toll on your body. I can tell you're weak; it's evident in your appearance, and you're very pale.'

'Don't worry, Mick, it's probably just from the lack of sleep.'

'What about the chest pains? You said yesterday that you had excruciating pains, have they gone?'

'No, but it's nothing to worry about. I'll be fine in a few days.'

'Kate, I think you need to see the doctor.' Mick looks at her sternly. 'That coughing is getting worse by the minute, never mind by the day!'

'Perhaps Mick's right, you don't sound too well. It'll do no harm to get it checked out,' Sadie sounds concerned.

'Okay, I'll go and see about it this week,' she mumbles, sounding extremely hoarse as she rubs her hand over her chest. She then gets up and begins to clear the dinner dishes.

'No,' Mick shakes his head in disagreement. 'I think you need to see him sooner rather than later, and put those down, Kate. We'll see to those.' He delicately removes the plates from her hands and directs her into the living room where he urges her to sit down on the sofa. 'I'm going to take a trip up to Doctor Devlin, see if he'll come down to view you today.'

'Wait till later, Mick,' my mother pleads as she coughes again into her handkerchief.

Mick frowns, 'No, I'm going now, it needs to be sorted. You didn't get a wink of sleep last night, I heard you up a few times in the middle of the night. I want him to see you today.' Mick holds up his finger. 'You stay right there and I'll bring you in a cup of tea.'

'I'll get the tea, Mick.' I stare at her in disbelief, taken aback at how pale she looks; her usual young, rosebud complexion is now that of a tired, gaunt old woman. I'm beginning to feel as concerned as Mick.

'I'll lie down, I'm feeling exhausted.' She settles herself on the sofa. She curls her legs and rests her eyes.

'I'll bring you in a cuppa.' I kiss her gently on her forehead; her skin feels unusually hot and clammy.

'Thanks, Molly.'

Mick follows me out to the kitchen. He leans close and whispers. 'Molly, keep an eye on her. I'll be back as quick as I can.'

'Okay,' I nod in obedience.

'Great, I'll not be long.' He glances at the others. 'Give Molly a hand to clean up this kitchen. You know the kind of your mother; she'll have a fit if the place isn't tidy when the doctor arrives.'

317

He places his peak cap on his bald head and looks around the kitchen for his coat. He spots it hanging over a chair and quickly retrieves it. He slips his arms into it and dashes out the door.

I watch from the window as Mick quickly jumps on his bicycle and hurries away; it's not long before he's out of sight.

Back in the living room my mother dozes on the settee. I kneel down and whisper in her ear. 'Mother, your tea's ready.'

Her eyes flicker.

'Do you want your tea?' I nudge her gently. She stirs and shakes her head, signalling a refusal. She begins coughing again, so fiercely her face turns bright crimson. She feels around the settee for her handkerchief, finds it, and uses it to cover her mouth.

A red substance spills into the tissue. 'Is that blood?' I gasp.

My mother frowns. It is clear from her expression she had hoped I hadn't seen the huge amount of blood that she has just coughed up. She clearly doesn't want to worry me.

'It's just a little, but it's nothing to be concerned about. I'll be fine.'

My thoughts return to Mick and how quickly he has dived out the door. He must've seen this happen too, that has to be the reason behind his speedy departure. 'Okay, I'll take your word for it,' I lie. 'Do you want this tea?'

'No thank you, darling, I don't feel like drinking right now.'

'Perhaps I can get you some food? You didn't take

much earlier. There's some soup left in the pot.'

'I'm not really hungry, love.'

'Are you sure? Mother you really ought to eat something.'

'I'll be okay honestly, darling. I'm in no mood to eat. I've no appetite, Molly.'

'Okay, if you insist,' I sigh helplessly.

The door bursts open and Mick enters, followed by Doctor Devlin. 'Come on in.'

Doctor Devlin gives me a curious look. 'How are you, Molly?' He kneels down by my mother and takes her hand.

'I'm fine, thanks,' I reply meekly.

'Well, Kate, I hear you're feeling slightly under the weather. Can you tell me a little about it? How long have you had the cough?'

He proceeds to pull out his stethoscope from his leather bag and places the two earpieces into his ears, before setting the chest piece on my mother's chest. Soon his eyebrows knit together in deep thought. 'Kate, is your cough wheezy or dry?'

'It's more of a dry, irritating cough,' she replies, sounding extremely weak, 'although I'm coughing up some mucus.' She threw a glance at me.

Mick interrupts, 'What about the blood, Kate?'

'I see.' He removes his stethoscope and replaces it in his bag. He brings out a thermometer and places it under her tongue.

'My goodness, Kate, your temperature is sky high. I'll give you some medication to bring it down. Molly, will you fetch some cold water and a sponge or a cloth? We need to

319

cool your mother down.'

I leave the living room at once and soon return with the items. Doctor Devlin soaks the cloth in the water and places it over her forehead. 'I was just saying to your mother, she looks as if she's lost weight from the last time I saw her, would you agree, Molly?'

'Aye well,' Mick interrupts, before I can answer. 'She does seem to have lost some weight, but she hasn't been eating properly the last few weeks.'

'I see, so have you lost your appetite too, Kate?'

'I suppose so. I don't feel like eating at the minute.'

'What do you think it is doctor, is it a chest infection?' Mick queries.

'No.' He shakes his head and looks directly at my mother, 'A dry, irritating cough lasting this long, high temperature, loss of weight and appetite, together with coughing up blood; I think it's more serious than a chest infection.'

'What do you think it is?'

'I'm afraid, Kate,' he pauses before continuing, 'I hope I'm wrong, but I think you have tuberculosis.'

A shocked, hushed atmosphere invades the room.

Chapter 34

Tuberculosis! My body freezes on hearing the diagnosis. It's a frightening disease, accounting for a vast amount of deaths of all ages. I don't know many people that have survived this dreaded illness. I glance at Mick; it's clear he feels the same anguish. He nods his head in agreement. He has obviously guessed that she has this disease.

Doctor Devlin releases a sigh, 'Kate, I'm afraid you may need to be admitted to hospital to fight this. I'm aware the wards are packed to their limits at the minute. I'll have to see what I can do; in the meantime you will have to be isolated from the others as much as possible.'

'That's fine,' she replies.

'Molly, I can hear talking in the kitchen, who's out there?'

'Sadie, Charlie and Anna.'

'Can you call them in? I need to have a word with them. I want to explain a few things regarding your mother's condition.'

'Okay.' I head for the kitchen. 'Listen, everyone, I've some bad news.'

'What's up?' Sadie asks.

'Sadie, it's not good. Doctor Devlin thinks mother might have tuberculosis; he wants a word with all of you.'

'No way!' Sadie screeches as she clambers from her chair.

They follow me into the living room in shocked silence.

'I'm sure Molly's told you why I've called you in.'

'Aye,' Charlie nods.

'I just want to give you some advice on your mother's condition. Tuberculosis is an infectious disease, caused by the bacterium mycobacterium tuberculosis. It's usually transmitted in airborne droplets, expelled when an infected person coughs or sneezes. Once the bacteria enter the lungs, they begin to multiply. However, the immune system usually seals off the infection at this point, with only about five percent of the cases spreading elsewhere in the body. As you know it can be life-threatening. Each of you must be careful when in contact with Kate.'

We all nod in agreement.

'Kate, I will prescribe you medication to fight this. You must ensure you take it, as instructed, in order for you to recover,' he says with a caring tone, 'Remember, when you cough or sneeze, please try to ensure you use a handkerchief at all times. It will help minimise the risk of spreading the germs into the air.'

'Okay, I will.'

Doctor Devlin smiles softly. 'Right, well, I'll leave you for now. I'll drop in tomorrow to see how you are. Take care, dear.'

'Yes I will, and thank you for your help,' my mother forces a weak smile.

He glances around the room, 'I don't want the rest of you catching this. Everyone must be so vigilant, and if any of you do show any signs of the infection please contact me immediately.'

Doctor Devlin walks towards the door; before he leaves

he stops and looks around. 'If you can arrange for Kate to be isolated in her own room, with as little contact with others as possible, it will be a great benefit to you all. Please also ensure that her handkerchiefs are disposed of properly after use.' His eyes fall on mine. 'I can hear a baby crying.'

Anna leaps off her seat. 'I'll get Shane.' She dashes upstairs.

'Okay, if there's anything else I can do for you, you know where I am. Goodbye and God bless you, Kate.'

'Thanks, Doctor Devlin,' my mother replies in a low voice, her beautiful eyes full of fear.

'I'll see you out.' Mick jumps to his feet.

'Okay, take care, I'll see you soon.' Doctor Devlin glances at each of us with a look of sympathy etched on his face.

I kneel beside my mother and take hold of her hand. 'You'll be okay, you'll fight this.'

'Of course I will.' She stops to cough again, a cough that appears to go on and on. 'I'll be back to my old self in no time, there's nothing to worry about, love.'

'Aye, well, if anyone can beat this, you can.' I try to sound as convincing as possible on the outside, whilst on the inside my tummy feels sick with worry.

My mother sits up, 'What's that noise?'

'What noise? I can't hear anything,' I shrug.

'Ssh, listen.' She holds a finger to her lips.

Thump, thump, thump, followed by soft whispers. Suddenly, the living room door opens.

'You'll never guess who's here!' Mick announces.

323

We watch, open-mouthed, as Donal shuffles in slowly on crutches.

'Donal!' My mother holds her hand over her mouth and stares at her son in disbelief. 'What are you doing here? I thought you weren't coming for weeks.' Her face lights up with joy. 'I only got your letter this morning.'

'I told you a little white lie. I wanted to surprise you. Ah, Ma, Mick's just after telling me you're not well, that's terrible news to come home to.' Donal looks really worried as he makes his way cautiously across the living room towards her, hobbling along with the aid of the crutches.

'Your leg, what happened to your leg, son?' she holds her hand over her eyes, 'Donal, what has happened to your leg?' she repeats.

'Never mind that, I'm more concerned about your health,' Donal shrugs his shoulders, as if to shrug off the question with it.

'Please, Donal, tell me what happened to you?' she questions again, sounding hoarser than ever.

He looks down at his stump of a leg. 'It had to be amputated from the knee down. It was too badly damaged to save. The doctors had no choice.'

Her face turns sour but before she can speak again, the dreaded cough dictates otherwise.

Donal sighs, 'But sure it could be worse, Ma, at least I'm still alive. That's the main thing,' he replies, attempting to sound as cheery as possible.

'If only you hadn't have joined the army in the first place,' she stops to catch her breath, before continuing, 'this would never have happened.'

Donal glances at me, our eyes meet briefly. 'Aye, well, there's no point in dwelling on it. I knew the risks before I went. And anyway, don't worry about me, there's no point in crying over spilt milk. I've no regrets.'

'So, that's why they sent you home then?' Sadie questioned.

'Aye, I think I can safely say, a one-legged soldier isn't any good to anybody, is he?' Donal laughs, trying to make light of the awkward situation.

I feel terribly sorry for him, but I just can't help myself and the words come blurting out. 'Well, it just goes to show you how fragile life is. You never know what's around the corner, do you? Life's far too precious for petty things.' I stare at him with a look of defiance but can feel my cheeks burning with guilt.

Seeing him back in the flesh brings back hurtful memories. There's no way I can deal with his childish behaviour again. I was at my weakest point in my life back then, but I've come a long way; I'm stronger now, much stronger. I can stand up to him this time. 'I'll make a fresh pot of tea.' I get up and make for the door.

'You're right, Molly, I agree.'

His words take me by surprise. I stop and turn around to face him. 'Good, I'm glad you do.' My heart is thumping. I really want to hug him and put the past behind us.

'I hear congratulations are in order, Mick's just told me you've got engaged. I'm pleased for you, and I'm looking forward to meeting Daryl.'

'Karl.'

'What?'

'Karl, his name's Karl, not Daryl.'

'Oh, right, sorry. Well, I'm looking forward to meeting Karl then,' Donal smiles sheepishly.

'Thanks. I'll get us a cuppa,' I reply making my way to the kitchen, thinking they are the most words Donal and I have said to one another in a long time. I'm interrupted by the living room door being opened once again. Nosy Nora's loud voice invades the area. What the heck does she want at this time in the evening? It's nearly time for the blackout. She should be in the house putting her children to bed. No doubt she's heard about Donal being back and has called in for a nosey. The curious, interfering sod makes me feel so angry at times.

'I was knocking away at the door – you mustn't have heard me – then I realised it was open all along. You never closed it properly,' Nora grins.

If I didn't know any better, I would have thought someone had just thrown plums at her face, her wee cheeks are so flushed. Perhaps she's on the booze already. 'Hello, Nora, what brings you here at this time of the evening?' I ask with a hint of sarcasm in my voice.

Nora ignores my question. Her attention is fixed on Donal and his missing limb. 'Gees, Donal boy, where the heck did you come out of, and what has happened to that leg of yours?' she folds her arms under her hefty bosom.

I sigh and roll my eyes. 'I'm away to make the tea.'

From the kitchen I can hear Donal filling her in on how he had got his leg injured in battle, and how the medical team had done everything they possibly could to save it. Soon the conversation changes to my mother's sickness. 'She's getting plenty of information for the neighbours tonight,' I whisper to myself.

'My goodness, I didn't even know you were sick, Kate, but coming to think of it, I didn't think you looked well the last day I saw you, thought you were quite pale looking, now, coming to think of it.'

'She's here for the night, by the sounds of it,' I sigh.

I place the cups of tea on the tray and make my way back into the living room.

'I hope you have a wee cuppa on that for me, for my mouth's like a fur boot,' Nora flashes me a cheeky grin.

'Of course, Nora, sure I wouldn't leave you out.'

'Gees!' Nora announces, ruffling her hands through her hair. 'Do you know something? I'm that busy chatting to you all about Donal and Kate. I nearly forgot to tell you what I came here in the first place for.' Nora rolls her eyes. 'That's not like me.'

'No, that's not like you,' I tease.

'No you're right it's not, Molly, I've usually a good memory on me. Well, did you hear the craic about that farmer's daughter?'

Mick holds up his hand and interrupts, 'Now, Nora, you know we don't like pointless gossip.'

Nora is aware her visits with scandal are unpopular in our home. 'Ah this isn't gossip. I can assure you of that, Mick. What's his name?' Nora rubs her head in thought, 'Mr Brown,' she bellows. 'Jack Brown's daughter, did you hear about her?'

Everyone nodded, signaling that we haven't heard anything about Jack's daughter, and, by the look on our faces, we don't want to hear.

'I just heard this today. Now you know me, I'm not one for tittle-tattle. I don't know if it's true or not, but I'm sure it must be and so I thought I'd better warn you anyway.'

Oh here we go again, I think. One minute she's telling us that she can assure us it's not gossip and then she tells us she can't be sure. Nothing changes with Nora.

Donal tuts impatiently.

'What is it, Nora?' Mick asks, sounding as if he couldn't care less what she says.

'I heard that his youngest daughter was out walking alone, out the back roads towards Muff, and got raped. Can you imagine, someone getting raped around here? Sure it's unheard off. It's ...'

My reaction to her news stops her from continuing.

Donal eyes me with suspicion as the tea tray slips from my hands, sending a clatter of cups to smash to the floor.

Chapter 35

'He loves me, he loves me not, he loves me, he loves me not.' I snatch the last remaining petal from the daisy. 'He loves me. Well, at least that's one comforting thought,' I whisper as I stare at the bald flower. I twist it between my thumb and forefinger before tossing it over my shoulder where it joins the others, scattered on the grass behind me.

'Talking to yourself is a sign of madness, don't you know that?' Emily laughs.

She startles me, making me jump with fright.

I look around. 'Perhaps I'm going mad then,' I reply in a slightly depressed tone. Emily collapses on the soft grass. I clutch my chest, 'Emily, you gave me a terrible fright there. You nearly scared the wits out of me, creeping up like that.'

Emily giggles. 'Sorry, I didn't mean to scare you. What's wrong with you now, love?'

'What's right?' I reply biting on my lower lip.

'Oh, I know, you're concerned about your mother. Mick's just after telling me about her. It's terrible news. You must be worried sick. She'll recover, Molly, she's a strong woman.'

'Aye, I hope so.'

Emily's eyes dart around the garden. 'She keeps this area beautiful. You can tell she puts a lot of work into it. I suppose you're looking after it for her at the minute.' Emily pauses, 'You're in a wee world of your own, Molly.'

I pluck another daisy and began to pull petal after petal from it, my thoughts a million miles away.

'I said, you're in a wee world of your own.' She leans closer and speaks louder into my ear, causing me to jump again.

'Gees, Molly, you're a nervous wreck today. There's something else bothering you, isn't there? Is it Donal? I was speaking to him on the way in. I hope he's not starting up all that nonsense again. If he thinks he's going to do your head in, he has another thing coming. I can't believe he's lost a leg. He seems to have accepted it, but I think it's all an act; he's just putting on a brave face for everyone.' Emily babbles on, she stops briefly to catch her breath. 'Molly, is it Donal?'

'No, no it's not Donal.' I rub a hand over my tired, puffy eyes, the result of yet another sleepless night. 'My head's so mixed up, I don't know if I'm coming or going at the minute.'

'Come here.' Emily puts her arm around my shoulder. 'Try not to be too concerned about your mother, she'll be grand. I know it's worrying for you, but she'll be okay.'

Emily lifts up my left hand. 'I hear congratulations are in order. Let's get a look at this ring. I hear from Sadie that it's stunning.' She gasps, 'Oh, Molly, it's beautiful. I'm so pleased for you. You must be full of excitement. At least the engagement is something to feel positive about at the minute.'

My gaze falls on my diamond ring. It sparkles brilliantly as it catches the sun. I'd almost forgotten about the engagement.

'Aye, but unfortunately so much negative stuff has outweighed the positive. The usual scenario in my life: as soon as something good happens to me, it's always followed with something doubly bad.' I twist the ring around my finger.

'Let's try it on, I want to make a wish.'

I slide the band off and hand it to her. She places it on her finger and turns it around several times, whilst closing her eyes tight to concentrate on her request. It's a tradition amongst the factory girls to make a wish when they try on an engagement ring. Frankly, not being one for superstition, I think it's a load of rubbish and something I never take part in.

Emily smiles contently before handing the ring back to me. I replace it quickly on my finger before blurting out, 'I guess you haven't heard the news about Mr Brown's daughter?'

'What about her? I haven't heard anything.'

My heart begins to thump. 'She was raped.'

'Raped? Jack Brown's daughter? What?'

'Aye, she was attacked around the same area ...' I stop, unable to continue.

Looking shocked and confused, her voice trembles, 'Molly, that's terrible news. Do you think it was the same ...'

I swallow hard. 'Aye, there's no doubt about it – of course it was him! He's done it to me and now he's struck again.' I bury my head in my hands. 'Dear God, what am I going to do?'

'Gees, Molly, I don't know what to say. I'm in shock, I can't believe it.'

I lift my head to look at her. 'It's my fault,' I reply tearfully.

Emily looks at me with so much love and pity. 'Don't think like that. Of course it's not your fault!'

'It is. If I'd gone to the police, this would never have happened. Karl's right; he warned me that he'd strike again, and now he has.'

'You've told Karl? How did he take it?'

I can't answer her. I'm overwhelmed with guilt and battle to hold back the tears, but it's no good; they fall from my eyes. 'My silence has allowed this to happen to that poor, innocent girl,' I sob.

'I can't believe he had the nerve to do it again.'

'No, I can't either. The sickening thing is he thought he got away with it with me, so he had the nerve to strike for a second time, or maybe it was his third, fourth or fifth time, God only knows. Oh, Emily, you've no idea how bad I feel right now. This news has me feeling like something's eating at my insides. That monster has caused so much trouble in my life; I'm never going to escape what he's done.'

'Oh, try not to blame yourself, Molly.' She sounds reassuring, but I can tell by her tone of voice that she agrees with Karl.

'I'll always blame myself; if only I had listened to you and Karl. I had the opportunity of doing something and I did nothing.'

'What are you going to do now? Are you going to make a statement?' Emily looks deep into my eyes. 'Molly, it's not too late to do something.'

'It's too late for Mr Brown's daughter. There's no point in going to the police now. Sure they'll be out looking for him anyway, besides, my family have enough on their plates without me adding to it again.'

'I can understand you not wanting to upset your family, but then again, Molly, there's never going to be a good time for this kind of news. You need to tell them and you need to go to the police. What happens if they never find him? What if Mr Brown's daughter wasn't able to identify him? Molly, you know who this rapist is and you must help in getting him caught.'

'No, I'm not going to the police,' I brush aside her protests.

'Why not?'

'I can't.' I pick up another daisy, and proceed to pull the petals one by one. 'My mother's not well. It's the last thing she needs to hear. She's over the moon with Donal being home, there's no point in upsetting her.'

'What do you think Karl's going to say?' Emily presses her lips firmly together. 'I know exactly what he will say.'

I sigh and throw the daisy over my shoulder. 'Aye, Karl will probably march me up to the police station.'

'Aye, and I hope he does! Think about it at least, Molly!' Her voice rises.

'I spent all of last night awake, thinking about it,' I shout back. 'That evil creep has caused me yet another sleepless night!' I squint my tired eyes against the glaring sun. 'Emily, what am I going to do?' I pause to take a breath; my body is now shaking uncontrollably. 'He raped me, left me pregnant and I've let him away with it, free to attack again. I wish I hadn't kept it to myself, but I did and I have to live with that! It's clear I've made the biggest mistake of my life. I really wish I had said something earlier, but it's too late now. It's too late now.' I twist my hair around my finger so tightly it hurts and wait for her response. Emily looks past me, her gaze fixated on something else. I turn around. 'What are you looking ...' my eyes meet Donal's, and standing next to him is Sadie.

Donal stares at me intensely. '*I* wish you had said something earlier too!'

Chapter 36

'Molly, you're going to tell our mother everything, and then you're going to the police, whether you like it or not!'

'I can't, Donal, she's too sick.'

'I don't care how sick she is, you owe it to her to be truthful. She will be devastated if she hears this from someone else, she needs to hear it from you!'

I bury my head in my hands and sob.

'Oh, Molly, don't cry, I didn't mean to upset you.'

'I can't help it, Donal. I've cried so much since the attack. I've no control over my tears anymore. I try to be strong, but I can't.'

'Is it any wonder you're tearful, Molly?' Sadie sits down on the grass next to me. 'You've had a terrible burden to carry.' She strokes my hair. 'Apart from Emily and Karl, does anyone else know?'

'Just Aggie,' I sniffle.

'You didn't have to go through this on your own; you really should've said something.'

'Donal, I was too scared to tell anyone else.'

Sadie takes hold of my hand. 'Listen, Molly, it's only a matter of time before the truth comes out, one way or another. A lie will go undetected for so long, but one day it will raise its ugly head to bite back; the truth always comes out in the end.'

I look at Sadie, then Donal. I know they're right. 'Okay,' I whisper, my voice barely audible. 'I'll tell her today.'

As Donal and I approach my mother's bedroom, my heart begins to thump in my chest. My whole body is shaking.

'Dear God, help me, please,' I whisper under my breath. I hold open the door for Donal to allow him to hobble into the room.

I sit on the edge of the bed. Donal sits on the chair opposite me. My gaze falls on the picture of the Sacred Heart of Jesus hanging on the wall above my mother's head. Jesus help me, please, Jesus help me, I pray to myself.

'Molly?' my mother coughs. 'Molly, you're shaking, what's the matter?'

Donal leans forward and gently squeezes my shoulder. 'Go on, Molly, tell her.'

'Tell me what?'

My eyes are glued to the picture.

'Do you want me to tell her?' Donal grips my hand.

I pull my eyes away from Jesus and look at my mother. My mouth opens but no words come out.

'Donal, what's going on? Look at the state of my daughter! What's the matter with her?'

'She has something to tell you, don't you, Molly?'

Silence wraps around me, the air charged with tension.

I look at Donal and suddenly the words come blurting out all on their own, 'I've been raped and Shane is the result.'

My mother's face has a blank expression at first as she glances from me to Donal, then back to me again. Her appearance soon turns to a sickening, sour look of despair. 'What?' she tries to yell, but she's too weak. 'Molly, my poor Molly!' She clutches her chest. 'Who did such an evil thing to you?' I sense a hint of anger in her voice. 'Why did you not say something before? Why did you go this long, suffering in silence? Why, why, why?' She pauses as the awful cough that

336

has invaded her life for weeks fiercely erupts.

I hang my head in despair and wait for her to continue. I can't answer any of her questions. My mind is spinning. I throw myself down on her bed and weep. 'I'm sorry, I'm so, so sorry, forgive me, please forgive me, Mother.'

The coughing stops and she appears so weak and fragile; she is barely able to speak. 'You don't need to be apologetic, you don't need forgiveness. It's not your fault. Molly, you've been through so much and you've been so brave, you could've easily crumbled completely.'

I look into her eyes and she smiles weakly.

'Brave? I wouldn't say I was ever brave. I almost did completely crumble. If it hadn't been for you and Emily I wouldn't have got through the darkest points in my life. In fact, I wouldn't be alive today, sure I almost killed myself.'

'What do you mean?' Donal asks.

My stinging eyes meet his. 'I wanted to end my life, I hated myself so much. I wanted to jump off the pier at Greencastle, and on another occasion I cut myself, wanting so badly to bleed to death.' I draw my sleeves up and hold my arms out. His face fills with horror at the sight of my scarred skin.

'If I get my hands on that brute, I'm going to kill him!' He waves his fist in the air. 'I'm going to ...'

'That's enough, Donal,' my mother interrupts.

I pull my sleeves down again. 'No, I'm certainly not brave.'

'Aye, Molly, you've been courageous. You fought on and you got your life back into some kind of normality, and that takes bravery.' She reaches out and takes my hand. I can feel her trembling. 'Did you go to the police?'

'No, no I didn't.'

'Can you identify him?'

'Aye, I can, Mother.'

'Then you need to report it. Don't waste any more time letting him roam free.' She reaches out to take my hand and continues slowly, 'You know if I was at myself I would go with you to support you, but unfortunately I can't. Molly, please don't let him away with it; it's likely that he's responsible for the attack on Jack Brown's daughter, and if he is, and is caught, the girl can get on with her life knowing he's behind bars. Perhaps she can't identify him. How do you think she will feel knowing that someone out there raped her? She'll hold a suspicion against every man she meets. Promise me you'll report this.'

'It's okay. I'll do the right thing.'

'I'm proud of you, love,' she whispers. 'One day you'll recover completely from this ordeal. Shane is such a beautiful, innocent child; open your heart and grow to love him, only then will you find true peace.'

'I've been trying, it's not easy, but I'll try harder,' I promise.

'Why did you not report this?' Donal queries.

'I feared no one would believe me. I know that might sound stupid, and, I feel silly even thinking about it.'

'We believe you, Molly, and would still have believed you even if Jack's daughter hadn't been attacked. You really should've told us from the beginning. We could've helped you in some way, instead I made life harder for you.' Donal hung his head in shame. 'I'm sorry, I've treated you so cruelly, I'm so regretful for my behaviour.'

'Don't worry about it.' It's rare for Donal to apologise, but when he does he means it from his heart.

'You need someone to go to the police station with you. I want you to go today, love. Go and get it over and done with.'

'I'll go with her, Mother.' Donal puts an arm around my shoulders. 'I really am sorry. I never expected you to bring us shame, and, I certainly should've known better. I'm sorry.' He holds out his hand.

'I'm not one for holding grudges. We'll put it behind us.' As I take his hand I catch a glimpse of my mother smiling softly.

'I knew something wasn't right surrounding the pregnancy. That's why part of me didn't push you to reveal who Shane's father is.' She pauses to catch her breath, 'I guess that also explains your moods after the birth.'

'Aye,' I nod.

Sometime later, Sadie's husband collects Donal and I to drive us to the police station. Our journey is overshadowed with the awkward silence. None of us discuss why we're making this trip. I'm glad. I'm not in the mood to talk it over in the car, and besides, Sadie has obviously filled Mark in on everything; I can tell with the sympathetic look he throws me as we climb into the back seat of the car. Every so often he breathes deeply through his nostrils and sighs with disgust.

The car pulls to a halt outside our destination, and at once butterflies arise from the pit of my stomach. I reluctantly get out and hold open the door for Donal. He struggles to maintain his balance as he reaches for his walking aids. My heart fills with sorrow at the sight of the blisters which cover the palms of his hands from the constant pressure of his weight bearing down on the crutches. He screws his face in pain and guilt overwhelms me again. A volcano boils up inside me, like never before, as the reality of how much damage that beast has inflicted upon my life and my family becomes crystal clear.

I march towards the steel gates with determination. 'I'm going to make sure he's caught and pays for his crime!' I announce.

Donal hobbles behind me, desperately trying to catch up.

On entering the building we come face-to-face with a police officer sitting at the front desk. He glances at us from the feet up and quickly looks away. He begins scribbling something down on a piece of paper, his head cocked to the side with his shoulder slightly raised, holding the telephone receiver firmly in place, as he listens to the caller on the other side. Minutes later, he replaces the receiver and turns his attention to me. 'What can I do for you, Miss?' He sighs, sounding tired and slightly fed-up. His eyes dart at the clock on the wall behind me and then back to me.

I take a deep breath and with a glimmer of defiance I state, 'I've got some information that may help you.'

'Oh? And what might that be?' he raises his eyebrows and bites on his pencil, appearing as if he couldn't care less what information I have for him.

'I've heard a young girl has been raped in the

Ballyarnett area.'

'Yes.' He leans over the desk, appearing more interested. 'Yes that's right.'

My words spill out, 'I was raped in that area too. I want to make a statement.'

His eyes widen, 'Okay, I'm, I'm sorry to hear that.' He appears attentive now, at the possibility of a serial rapist in the area. 'I'll get someone to take your testimonial. I'll be back in a minute.' He bounces off his chair and disappears down the corridor, returning in less than a minute with a tall, older gentleman.

'Hello, I'm Sergeant Caldwell. I'm in charge of this investigation.' He peers over his glasses and holds out his hand. 'And you are?'

'Hello, Mr Caldwell, I'm Molly O'Connor.' I shake his warm hand.

'Hello, Molly. Would you like to follow me and I'll get a wee report from you.'

'Aye, thank you, sir.' I follow him down the long corridor, poor Donal lumbering behind. We stop outside a room on the left-hand side and enter it. The room is empty, apart from a small wooden desk and two chairs on each side. Donal and I sit down whilst Sergeant Caldwell closes the door and sits facing us. He draws his notebook from his pocket and removes a pencil from behind his ear.

The air smells musty and it's so overwhelming it makes my stomach churn. I stare past him. My gaze fixes on the cracks on the wall behind him. My thoughts are interrupted with a sharp nudge in the ribs from Donal.

'He was just asking you to tell him the sequence of events.'

'Oh, sorry, I was just thinking ...' I stop myself from telling him how the walls need fixing. It isn't difficult to remember the events of that dreadful night. The memories come flooding back, as if it had happened only yesterday. They are as clear as crystal in my mind; traumatic events have the ability to embed every last detail in the brain.

He listens and scrawls every bit of information onto the piece of paper in front of him. 'Erm.' His glasses slip down the bridge of his long, pointy nose. He pushes them back into place before continuing, 'Molly, the area that you have described sounds familiar to the place Miss Brown alleges she was attacked. It's more than likely that we're dealing with the same person here.'

Donal nodded in agreement, 'Aye, it sounds like it. What are you going to do now, sir?'

'Well, thanks to Molly, we're now in a position to arrest this man and bring him in for questioning.' He gave me a sympathetic smile. 'Molly, I just have to go and grab something I would like to show you. Can you wait a minute?'

'Of course.' He leaves the room and I sit back in the chair. Relief sweeps over me; it's over. I can relax now.

'Are you okay?' Donal takes my hand in his and gives it a reassuring squeeze. 'I'm proud of you, Molly. You did well to bravely face your past,' he smiles softly.

'Aye I'm feeling fine,' I tell him, but really I feel quite sick.

'Molly, I'm sorry again for the way I treated you, just

listening to you give your evidence has brought it home to me how much you suffered. I'm disgusted with myself. I should've been there for you. I'll be honest with you, I came back still carrying some of the pain and anger that drove me away, but I've tried my best to put it behind me. You're probably wondering why I treated you with such hostility.'

'Aye I did, I couldn't understand it. I thought you above all people would've stood by me.'

'For crying out loud, Molly, you were sixteen and pregnant. Sixteen! And I seemed to be the only one that digested how awful a situation that was. I'm your eldest brother, your only blood brother! I'm supposed to protect you. In my heart it felt like I had let you down.' He lowers his head as a solemn expression develops on his face. 'Most of all, Molly, I thought I'd let our father down. I believed at the time that if he had have been alive, you wouldn't have got into the mess you were in; but now that I have learned the truth regarding the pregnancy, it's clear that neither him nor I could have prevented that from happening. I'm sorry, Molly. I've really let you down, I've let you down badly.' A silent tear escapes from his eye and rolls down his cheek.

I observe the etched lines formed around his eyes on his once young and handsome face. The strain of everything has clearly taken its toll on him. 'Donal, you don't have to keep apologising. I'm the one that should be sorry. I feel guilty you felt you had to leave home. And the worst about it, you returned with one leg!'

Donal laughed. 'Hey, don't worry about that, I don't feel bitterness. I've decided to accept it; sure as I keep saying,

343

it could be worse. I could be buried six foot under by now. I'm just glad I'm still alive, Molly, and that's the truth.'

The door creaks open and Sergeant Caldwell returns holding a small bag in his hand. 'Sorry to have kept you waiting. I just got held up chatting to one of my officers about another case. You'll both be glad to know, I've sent a few officers out there to arrest him. Now, I want to show you something, Molly. We searched the scene of where Miss Brown was attacked and I found this.' He opens the bag and spills the contents out into his hand.

I gasped at the sight of my mother's bracelet.

Chapter 37

Mick stares at the policeman before his eyes. 'What's up?' He gazes at him from head to toe.

'I'm looking for Molly O'Connor, is this where she lives?'

'Aye, it is indeed.'

'Great, can I have a word with her?'

'You can. Come in.' Mick holds the door open and beckons him inside. 'Cold day out there, some change in the weather.'

'It sure is.' He rubs his hands together, before moving into the warmth of the hallway.

The living room door is ajar; the sight of him stepping inside startles me. My head is throbbing, each temple pounding with this matter constantly in my thoughts. I wonder if I've done the right thing, going to the police.

Mick opens the living room door wide. 'Molly, this gentleman would like to have a word with you.'

I shift uneasily to the edge of the sofa.

'Hello, Molly.'

'Hello, sir.'

'Molly, I thought I would call in to inform you that your attacker has been arrested and charged with both the assault on you and on Miss Brown. He will appear before a judge to be sentenced later this month. You'll be pleased to know that he has been remanded in police custody.'

I sigh with relief, 'That's great news, thank you. I appreciate it.'

'No bother, you're welcome.' He throws me a sympathetic look.

I sit back at ease and rest my aching head against the sofa. 'I'm thankful he's caught, at least now he can't harm anyone else.'

'That's true, but the thing is, Molly, you'll be required to attend the court hearing and give your evidence, is that okay with you?'

'Aye,' I nod. 'I knew I would have to give evidence, I've no problem with that.'

'Good, I'll be off then. Take care.'

The courtroom falls silent as all eyes watch him make his way to the stand. He no longer looks like a beast, as he did so that night. Today he appears like the boy next door, with his hair combed neatly to the side, not a strand out of place, and dressed in a fine suit and spit-polished boots.

With my mother being too weak to attend the hearing, Karl, Donal, Mick, Sadie and Emily come along to offer their support. The entire Brown family is in attendance, and every so often they shout angrily at him. He, on the other hand, is accompanied by his mother; no other family or friends have joined him. She sits nervously poised in a floral dress, her hair scooped back in a tight bun. Now and again she fiddles with the pearl necklace that hangs loosely around her neck.

He sheepishly clears his throat, and, when asked if he is responsible for the crimes, he pleads not guilty.

'You're guilty alright, you dirty ol' git!' Jack Brown stands up and waves a fist in the air. 'You'll get what's coming to you, you filthy ...'

'Mr Brown, that's enough. If you interrupt this court again I will have no choice but to have you removed,' the judge says with a stern look etched on his.

'Aye, whatever. Wait till I get my hands on the dirty brute!' he mumbles before sitting back down on the wooden bench.

The court continues. After Miss Brown gives her evidence, it's my turn to take the stand.

I take a deep breath and bravely walk to the front of the room, remaining calm and dignified. I'm not sure where I get my strength from, but I manage to hold myself together through the gruelling process. My evidence is flawless; the scene of that awful night plays in my mind, like an image from a projector onto a huge screen, and not a single detail escaped my memory.

I can't bring myself to look him in the eye, but I do observe how he hangs his head in shame. He comes across like a broken, confused mess of a being and somehow I feel sorry for him. For a strange reason, my heart goes out to him; he appears so weak, no longer the powerful monster that attacked me on that cold December night.

He catches me staring at him. I glance away, willing myself to become invisible. My eyes fall upon his mother, but she isn't looking in my direction. Her eyes are glued on her son. Her face is pale and withdrawn, and covered in dense wrinkles, making her appear much older than perhaps she is. She doesn't accept that her son is capable of rape. On the way into court she grabbed hold of my arm and whispered in my ear, *'Everyone is making a big mistake. The truth will come out in the end!'* She shook her walking stick in the air and pointed it directly at me.

'Miss O'Connor!' The judge's voice snaps me out of my trance. I look at him with fear. All eyes are on me, staring through me, making me feel like a caged animal with nowhere to run. 'I'll ask for the third and last time, Miss O'Connor, have you anything else that you would like to share with the court?'

'There is,' my voice tremors. 'I gave birth to a son as a result of the attack.' My body trembles. 'His name is Shane and *he* is the father.' I point a shaky finger at the accused.

The courtroom fills with 'oohs and 'aahs' and then a hushed silence. I shift my gaze onto his mother. After the news of the pregnancy is announced, the shock is too much for her. She grabs hold of her chest and releases a terrifying wail, like a crazed banshee, and her screams echo throughout the room.

'Shane is the result of the rape, there's no running away from it now!' I yell, turning my attention back on my attacker. I observe how he almost falls over with the surprise bombshell. He wasn't expecting that announcement. He appears as if he has had a good kick in the teeth. He lowers his eyes, unable to hold my stare, lips quivering. The bolt from the blue is too much to digest. Suddenly he begins to cry like a baby.

The court stops for lunch and we are informed that it will resume in the afternoon, with the verdict expected.

My body is in turmoil with nerves; they run rampage through my being, twisting and churning my stomach, until I almost feel as if I'm going to throw up, or worse, pass out altogether.

Karl holds my hand. 'You did well, Molly. He's bound to be found guilty. I'm so proud of you, honey.' He gives my hand a light squeeze and smiles softly. His aqua eyes are soft and full of love. I lean my head against his shoulder. I know, no matter what the verdict is, I'll be safe with him.

I smile weakly. 'I hope so. I need closure on this, we all do.'

Karl peers at his watch. 'We need to be getting back in, the court is starting again at two, it's almost that now.'

We return to our seats. The atmosphere is tense, but I feel much calmer now than I had done earlier. We wait patiently for the court to begin.

The judge appears and I hold my breath as I watch him take his seat and sit down. He clears his throat. My heart begins to pound as we wait for his response.

'Good afternoon and welcome back. Before I give my verdict, the defendant's solicitor would like to read a statement from the accused.' He nods. 'You may stand up and deliver it now.' He beckons him to commence.

My stomach does a somersault. I throw Karl a quizzical look. 'I wonder what this is about.'

Karl shrugs. 'This sounds interesting.'

Donal raises his eyebrows. 'Aye, wonder what's up?'

The solicitor holds a piece of paper in his hand then waves it in the air. He glances at me, then the Brown family, and back to me again. 'This is a statement from the defendant. He has altered his plea to guilty.'

The room fills again with gasps. His mother lets out

another wail and again clutches at her chest. Karl grips my hand and I breathe a sigh of relief, but wonder what has made him change his mind.

He begins to read the statement aloud.

'I have decided to change my plea. I am guilty of both attacks. I am sorry for the damage I have done to both girls and hope they will one day forgive me. On hearing that I fathered a child as a result of my actions, it has made me realise how much my behaviour has affected others. I am truly sorry.'

The solicitor looks at me again before continuing. 'Ladies and gentlemen, my defendant is a broken man who doesn't know what came over him to cause him to carry out the assaults. I can only say from listening to him that he is a very lonely, confused and mixed-up person, who truly is remorseful.' He pauses. 'In saying that, I cannot make excuses for what he has done, I can only try to assure you that he is genuinely regretful.'

'The crafty brute, I'm not falling for that nonsense,' Donal whispers.

Karl shook his head from side to side. 'He has some nerve!'

The judge nods in agreement with the solicitor. 'I do believe that this young man is remorseful. I praise him for his bravery in admitting the offence. However, I must also condemn him for his cowardly actions in attacking two young vulnerable ladies, leaving them scarred and traumatised for life.' He turns his attention to the defendant. 'You, young man, have committed despicable acts, and so I have no choice but to send you to prison. I only hope that you do learn from your mistakes and that you will never carry out such cruel and cowardly deeds again.'

The brute looks away, his face covered with shame. My eyes meet his gaze, as he is being taking away by two police officers. 'I'm sorry,' he mouths, before disappearing out of sight.

His mother throws me a sympathetic look, the wrinkles around her mouth deepen as she purses her lips. Her eyes water. She leaves the room in silence wiping away her tears, a broken woman, another life damaged forever.

I feel sad for her, my heart aches with the pain he has caused us all. Jack Brown's daughter is clearly troubled by the whole matter. She quickly leaves, weeping bitterly, with her family surrounding her.

The next few weeks are filled with pity for Shane's father. In a strange way, I'm eventually beginning to feel that I can forgive him. Maybe getting it out in the open has helped. I no longer have to bottle it up. Perhaps knowing that he is in jail and sorry for what he did is comforting. I no longer feel the anger of thinking he got away with it. The matter is done and dusted as far as I'm concerned. I can forgive him, but I will never be able to forget the incident. I just have to learn to live with it and accept it's a part of my past that has happened, and Shane is the positive outcome of a bad situation.

I become the talk of the street for weeks. Every time I leave the house, to fetch water from the well, I can sense eyes on me and they look awkward as they try to cover up their guilt of their secret talks behind my back.

Hushed silence is all around, but I no longer care. I'm free, I didn't do anything wrong. I did a brave thing by going ahead with the pregnancy. I can hold my head up high, and the neighbours can think what they like.

News of Mrs Flannigan's sudden and unexpected death spreads throughout the countryside like wildfire, and soon I'm no longer the main topic of conversation. In a way I'm relieved the neighbours have something else to focus on.

According to Nosy Nora, 'The ol' biddy died of a massive heart attack in the back-yard.' Rumour has it she was found by someone going in to pay his weekly debts. The entire countryside is elated by her passing away, most of them owing her a fortune. The way they look at it, if she's dead, their debts are dead too. Many are actually celebrating.

I stand getting drenched in the pouring rain, at the bottom of the street, as I wait. If anybody were to see me they would think I'm a crazy lunatic. The rain pelts down soaking through my clothes. It came on quite sudden and unexpected and it is falling faster by the minute. Oh to heck with it, I may as well wait. There's no point in turning back, I'm soaked now anyway, I think.

The sound of horse's hooves, trotting down the lane and onto the road, makes me turn my attention in its direction. 'At last,' I sigh, as I watch the hearse make its way down the muddy road. Slowly it draws nearer. My heart sinks at the sad sight before my eyes: Mrs Flannigan's remains are being led through the countryside by the horse and cart, her body lying in a lonely wooden coffin, with only three other people following behind.

She may have been hated and despised by the locals for swindling their money with her huge interest on her loans, and it is true, I didn't have much time for her, seeing all the years she left my mother penniless, however I bless myself and bow my head in silent prayer for her soul as her remains pass me by.

It's sad to think she died as she had lived, a sad, lonely woman, no friends and no family, only three neighbours to accompany her to her place of rest. Her only son absent from his mother's funeral, it's a pitiful sight.

I owe it to her to pay my respects; after all, she was Shane's grandmother.

Chapter 38

I run my eyes over the contents of the letter and gasp, 'I don't ...' I shake my head in shock.

'What's up?' Donal lifts his head up from his breakfast briefly, before shuffling a heaped spoonful of porridge into his mouth.

'You're not going to believe this,' I pause and read over the letter again. I scan every word and take a deep breath before continuing. 'Donal, Mrs Flannigan has stated that everything is to be left to me: her entire estate, all its belongings and all of her money!'

'What?' Donal gets up quickly from his seat and almost topples over. He reaches out and grabs my arm and peers at the document over my shoulder. 'Whoa, Molly, that's great news!'

'Is it?' I make a face. 'I'm not so sure.'

'Why wouldn't it be?' he shrugs dismissively.

'Well, think about it, what would I want with her stuff? Why the heck did she leave it all to me?'

'She's left it to you because she wanted you to have it! I don't know, maybe she felt guilty for what her son put you through, or then again, maybe with him in prison she realised Shane was the only family she had left. With regards to your question of what do you want with her stuff, I can think of plenty of things you can do with her belongings. The ol' biddy was minted, she was rotten with money, you can do loads with it.'

'Aye I know,' I sigh. 'You're right; she must've felt some kind of guilt. Oh look, there's another letter attached.'

'What does it say?'

'It states that she would like Shane to have a comfortable life, and that I should use the inheritance to build my own life up again.'

'Good on her!' he laughs. 'The ol' miser had a heart after all then! It just goes to show, people can surprise you.'

'Oh, Donal, my heart feels a terrible sense of sadness. She obviously accepted the fact that her darling son was guilty. That must've been a bitter pill for her to swallow.'

'She must've done.'

'If she's bequeathed everything to me, she obviously hasn't left anything at all for him. What's he going to do when he gets out of prison? Donal, I can't accept the inheritance, it wouldn't be right.'

'Are you mad? Don't you worry about Peter Flannigan and what he's going to do, that's his problem. As far as I'm concerned he's made his bed, he can stay in it! Ol' Flannigan obviously thought the same. Perhaps not leaving him anything is her way of punishing him for his crime. Then again, maybe she just wants to make amends for what he did, but whatever way you choose to look at it, you're going to be a very rich young lady! She left her inheritance to you so enjoy it, Molly. You're taking it, you deserve a bit of happiness in your life.'

'Do you know something Donal? You're right, to heck with her son. I will accept it.'

I bounce upstairs to tell my mother the news, feeling like a millionaire. My mood changes on seeing her. She looks unusually pale today. Her condition appears to be getting worse instead of better.

I sit at the edge of the bed and I'm shocked to find the sheets soaking with sweat. 'Mother, I need to change these sheets, you're drenched. Come on, take a grip of my arm, I'll help you out onto the chair.'

'Thanks, love.'

She grabs hold of me, and gently I help her onto the seat. My heart aches at the sight of her. Her hair clings to her pale face in unruly, sweaty strands and she seems so weak.

'I don't feel too well today, Molly,' she whispers.

'No,' I frown, 'you don't look good.' A boulder forms in my throat; it's painful to see her so sick. 'I've some good news for you.'

'What is it, love?'

'Mrs Flannigan has left her entire estate to me. She's left me everything!'

'Oh my goodness, that's wonderful news.'

'At first I wasn't sure I should accept it, but I've changed my mind.'

'Molly, she wouldn't have left you all her belongings if she didn't want you to have it. Take it, love, I know you'll put it to good use. But remember, money can be the root to all evils, don't let it ruin you.' She gasped breathlessly, 'Oh, my knees and ankles are so painful.'

'Let's take a look.' I examine her joints and discover quite a bit of swelling in both her knees and her ankles. My heart sinks.

'I'm so exhausted today, Molly.'

'I'm going to get the doctor to examine you.'

'Please do.' She nods in agreement. 'That was a decent gesture from Mrs Flannigan but remember what I said – don't let riches destroy you.'

An idea strikes me regarding the money, but first I need to concentrate on helping my mother. I'll put my plan into action later.

Within seconds of seeing my mother, Doctor Devlin appears concerned. 'Kate, I'm afraid I have to transfer you to hospital. The swelling in your joints is an indication that the disease has spread to other parts of your body. I'm sorry, but your condition is deteriorating.' He sounds extremely concerned.

She smiles weakly. 'Okay.'

It's so typical of her, not a word of complaint and always a little smile regardless of the situation.

Within hours she's transferred to hospital. Donal and I stand with Doctor Devlin, and we watch as she is wheeled into one of the rooms. 'You'll have to wait here,' a nurse says.

'I was hoping that your mother's immune system would isolate the disease in her lungs, but now that it has spread I'm afraid you all should prepare yourselves for the worse possible scenario. It pains me to say this, but this could prove fatal.' Doctor Devlin places his hands on my shoulders and gives me a light squeeze.

A dense sadness sweeps over me as Donal's eyes meet mine and we both fall into each other's arms and sob.

It's a terrifying situation. The thought of losing such a strong role model in our lives is too horrible to contemplate. All those times my mother stood by me, lifted me up when I fell and encouraged me to struggle on with life, come flooding back into my memory. She was my strength when I was at my weakest, my voice when I couldn't speak, my rock to lean on, in fact, she is my life, my all. I wouldn't be the person I am today without her guidance and support. How will we cope if we lose her? She sacrificed her life for us, always working hard to maintain the family.

Not only has she been a huge impression on me, she's helped so many people. All of the little things she's done for her family, friends and neighbours over the years, they seemed too little to notice at the time, but looking back now, they also had an impact on our lives. Her honest approach to life and the examples of selfless love that she showed to others throughout the years have taught us the true meaning of our existence. We're all on a journey; we should do as much good as possible for those we meet along the way.

Three days later we are informed by the medical staff to remain at her bedside as she gets sicker and weaker by the minute.

Mick, Sadie, Donal, Charlie, Anna, Father McGroarty and I gather round her bed and pray continuously. Doctor Devlin stands behind us in stillness.

At three o'clock, we kneel and pray the rosary. Just as we end our prayers, I observe my beautiful mother opening her eyes; she smiles weakly at each of us. Her chest rises and falls for the final time, unable to rise again, as she takes her last breath and passes peacefully away.

'A saint has gone to Heaven,' Father McGroarty whispers as he makes the sign of the cross on her forehead and kisses her cheek.

I feel a hand on my shoulder. 'Your mother's suffering is over,' Doctor Devlin says in a low voice, with sympathy in his eyes.

Together we weep in silence; the only sound to be heard is sniffling from each of us.

My heart is torn to shreds with the shock of her gone so quickly, so unexpectedly. The pain is intense. The numbness of losing her has left us speechless. We had expected that she would get better, none of us prepared ourselves for this day, but, then again, how can you prepare to say goodbye to someone you love? How can you prepare to lose a parent?

My dear mother had lead a good life. She was a holy, sincere woman, one that never missed Mass, got Masses said for the souls in Purgatory, gave to the needy and rejected slander and gossip; surely if anyone is looking down at us from Heaven above, it's her. These thoughts are my only consolation, and the only thing to bring me any kind of comfort because right now I want to die with her.

The sun bounces its rays of light all over the countryside. The brightness brings with it a sense of warmth and happiness. My mother loved days like this. Today, as we prepare to bury her, no amount of sunshine will bring any of us joy, it's a sad day for all. Saying our final farewell to her is one of the hardest things to do.

I don't want the wooden coffin, containing my darling mother, to leave our home. Knowing that it's being taken to be placed down a six foot, muddy hole is an unbearable image in my mind. It will finalise the fact she's gone, never to return to her home again. Never will we witness her up to her arms in flour, never will we find her in her garden, covered in mud, never will we hear her sweet melody, and never will we smell her cooking or witness her bounce Shane about in her arms. My heart is breaking.

Just as they are about to close the coffin, I choke on my tears and weep uncontrollably and, without realising, I throw my stressed body across it and grip the casket tightly. 'No, no, no!' I sob my heart out. 'Please don't lock her up in *that!*' I cry.

Eventually Mick and Charlie gently pull my fingers away.

'You have to let her go, Molly,' Charlie whispers softly. 'Let her go.'

'I don't want to!' Warm tears flow down my flushed cheeks.

Karl places his strong arms around my waist and gently draws me away, 'Come on, honey, they have to take her now.'

I bury my face in his chest and cry like a baby. I can't watch my mother being carried out the front door.

Outside, a crowd of neighbours and friends have come from all over the countryside to bid their farewells to an amazing lady. I walk in a trance behind her coffin, through the packed street and onto the same road that I had watched Mrs Flannigan's remains pass by only weeks earlier. My legs feel like jelly. My mother's funeral is the opposite from the scene at Mrs Flannigan's: no rain in sight today and a huge crowd to follow her remains to the church, unlike the three people that had turned out for Mrs Flannigan.

Strangers on bicycles come to a halt, and the men remove their peak caps and bow their heads in prayer as the cortege passes them.

Inside the chapel, the seats are quickly occupied with mourners. The sound of sniffles can be heard through the hushed silence.

Father McGroarty conducts the service. It is evident at times that he struggles to prevent himself from breaking down crying. I listen carefully as he pays his tribute to my mother.

'I'm saddened at the sudden death of Kate O'Connor. Kate's bereavement has brought both shock and sorrow to us all. Her passing will be a huge loss to her family and friends, but especially to her brother Michael, children Sadie, Donal, Molly, Charlie and Anna and little Shane. Kate's death will also be a great loss to myself, for she truly was a great friend to me throughout the years, and I'm sure you will all agree her death will be a great loss to the community as a whole, for Kate was sincerely a wonderful, kind, considerate friend and neighbour to everyone.' He pauses to wipe away a tear before clearing his throat to continue, 'Kate has been an inspiration to all that knew her, and she has especially inspired me as I witnessed throughout the years her true love for her family and a devotion to her faith, which was exceptional. She treated everyone equally, and refused to judge or contribute to slander or gossip in any way, always seeing the good side in everyone she met. They say only the good die young; well, Kate was one of the good ones, dying at the young age of forty-six, she truly was a saint on this Earth and I feel privileged to have been friends with such a wonderful person, a woman who at all times triumphed over evil, generated good and went about her life with as little fuss as possible. Even in her last weeks, through all of her misery, she refused to make hassle or complain. She accepted her suffering as a gift from God and she died like she lived, in a peaceful and dignified manner. If anyone is sure of entering Heaven, it's Kate. Let her life be an inspiration to all of us, for she was beyond doubt the most decent lady I have ever met, and I hope her family take great comfort from the fact that they were privileged to have such a wonderful, saintly person in their midst. Please join me in praying for her soul. Eternal rest grant onto her oh Lord, and may the perpetual light shine upon her. May her soul and the souls of all the faithfully departed, through the mercy of God, rest in peace. Amen.'

Silent tears roll freely down his cheeks; it's an emotional sight.

The moment of placing my mother's body into the lonely, murky hole in the ground is the time that I've dreaded the most, and perhaps the most difficult thing for us all to witness. As the coffin is being lowered into the ground each of us in turn steps forward to throw a single white rose into the grave. As I approach I linger at the side of the grave before throwing mine in. I watch as the beautiful flower falls from my hand and drops onto her casket. Father McGroarty sprinkles some holy water and begins to pray a decade of the rosary. My mind is in too much turmoil to concentrate in joining in with the prayers; all I can see in front of me is a wooden box containing my beautiful, precious mother. I have an overwhelming urge to jump into the grave and be with her. Thinking of her here in this desolate place alone, night after night, is traumatising. I want to pull open the lid, lift her out and breathe air back into her body. The whole event feels like a terrifying dream.

My thoughts are interrupted when Shane – who has been standing holding Sadie's hand – releases his grip from her and begins to frantically look around as if searching for someone in the crowds. 'Mama,' he announces. 'Where's my mama?' he quizzes, as his little, innocent eyes search the unfamiliar faces in front of him. His eyes scan everyone in search for the woman that brought him up as her son. My heart sinks deeper. The poor child; little does he know the lady he is looking for is never going to be seen in his life again. His mama has gone, but his mother still remains. He rubs his little eyes with his chubby hands and begins to cry, 'I want my mama.'

I bend down and scoop my son up, the son that I have rejected for so long, and lift him into my arms holding him close to my chest, 'Your mama's gone to heaven, she's with the angels,' I whisper. He looks at me with huge tears in his round eyes, too young to understand why she is no longer here. I rock him gently in my arms and kiss his tear-stained cheeks until he stops crying. Contently he snuggles his little head onto my shoulder. I press my lips against his thick, soft curly hair. 'Your mama's gone but your mother's here, and it's time I began being a proper mother to you.'

Chapter 39

The cool breeze brushes against my cheek and flattens Shane's blond curls as it swirls around us. He holds his small, pudgy hand in mine and raises his free hand to point across the calm water as the gentle waves lap softly against our bare feet and lick against the rocky shoreline. The tide is on the turn.

'Boat, Mammy!' he shrieks. His blue eyes sparkle with excitement. 'There it is!' he exclaims as he dances about my feet, fascinated at the sight of the vessel before his young eyes.

I catch sight of the boat in the distance behind the lighthouse.

'Aye son, Mammy sees it.' I smile contently and watch him bounce up and down at the shore's edge, causing the water to splash in all directions.

We observe the black fishing trawler crawl slowly towards the pier, sending tiny ripples to spread across the lough. It moves along at a snail's pace through the sea, the fresh tar of the boat reflecting in the soft sunlit waters. I lift Shane into my arms, ensuring he gets a better look. He chuckles with excitement as he wriggles his toes about, sending the water to drip from his feet and fall onto my skirt.

'I'll be soaking wet by the time we get home if you keep kicking about like that,' I laugh and blow raspberries on his delicate cheek.

He giggles and flings his feet mischievously about a little more. 'You're a little rascal.' I ruffle his hair playfully and tickle under his chin.

'I love you, Mammy!' he announces as he wraps his

arms around my neck and plants a kiss on my cheek.

'I love you too, Shane,' I reply, my heart wanting to burst with joy. 'I love you so much, son.' I cling tightly to my child for a few moments and rock him gently in my arms. 'I love you with all my heart,' I whisper as I struggle not to cry.

'Right, let's go, son, we'll meet them getting off.' I place Shane back down onto the sand and take his hand. We walk barefoot on the soft, cool beach, the sand slipping gently through our toes. It generates a therapeutic sensation.

The sky is laced with a pinkish glow on the horizon, indicating that it's almost teatime. The mirror image of the soft sun dances on the calm waters; it's a beautiful summer's evening.

We make our way to the moss-covered pier just in time to catch a glimpse of the two familiar bodies emerging from the trawler. I wait as they tie the boat up before they run up the smooth, worn steps that lead to the top of the pier. The strong aroma of fish and seaweed lingers heavy in the air.

'Salmon for dinner tonight, honey,' Karl beams as he approaches us. He proudly holds it in his arms. A grin forms from one end of his face to the other. He lifts the fish in the air to display his fine catch. 'Have you ever seen one this big, son?'

Shane's eyes go wide with amazement. 'No!'

'Look at the size of it!' I gasp. 'How will I fit that boyo into the oven?'

'Molly, don't you worry about that, love. We'll get it in one way or the other,' Paddy laughs and licks his salt-cracked lips. 'There's nothing like a fresh piece of salmon for dinner.'

He glances at Karl. 'That's a fine one that is; well, at least for a man that's still an amateur at the ol' fishing game.' He playfully pats the top of Karl's head.

'Hey you, less of the amateur,' Karl replies in his strong American accent. He grins back at Paddy. 'With a catch like this, I'm becoming a real pro.' He winks, 'Isn't that right, Molly?'

'Oh, whatever boys, whatever.' I roll my eyes and wave my hand dismissively.

'Wait till you're my age and have the experience that I have before you call yourself a pro. For now there's only one professional, you remember that, sunshine!' Paddy jokes and his face lights up. His eyes twinkle like stars in his weather-beaten face.

Soon the area is buzzing with activity with others returning from sea, and in no time the pier is lined with boxes of fish piled high ready to be transported away in handcarts.

The banter between Karl and Paddy continues as we set off walking the short distance through the village of Greencastle until we arrive at our destination. In the sky above us the sun still shines brightly, glinting blindingly off the whitewashed cottages in the village, the blue of the sky reflected in the tiny windows. Every now and again along the way Paddy will stop, remove his cap, and chat to the villagers and of course show them Karl's fine catch.

Just before my mother died, thoughts of how poor she had been throughout her life came flooding into my mind. She died as she lived: poor in pocket, but rich in spirit. When she warned me not to let money ruin me, as she lay sick in her bed, it was then that I decided to use the cash that Mrs Flannigan had left me and share it amongst the poor. After all, it was their money that she had taken off them over the years.

Soon after the funeral, Emily and I set off to retrieve the money from the house. It gave me something to do and helped to take my mind off the loss of my mother.

Emily had her own bicycle and I borrowed Mick's. Our plan was to get the cash then cycle around the countryside, distributing it fairly amongst everyone.

It felt odd turning the key in the door and entering into the grand home. My feet bounce on the soft crimson carpet as it cushions my every step. In all those years of coming here as a youngster, never did I imagine that one day all this would belong to me.

The air is musty and stale. I run my finger along the piano that I had admired as a child, sending the dust to scatter.

'This is a beautiful place, Emily, but I could never live in it.'

'What do you plan to do with it?'

'I'm going to sell the house and use the finance to buy a home for Shane and I somewhere else.'

Emily looks over her shoulder as she holds an expensive vase in her hand. 'I can't blame you. I wouldn't live here either if I were you, not under the circumstances.' She pauses briefly. 'Molly, this must be worth a small fortune, look at it,' Emily said, holding the delicate piece of porcelain cautiously in her hand.

'Do you like it?'

367

'Aye, it's beautiful.'

'Take it with you, I don't want anything in here.' I gestured casually.

'Molly, I couldn't,' she replied as she placed it back on the shelf.

'Emily, take it! Really, I want you to have it. I'll not let you leave here today without it,' I smile.

'Are you sure, Molly?'

'Of course I'm sure.'

She nods in agreement. 'Okay, I'll take it. I'll give it to my ma. It'll cheer her up. Thanks, Molly.'

'You're welcome. If you see anything else you like just take it.'

It took us a few hours to search the house. Mrs Flannigan had stashed her cash in every nook and cranny: we found money under her mattress, inside books, vases and even a load of notes in an old, cracked teapot. We then came across a rusty biscuit tin that she'd kept under her bed. I couldn't believe my eyes when I opened it to find that there were hundreds of pounds crammed inside, along with a book. I flick through the book and gasp. 'Great!' I exclaim. 'Just what I need.' I smile. 'Look, Emily, every name and address of all the people that owed her money is listed in this,' I wave it in the air, 'We can use it to distribute the bucks.' I almost fall over with excitement.

'Oh, Molly, that's fantastic. You're not going to believe this, there's more in here too.' Emily had opened a jewellery box and found a stash of notes amongst the diamond necklaces and earrings.

'Gees, she was a terrible woman for hoarding stuff.' I shake my head in disbelief. 'It's mad to think, Emily, she had all these riches and stored them up over the years, only to die and leave them behind. The silly fool, she could have enjoyed it while she was alive but instead she decided to lead a life of unhappiness as a result of her greed.' I sigh with sorrow.

'Aye,' Emily agrees. 'But do you know something, Molly? Look around here; she had all the material things she needed, but that money was no good to her. She needed happiness in her life, not this.' She lifts the notes in the air and lazily drops them back in the box. 'All the money in the world can't bring you true happiness.'

I feel a pang of regret for the old woman. Emily is right, Mrs Flannigan died as she had lived: a sad, miserable, lonely old woman, again the opposite to my mother. 'Aye, that's true. I can't help but feel sorry for her.' I bow my head and silently pray for her soul. If anyone needs a prayer or two, I'm sure it's her.

Once we had searched every room and were satisfied that all of the money was gathered up, we set off on our journey to give it back to the people it belonged to. As I knocked on their doors and handed over the cash, the shock and gratefulness in their faces was overwhelming. I hadn't imagined giving to others in need would feel so good; it was satisfying observing such joy. We continued until evening fell upon us.

'We'll make this our last house to call to today, Emily. We need to get back before the blackout starts.' Soon it would get dark and all lights would have to be put out. I push open the creaky wooden gate and we walk up to the door and tap on it gently. No one answers. 'Maybe they didn't hear the knock.' I rap harder this time. The door is opened by a beautiful, young woman. We can tell that she has been crying; it was clear by her tear-stained face and swollen red eyes. Three young children cling nervously around her, one hugging her legs and the other two clinging tightly to her waist. The sadness of all the children is evident in their tiny faces. My heart sinks as I begin to feel pity for this family. I sense something terrible has happened to them.

'Hello,' I announce. 'I'm sorry to bother you.' I smile weakly at the broken-hearted lady before my eyes.

'You're okay, what can I do for you?' The lady wipes a tear from her cheek with the hem of her apron.

'Maybe this is a bad time,' I reply sheepishly. 'I can come back tomorrow.'

'No it's okay, love. Never mind me. I'm just feeling a bit down at the minute.' She looks at her three children before whispering, 'I've just buried my husband yesterday ...' She pauses to catch another tear.

'Oh dear, I'm so sorry to hear that.' A huge lump gathers in my throat. I know what it feels like to lose someone so close. I try to swallow the boulder and dip my head to secretly blink dry my tear-filled eyes.

'TB,' she sniffles through more tears, 'he died of tuberculosis. He had just turned thirty.' Her red-rimmed, puffy eyes gaze into the distance. 'He had his whole life in front of him, but was snatched away so young by that awful disease.' She covers her eyes with her hands and my heart sinks deeper at the sight of the waterfall of tears seeping through her fingers.

I remain speechless. The wounds of losing my mother to the same illness are still raw and my heart goes out to this woman. I feel every bit of her pain. The lump in my throat grows in size as I struggle not to cry. 'My mother passed away two weeks ago with the same ailment,' I reply hoarsely.

'Oh.' She covers her mouth. 'I'm the last person you need to meet. I'm terribly sorry to hear that.'

'Aye, well, I suppose we don't remain here forever.' I reach into my pocket to retrieve some money. 'You've probably heard that Mrs Flannigan has passed away.'

'I did hear that,' she nods. 'May she rest in peace. She wasn't much liked around here. I don't hate her like some of the others do; without her loans my kids would've went hungry on many occasions in the past.'

'I suppose you're right.' My gaze falls on the three youngsters. They look so pitiful, like little sad cherubs. 'Well I've some good news for you. I've inherited her belongings and I've decided to return some of the money that she's gained off folk like you.' I hand her the cash and I'm shocked to witness her cry again.

Through her sobs she manages to reply, 'God bless you, love! I didn't have my dinner today and I didn't know where I was going to get food for my kids tomorrow, I'm totally penniless. You're a godsend today, God has answered my prayers.' She reaches over and hugs me with so much gratitude and genuine love.

I'm moved by this woman's plight, and remember how my mother went without her dinner the first Christmas after my

371

father had passed away. Having no husband to support us only increased my mother's struggles with poverty. When a father is removed from the household, many families fall apart. I reach into my pocket to retrieve the remainder of the cash. 'Take the rest of this. It will help you bring your children up.' I open her hand and place the money in her palm.

'My goodness, no way, I couldn't take all of that, please give that to someone else that needs it,' she pleads.

'No, I want you to take it. Don't worry about the others. I'm going to sell the belongings at Mrs Flannigan's to raise cash for them. Everyone in this book will get their fair share. I'll go now, take care. God bless you and your children, my thoughts are with you at this difficult time.' I back my way down the garden, before she could hand back the gift.

'Thanks, dear. God bless you!' She waves until I'm out of sight.

It wasn't long before I had placed the house up for sale and sold it. I gave her animals to Mr Brown. I thought he could benefit from them and besides it was the least I could do after all the years of annoying him as a child. Once I was satisfied that every name in Mrs Flannigan's book had received a share in the funds, I used the remainder to buy a delightful three-bedroomed cottage in Greencastle overlooking the shores of Lough Foyle. I packed our belongings and Shane and I left Derry to start a new life in Donegal. Before leaving, I removed a small piece of the rose bush that my mother had planted in memory of my father, and I placed it in the front garden of my new home. Each time I look at the beautiful plant, I smile at the memory of how much peace my mother got from it, a tranquility that I now receive when my gaze falls upon it. It feels as if I have part of both my parents with me in my new surroundings.

A year later, Karl finished his service with the Navy and we got married. He moved in with us.

Aggie and Paddy are thrilled that we have decided to start a new life in the cottage next to them. They always said my heart is in the beautiful Donegal, and I guess they're right.

My relationship with Donal has grown stronger and stronger. He regularly comes to stay for weekends, and we have now become closer than ever before.

I vow to put the past behind and move on. It isn't easy, but time is an amazing healer. Life is too short to look back on events. I have learned that I cannot change what has happened but I can change my future and I'm going to make it a happy and loving one for Karl and Shane, Shane the son that I now love with all of my heart.

I promise that no matter what the future may hold for my family, there will be no more hush-hush.

35978151R00213

Made in the USA
Charleston, SC
22 November 2014